ICE
GENESIS

"It's all true, except where it's not."

ICE
GENESIS

by

KEVIN TINTO

Three Dog Publishing
41 Mercury Ave
Tiburon CA, 94920

Publisher's Note:

This is a work of fiction. Names, characters, places, and incidents are fiction, except when they are not. Any resemblance to actual people, living or dead, or to businesses, companies, events, institutions, or locales is completely coincidental. ICE GENESIS/ Kevin Tinto – 1st ed. – v1.6

Anasazi bowl patterns–public domain, courtesy of the Chaco Culture National Historical Park, USNPS.

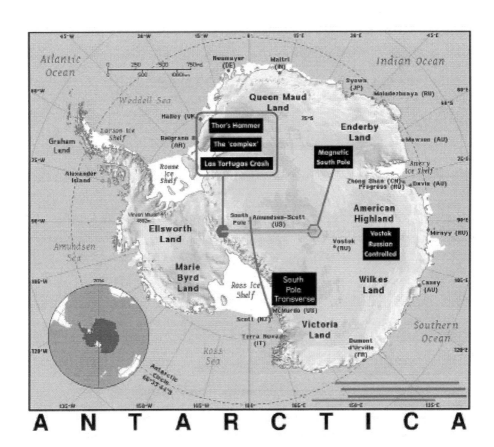

ANTARCTICA

AUTHOR'S NOTE

"The extraordinary disappearance of the Anasazi/Mogollon cliff dwellers from the American Southwest has been well document-ed but never solved. Why Native Americans who lived and pros-pered peacefully on the mesa tops for thousands of years suddenly abandoned these villages for precarious cities lodged in the cliffs around the year 1200—and for only a period of some two-hundred years, before disappearing—remained a mystery. Until now."

If you've come this far, you've seen this quote before. It is placed prominently in the opening pages of ICE. A lot of time has passed since the Ancients, as we refer to them in ICE GENESIS, lived in the cliff dwellings. It almost feels like the same amount of time has passed since ICE was first published.

Just another indie debut among millions of the same, sparring for reader attention. The cover price of any book is inconsequen-tial to the time and attention readers take out of their busy lives to read and finish a novel. While selecting a Netflix movie might 'take two hours out of your life you'll never get back' a book could be ten times that commitment—or more.

If you're reading this, for better, or for worse, you sat down, took a look at a pretty cool cover, and read one page, maybe even two of ICE. Two led to three, and by ten, ICE had already won the one-out-of-a-hundred, indie lotto; you'd turned to page eleven. Four-hundred and seventeen pages later, Jack and Lea had sucked up a significant chunk of your free time. For that I say, thank you!

The ICE series is three books. ICE, ICE GENESIS and ICE REV-ELATION. I'm well along on ICE REVELATION. Look for IR in the fall, 2018.

That's enough from the author. After all, you've been waiting extra-long for ICE GENESIS.

Find that special reading place, shut off that phone, get out a parka if you chill easily....

Here it comes....

For My Dad
James Halliday Tinto

&
Bobo

PROLOGUE

Commander Gus Beckam hauled himself out of the sleeping cocoon constructed from fragments of burned aircraft insulation, cargo blankets, and anything else the survivors had been able to salvage from the fuselage of the Russian Antonov.

The reprieve from what should have been vaporization, courtesy of a nuclear detonation, had been, apparently, only delayed. It had become obvious after more than ten days: no one was coming to rescue them. While Beckam would have liked to blame that on Fischer and the President of the United States, he suspected they'd spotted no overflights of any kind because of the electronic-communications disruption. Even basic Global Positioning Signals remained in full blackout.

As for Beckam's team's unexpected survival, Beckam's best guess was that two of the three Isomer-Hafnium warheads had not detonated. The explosion, although substantial at two kilotons, had been a whole lot less destructive than he'd anticipated.

Prior to the detonation, Beckam and six of the surviving SEALS had taken a defensive position inside the burned-out fuselage of an Antonov transport that had crashed at the remote Antarctic site weeks before. The AN-12's fuselage provided a perfect defensive position from which to set up a lethal spread of fire, pinning the newly arrived Russian troops down for the few minutes necessary to enable Paulson and his B-29 to take off from the primitive ice runway. The fact that Paulson's plane had cleared the runway with only one of the World War II-era radial engines blowing smoke was beyond what Beckam had thought possible. His last view of the vintage bomber had been on the Antarctic horizon, the aircraft still gaining altitude. Watching the old B-29 disappear into the frigid air was the last thing he remembered before the detonation.

Beckam's first experience with the Iso-Hafnium devices had been on a mission to destroy an Iranian nuclear facility. Like characters out of a Tom Clancy novel, Beckam and twelve hand-picked SEALS had flown automated, terrain-hugging jet-wings to the bomb-drop site and parachuted in, while the state of the art jet-wings flew themselves off shore and were captured in what looked like a massive catcher's mitt made of netting, strung across a carrier deck. Once the mission was completed, his team bugged out, transported out by Osprey aircraft. When the Iranian facility inexplicably exploded minutes later, wiping out all the offending hardware and every nuclear scientist in the deeply buried facility, the POTUS had shrugged while the press went nuts.

"It appears to be an industrial accident created by the Iranian nuclear industry," was the U.S.'s official statement, the truth remaining a closely-held secret until being declassified many years down the road.

Beckam's mission to Antarctica, on the other hand, had been billed as a 'milk run.' "A simple mission," the orders read, "requiring the removal of civilians caught in the epicenter of an American-Russian diplomatic dust-up."

Of course, it had turned out to be the opposite.

While engaged in a fierce firefight, the SEALs had done their best to stack debris against the aluminum skin of the fuselage, fortifying the interior against the coming explosion.

The blast wave of the Hafnium detonation tossed the Antonov's fuselage across the Antarctic terrain like an underhand softball pitch. After touching back down on the ice, it had tumbled over an ice dam, finally coming to rest on the downside of an icy slope more than five hundred meters from where it had originally touched down.

The SEALS had been spun around inside the aircraft like agates in a rock polisher. The survivors: Beckam, his Executive Officer Lt. Danny Frantino, and the Clay twins. Beckam and the Clay twins had suffered a variety of cuts and bruises, and Liam Clay had lost his front teeth. Danny had gotten the worst of it, with injuries including a fractured femur, spinal contusions, and a class-A concussion.

What had saved them from the Hafnium bomb's lethal gamma radiation was the combination of distance from ground zero and simple topography. The Russians had cleared ice with a dozer flown in to flatten a working runway. The cleared ice had been pushed up into piles, and the fuselage had come to rest behind one of these piles, partially shielding it from the radiation.

Nonetheless, all four of them had minor symptoms of radiation sickness: nausea, vomiting, the dreaded in-the-field diarrhea, and mouth sores. Given they had survived more than ten days and the symptoms hadn't gotten worse, Beckam figured they were destined to survive the radiation dosage. They'd likely pay for it in ten or twenty years with variety of rare cancers. They could only hope the VA's medical system would be in a whole lot better shape by then.

One lucky break was the survival of the Clay twins. If Beckam ever needed two SEALs for back-up in a dodgy situation, he would have chosen Liam and Lenny. Not that they didn't come without their risks. If you wanted to stay out of jail in Virginia Beach, you'd avoid them like the plague. The boys were naturals at drawing fire, whether from enemy combatants on the battlefield or the local rednecks who made their way to the beach for a night of boozing at Fran's Ready Room or one of the other VB watering holes where non-deployed SEALs could be found.

Beckam had sent them out on the ice, combing the wreckage blown for miles in every direction for medical supplies, food, and fuel for the two stoves they'd managed to resurrect. It hadn't been easy, most of the debris having been covered in a layer of ice blown over during the blast. But they'd found enough to survive on. For a time.

"We can't stay here forever, Boss."

Frantino was finally awake, looking clear-eyed but worn.

"How's the pain?"

"On a scale of one to ten, a twelve—way better than twenty."

"Need a shot of the good stuff?"

"Always, but my dealer says his supplies are tight. I'll just hold out."

"The Clays are looking for more meds," Beckam said. "Morphine's in short supply, so try and bite down on it if you can." Beckam checked to made sure Frantino was tucked in and warm as possible in the penetrating cold. "I had hopes Antarctica might work out as a get-away-from-it-all, retirement option, but I'm starting to have my doubts."

Frantino nodded, managed a weak grin. "You know the Russians made a tactical airdrop somewhere out there on the ice. I think it's time we take the bull by the horns and rescue our own asses."

"Reading my mind, Danny." Beckam patted Frantino gently on the shoulder. "The Clays are feeling strong and I'm sick and tired of this hotel. Given the atmospheric interference, planes won't be flying over us any time soon."

The sound of the makeshift door in the creaky fuselage turned both men's heads. The Clay brothers had finished their treasure hunt. Except it seemed that they'd returned without any real treasure, only Heckler & Koch automatic weapons slung over their cold-weather combat gear.

Beckam said, "Come on over, guys. I'm about to make a command decision."

Liam Clay winked at his brother. "Boss, if this is a personal-hygiene inspection, I can tell you right now we're not gonna pass."

"No shit. I can smell you clear across the ice. No worries. We're on modified grooming standards until we reach civilization." He winked. "No, what I'm saying is, Danny and I are sick of this dump. Sorry, Frogs, but it's time to leave this slice of heaven."

Lenny's eyes widened. "No shit? We're outta here? You got a plan?"

"That's why they pay me the big bucks. I always have a plan."

Liam high-fived his brother. "I was damn sure I was gonna die, a handwritten note pinned to my chest: Cause of death: Vienna sausage."

Beckam chuckled. The Russians had left cases of Vienna sausages stacked around the camp and in the Antonov. He and the boys had been living on VS for the duration.

"Our tactical situation," Beckam said, "is that we've had no visual contact with aircraft since detonation. Negative communications and no GPS. We can assume the same goes for the Russians' GLONASS satellites. Otherwise we would've seen their planes by now. Two possible scenarios: The alien structure emitted a high-energy beam when the civvies breached the interior, and the energy burst either destroyed communications and global-navigation satellites or rendered them inoperable."

"So here we are," Liam said, "twenty-thousand klicks from Virginia—sitting in the reefer from hell and a communications blackout. I think that about sums it up." He looked to his brother.

Lenny held up his H&K. "Yeah, but look at the upside—we're destined for the history books. First firefight of World War III, right here. This baby here's headed for the Smithsonian."

Beckam removed a plasticized map of Antarctica from his pocket and unfolded it. "We've got plenty of stove fuel to melt ice, at least enough for a week, maybe two. When the fuel runs out, we'll have to have scoop it into the bottles, and wear them inside clothing in order to make water. A short-term solution at best." He used a gloved hand to point out a spot on the Antarctic map. "Our position is here. The nearest survival point is here." Beckam drew an imaginary line with his finger from their position near Thor's

Hammer to the center of the South Pole. He tapped on the South Pole and said, "Amundsen-Scott's around five-hundred kilometers away as the crow flies."

Frantino croaked, "A long walk, even on a nice summer day."

"Right. Plus, we're deaf, dumb, and blind. Without dependable GPS, regardless of how we got there, we'd likely miss it. No need to discuss in detail the ramifications." Beckam moved his finger to the center of the magnetic South Pole, north of the geographic South Pole and a thousand kilometers from their current location. "See what happens if we use a compass and navigate straight for the magnetic South Pole?"

"Yeah," said Liam. "We miss Amundsen-Scott by half a continent and end up in Nowhere, Antarctica."

"Right. However, the South Pole Transverse runs here." Beckam drew a straight line from the large American base at McMurdo, located on the coast, to Amundsen-Scott at the bottom of the globe. "The highway's an overland route used during the summer months to transport supplies and equipment to Amundsen-Scott from Murdo. It's marked by a series of flags running the entire length, around a thousand klicks."

Liam nodded. "We'd still have to find those flags, then?"

"Negative. The summer traffic leaves pretty clear tracks grooved into the ice. If we set a course for the Magnetic South Pole, even if we're off a few degrees, it won't matter. We'd have to cross the Transverse here." Beckam showed how they'd bisect the South Pole Transverse on a path to the Magnetic South Pole.

"Once we hit the Transverse, we make a left turn and follow it right up to Amundsen-Scott. Assuming Amundsen hasn't been blown up, all we need is a deck of cards while we wait out a rescue. I'm discounting any chance that the Russians have occupied it, for now. Even if the base's been destroyed, it's riddled with tunnels dug under the ice during the last fifty years: under-ice food storage, snow-cats, fuel and more. We'd find shelter and plenty of food, enough to survive on until we figure out our next move." He shrugged. "And if the Russian are there? We go out in a blaze of glory."

Liam elbowed his brother. "Could be a quite a stroll, bro. Not that I couldn't do it."

"Affirmative," Beckam replied. "I have no interest in setting the Guinness Book of World Records for dumbass crossings of Antarctica using a Boy Scout compass, walking stick, a can of sausages, and a Sierra Club space blanket."

"Note to Boss," Frantino said, raising a shaky hand. "I can't walk."

Beckam grinned. "How could I forget? We know the Russians made a tactical drop of support gear for the airborne platoon we engaged prior to the detonation. My best guess is the drop was over here." He pointed on the map to a location south of their position. "Far enough out to avoid parachuting gear into a gunfight. Maybe ten, fifteen klicks out. Without GPS navigation, getting back will be a risk. If we were Army Rangers, we'd be crying for Mama after the first klick, but we're SEALs."

The brothers nodded in unison. Frantino managed to raise his eyebrows in solidarity.

"All righty, then," said Beckam. "An Arctic-spec drop for Spetsnaz commandos will contain food, ammunition, weapons, shelter, meds, and most important...transportation. You'll take along tools scattered around our aluminum home here. Given no GPS and zero-visibility windstorms blowing up without warning, you'll use them to mark your trail out and back. Use a compass azimuth and the reciprocal. Straight out, ten klicks and back. Use binoculars to eyeball the terrain off the azimuth for the supply drop. Then straight back. Don't chase ghosts. If the weather breaks bad, you don't want to be guessing the return bearing. Got it?"

"Understood," said Liam.

His brother nodded. "Got it, Boss."

"If we're in luck, they over-delivered and dropped a few Taiga snow machines with fuel, sleds, and toboggans. Those are the tops on our shopping list. And, boys?"

The twins lifted their chins, awaiting his order.

"One more thing," Beckam said, "and you'll like this one. You find any Russians? Kill them clean and quiet."

L eah dodged piñon pines, hurdling roots and rocks, but no matter how hard she tried to keep up, she continued falling farther behind. Her lungs burned, sucking the thin air of the 4,500-foot elevation as the hunting party continued to range ahead of her.

The hunters were five Native Americans from three different tribes, and the last time they'd stalked deer had been during the late Middle Ages, when King John Lackland ruled England. Leading them now was Appanoose, a Lakota by birth who had no business living in a cliff dwelling in southern New Mexico. Appanoose had a powerful physical presence and an attitude to match, which had quickly made him the de facto chief and shaman for the twenty-seven others.

Certain other traits separated the leader from the rest of the Ancients, as Leah had dubbed the survivors: While the others still seemed to suffer certain after-effects from their rescue from the stasis units almost three weeks ago—never mind the plane flights, medical examinations, strange foods, sounds, lights—Appanoose never seemed even slightly startled, shocked, or uncertain. Instead, he served as a steady, imperious presence among the other

Ancients, seemingly having risen, by default, to be their leader in this strange, new world.

Leah had tried to engage Appanoose on more than one occasion during the seven days since the Ancients had arrived at the Settlement, twenty days since Leah and her companions had touched down at Holloman Air Force Base after the nightmare in Antarctica.

The Settlement was a re-creation of a village typical of the time period in which the Ancients had lived. Leah's utopian concept of returning these people to their traditional lifestyles hadn't gone so well. No. Strike that. So far, it had been an utter and complete failure. Whenever she tried to engage the Ancients in traditional Native American activities, they simply stared at her. Only when the shaman spoke to them in low, reassuring tones would they act, rarely doing as she wished. And the shaman never, ever spoke to Leah directly.

So far, Appanoose and she had agreed on only one thing. When the Ancients had arrived at White Sands, they'd been dressed in one-piece, military flight suits, drab olive in color, with sneakers and jackets. In advance of their arrival, Leah had gathered as much traditional clothing as she could find: buckskins, furs, and moccasin-style footwear, all period-accurate. Seeing the native garb, Appanoose had immediately ordered the Ancients to discard the modern clothing and don the traditional wear.

For her part, Leah had tried to follow suit, also wearing the skins and furs and moccasins, but it was so cold in these New Mexico mountains that she'd given it up after less than a day, returning to the flight suit, long underwear, a down parka, and hiking boots. Her longtime friend and fellow archaeologist Garrett Moon had opted for a mix. He wore the flight suit but, instead of the down parka, he wore buckskins and furs over the military jumpsuit, cutting quite the handsome figure, as Leah had assured him.

Like Leah, Garrett had no chance of keeping up with the Ancients as they hunted. Leah had expected the Ancients to be tougher and fitter than modern-day humans, but she and Garrett had soon realized that their speed and endurance were at a completely different level. For one thing, they seemed impervious to the cold. Half the time, they went barefoot, despite the frigid time of year.

Today had been the best day so far in the Settlement's one week of existence. Almost enough to make Leah feel encouraged. Perhaps the Ancients were acclimatizing to their environment, as shown by their sudden willingness to form the traditional hunting party that she was trying to keep up with now.

Leah wasn't a hunter—and, frankly, didn't like anything about it—so she'd had no idea what to expect. The warriors armed themselves with hand-carved spears made of pine. Between six and eight feet long, the weapons featured no exquisitely hand-chipped obsidian heads. Instead, they'd been sharpened to a needle point, with the back of the spear shaft shaved down significantly, perhaps to provide better throwing balance.

Many of the warriors also carried military-spec, black, stainless-steel knives. That had not been part of her plan. Leah had raided a number of museums for artifacts, including spear points and axes, then arranged for the items to be delivered to Holloman Air Force Base, where they were bundled up and flown by helicopter to the Settlement's designated landing zone about ten kilometers away. Far enough, she'd hoped, that with a proper approach the sound or sight of the Black Hawks wouldn't frighten the Ancients. Yet, somehow, within forty-eight hours of having established the village, at least six of the warriors had come into possession of what Leah learned were ONSP2-BRK Air Force Survival knives—the type carried by the Air Force personnel who manned the Settlement's interior perimeter. Sure enough, within a day, a number of the perimeter guards had reported that they'd 'lost' their knives. Clearly, the handful of Ancients, led by Appanoose, had 'procured' them under the cover of night with stealth and dexterity that could have rivaled that of The Artful Dodger and Fagin from Oliver Twist.

The Air Force security personnel of course, wanted the knifes back, but when Garrett approached Appanoose, he'd been rebuffed immediately by the shaman's customary single head-shake.

The Ancients had since put the knifes to good use, tackling a wide variety of tasks, from cutting firewood and prying rocks free to creating their lethal wooden spears.

She hadn't told her husband Jack about the knives...yet. She expected he'd tell her that she shouldn't be surprised – that the Ancients had already proven themselves willing and able to murder when threatened, as proven by the evidence Leah had originally uncovered in their centuries-abandoned cliff dwellings. Evidence that had originally sent her to Antarctica.

If asked, Leah said that she felt no threat from these people at all. But the truth was, walking about the Settlement was increasingly reminding her of cage-diving with great white sharks—sans the cage.

Leah pushed pine boughs away from her face as she continued chasing the Ancients. Her jog slowed to a walk when her lungs and heart could take no more. She stopped and put her hands on her knees, panting for precious oxygen. She turned to look for Garrett Moon. Nowhere to be seen.

Leah stripped off her parka and tied it around her waist. She'd gone from freezing to sweating during the chase. She reached blindly for the water bottle that should have been hanging on her side. At some point during the past four or five miles, it had slid free of the nylon holder.

Garrett appeared moments later, jogging along at a steady pace. Leah had tried to keep up with the Ancients by sprinting, then jogging until she was gassed. She should have taken Garrett's approach: slow and steady. He hardly looked winded.

He pulled a water bottle from inside his buckskins and handed it to Leah. "I saw it pop off maybe two miles back. Rolled down that hillside."

She sucked down several deep mouthfuls of cold water before handing the bottle back to Garrett. "There's no way I can keep up with them. How can these people, who haven't exercised in more than eight-hundred years, run like freaking deer?"

Garrett shook his head, then shaded his eyes, scanning ahead for any sign of the Ancients. "We'll never catch them. Want to turn around?"

"What? And look like a major league powder-puff in front of that arrogant bastard Appanoose? No thanks. I'd rather have a stroke and go out on top."

Garrett grinned. "Age before beauty."

"Am I looking that worn-out?" Leah said, with a smile. Garrett and Leah were not related by blood, more like sister and brother than a pair of Native American archaeological fanatics. Garrett had a tough upbringing on the Navajo Reservation, and Leah's dad, also a noted archaeologist, had taken Garrett under his wing. Leah had been just three or four at the time. Duncan Andrews took Garrett Moon out on archaeological digs in New Mexico, educating him about his amazing ancestors, long before Leah was out of grade school. When Garrett had turned eighteen, he'd enlisted in the Air Force and served twenty years until retirement as an aircraft mechanic. Once out of the Air Force, he'd bought his own Cessna 172 Skyhawk, and with time on his hands, began flying Leah around the southwest in search of her nirvana: undiscovered Ancient cliff dwellings. Dwellings that had not been swept clean of artifacts and information over the past thousand years.

Leah judged that she'd recovered enough to jog once more. She held the pace for five minutes, eyes on the path to avoid tripping on the tree roots, rocks, and small washouts that dotted the trail.

Without warning, an arm reached out and grabbed her, pulling her off the trail with such force, she might go head over heels, perhaps even tumble down the hillside. Instead, the hand yanked her back from the precipice.

Leah found herself staring into the piercing eyes of Appanoose, his face expressionless as he gripped her shoulders tightly. She was about to open her mouth and give him a piece of her mind when he pulled her closer and uttered one word in Navajo:

"Nizéé'."

Silence.

Leah knew the word, as did Garrett. What didn't make sense was how Appanoose, a Lakota, knew Navajo. Could he have chosen to use that language because he somehow knew Leah spoke it but not Lakota?

Appanoose stayed hidden with Leah behind a piñon pine until Garrett came shuffling up the trail.

"Ooljéé'."

Garrett stopped in his tracks. Ooljéé' translated as 'moon' in Navajo. Appanoose had taken to calling Garrett by his given name.

Leah kept her mouth shut, as instructed, while Appanoose, using hand signals, indicated that they should follow him...quietly. He led them across the deer trail, then down a slope where the trees dispersed into a large meadow. Grazing in the meadow were a doe and two button bucks—likely the doe's offspring, perhaps six or eight months old. None of the other warriors were in sight. Leah glanced back into the eyes of Appanoose, and he nodded in the direction of the deer.

Leah felt nauseated. The idea of the warriors chasing an old buck had been distasteful enough. But to see Appanoose planning to kill this helpless doe and her two young bucks with those sharpened spears.... She felt bile rising. Beads of sweat broke out on her forehead. She would have given *anything* to be *anywhere* except right here, right now.

She gauged the distance to the doe and her bucks. At least 100 meters from the tree line in every direction. Even with a perfect spear toss, it was a long shot. And if the deer bolted too soon...impossible.

Appanoose slowly raised his hand up, palm open. When he closed his hand into a fist, it was if he'd never been there. The space where he'd stood was empty. Leah watched in stunned silence as the warriors burst out of the forest from all points of the compass at inconceivable speed.

They covered the hundred meters in less than five seconds. Before the deer could raise their heads, they were surrounded by all five Ancient warriors, including Appanoose, spear raised above their heads, frozen in launch position.

Leah shut her eyes and covered her ears. She couldn't stand to hear the sound of the deer screaming as they were speared. Seconds later, she opened her eyes. The warriors still stood frozen, spears prepared to strike, the deer surrounded and too terrified to move.

Suddenly, Appanoose flipped his spear vertically and stepped back. The other four warriors did exactly the same. The deer, sensing an opening, bolted for the protection of the trees, leaping in huge, three-meter gallops.

Leah stood, mouth opened, in stunned silence as the warriors walked toward Garrett and her. When she found her voice, she asked Garrett, "What the hell did we just witness?"

"Don't know but I'm guessing we're about to find out."

Appanoose turned to the other warriors, speaking to them in low tones. They nodded and sprinted across the meadow and into the tree line, headed back toward the Settlement.

Appanoose approached the two modern humans, then pulled Garrett aside and spoke to him. Leah felt irritation welling, and she walked forward several steps, not willing to let Appanoose keep her out of the conversation.

"What did he say?" she asked.

"I asked him why they allowed the deer to go free. Deer are an important source of food for the Settlement. He said they don't kill needlessly. I repeated that they needed to hunt—that they needed a source for food. It's winter, and they can't plant and grow until spring."

"What did he say to that? 'We don't need to eat?' We know *that's* not true."

"Nope. He said it was a crime to unsettle the balance of nature, for sport, or exhibition. Then he gave me that sly look and said, 'You provide all the food necessary.'"

Leah turned to Appanoose, who was looking up at the heavens. It was getting to be late afternoon. He nodded skyward. "Cha-hałheeł." Then he pointed at Leah's parka and added, "Hak'az." With that, he gave a nod and raced down the deer trail, following his warriors.

Leah thought she understood his gist. "I gather he said it's getting dark and we're gonna freeze our asses off."

"Yep, pretty much." Garrett sighed and looked at her. "Well, we've got a whole new set of complications now. And they've got nothing to do with the cold."

Leah blurted it out for him. "They aren't human, are they? You saw how fast they closed on the deer. Covering a hundred meters in, what, five seconds? That cuts the world record in half." She took a deep breath. "As much as I'd like to keep this to myself, I have to update Gordon. If Wheeler finds out what they can do, he'll roll in here in no time and take the Ancients. Study them to make super soldiers, or something equally hideous."

Garrett nodded. "Also, Appanoose just made a pretty clear statement to us: we can take our whole return-to-a-traditional-way-of-life plan and shove it up our asses."

2

Leah crawled out of her mummy sleeping bag, immediately sweeping the area with outstretched arms, searching for her wool gloves and matching wool pullover cap. She was physical and mentally exhausted from yesterday's lesson in humility from Appanoose and his warriors.

She glanced at her sport watch: past eight a.m. She could imagine the shaman, pointing toward the sandstone overhang where Leah slept and uttering the Lakota word for 'Snow Flake.'

Well, from what she'd learned yesterday, not even the strongest Navy SEAL could compete physically with the Ancients.

Leah dressed as quickly as her sore limbs and back allowed, donning two sets of long underwear, then sliding into the flight suit. That done, she slipped on her running shoes, once gray from the factory, now a permanent shade of red from the local trail dust.

She had to shade her eyes from the bright, blue skies after the relative darkness of the overhang. The Settlement was bustling this morning. The women, who Leah had nicknamed fierce-femmes, were busy cooking the government-supplied corn and beans, traditional staples of the agriculturally-oriented Pueblo and Navajo diets. Appanoose was busy directing his warriors as they wove together a series of long, pine branches that had been cut and stripped of bark. Garrett Moon stood nearby, arms crossed over his chest and brows knit in concentration as he observed. Leah limped in his direction, brushing knotted, gray-streaked brunette hair out of her face and stuffing it under the wool cap.

"What's going here?" she asked.

"Sweat lodge," said Garrett.

"Think Appanoose needs a little heat to work those tight muscles after yesterday's hunt and hike? Or rather, just hike...."

Garrett chuckled. "Not likely."

"What time did they start this?" she asked.

"Think they've been working on it all night. They started by hunting up these pine branches, then cutting and stripping them."

She shook her head. "I was sure until yesterday that their lack of sleep was due to anxiety and stress. But after watching them crush the hundred-meter-dash world record—barefoot—I'm inclined to believe they just don't need much sleep."

"Ditto for exposure," Garrett said. "They're impervious to cold weather." He glanced over. "One more thing—we're gonna need another delivery of corn and beans to the supply LZ."

"Noted. They're eating us out of house and home. The original stock should have lasted weeks. Ancient metabolisms seem way, way faster than ours."

Garrett said, "How is it that Gordon didn't pick up on this?"

"The clues were there," she said. "Gordo said the Ancients were in excellent health. Beyond what he would expect from peoples living a hard existence in the ancient past. I didn't see any evidence they could run at gazelle-speed until a few days ago. I'll take the satellite phone up on the mesa and call him—as soon as I regain use of my legs."

"Diyin Dine'é! Diyin Dine'é!"

Leah watched K'aalógii running among the Ancients, her deer-like feet barely touching the ground.

"Uh oh," Leah said. "Gotta be a helicopter."

"Diyin Dine'é" translated roughly in Navajo as "Angry Gods." The young girl K'aalógii was the only Ancient that still used the outdated term to refer to the security helicopters working the perimeter of the wilderness area. The military pilots were under strict orders never to overfly the Settlement, and mostly they complied. Despite that, the Ancients heard the helicopters daily, though Leah and Garrett could neither hear nor see the Black Hawks.

Add another gift to the Ancients' enhancement package, she thought.

A couple of minutes later, she finally heard the sharp *thwap* of rotor blades echoing off the canyons. A Black Hawk was inbound... from the wrong direction and wrong altitude.

Really, guys? Another navigational error?

Leah shaded her eyes. Sure enough, here came a Black Hawk, fudging the No-Fly Zone. She hadn't called for support and wondered why the crew was approaching from the wrong direction. Several of the Ancients jogged toward the sound of the approaching Black Hawk, shading their eyes while Garrett tried to direct them back to the Settlement.

The Black Hawk made a sudden roll away from the Settlement and inexplicably pitched downward, losing significant altitude in the process. Either it had suddenly occurred to the pilot that his next flying job was going to be supporting well-drilling in Mozambique, or else the Black Hawk had suffered a mechanical issue and was in trouble. Leah had already seen the result of one Black Hawk crash when a rotor clipped a towering pine tree while landing. The Black Hawk had spun itself into a pile of parts, sending shrapnel in every direction for two hundred meters or more.

That crash had killed Glen Janssen, the forest ranger who had entered the cliff dwelling after Leah and shown her discovery to Teresa Simpson, then the Bureau of Land Management director. Following his death, Leah had worried that the Genesis Settlement might be cursed, and nothing since that crash had convinced her otherwise.

As the Black Hawk continued its steep descent, Leah could only assume the worst:

It's gonna crash.

3

"I'm going to the supply LZ," she told Garrett. "If the helo is in trouble, he'll be headed there—it's the only good clearing for miles around." She hesitated. "Are you okay here by yourself?"

"As long as I don't piss off Appanoose, there's a better than fifty-fifty chance I won't have my throat cut while you're gone."

Leah stopped dead and gave Garrett a look. "That might have been a funny a few days ago."

Then she turned around, braced her sore body for the road ahead, and ran.

Rather, she first tried running, then resorted to jogging along the steep, deer-trail switchbacks. Quickly, her pace devolved into a hobbling walk-jog, her muscles resisting anything resembling yesterday's adventure. Fortunately, she didn't have to run all the way to the Landing Zone.

Her other transportation option between the Settlement and LZ had also been provided by the military: An Army Special Forces-equipped electric quad runner. It was similar to the four-wheel, off-road vehicles that every redneck and rancher in New Mexico owned. But then again, not. The Army's electric version was equipped with high-tech options such as a suspension system that rode on magnetic fluid and a computer-adjusted suspension system to smooth the ride. Powered by a Tesla-like rechargeable lithium battery, the quad could roam more than a hundred miles at thirty miles per hour and achieve a neck-breaking top speed of sixty—all while making no sound whatsoever.

Perimeter security had built a camouflaged 'hide' two-kilometers north of the Genesis Settlement, deep within the forest. By the time she finished the 2K run, Leah was, once again, sucking her lungs inside out. On a more positive note, her leg muscles had finally given in, and she'd been able to run about half the distance to the hide.

Once she reached the branch-camouflaged hide, she pulled out the Ontario Survival Egress Knife that she needed in order to free the quad. Quickly, she cut the green, braided line that locked a pine-bough-woven 'door' in place. With the door free, Leah reached in and gripped the vehicle's handle bars, using all her weight to muscle the quad out of the piñon shelter. After several f-bombs and other curses worthy of her mechanic friend Mac Ridley, she hauled the quad clear.

Leah swept the helmet off the seat and tossed it back into the hide. The 'brain-bucket,' as security called it, had a tendency to slide down over her eyes. A fact she kept to herself when interacting with the security personnel. No need to reinforce any bogus "girl" stereotypes, despite their repeated advice to wear the helmet and the armored dirt-bike jacket, she wore neither.

Leah re-secured the hide, flung a leg over the quad, and pushed the red power button center-left of the display. When the display lit up and the LED lights flashed green, she rolled on the throttle, just enough to get the four-wheeler moving. The last thing she needed was to leave a pair of non-native, peel-out skid marks right next to the hide.

Several hundred meters north, Leah descended into a solid sandstone wash and 'put the spurs to it!' climbing out the opposite side, as one Texas-born soldier had shown her. Unfortunately, she didn't take into account the incline, which forced her cen-ter-of-gravity backward, sending the front tires skyward into a wheelie, the quad nearly flipping over backward and trapping her underneath.

Leah cut the throttle, and the quad slammed down on the front tires with such force that she banged her forehead on the control panel. An instant reminder of why she needed the damned hel-met. Leah had spent hundreds of hours driving ordinary quads in the desert during her archaeological fieldwork, but none even approached the torque or speed of the Special Operations, com-bat-qualified quad.

"Whoa, Nellie," she whispered. "That's it. Let's go."

Coasting down the opposite side of the wash, Leah sucked in a deep breath, moved her weight forward over the handle bars, twisted open the throttle, this time keeping the front tires, mostly, on the sandstone as she sped toward the Supply Landing Zone.

4

As she approached the LZ, Leah saw that the Black Hawk had succeeded in making a landing with all its parts still attached. It had already powered down and, upon closer inspection, appeared unharmed.

She parked the quad under a tree, suddenly less relieved that the helo hadn't crashed than irritated by this latest incursion into the No-Fly-Zone.

She peered into the Black Hawk. No sign of the crew. She scanned the tree line. Sure enough, three guys in flight suits moseyed out of the forest.

Taking a leak behind a tree, she thought, holding back a grin. *Glad to see they've been trained in wilderness-survival techniques.*

Anticipating a tongue-lashing from the famously temperamental archaeologist, the two pilots and even the crew chief raised their hands in surrender. The command pilot, wearing captain's bars, took a step ahead of his crew. "Dr. Andrews! Hold fire! Not our fault!"

She gave them her best effort at a scowl but couldn't hold it. "Captain Hutchinson, Lieutenant Cruz, and Sergeant Bruce. What's wrong with you guys? You know if you make your approach from the south, you're violating our basic security protocols."

The twenty-something, fresh-faced combat veteran said, "Yes, ma'am. You've briefed us many times—we tried several times to contact you via the satellite phone, but had no luck raising you."

Oh yeah, she thought. *Again, the satellite-phone issue.* "You know I can't tote a satellite phone around the Settlement," she said, formulating a best-defense-is-a-good-offense strategy on the fly.

The pilots glanced at each other, confused as to the proper course of action. They stepped back in unison as she approached within arm's reach.

"What?" Leah asked, raising her arms.

Hutchinson grinned, but he was smart enough not to say anything. The crew took another step back.

"Relax. Boys. As much as I might want to, kicking your asses isn't my style."

"That's not why they're backing up, love."

Leah spun as Jack Hobson sauntered out of the piñon.

"Jack!" Leah sprinted toward the handsome climber and was ready to throw her arms around him, when he also stepped back, raising both hands defensively.

"Is this the greeting I get?" she said, more hurt than angry. "I'm pretty sure I haven't caught the Black Plague from the local rodent population."

Jack put his hands on his hips. "And you thought my climbing gear reeked after six weeks on Everest? Damn, girl, you are downright...." He feigned a shiver.

Leah had been living and working in the cliffs with the Ancients without a bath for seven days now, dressed in the same flight suit, which had absorbed smoke, body odor, and more. She'd cooked the government-supplied corn and beans in period-accurate pottery, choked down smoke on the underside of the sandstone cliffs, gathered wood until her hands bled. She'd gone so 'Ancient' that she no longer noticed the aroma. She took a deliberate whiff of herself and the stench hit her like a slaughterhouse during a heatwave.

Jack was being polite.

Leah reached up and kneaded her stringy hair, then studied her hands. Her nails, rarely manicured at the best of times, were unrecognizable. Her hands were grimy, the knuckles covered with cuts, scrapes, and burns, the aforementioned nails jagged, broken, and dirty.

"Oh yeah...well, you know, I've been busy. Sorry, guys!"

Without warning, Jack reached out, picked his wife up, and hugged her tight. He set her down, leaned over, and gave her a deep kiss.

"Wow, "she said, wiping at her mouth, mortified at how far out of touch she'd gotten with her real life away from the Ancients.

"I tried the satellite phone for two straight days," Jack said. "Nada."

Leah unconsciously wiped her hands on the skins, to no effect. "I'm sorry. I've been so immersed with the Ancients, and it's a pain to carry the thing around."

"Leah. I've got to be able to get in touch with you." Jack pointed at the Black Hawk crew. "Security has to be able to stay in contact. Don't forget, there're a lot more people involved in this beyond you and Garrett."

Leah simply nodded in agreement.

"Don't blame Captain Hutchinson for buzzing you," Jack continued. "He screamed bloody murder that you'd draw and quarter him if they approached from the south." Jack gave her a guilty smile. "Truth is, I wanted to get a look at the Settlement from the air."

Leah nodded. "Well, no harm done. The truth is, the Ancients don't run away from the helicopters anyway—they run toward them. The chuck wagon, rolling in."

Jack seemed to sense her distress. "How is your plan working out?"

She winced. Despite her personal pledge to stay positive, even if it required an Academy Award-winning performance, Jack had definitely picked up her malaise. She could hear it in his tone.

"Not so good, for all of the above reasons and more. We can discuss."

"Could it be our esteemed expert on all things 'Star Trek' had it right." Jack crossed his arms, mimicking Marko Kinney: "'The Prime Directive. Rule Number One. Never introduce advanced technology to naturally developing, less-advanced cultures and expect good things. It's always a recipe for disaster.'" He shrugged. "You don't mess with the Prime Directive."

Leah gave him a pained smile. "A little late to undo that, isn't it?"

"A little late to undo a lot of things," Jack agreed.

Leah gave a small laugh. "At least our extraterrestrial friends had the good sense to put those people to sleep. It's like herding cats over there." She glanced over to see Hutchinson already in the command seat, ready to spin the turbine jet engines on the Black Hawk.

"Wait...don't tell me you forced Hutchinson to risk his career overflying secured airspace just to get my attention. Not that I don't appreciate it."

The expression on Jack's face meant bad news.

"What is it, Climber? After what we've been through, how bad can it be?"

"There's news, Leah. I felt this should come from me directly— instead of through Gordon, or someone else."

"Bad news? Tell me something I don't already know."

"Okay. First, the President."

"About time." Leah rubbed her hands together. "This is gonna be good. So, have you had a chance to water-board the SOB yet?"

"No." Jack drew in a breath. "Wheeler's not going anywhere. And he's keeping most of his staff intact, including Fischer, like Antarctica never happened."

"Are you kidding me?"

Jack nodded, his expression still ominous. "Let me give it to you straight. We're in a world of hurt right now. The Southern Ocean was the scene of a short but epic sea battle between us and the

Russians. That high-energy beam we triggered breeching the complex is raising hell over the continent of Antarctica. It knocked out all satellites in the area. Ditto radio and GPS. And to make matters worse, this bizarre blackout is spreading northward into the Southern Ocean."

She motioned for him to continue.

"That means that our forces, and the Russians' are increasingly deaf, dumb, and blind the closer to Antarctica they get. The American base at McMurdo was evacuated before this anomaly reached the Ross Ice Shelf. Further inland, whole different story. Amundsen-Scott base at the South Pole couldn't be evacuated, and there's been no contact with them since we left the ice. Several aircraft-carrier-based aircraft sent to do reconnaissance over the continent crashed, for unknown reasons."

Leah covered her mouth in shock. "I'm sorry, Jack. I'm so immersed in the Settlement that I forget you and Paulson are trying to prevent a nuclear war." With effort, she pasted on a smile. "So, how's it going over at Diaper?"

"Actually, we're just getting started over at DARPA." He enunciated the word carefully to counter her snide nickname for the agency. "First, we're cataloging the artifacts recovered from the facility, including the surviving stasis units," he said, referring to the high-tech pods in which the Ancients had been sleeping in stasis. "Kyra, the director, is brilliant, and she was briefed in detail on the whole Wheeler/Fischer debacle. One of the first things she said was that they both ought to be shot in the kneecaps and tossed into the mouth of a live volcano—so, I was instantly at ease." Jack's eyes opened wide. "Not to mention, she's a world-class triathlete. She takes a couple hours each day to work out. I'm the only one who can keep pace with her on a run—so of course, she loves me."

Leah pulled back, her eyes narrowing. "And her name's Kyra?"

Jack grinned. "Dr. Kyra Gupta. I can fill you in on the ride to Holloman. I told Gordon the chances were slim you'd leave the Settlement, but he was insistent I get you over to his slice of medical heaven for an hour of debrief. Plus, we can spend a little time together. A welcome change from the nightmare in Washington."

"Hm. No surprise Gordo wants to see me," Leah said. "I wondered as much when I saw the Black Hawk inbound without an appointment. Well, I'll give you all the horrific details on the way to Holloman."

Dr. Gordon, was tasked with the first medical examinations of the Ancients. He'd been so horrified at their future as lab rats, he'd helped Leah escape the facility at White Sands with the first of the awakened, and also the youngest: K'aalógii.

"Sounds like we all have bad news," Jack said. "Can Garrett handle the Ancients alone?"

Leah nodded. "He knows I was headed here." She felt the tension draining from her body. "Besides, he's got a better relationship with the Ancients than I ever will." She paused for a moment. "How about Marko? Is he still bomb-sitting? Complaining?"

"If so, he's talking to himself. We're on radio silence with him unless he needs to report an emergency."

"You mean like, 'I did something and the warhead's now making pre-explosion noises?'"

"Not even enough reason to break radio silence. Only in the unlikely event that a Special Operations Team comes sniffing around."

"You know they're looking...."

"As long as we provide no clues, they're not gonna find the location. That's why I gave him a PlayStation 3 with strict orders not to leave under any circumstances."

"He's got a PlayStation?"

"I kid you not. It's one generation back from the PlayStation 4, but how else are you gonna get a long-haired millennial like Marko to sit for days, maybe weeks, without searching for the nearest Taco Bell?"

"He might have scored the best job of all, in retrospect," Leah said. "Unlimited food. Sleep all day. Playing idiot video games all night. Like a pig in shit."

"Exactly how I pitched the job to him. The fact he is babysitting the warhead didn't seem to rattle him too much. The codes...that was a different story."

Leah stopped. "Jack—you didn't give Marko the codes..."

Jack nodded. "The only way the warhead continues to keep us alive is if there's a threat. If they thought we were only storing it, we'd have all been rounded up and shuttled out of country by now."

"But Marko? Enter bomb codes? Of all the people? I mean—seriously—he can't pour milk on cereal without spilling half of it on the table."

"I sealed the codes in an envelope and told Marko to keep it on his body at all times. He suggested his underwear—I told him inside a sock would be better." Jack smiled and shrugged. "Worked like a charm. I assume. He has no idea how to enter the codes. However, if we have to make a hardcore bluff, it's impossible to do if we have the warhead, but no codes in hand."

She glanced in the direction of the Black Hawk, which was ready to go. Hutchinson waved her over after making eye contact, then added his standard, 'stay away from the tail-rotor' signal: his hand slicing across his throat. It was an effective reminder.

Leah sighed. "Okay, let's do this." She inhaled deeply, cleared her head, then stepped up to Jack and hugged him again. "Hold your breath, Hobson."

"No need," he said, pulling her in tight.

5

Marko Kinney was by nature a night owl. His last real job had been working as a night stocking clerk for one of the two Whole Foods Markets in Albuquerque. He spent his daylight hours rock climbing, sleeping, and eating. Sometimes in that order, sometimes not. On the whole, he wasn't impressed with watches, clocks, or schedules. To avoid being late for work, he'd parked his beat-to-crap Toyota Four-Runner in the Whole Foods Parking lot around 8 p.m. He'd slide into the back of his climbing-gear-stuffed truck, close the door on the camper top, and sleep until his shift supervisor banged on the side of the truck twenty minutes before he was scheduled to clock in at midnight. Marko wasn't the only time-impaired employee working the graveyard stock shift; there were always two or three additional beater trucks parked out back. The supervisor used the same alarm system with them all, the only way to ensure that his graveyard crew came to work on time.

How times had changed. Now, instead of stressing over his midnight shift at a grocery store, Marko was babysitting an exotic nuclear warhead that could vaporize him and a good portion of the desert in an instant. Or, best case, make him a target for a lucky soldier with a high-powered rifle.

F*** Me....

His current location was unknown to all but a handful of people, including Jack Hobson, Jack's billionaire mountain-climbing client and friend Al Paulson, and the crazy-ass old pilot Luke Derringer.

Getting here had been as scary as anything Marko had experienced in his daredevil life. Old Luke Derringer had done everything but kill them flying a hot-rodded, single-engine Cessna between a series of cliffs and down onto a smooth, sandstone wash in the narrow canyon in southwestern New Mexico. Despite having been in dangerous situations before, Marko experienced a new level of 'pucker' with Derringer almost flying them into one rock wall after another.

Finally, on solid ground, they'd hustled the Hafnium bomb off the aircraft as old Luke pointed out, with trembling hand, a series of sandstone caverns carved into a nearby cliff face. They'd stashed the Hafnium warhead deep within one of the water-carved caverns, which had become Marko's new home.

The warhead, which Marko had christened 'Freddy Krueger,' slept soundly in the cavern, mere feet from Marko's own bed. His job was to live with the warhead twenty-four hours per day, with strict instructions to stay concealed; permission to leave only in case of *dire emergency.* Jack had defined *dire emergency* as either heart failure or heart failure combined with a paralyzing stroke.

Jack had acquired several cases of MREs—Meals Ready to Eat, the modern military version of K-Rations. In addition to the MREs, Jack had left him an inflatable mattress, a couple of expedition-quality, goose-down sleeping bags, and a Marmot Midgard mountaineering tent colored in an eye-pleasing fusion of terracotta and pale pumpkin. Designed for two with a floor dimension of 93" x 56", it had become Marko's home within a home for the foreseeable future.

Marko had said he'd do it—joking only, of course—if he could take a PlayStation along with him.

"No problem," Jack had replied, nonplussed. "We'll set up a lithium battery power station, operating through an inverter. Think of it as a small version of a Tesla power system. You won't be able to play online with the rest of your geek buddies, so let me know what games you can play solo. But don't plan on gaming day and night if you want to stay warm. We're rigging portable ceramic tent heaters to operate off the same system. It should provide a week's worth of power if you're using common sense and conservation."

Naturally, Jack had thought of everything.

"In addition," Jack had explained, "we're including a small wind generator and solar panel recharger. You *cannot* set this gear up outside the cavern. The entrance to the cavern is facing southeast. The sun should provide you six hours a day of solar recharge by hitting the panel *inside* the cavern. The wind generator can generate power any time the winds are blowing out of the south. When storms are inbound, and the winds shift south, it will generate power. You can position the generator at the mouth of the cavern at night, but you've got to remember to get it out of sight before sunrise. The wind generator also makes noise, so use common sense."

"Yeah," Marko had said sullenly. "That all sounds, you know, workable, except for one thing."

"Lemme guess…. Bathroom facilities."

"If I can't leave the cavern, it's gonna get kind of nasty in here quick."

"What? You can't hold it for ten weeks?"

"I might if you forced me…."

"I'm leaving it to you to get creative, Marko."

Creative. That was one word for it.

6

Leah sat in the portable conference room inside a secure aircraft hangar at Holloman Air Force Base, a steaming-hot cup of coffee and a pack of genuine Hostess chocolate Cupcakes served on a plate supplied by Dr. J. Alan Gordon.

Her visceral sense of failure had only been magnified by her ever-so-brief return to civilization. Her hair was still wet from the ten-minute steaming shower she'd requested upon landing at Holloman, but she'd elected to leave it stringy, dingy, and dirty—it seemed bad form to return to the Settlement with her hair shampooed, conditioned, and scented lilac.

Gordon walked into the conference room unannounced, clutching a stack of folders to his chest. He dropped the mass on the table and slumped into a chair. He'd lost considerable mass around the waist since she'd seen him a week ago. He would never win any fitness awards, but now he appeared frail and unhealthy, blue veins working up his wrists in ornate patterns, skin even paler than normal.

Pressure and stress, she thought. *A stone-cold killer.*

Gordon was a research geneticist and graduate of Armed Forces Medical School, but you wouldn't have known it by looking at him. His blow-dried comb-over and mustache gave him a strange resemblance to BTK serial killer Dennis Rader.

She skipped the pleasantries and nodded at the pile of paper. "Handouts?"

Gordon looked up at her, confused for a moment. "Handouts? No. Just ongoing research...never stops, you know."

"Excellent", she said, surprised Gordo hadn't mentioned the Ancients. "No handouts," she said. "Well, I'm guessing you didn't invite me up here for Netflix, coffee, and cupcakes."

Gordon pushed his glasses up his nose. "Where's Jack?"

"Jack took the flight suit I'd worn seven days in a row and tossed it in a Dumpster. Leah waved it off. "Long story. Anyway, he should be—"

Jack pushed open the door and stepped up into the room. "Sorry if I'm late." He plopped into a chair next to Leah, snatched her coffee cup, took a sip, and grimaced. "This is awful."

Leah snatched the cup back, then took a quick, protective bite of her cupcake. "I don't know what you're talking about," she said through a mouthful of crumbs, one hand trying to cover it up. "It's divine."

"If you say so," Jack said, eyeing her.

"Remember," she said through another bite, "I've been drinking stream water and eating pine nuts and squirrel intestine for what feels like eons."

Gordon failed to acknowledge the humor. "Am I to gather that the Genesis Settlement is not meeting your expectations thus far?"

Leah washed down the pastry with the last of her coffee. "If you're asking whether it's FUBAR, my military-scientist friend, you're right on target." Leah proffered the empty coffee cup. "Got any more of this sludge? I need a refill before delving into the details."

"Sorry about the coffee." Gordon paused. "Could I offer you real food...?"

Leah swallowed a sharp retort, unable to resist the thought of an actual, modern meal. "That'd be great. Just what I need to push me over the edge. One good meal and I'll be out of here so fast it'll make your head spin." She gave the doctor a wave of the hand to get him moving and waited until the door clicked shut behind him. A few minutes later, Gordon kicked the door open and carried in a fresh carafe of steaming coffee and a tray of Hostess pastries.

Jack raised his eyebrows at the "real food."

Leah rubbed her hands together. "Now we're talking." She poured a cup of coffee, grabbed two more cakes, and slid two more over to Jack. "We're guessing you didn't call me here to say we're being shut down."

Gordon blinked. "No. If I heard anything of the sort, I'd have flown out to the Settlement immediately."

"Excellent response, Gordo. You do know that was a test. Here's an FYI that's gonna blow your skirt up." She leaned toward the doctor to making her point more dramatic. "The President and his cronies, including Fischer, are still in power—and going no-where."

Gordon's eyebrows rose but he didn't comment.

Jack spoke instead. "There are matters I can't talk about—speaking of national security. None of it impacts the Genesis Settlement." Despite his reaction earlier, he polished off a pastry in two bites, then wiped flakes of frosting off the table. "I already told Leah most of this, but I'll repeat it so you have an update and can brief your people here."

Gordon nodded. "As we don't get any classified briefings here, it's much appreciated."

"Yeah. I figured. Okay, well...the Southern Ocean resembles the DC Beltway during rush hour. Ships, submarines, aircraft, and aircraft carriers increase in number daily. The Russian Fleet is schooled up off the Antarctic coast, using South Africa for resupply. After the planted nuclear detonation blew up the alien facility, there was an intense sea battle, resulting in the only sea-ready Kirov-class Russian guided missile cruiser, the *Pyotr Velikiy*, being sunk with its two escorts. It engaged Navy surveillance aircraft with missiles, shooting down at least one. Two more disappeared and it's thought they also were shot down as well. So the *Pyotr Velikiy* had it coming, for what it's worth. The loss of life is estimated at more than a thousand Russian crew."

"You didn't tell me that," Leah said quietly.

Jack nodded. "And I'm not done yet. We've lost an unconfirmed number of Navy strike aircraft, and two aircraft-carrier battle group escorts were sunk by Russian aircraft operating out of South Africa with air-to-air refueling. Some of the Russian air-to-air tankers have been shot down or disabled. One Los Angeles-class attack submarine is missing, and intelligence suspects one or more Russian submarines were also sunk by carrier-borne anti-submarine aircraft using a classified, super-smart torpedo."

Jack stopped to catch his breath.

"The slightly good news is that neither the United States or the Russians have gone nuclear, beyond the original nuke Wheeler detonated to destroy the alien facility. After that first bloody battle, both sides decided to back off and take a breath. With three carrier battle groups in the Southern Ocean, the US has air superiority, forcing the Russians away from the continent. But it's a sure bet that subs and bombers with nuclear payloads are on station. For now, the restraint both sides have shown—at least regarding nuclear weapons—is why we're able to have this conversation today. But the bottom line is, it's all balancing on the edge of a razor."

Leah was still trying absorb what she'd just learned when Gordo spoke. "How much do the Russians know...about the non-terrestrial technology?"

"Good question," Jack said. "Clearly enough to send a plane-load of airborne commandos shooting first, asking questions later."

"Well," Leah said, "as far as I'm concerned, we should make all the information public."

Gordon gave her a stern but slightly confused look.

"Seriously," she said. "You want to take the violence out of drug-dealing? You make drugs legal. Same principle here. Hoarding information only increases the tension and the chance of a radical miscalculation."

Jack said, "If we're spreading the goods around, does everyone get a piece of the action? North Korea included? Where do we draw the line?"

"Quite a chess match," Gordon said, "with a frightening end-game."

"Exactly."

"Speaking of which," said Gordon, "how long do you think you can hold our government hostage with your weapon?"

"Hey," Leah said. "You know better than anyone that we're dealing with a corrupt executive branch that'll commit mass murder at the drop of a hat. Yeah, it's messed up, but 'Freddy Krueger' is the only thing standing between us and a bullet in the back of the head." She aimed her finger and pulled an imaginary trigger. "And by 'us,' I mean you, too."

Gordon shut his eyes for a second, then nodded in agreement.

"Sorry if I sound harsh, Gordo. You know this whole situation is a disaster." She watched the doctor closely, wondering whether he too had observed the Ancients' physiological anomalies. "You're up. If you have bad news, spit it out."

Gordon removed and cleaned his glasses, a familiar nervous tic.

Leah and Jack waited for him to speak.

"We've done some additional analysis on blood samples taken from the Ancients. The results are confusing, startling, and perhaps even ominous." He glanced over at Leah. "Have you witnessed anything you'd classify as odd in behavior, or, have they suffered seizures, bleeding, anything that might could be mistaken for a stroke?"

Leah calmly tore open another cupcake wrapper and stuffed half the pastry into her mouth before offering Jack the other half. "Nothing of that nature, no. Now, if you'd asked whether they could cut the world record in the hundred-meter dash in half—barefoot over rugged ground—or sit nude in twenty-degree weather like they just climbed out of a hot tub in Telluride.... Or if you asked about their hearing, which is at least ten times as sensitive as ours.... Yeah. You'd have me there."

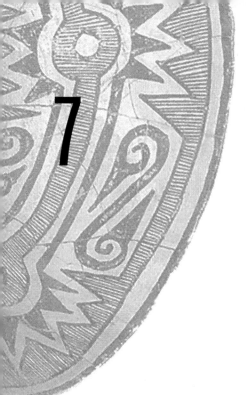

Gordon remained speechless for a moment. "You've noticed...*abnormalities?* You know as well as anyone that there's a *plausible risk of catastrophic consequences* if the Ancients—"

"Don't get your shorts in a twist," Leah said. "Your own tests already showed them to be free of contaminants, parasites, and infectious diseases."

Gordon took a deep breath. "Dr. Andrews, I understand and support your desire to prevent these peoples from suffering un-necessarily. However, if you are witnessing anomalies, you are required to report them. *At once.*"

"Well, your call to arms was well-timed. If Jack hadn't flown a Crash Hawk at tree-top level into the supply LZ, I was planning to contact you via satellite phone today."

Gordon seemed placated, curiosity quickly overtaking his irri-tation. "Can you describe what you've observed?"

"Yesterday, I watched Appanoose and four of his warriors close on three deer, from a distance of at least a hundred meters, in less than five seconds.

"That's impossible—for humans," Gordon said.

"Funny you say that, Gordo. That's exactly what I told Garrett. Let me run down the list: They're all pretty much impervious to cold. They hear inbound Black Hawks from miles out, minutes before Garrett or I hear the faintest sound. And they have little or no need for sleep. I'm almost a hundred percent sure they weren't exhibiting these characteristics when we first took them to the Settlement. Oh, yeah. One more thing. They're eating us out of house and home at an incredible rate. They must be slamming fifteen-thousand calories a day, and that's not easy to do on beans and corn. The cooking fires never stop."

Gordon had been making notes while Leah described her observations. Now he drew a deep breath and dropped the pen on his yellow pad. "That could be consistent to what we've seen within the blood samples over the past forty-eight hours. As you know, the initial physical examinations were 'abnormally normal' for people from their historic time period. In other words, their health was perfect, across the board, on every test. Naturally, we theorized that the stasis units also served to heal past injuries, maybe even repair organs, remove parasites, supercharge the immune system." Gordon's eyes sought Leah's. "The fact that you're beginning to see these...modifications fits our analysis."

He took three sheets of paper out of the top folder and passed two along to Jack and Leah. The pages were filled with columns of numbers, similar to what Leah saw when given her annual physical. A long list of blood tests. In this case, one list had a date of about fourteen days ago, another long list featured numbers and notations, dated yesterday.

"These are blood tests conducted upon arrival, and additional testing using blood from the same numerical samples. Red blood cells degrade progressively during refrigerated storage. Typically, we don't see real degradation in cells for weeks...."

"Are their red blood cells degrading abnormally fast?"

"No," Gordon said. "The opposite. The red blood cells in the samples have increased in both count and size of cell—increased *significantly*—over the past two weeks."

"That sounds like cancer," Leah said. "If it's even possible in a test tube."

"Cancer, I could explain. And frankly I'd be more comfortable if that's what the Ancients were presenting. But these cells are mutating and the counts are growing at an alarming rate. An impossible rate."

Jack said, "I could use some of that blood enhancement. Can you imagine the increase in body oxygenation at altitude? I could jog to the top of Everest and do it in a swimsuit I'd be so flush with O2."

"If you didn't die of a stroke before you reached the summit," Gordon said. "That's why I asked if Leah had witnessed anything that could match stroke symptoms."

Leah felt her anxiety growing. "Gordo—are you saying they could be suffering from polycythemia?"

"Yes. A condition in which there are too many red blood cells in the blood circulation."

"That causes strokes?" asked Jack.

"Yes," Gordon said. "When the body has an overabundance of red blood cells, blood is susceptible to clotting. A blood clot can cause stroke, heart attack, organ damage. It is lethal in some instances. In the case of the Ancients, from the samples we have tested, this abnormality is present within all our Ancients. In one case, it's accelerating well above the median." Gordon paused, appearing hesitant to say what he was thinking. "Our Ms. K'aalógii is suffering this growth condition at a faster rate than the rest of the Ancients."

Leah closed her eyes for a moment. She clenched her fists underneath the conference table, and drew in a deep breath to keep from getting emotional. "Tell me what we have to do, Gordo."

"At the very least, I need a fresh sample of her blood, immediately. Ideally, I'd want her here—where we can do a complete work-up and a wide series of tests. You alluded the shaman has become extremely protective of the Ancients. I would prefer a blood sample, over having you and Mr. Moon suffer injury or death at his hand...." He hesitated. "I'm wondering if it might be time to 'isolate' him from the rest of the Ancients. For your safety—and that of the Settlement." Gordon leaned away, as if he expected Leah to pick up a chair and toss it at him for the very suggestion.

Instead, Leah glanced up and studied the false ceiling for a moment. "I think that might be a very good suggestion, Gordo. His sway over the Ancients is growing by the day. I'll ask him if we can take K'aalógii for testing. I'll tell him her health is in danger. But if he refuses, then we'll need to act fast."

"Here's a head twister," Leah added. "We're on this hunt yesterday. Turns out, the entire event was staged theatre. Me and Garrett, the sole audience. Needless to say, he got his point across. But, he could have made the same point at the Settlement, without so much as getting up off his ass. Why would he do that?"

Gordon glanced back and forth between Jack and Leah. "I'm sorry. What hunt?"

Leah waved her hand. "He had three deer, good as dead, and walked away, then said something to the effect, 'I'm not hunting deer when I've got three square meals a day provided freebie.' He did not bother to add, 'I hope you enjoyed he six hours climbing over hill and down into ravine', but I got the message. Appanoose took hours to make a point he could have easily made to Garrett, then turned his back on me. Why?"

Gordon said, "As a teaching professor, I can tell you that demonstrating a point with an experiment, specifically one your students are invested in—gets the best result."

Jack nodded in agreement. "It does sound like Appanoose is taking time to school you. Didn't he give you some advice before he sprinted back to the Settlement, at the end of the hunt?"

"He said it was getting dark soon—and when it got dark it was going to get cold. That we should hustle our asses back to the Settlement, post haste."

Jack grinned. "See? Mr. Warm and Fuzzy. As much as he's pushing back at you and Garrett, he took time to make a point you already knew to be true. Perhaps a touch of 'playing nice' after giving you blisters. He's turning into the master of head games. We just need to figure out his game plan."

"Yeah. That threw me. He generally treats me like a stack of wet firewood." Leah said. "Plus, he didn't bother to cut our throats with the knife he stole from the perimeter security—so I have that in the positive column—today anyway."

"Day is still young…"

"Jack!"

"Kidding—still, we could be playing with the biological equivalent of Chernobyl, here. Maybe that's why these people were not returned home, why they were isolated in a sealed lab in Antarctica."

"That brings us to our current quandary," Gordon said. "I have not yet updated Mr. Paulson or anyone else in Washington about my findings. And there's no doubt that the Genesis Settlement, at least as Dr. Andrews envisioned, will cease the instant I report my findings. The Ancients will be quarantined for scientific and safety reasons. But clearly these individuals could turn aggressive, even dangerous, if the government tries to round them up."

"That's a given," Leah said, "if Appanoose is in charge when the round-up begins. I have no doubt, if challenged, they can be lethal."

"I want you and Garrett out of there," Jack said. "Don't even return to the Settlement. I'll go in there myself, tell Garrett you've come down with pneumonia, you've had to be hospitalized, and that he's needed for a fast debrief—anything to get the two of you safely away before the shit hits the fan."

"I hate to tell you guys, but I have a feeling that we're all underestimating Appanoose. He'll smell this double-cross coming a mile away." She turned to Gordon. "This comes down to you, Gordo. How soon are you planning to report your findings? When you report, we'll be lucky to have twenty-four hours before a platoon of Special Operations fast-rope into Gila and all hell breaks loose."

Gordon paused before answering, his expression conflicted. "Reporting could result in your death, and Mr. Moon's as well, following your line of reasoning. I hesitate to report results that could be misinterpreted without additional testing and analysis. I suggest we follow your plan. See if you can free Ms. K'aalógii for a medical work-up... That will also guarantee that she's not at the Settlement if...violence should break out."

Jack said, "If the shaman won't free K'aalógii, you and Garrett have to get out of there—as fast as you can. I'm not leaving until I know that you two are safe."

Leah closed her eyes, feeling a throbbing migraine starting to poke her left temple. That poke would soon turn into a ballpeen hammer. "I need another Gus Beckam. Someone I can trust, who can stand up to Appanoose." As quickly as she said it, Leah winced. The death of Navy SEAL Gus Beckam and his team was still a painful reminder of what had gone wrong in Antarctica.

If I'd only minded my business, as I'd been warned, none of this would be happening.

8

Liam and Lenny Clay stood beside the wrecked Antonov fuselage while Beckam gave the skies and horizon a quick look-see with binoculars. Wind had kicked up and visibility had closed in to less than half a mile.

Beckam swung his handheld compass in the general direction they'd spotted the first wave of Russian airborne troops. "I have the outbound bearing as one-niner-five," Beckam said, glancing once again at the compass. "The reciprocal is...one-five degrees on your return."

Liam Clay checked his compass. "Got it. We're good to go."

"Okay, Frogs. Get it done."

The Clay twins skedaddled.

The adrenaline rush of a combat task, and a battle plan does wonders for mental health, thought Beckam.

"If there's commie gear out there, they'll find it," said Frantino from inside the fuselage, his thumbs-up barely visible above the stacks of junk surrounding him.

"I'm not sure commie describes the current political situation in Russia," Beckam replied. "More like cult-of-personality?"

"Yeah. Well. Commie still works for me."

Frantino dropped his hand to his side.

Danny was getting weaker, Beckam noted. His survival, and their own, depended upon getting out of town, and fast.

Nine hours later, Liam Clay stuck his head back into the wrecked fuselage.

"Pay dirt?"

"Hell yeah, Skipper. Maybe ten klicks right on the azimuth. You called it. They air-dropped enough gear to move in permanent. The pallets are cemented in snow and ice, compliments of the detonation. Lenny's getting a jump on cutting through the ice with his MK-3, but we could use a shovel or, even better, a pick-axe."

Beckam was delighted—especially on behalf of Frantino. "There'll be a shitload of tools strapped in with the gear—right on top if they offload the same way we do. Let's see what we have around here that can get the party started. Once we break a pallet or two open, it'll be the land of milk and honey."

Searching in and around the fuselage, they soon located several four-centimeter-diameter sections of loose steel pipe. "This ought to work fine as an ice-chipper," Beckam said, holding up a meter-long section.

He walked over and knelt beside Frantino. "Hang tight, Danny. We'll be back inside five hours with transportation out of this dump."

His executive officer coughed and squeezed his eyes shut before speaking, "I'm good, Skipper." He lifted a gloved hand and grasped Beckam's.

Beckam grinned and grabbed Danny's hand in both of his. "I think our rotten luck is changing."

"Get 'em, Boss. And bring back something to eat besides Vienna Sausage."

Beckam nodded in agreement, then patted his XO on the shoulder "Roger that." He spun and found Liam Clay waiting impatiently with a pipe in one hand and his MP5 slung over his shoulder.

Beckam and Liam traced the prints the twins had laid down on the outbound azimuth. Liam quickly overtook Beckam, setting a fast pace toward the Russian airborne drop. Beckam paused for a breather, catching a glimpse of the sapphire-blue ice cap that covered whatever remained of the alien lab. For kilometers around the detonation site, the ice glimmered a light shade of pink— shards of the signature red granite of Thor's Hammer, now blown to smithereens and dusting the terrain in all directions.

He set out again, following Liam's trail.

Amundsen-Scott was their best bet for Danny's survival, and their own. He had a knuckle sandwich all ready to serve, with a side order of kick-to-the-head, if he managed to get off the ice and locate Stan Fischer or anyone else, including the President, who'd had something to do with this cluster. The thought of squeezing the presidential advisor's neck between his bare hands increased Beckam's speed over the ice. He caught up with Liam Clay and passed him, the growing sense of hope putting a fresh spring in his step.

J ack leaned back into the web-and-aluminum seating of the
Black Hawk helicopter. He had just lifted off from the meadow at the supply Landing Zone, headed back to Holloman after the meeting with Gordon and spending time with Leah. Jack
was well-adjusted to living within a hazardous environment,
death a single mistake, one slip, one screw-up of any kind, away.

Watching Leah rolling down the trail on the quad, knowing she
was returning to a potentially lethal situation, was harder to en-
dure than descending Everest with a storm inbound, out of oxygen,
and frostbite already working back from your nose into your brain.

Leah was emotionally invested in the Settlement, violently opposed to the idea that her people end up as lab rats in some off-
shore, black research facility. He couldn't talk her out of returning
to the Settlement, regardless of the looming danger.

The only thing he could do was park himself at Holloman Air
Force Base with a Black Hawk on standby. Alerting the perimeter
security personnel would only create the disaster they wanted to
avoid.

Leah and Garrett were on their own, and Jack desperately
hoped Appanoose agreed to allow K'aalógii to be removed from

the Settlement. His instincts said the chances of it happening were remote. The Lakota shaman had made it clear to Leah and Garrett that he was done with interference from outsiders—terrestrial or not.

While he waited at Holloman, Jack had his own responsibilities. In bare-knuckle negotiations following their return from Antarctica with the U.S. government's own nuclear bomb, Al Paulson, now Chief of the National Security Council and unofficial Wheeler watchdog, had made Jack Hobson his direct link into DARPA. Stan Paulson the former NSC Chief had been demoted to Special Presidential Advisor.

For more than fifty years, DARPA had been the tip of the spear when it came to identifying and funding breakthrough defense technologies in the name of national security. To say DARPA had hit the jackpot by being tapped as the lead agency researching the discovery of the non-terrestrial technology they'd brought back from the facility in Antarctica was a vast understatement. Working with the agency under Kyra Gupta, Jack had two key responsibilities. He was one of a handful of surviving individuals who had been inside the complex before Fischer's black-ops CIA team had ransacked and then nuked the alien structure. Consequently, Jack had spent hours with DARPA engineers and artists, describing every detail of the inside and outside of the complex. Just when he thought he'd described it down to a molecular level, he'd be called for another session, where sure enough, they'd pull fresh details out of him.

Jack was also tasked with developing non-technology-driven techniques for finding and identifying additional non-terrestrial sites, if they existed. Having worked all around the globe as a climbing guide, on numerous adventures, Jack was uniquely qualified for this task. The theory went that he might be able to link historical cliff- and cave-based dwellings cities with regional history, legend, and mythology to find other sites where the non-terrestrial entities might have carried out snatch-and-grab programs among other local populations.

Jack had told anyone who would listen—and many who wouldn't—that this historical-cultural-archaeological approach was unlikely to yield results. But the discovery of the Antarctic facility and the implications of foreign nations getting ahold of such technologies had created turmoil at the highest levels of government. Pointless it might be, but the search for other sites would continue, with or without Jack Hobson.

Thus far, only one location on the globe seemed remotely worth pursuing: eastern Turkey. Specifically, an amalgamation of cliff dwellings in ancient Cappadocia, the mythology associated with Mt. Ararat, and a mysterious hot spring on the shoulders of Ararat that had been named Jacob's Well.

He hadn't told Leah that he'd been named the chief candidate to lead that mission. The timing seemed wrong, given how off-the-rails her plan for the Ancients had gone in such a short period of time. Not that the timing could ever be right.... He already knew the words she'd use, line by line. Doubtless the same words Leah had found so effective when she'd booted him out for taking a large cash payment to guide an unqualified, eight-thousand-meter-peak climber. An amateur climber named Al Paulson.

Jack looked down on the terrain speeding underneath the Black Hawk, as Hutchinson made a bee line for Holloman. He had one major concern. It had gotten to the point, that he'd begun having theatre-quality nightmares, with a variety of scenarios always ending in a blinding flash.

Marko Kinney.

His plan for Marko to babysit a nuclear weapon that had the potential to wipe out every single living thing in New York City or Chicago or Albuquerque was the most tenuous part of their post-Antarctic survival plan, hatched and successfully implemented by Paulson. Simply stated: without the Hafnium warhead, there was no guarantee, even with Paulson's political allies, that they wouldn't be rounded up and sent off-shore. They posed an incredible threat to Wheeler and his remaining administration, and the information they all possessed was worth millions of dollars on any market.

Marko had limited patience for anything that resembled structure, and while he grasped the importance of harboring the warhead, having seen one detonated live, that didn't mean he couldn't snap after being cooped up in a cavern for weeks on end.

Marko was a liability on every level. He had the same knowledge as everyone who had survived, making him a target for both governmental agents, and the media, if they ever cornered him— so there was no way he could be cut loose on the streets anytime in the near future.

Jack decided, right then, that he needed another plan for Marko. All it might take to set him off would be a Big Mac wrapper that had been blown in during a windstorm.

10

Leah stashed the quad inside the hide, making sure to plug in the solar-charging system. She even returned the helmet that she'd so casually chucked aside back to its checklist position on the vehicle's seat. As she closed the door to the hide, she vowed to wear the helmet on future rides, having imprinted the quad's handlebar pattern on her forehead earlier in the day.

After taking a deep breath and rubbing her face and hair with dust and pine needles to eliminate any lingering scents, Leah jogged down the deer trail toward the mesa. She stopped at the same overlook from which she'd viewed the Settlement that morning.

Closing her eyes, she drew in a deep breath. When she exhaled, she imagined casting aside all the trappings of modern civilization that she'd enjoyed only hours before, thus making a seamless transition back into "Ancient" mode.

High cirrus clouds and a visible ring around the setting sun whispered that a storm was inbound. Probably meant rain, maybe even snow at this altitude, which would only add to the perpetual chill.

"Láiish!"

K'aalógii had spotted Leah and was sprinting toward the deer trail connecting the mesa top with the Settlement below.

Leah felt an upwelling of warmth inside. At least one of the Ancients cared about her.

"Láiish!" K'aalógii shouted again, waving her arms, her face lit with joy.

Leah grinned. She'd only been gone for most of a day, but K'aalógii made it seem as she'd been missing for a hundred years. The girl ran up the trail at a pace that would have exhausted a world-class athlete, skipping the trail's switchbacks to climb on all fours up near-vertical rock and sand, saving time and distance and reaching Leah in a fraction of the time it would have taken Leah to descend the deer trail at a dead sprint...had she been inclined to risk breaking her neck.

She and K'aalógii shared a secret that should have made the scientist, Dr. Leah Andrews, ashamed to hold the title. When one of the Settlement's initial food deliveries had been dropped off by Black Hawk, she discovered that the military had included cases of packaged Corn Nuts, not corn kernels, as instructed. In a fit of weakness, Leah had stashed a case of the Corn Nuts in the hide before returning the rest. Every now and again, she made a run to the hide and filled a pocket or two of her flight suit with small plastic bags filled with Corn Nuts. The salty snacks were a delightful guilty pleasure, supplementing the bland corn-and-bean diet she shared with the Ancients. One night, in a moment of weakness, she'd given K'aalógii a handful, telling her it was a special treat, but a secret only between them.

Now, any time Leah returned after a longer-than-normal absence, K'aalógii ran to her in hopes of getting another handful of Corn Nuts. This time however, the girl didn't have her hands out for the special treat; instead, she seemed more flushed and excited than normal, grinning as if she'd decoded the key to the universe.

She spoke in Navajo, including a mix of Apache and Pueblo words. "I know why you have been gone!"

Leah didn't know if she should be amused, or alarmed. K'aalógii always asked Leah where she went when she 'disappeared.' To which Leah typically replied vaguely that she was 'looking after' the Ancients. Now she responded with what she hoped was a non-committal facial expression. "You do?"

"You're preparing for our arrival into the Fifth Domain."

Leah blinked. This was the first time K'aalógii or any of the Ancients had mentioned anything that might relate to mythology.

"The 'Fifth Domain'?"

K'aalógii spun and pointed at Appanoose.

The shaman was watching from below, no doubt grasping, if not hearing, the gist of their discussion. He locked eyes with Leah, his expression one of undeniable disapproval. Appanoose forced his way through the warriors and climbed swiftly up the deer trail toward Leah and K'aalógii. As he neared them, he signaled that K'aalógii should approach him. When she did, he laid a gentle hand on her shoulder and guided her a few steps away.

"Hey," Leah said loudly in plain English. "Hey! I'm having a conversation here."

No response from Appanoose.

"Just because you're a big fish in a small pond," she continued inanely in English, "don't think you can just interrupt my discussions at any time."

He responded with a withering glare, then turned his attention back to K'aalógii, kneeling and whispering to her at eye-level. Leah thought he sounded more like a patient teacher instructing a student than an authority figure scolding an errant child. K'aalógii listened attentively, eyes wide.

Appanoose stood and regarded Leah, his countenance now merely a disapproving scowl, absent of all menace. He turned and strolled back down to the Settlement, strutting in a manner that seemed custom-made for the approval of his followers.

Arrogant jerk.

Leah felt the small hand of K'aalógii taking hers.

"Doo shił bééhózin da," she said, her eyes downcast.

"But why?"

"He says I can only speak of the 'Fifth Domain' with him. It is only for us." K'aalógii nodded, as if agreeing with her great leader. "We are special."

Leah smiled her approval. "You didn't need to tell *me* that."

K'aalógii beamed and giggled, then wrapped her arms around Leah and embraced her tightly enough to squeeze the air out of Leah's lungs. Another reminder that the Ancients inhabiting the modern world bore only a surface resemblance to those who'd lived on these mesa tops and in the cliff dwellings a thousand years prior.

Garrett Moon emerged from a thick grove of piñon, his arms loaded with a stack of firewood. Two fierce femmes and one male warrior followed, also heavily laden.

Leah pointed at Garrett and told K'aalógii, "Go help Moon carry the firewood."

K'aalógii bolted toward Garrett, dust kicking up from the rear of her bare feet, at a pace a world-class sprinter couldn't hope to match. Leah jogged behind her down the sandy path, intercepting Garrett as he dropped the load of wood under a sandstone overhang. Leah spoke in a whisper to K'aalógii in Navajo, telling her to warm herself at the fire and dangling the promise of a 'ch'iyáán spéshelígíí,' a special treat, for her later.

K'aalógii bolted away. She appeared healthy and happy. Leah was having a difficult time matching up the information she'd gotten from Gordon with what she was witnessing right now.

Once K'aalógii was out of range, Leah filled Garrett in on the meeting with Gordon, his findings, and the need to get K'aalógii to Holloman for testing. And their concerns about Appanoose.

She saved the worst for last. "The bottom line is, our dream for the Settlement was righteous but fatally flawed. These people are every bit as intelligent as we are—the idea that we might create a version of the San Diego Zoo on steroids, was naive and cruel." She placed a hand on his shoulder. "I'm sorry, Garrett. I know this is an experience that I can't even fathom. A chance for a modern Navajo to interact with living ancestors."

Garrett nodded. "I saw this coming." He sighed as he took a glance at the shaman. "I have a feeling if Appanoose had been a warrior and chief a little later in our history, things might have turned out a whole lot different."

"Well," said Leah, "unless we can think of something, and think of it fast, we'll repeat history in a matter of hours. If Appanoose refuses to release K'aalógii, then Gordon has no choice but report the Ancients are undergoing non-human, physiological changes. Wheeler and his crew will send in a team of special ops thugs; they'll make the same assumptions that we have, that they're harmless cave dwellers who'll scatter at the sight of a flare gun. But what they won't believe is that Appanoose and his warriors could easily 'ghost' an entire platoon of commandos before they knew what happened."

Garrett nodded again. "Of that I have no doubt." He paused for a moment, clearly hesitant to say something. Then he said it. "I have to get you out of here, before that happens."

"No, we both have to get out of here—and try and save as many as we can. Somehow."

Garrett Moon shook his head. "I'm not leaving, Leah. These are my people. I know they won't submit. They survived a last-stand nearly a thousand years ago, and I feel with every strand of my Navajo DNA that they won't be captured again."

Leah stood, arms crossed, watching as the Ancients heated river stones on a fire next to the newly constructed sweat lodge. She was still devastated by what Garrett had said only hours ago: *I'm not leaving, Leah. These are my people.*

She didn't have the emotional strength to do battle with him this evening. She'd approach him in the morning, and then contact Jack on the satellite phone with the news. Of course, the worst-case scenario might be delayed for days or weeks if she took K'aalógii back to Holloman with her. But instinct told her that Appanoose would reply to their plan to take K'aalógii away for testing with his standard headshake: *No Chance.*

In another ironic development this day, the Settlement hadn't had enough skins to finish constructing the sweat lodge, so Appanoose had rifled through Leah's gear bags, finding two large plastic tarps and layering them on top of one another to cover the dome-shaped pine structure.

The sweat lodge that the shaman and his people had completed was classic Lakota. An earthen rise and fire pit just outside the door flap: the fire representing the sun and the mound of earth representing a crescent moon. The sun and moon mounds together represented the universe, the sweat lodge the earthbound world. Lakota sweat lodges were serious business; inside, participants underwent rebirth.

When the stones surrounding the fire were nearly as hot as the fire itself, the Ancients lifted the stones out with two lodge poles and quickly transported them into the center of the sweat lodge. Once each stone was positioned in the center of the lodge, the warriors exited, and dipped the poles into a shallow depression filled with water. This prevented the poles from burning while transporting the next, blistering hot stone.

Garrett shouldered up next to Leah. "I stuck my face inside the lodge this afternoon. There's no way we'd survive inside. It's at least thirty-degrees hotter than any lodge I've ever been in—more like a sauna—at least a hundred and thirty, maybe a hundred and fifty degrees."

Leah shook her head in disbelief. Ten minutes in a sauna made her dizzy. A sweat lodge ceremony continued for hours and hours.

"Appanoose seems to be taking the Ancients into the lodge five at a time. How long has this been going on?"

"They finished building the lodge about noon—so maybe ten hours now."

"In ten hours, he's taken three sets of five Ancients inside for a purification ritual? How long does each ritual last?"

"Two hours—sometimes more."

"So Appanoose has spent at least six of the last ten hours in that heat? How can he survive temperatures that would cook us inside out?"

Garrett gave Leah a sideways glance. "From what I can tell, he started with the youngest first. K'aalógii was in the first group."

Leah was stunned that Appanoose would risk subjecting his people, especially young K'aalógii, to such dangerous temperatures.

"When I got back to the Settlement, K'aalógii was bubbling with excitement. She couldn't wait to tell me about the 'Fifth Domain' and how I was destined to guide them to their destination. You saw Appanoose. He wasn't at all pleased that she was telling me this. I thought maybe she was just trying to make sense of it all—using Indian mythology to explain what had happened to them."

Garrett said, "I've noticed the Ancients who have gone through the ritual look more like they've attended a religious revival. Baptized in the pond, or whatever. At first, I thought they were just happy to get out of that oven.... Now I'm not sure."

Leah studied the lodge as the warriors continued to heat rocks, then stack them inside. "Appanoose knows a whole lot more than he lets on—and more than the others in the Settlement. Whatever he's telling them inside is boosting their hope for the future."

Garrett nodded. "He'd make a pretty good Charlie Manson. He's got that kind of charisma, and he knows how to manipulate people—including you and me."

"I'm wondering what exactly Appanoose is handing out inside the lodge while the flap is down. You think they are getting high on cactus?"

"The only peyote I know of is up around Smith River. That's a long-ass haul from here. But we know the Ancients can run like the wind, and if their sense of smell is improving at a similar rate...." Garrett shrugged. "If Appanoose wanted 'buttons,' he'd probably find 'em without much trouble." He turned to her. "What's your plan?"

"Tomorrow morning we'll have a sit-down with Appanoose. We have to convince him to allow us to 'borrow' K'aalógii from the Settlement for testing, perhaps treatment. If he won't cooperate, I wouldn't give a nickel for our chances of surviving the next forty-eight hours."

11

At first light, Leah took Garrett aside. "Whatever we do, I don't want to piss him off. We want to be firm on K'aalógii, but not combative. He's got to understand their bodies are undergoing changes he can't explain. For K'aalógii, the 'changes' could be dangerous. I want you to handle the discussion. Your language skills are way better than mine, and you can remain calm no matter what he says."

Garrett flashed a grin. "Don't piss him off? Is that even possible when you two mix it up around the fire?"

Leah ignored the comment. "Go over there and get us a meeting *like a boss*."

Garrett walked over, gesturing his desire to engage in a private discussion. He leaned in to Appanoose and whispered, making the same sort of hand signs and movements that Leah had seen him use on other occasions when engaging with the leader.

Garrett turned and waved her over. He'd gotten an agreement for a private discussion. When Appanoose beckoned, Leah advanced toward his fire. After watching Appanoose 'preaching' to the Ancients, she'd christened his over-sized fire pit and circle of cut logs the *Shaman's Basilica*.

Once seated, Appanoose motioned to one of the warriors who stood a respectful distance away. The young man suddenly appeared at the shaman's side. Appanoose whispered in his ear. The warrior backed reverently away, turned, and chose several choice pieces of firewood from the wood pile, adding them one by one. The fire grew with each new piece of wood, warming the sitting area against the near-freezing temperatures.

When Appanoose was ready, he gave his standard sharp nod.

Garrett leaned forward and spoke in precise Navajo. Appanoose nodded sharply each time Garrett made a point.

Leah understood much of what Garrett said: a soft-spoken plea to allow Leah to take K'aalógii away from the Settlement for, at most, a few days. He hit all the key points, and Leah was encouraged each time Appanoose gave one of his sharp head nods while Garrett addressed the changes taking place within the Ancients' bodies.

When Garrett sat back, he invited Appanoose to reply. The shaman spoke in rapid-fire Navajo, far too fast for Leah to follow, using his hands as he spoke to convey key points.

When he stopped, Leah leaned over and asked, "Is it just me, or did his Navajo get a whole lot better just now?"

Garrett nodded. "Uh, yeah. Turns out his Navajo is pretty good."

Bastard Lakota has been sandbagging us the entire time, Leah thought, but maintained an even expression. "I only caught a word here and there. I heard him saying, 'Inipi,' with almost every headshake. That's the Lakota term for a sweat-lodge rebirth, right?"

"Yeah. He had a few things to say about the lodge," Garrett said. "He agreed to allow you to take K'aalógii for two days—no more."

Leah couldn't hold back the overwhelming relief. "Thank God," she said, breathing into her hands while rocking back and forth.

"But...."

"What?"

"He wants quid pro quo," Garrett said.

Leah froze. If the shaman wanted something in exchange for allowing K'aalógii out of the Settlement, it wouldn't be extra sugar for his coffee.

"I couldn't possibly guess.... Tell me."

"You have to do a re-birth ritual with him. Privately."

"The sweat lodge? There's no way! Not as hot as he makes it. I wouldn't last three minutes in there, much less two or three hours."

Appanoose pointed directly at Leah. "Inipi!"

Before Garrett could object, she held up a hand, cleared her throat, and said, "Lą́'ąą."

Appanoose gave a little extra snap to his single head nod upon Leah's sudden agreement to his terms. He leaned forward, addressing her directly and said one word. "Kičháǧa."

"Bee ánáádí'ní," Leah replied. A basic Navajo term meaning she didn't understand, or grasp what he was communicating.

"Kičháǧa," he repeated.

Leah glanced over at Garrett in frustration and whispered in English, "I don't have a clue what he's saying."

Garrett leaned over and whispered, "Pretty sure that's Lakota, not Navajo."

Leah felt a flush of irritation. "Why is he jerking me around? He speaks Navajo."

"Could be he doesn't know the term in Navajo." Garrett pulled back and grinned. "More likely, since you're the big cheese, he thinks you ought to speak Lakota."

Leah kept an eye on Appanoose. "He really enjoys pushing my buttons."

Garrett nodded. "And he's gotten damned good at it, too."

Appanoose extended an arm and pointed south. "Kičháǧa!" He sat back on the logs, looking more irritated than Leah felt, if that were even possible.

Clearly frustrated, the shaman drew a deep breath, pointed south again, and sounded out a different word: *Ant-Arc-Tikke.*

Leah looked to Garret, then back at the shaman, dumbfounded. *He knows the modern name of the bloody continent? Apparently, he listens as well as he speaks.*

Garrett shrugged. "Sounds to me like he wants you to deliver him back to Antarctica."

12

Only one person aside from Gordon was more relieved that Appanoose had allowed K'aalógii out of the Settlement: Jack Hobson. After a restless night on base, he'd gotten a satellite phone call from Leah at noon. Saying that she'd hiked to the mesa top, Leah proceeded breathlessly to tell Jack that Appanoose had agreed. K'aalógii could be returned to the Settlement within two days. *'The fact that he agreed, without conditions is a miracle in my opinion, Climber,'* were her exact words.

Leah told Jack to have the Black Hawk at the supply Landing Zone no later three that afternoon. She didn't want to allow Appanoose time to change his mind.

Jack glanced at his watch. It was two-thirty and he was the only passenger aboard the Black Hawk. This time, Hutchinson and Cruz flew their approach by the numbers, coming in from the north and staying low over the treetops. Finally, the Black Hawk flared into a hover, and Hutchinson worked the Black Hawk skids, landing dead center of the SLZ. Jack waited until crew chief Sergeant Bruce had given him the 'all clear' before hopping out of the Black Hawk and onto the grass.

Before he had time to stretch his legs, Leah braked the quad to a stop at the SLZ perimeter. K'aalógii sat behind Leah on the quad, holding on tight around Leah's waist, the oversized helmet down over her eyes.

Leah swung her leg over the front of the quad and slid off, grabbed K'aalógii, and lifted her off. K'aalógii wore her native clothing. This time of year, at this altitude, temperatures were crisp, even during the day. Today it was in the low 40s, but K'aalógii wore no skin boots or moccasins.

Though Leah had described this particular superhuman trait in detail, Jack still couldn't help but stare at the barefoot child in the near-freezing temperatures. Leah grasped K'aalógii's hand and walked toward the Black Hawk, waving at Jack and smiling at the same time. K'aalógii seemed totally at ease, seemingly having assimilated into the high-tech, modern world without effort.

Kids, Jack thought. *Five minutes after you give them the latest gadget, they're bored and looking for the next cool toy. Helicopter rides and quads are already yesterday's news to the eight hundred-year-old young woman....*

K'aalógii, put her hands over her mouth and giggled, then pulled Leah down and whispered in her ear.

Jack crossed his arms and winked. "Something about me?"

"Might be," Leah said. "You know us girls...we have secrets."

"Your chariot is warmed up and ready to go, my queen," Jack said, sweeping an arm toward the waiting Black Hawk.

Leah had arranged to supply Gordon with two aircraft hangars at Holloman Air Force Base. In one hangar, they had installed a series of portable hospital and support facilities, recreating a sophisticated research lab. FEMA trailers had also been moved into the hangar and served as the mobile homes, offices, conference rooms, even dining facilities. The second, adjoining hangar was used to move personnel into and out of helicopters in a secure setting.

Hutchinson set the bird down on the pad assigned to the Genesis Settlement. From there, it was towed into the hangar, and the structure's massive hanger doors closed behind it.

⌐◡◠◡◠⌐

K'aalógii was hungry, as usual, so first they took her into one of the private dining trailers. She was working on her third bowl of chicken noodle soup while Jack and Leah sipped coffee.

"So," Jack said. "You sit down with Appanoose, give him the facts, try to look sad, and, boom, he agrees to allow K'aalógii off-site without so much as a side glance?"

Leah glanced down into her coffee cup. "That's about it," she replied. *Not the best time to tell him I agreed to a ritual in the shaman's sweat lodge.*

"Gordon has K'aalógii for two days," Jack said. "How long before he calls in his report?"

"I'm encouraging him not to jump the gun," Leah said. "It's unlikely he can come to any conclusions soon. Testing. Then analysis. I'm voting for a slow, careful analysis, you know?"

Jack nodded. "Anything else happen at the Settlement? Ancients levitating—that kind of thing?"

Leah simply gave him the 'look.'

"No levitating, but here's a newsflash: When I returned yesterday, Appanoose and his boys had constructed a sweat lodge, and he's been hosting purification rituals inside, non-stop. He takes between three and five of the Ancients inside, the flap closes, except when he requests more hot stones, and they don't leave for two or three hours. As Garrett said, they come out more serene than born-again Christians after a revival baptism."

Jack smiled at that. "Sounds more like a peyote-fest, if you ask me."

Leah nodded. "Garrett's first thought. He also said K'aalógii was in the first group to enter the sweat lodge. He started with the youngest first. When I got back, she ran up to me with her eyes lit up like a Christmas float. She said that Appanoose told her I was responsible for delivering the Ancients to the 'Fifth Domain.' When 'Noose' saw her talking to me, he was none too happy and terminated our discussion right then and there."

"'Fifth Domain'? A Native American version of Heaven or something?"

"There is Native American mythology related to moving through a series of Worlds, which I guess could translate as 'Domains,'" Leah said. "Given what these people have been through, it could mean just about anything. Whatever the 'Fifth Domain' means, it must be like eternal Club Med, based upon the serene glow the Ancients sport when they exit the lodge ritual."

"Hmm." Jack thought for a moment. "Have you asked yourself whether Appanoose is *really* Native American, or maybe one of our 'Visitors' in a clever Halloween costume?"

"That's a bit of a stretch, Climber. On the other hand, far be it from me to rule it out, given what we've seen. The mythology, as we understand it, relating to 'Worlds,' not 'Domains,' involves a common theme found in may religions. The destruction of the Earth through human immorality evil, wickedness—and so on. However, by transitioning to the 'next world,' you're given a chance to fix all your faults—give life another shot, having learned your lesson, so to speak. These are very, very old stories and beliefs, passed down for hundreds, if not thousands of years. It's possible that Appanoose is preaching the old-school mythology."

"Oh, good," said Jack. "I'm so much more at ease." He glanced up. "You're sure about all this stuff?"

Leah gave him 'the look,' again. "Seriously, Jackson? No, you got me. I read about this after opening a box of Cracker Jacks. I'm an archaeologist. Remember?"

"But would these Ancients, a mix of cultures...would this really be something they'd believe?"

"Without a doubt. Remember, within the Native American cultures, passing down stories, repeating them over and over; perhaps the most important task, after survival. There's no question in my mind this stretches back hundreds, or thousands of years.

"You think Appanoose believes this?" Jack asked.

"If he doesn't, he's using it for his own purposes. Garrett said he has Charlie Manson charisma. Because he's the shaman, no one questions what he says. So far, I'd say as leader of the Ancients, he's done a pretty good job of averting panic within the ranks, and, apparently, he's given them something to grasp that offers an alternative to death and disaster."

Jack nodded and then said, "You know what that is?"

"Hope," Leah replied. "Something we could all use a good dose of right now."

"What's your plan? All we've done is bought more time—and not very much."

"Fortunately," she said, "given Gordo's meticulous nature, I doubt we'll have to convince him to take his time on K'aalógii's analysis. Meanwhile, I'll have to come up with options, and I'm counting on you and Paulson to back me up."

"Al's definitely become a genuine, behind-the-scenes, heavy-weight player in Washington. Whatever you decide, he'll back you up." Jack glanced over as K'aalógii lifted the bowl and slurped the last of the soup. "So Garrett's handling Appanoose on his own?"

"Yeah. I'm about as useful as tits on a bull at the Settlement anyway. I'm not Indian and I'm bossy. They respect Garrett. So I'll stay here with K'aalógii during the testing, then take her back to the Settlement. If Gordo finds something that throws him into hysterics, I'll figure it out."

She reached out and grabbed Jack's hands. "You plan on stay-ing here with me?" She waved her hand around the inside of the dining trailer. "Not quite eternal Club Med, but romantic, none-theless."

"There's nothing I'd like more, love, but my fifteen minutes of Washington fame peaks tomorrow morning. Wheeler and Paul-son have scheduled a briefing in the Situation Room at the White House with all the players, including Teresa Simpson. Even Fisch-er. Kyra and her people have made some discoveries regarding the recovered 'artifacts.' My job is developing tools and the means to pinpoint any other existing alien facilities. I have to make a 'presentation.'"

Leah nervously tapped her fingernails on the table. "Anything I should know? There's nothing about the Genesis Settlement on the agenda?"

"Nope. Wheeler's leaving you alone, as you asked."

Leah leaned over and kissed Jack. "I know I can count on you to protect the Ancients."

Jack didn't respond. Based upon what Leah had said, the endgame for the Ancients was going to involve a lot of spilled blood—on both sides.

13

The ice-encrusted pallets appeared as a series of giant, misshapen pearls on an otherwise smooth surface, stretching to the horizon. The Russian airdrop had been textbook, the ice-covered pallets lined up in a perfect, five-hundred-meter string.

A bizarre and macabre monument to dead heroes....

Lenny Clay had just finished cutting away the ice from the top of the first pallet with his combat knife. The razor-sharp blade slashed the strapping on the pallets in a single stroke.

"We're in business, Boss!"

He used the knife to hack away more ice, under which treasure gleamed. "We've got two Taiga-551s right here with fuel, ammo, shovels, and an assortment of tools stacked right on top."

"Beauty," said Beckam. "Let's get it done and get hell out of here."

The Clay twins finished freeing the remainder of the pallet, using the Russian-supplied shovels and picks. Twenty minutes later, they were pushing the first of the two Russian tactical snow machines off the pallet and onto the ice.

Liam fueled the Taiga, swung a leg over the machine, and hit the starter button. The 500cc engine started with a roar. He glanced at the instruments and gave Beckam a thumbs-up. He shouted over the din of the 4-stroke engine running smoothly in high idle.

"Good to go!"

Beckam examined the tow toboggans packed alongside the Taiga. They were designed to be loaded with gear, or wounded, and you could string as many behind the snow machine as it would haul.

He shouted over the roar of the Taiga. "I'm taking the sled with two toboggans, loading up Danny, and the balance of our gear. Free up another Taiga, hook up two toboggans and load all the gear we'll need for an extended, cross-ice holiday."

Liam nodded. "I got fuel, food, weapons, communications, tents, and winter-spec-clothing at the top of the list. Anything else come to mind?"

"Electrically-heated vests, pants, and base layers. Climbing gear. Lines, harnesses, and at least one of those aluminum, snow-machine crevasse bridges."

"Mountain-climbing?"

"Unlikely. But in case we run into bad guys, we could anchor ourselves into a crevasse, making it almost impossible to root us out without taking heavy casualties."

Liam grinned. "That's why you're the boss."

Beckam studied the pallets stretching out into the distance. "Search for satchel charges, too. Once we get everything we need, we'll use whatever explosives the Russians included to blow the rest of the pallets. No use gearing up a crew of bad guys who decide we'd look good on the mantle—and giving them the tools to do it."

Lenny brushed ice out of his beard, then said, "There's a chance one of these Taigas is gonna go tits-up before we reach Amundsen. Should we find a third snow machine, so we have a spare?"

Beckam nodded. "Good thinking. We can always dump one in a crevasse if we don't need it. We could also use a couple of the pallet parachutes. They're blown to shit, but gather 'em up anyway."

"What are we gonna use those for, Skipper?"

"Camo. It won't help with infrared weaponry, but white nylon on ice is better than a stick in the eye."

14

Al Paulson faced President William Wheeler, sitting sideways on a couch in the Oval Office. The billionaire businessman sipped on piping-hot coffee, served in classic White House working china complete with gold trim and a matching saucer.

President William Wheeler sat behind his enormous desk, his face frozen in a forced, neutral expression. The animosity between Paulson and Wheeler, already at a boiling point, had gotten worse throughout the closed congressional hearings, in which Paulson had testified under oath about everything that had happened in Antarctica, leaving nothing out, including his then, but now demoted, National Security Advisor Stanton Fischer's attempt to eliminate Paulson and his expedition-mates after their discovery of the non-terrestrial facility, not to mention the deliberate detonation of a highly classified nuclear device, the sacrifice of a platoon of Navy SEALs, and, in an act of war, the elimination of an unknown number of Russian Spetsnaz commandos.

A compromise, worked out between political rivals, kept classified the discovery of alien technologies and preserved, eight-hundred-year-old Native Americans. The President and his team, while censured for the heavy-handed and poorly executed operation, had been cleared of all criminal charges. Given the looming potential of a nuclear conflict with the Russians, the critical fact of the U.S.'s exclusive possession of the alien technology was enough to save Wheeler's administration, despite all the unfortunate errors made along the way.

Thanks to the nuclear brinksmanship that Paulson and Jack had been forced to engage in, Paulson was now the president's National Security Advisor and remained in the loop on all decisions coming from the Oval Office. Wheeler had been forced to clean house within his Cabinet, but Stanton Fischer remained onboard as a Special Advisor.

Paulson suspected that was because Fischer knew where all the skeletons were stashed in Wheeler's political closets. Otherwise, Fischer would've made an excellent political scapegoat for everything that had gone wrong in Antarctica—and for the resulting quasi-hot war with the Russians.

The status of those who had survived the events on the ice would also remain classified—a matter of national security. Similar to witnesses living under federal protection, all participants of the Paulson Expedition were 'guaranteed safety,' assigned protective Secret Service detail, if traveling, and sent to live in secure, secret locations. Mac Ridley and his crew of mechanics had since taken up residence at Camp David, a national-security precaution, given their taste for whiskey and resulting loose lips. Some early grumbling had been quelled by gourmet meals and a liquor reserve fit for a president, along with free run of Camp David. Marko was sequestered with the warhead.

That left the only real loose end—Luke Derringer. He had refused to leave the airfield. Jack and Paulson had agreed to allow him to stay at the remote airfield, armed to the teeth. With Paulson's 'agreement' in place, and a pack of opposition senators dying to get rid of Wheeler under any circumstance, they'd all agreed to leave the old man out at the airfield. It would be political suicide for Wheeler to make a move against any of the Antarctic survivors.

Another part of the grand deal had been the creation of the Genesis Settlement, with Leah running the show.

As for Jack Hobson, Paulson had needed another person he could trust in the defense and national-security loop besides Teresa Simpson, who had left the BLM to take a job as Paulson's second in command on the National Security Council. Ultimately, Jack had been appointed a Senior Advisor at DARPA, a useful position, given the government's laser focus on the alien technology.

Through the process, Paulson had come grudgingly to respect Wheeler's toughness. He never backed down from Paulson, regardless of how wrong-headed his decisions. Maybe it was the desk he sat behind: the priceless "Resolute Desk," made from the oak timbers of the British ship *H.M.S. Resolute*. A gift from Queen Victoria in 1880. The White House might be leveled in a nuclear attack, but Paulson felt sure the Resolute Desk would soldier on without so much as a scratch. However, Wheeler's health had degraded visibly. These days, he looked gaunt and pale, and he'd developed an unnerving tic that made him appear to be constantly telling himself 'no.'

"Go ahead," Paulson told the President. "Say it."

Wheeler pushed his coffee aside. "You are a traitor to this nation and an extortionist. Kick your feet up in the Oval Office, while you can." He checked his watch impatiently.

Paulson eyeballed the President for a long moment. "See, Willie, this is a perfect example of why you're struggling through this. You let a guy like me get under your skin, but if you had half a brain, you'd be a whole lot more concerned about a hundred megatons dropping on the eastern seaboard than a straight-shooter like me—who's only trying to keep the country from going completely off the rails while making you look good in front of the American people."

"My concern is a small gang of domestic terrorists holding this nation hostage with a lethal nuclear device. That's the *real* danger here."

"I'm not any happier about that than you are," Paulson said. "But through bad behavior and poor decision-making, you've created this situation yourself. Once I'm sure our throats won't be cut the second we give up the warhead, I'll provide the whereabouts. Trust me, Willie, we're not happy about having to babysit that 'thing.' I saw the result of a detonation first-hand—remember?"

The President did not respond, but his head twitched. Twice.

Paulson quelled his mounting irritation. "For better or worse, Mr. President, we're all in this together. That you seem obsessed with me is mind-boggling. I could have gone to the press and lit you up like the Fourth of July. I don't expect us to become best buddies, but we have to team up, at least temporarily."

The expression of pure hatred conveyed the President's reaction to Paulson's most recent attempt at conciliation.

A secret service agent opened the door at the back of the Oval Office. "Mr. President. Mr. Paulson. We're ready for you in the Situation Room."

Wheeler and Paulson stood, Paulson waiting for the President to step from behind his desk and take the lead. His time in the military had taught him an important lesson.

You don't respect the man. You respect the rank.

That didn't mean he wouldn't have to get rid of Wheeler in the near future.

The President was on the edge of losing it.

15

The Kremlin, Moscow

Colonel Konstantin Yaroslavl didn't have a chair at the conference table. Those seats were reserved for the President, the highest-ranking generals, admirals, ministers, the President's Chief of Staff, Deputy Chief of Staff, and key aides—better known as *Kremlin Korichnevyy Nos*: Kremlin Suck-ups.

Yaroslavl wanted no part of the political process and was uncomfortable simply attending conferences at this level. When things didn't go as planned, red became blue, and anyone associated with red was purged. If he were lucky, any intelligence briefing would be handled by his superior officer, General Valentin Petrov. Briefings were dangerous in all political settings, never more so than here, and under these circumstances.

There was a rumor that an American insider with connections at the very top of the government, would, for the right amount of money, provide detailed intelligence about the entire Antarctica operation. Yaroslavl was skeptical. The number of times these over-the-transom information sellers actually had something of value, he could count on one hand. However, he had to admit, that 'handful' had done serious damage to US intelligence and their military, and had ousted more than a few double agents—who were quietly rounded up and shot down in the basement of some Moscow counter-intelligence site.

While they were still waiting for this 'eye-popping' information that they'd been promised, the Kremlin had learned through other sources that the Americans were so paranoid about what they'd discovered that they were expending massive resources to secure any similar 'sites,' while also acting as if the Antarctic continent had suddenly become American sovereign territory. The Russians had drawn the line there—and drawn American blood as well.

The room went dead quiet as security scurried near the doors. The President was about to enter. Everyone stood, most smoothing their uniforms or adjusting their out-of-place comb-overs. In strolled the President, cloaked in his typical casual clothing, as if he preparing to take a stroll in Gorky Park. He winked at the hostess setting up coffee and cakes, then nodded at the security staff, who efficiently escorted the service people from the room and closed the door.

The President pounded on the table. "Valentin...."

Yaroslavl stiffened. The first salvo was aimed right at his boss, whose anxiety was palpable. He'd told Yaroslavl before the meeting that his ass would be on the line.

"The rumors are the Americans found a buried spacecraft of alien origin—then cut it up and sent it home." The President gave Petrov an icy stare as the seconds ticked by. "Yes? No?"

Yaroslavl expected to see Petrov stumble, then be verbally gutted like a fish, but instead his superior officer turned, made eye contact with Yaroslavl, and handed over the noose with a sharp nod.

Yaroslavl swore under his breath, military discipline and his survival instincts preventing him from giving away any outward expression.

He cleared his throat as he gathered his thoughts. "We have an evolving condition. Communications are disrupted over much of the Southern Hemisphere—and getting worse across the balance of the globe. Maintaining communication with our forces in the Southern Ocean is nearly impossible. We sent a third recon unit after the first two teams were killed in transport aircraft crashes—one shot down by the Americans, the second, unknown. We've had no further contact with any of the teams, nor the aircraft that air-dropped them in to the continent. We should consider those assets lost as well."

All eyes focused on him as he addressed the President's question: "We are waiting for the expected intelligence on exactly what was discovered."

The President nodded but did not soften his glare. "So, you guarantee we can eliminate the American naval forces blockading our access to Antarctica?" He pounded on the table to make his next point. "We...must...have access...to Antarctica."

Yaroslavl felt a flash of vertigo, envisioning the inevitable: the launch of nuclear warheads unleashing an unstoppable and apocalyptic escalation.

"Yes. Guaranteed."

16

The Situation Room, better known as the John F. Kennedy Conference Room, anchored the basement of the West Wing in the White House. Remodeled and updated, it nevertheless felt like a well-lit, high-tech subterranean fortress. Its cream-colored walls were lined with flat-screen monitors linked to the government's communications systems around the globe. This allowed the President real-time contact anywhere on the planet at any time, including spec-ops commandos on the battlefield wearing helmet and body cams.

A wood-grain conference table dominated the limited interior space with traditional seating for twelve via high-back, black leather swivel chairs. Surrounding the perimeter were chairs set up for key aides and lesser officials.

Seated at the conference table: Admiral Kelly Rush, the Vice Chairman of the Joint Chiefs; CIA Director Jorah Frohman; Air Force General Tommy Mattson; Army General Erik Heller; NSA Director Leonard Prince; Stanton Fischer; and Teresa Simpson.

Vice President Frederick Holder and Chairman of the Joint Chiefs Marine General Gilman were not present but aboard an Airborne Command aircraft. In case of a surprise nuclear attack, key members of the government were sent to secure classified facilities or Airborne Command centers, thus preserving a portion of the civilian and military chains of command.

Everyone stood as Wheeler and Paulson entered the room. Wheeler nodded a greeting, patting Admiral Rush on the shoulder and sitting at the head of the conference table. Al Paulson took the empty chair immediately to the President's left, and Teresa Simpson sat to the right.

Paulson winked a greeting at Teresa. At a critical moment during the Antarctic crisis, Teresa Simpson, then Director of the BLM and Leah's former boss, had gone rogue and provided critical assistance, to both Paulson and Jack Hobson. Paulson had made sure to negotiate both her ongoing safety and a new position within the administration, working directly for the billionaire.

This was the first time all the major players, including Jack Hobson, Stan Fischer, Al Paulson, and William Wheeler would be confined together in tight quarters.

Within the White House, rumor had it that "those in the know" had started a pool, betting on exactly how long it would be before a fistfight broke out in the Situation Room, requiring Secret Service to bust in and break it up. The odds favored the first five minutes.

DARPA Director Kyra Gupta tapped Jack on the shoulder. "You hanging in okay?"

Jack turned to her and raised an eyebrow. "Helicopters are flying coffins—I never get comfortable once it's off the ground." He shrugged. "I'll be fine."

Kyra winced. "Is that fear rooted in personal experience?"

"Three times—once I was the only survivor. Didn't even get a scratch." He shrugged. "That'll mess with your head."

"And then you were nearly shot down over Mexico...."

"Actually, they never even tried, though they easily could have."

She nodded. "The benefits of nuclear protection."

"While it lasts," he said with another shrug. "When and if I hand over the Hafnium warhead, there's no question—I'll be booked on a CIA black cruise, faster than you can fly this sucker down to South Beach for a margarita."

"Well," she said, "you brought up the topic, not me. But let me make my pitch again for giving up the location and allowing us to get the warhead secured. You know the volume of damage resulting from detonation, intentionally or by miscalculation." Kyra touched his arm. "You're under my protection, Jack. I'm on your side. Right now, we're in charge."

"Thanks," he said, "but I saw a lot of friends, including a group of loyal Navy SEALs, sacrificed after repeated assurances to the contrary. I tested Wheeler and he screwed me more than once. That'll never happen again."

"Regardless, you're a professional and part of my staff. In twenty minutes, you'll be on the hot seat in the Situation Room with Wheeler and members of the cabinet. Tell me right now if you plan to sprint across the top of the conference table and tackle him." She added a grin. "Jack Hobson, I swear, I will turn this helicopter right around...."

Jack leaned back in his seat, chuckling. "Hey, that's totally in Wheeler's hands. If he mentions Leah in anything but glowing terms, I'll have my hands around his neck before the Secret Service can unlock the door."

Secret Service agents escorted Jack and Kyra from the helo into the White House, where IDs were checked for, what felt like, the hundredth time since he'd met up with his boss for the morning's trip.

Secret Service guided them into a secure elevator that descended to the Situation Room. Once more, Kyra quietly cautioned Jack to maintain his composure. They had a job to do, and theatrics wouldn't be in anyone's best interest, given the political and geopolitical tinder-box they were all tip-toeing around.

"Yes, Mom," Jack whispered back.

The elevator doors opened; Kyra stepped out of the elevator with Jack directly following.

"The President's ready for you, Dr. Gupta," a Secret Service agent said.

Kyra smoothed her skirt one more time as the doors to the Situation Room swung open and every pair of eyes in the room focused on Jack. Or so it felt. He recognized most of the faces from the endless briefings and interrogations he'd undergone since returning from Antarctica, but only two reacted when he nodded a greeting: Paulson and Teresa Simpson.

Stan Fischer sat expressionless, the faint marks of his last fist-to-face contact with Jack fading but still visible.

At least the swelling's gone down. Jack also noted that Fischer had lost weight, his hair had thinned, and his once-ramrod-straight posture was gone. He appeared mentally and physically beaten down. So much so that Jack *almost* felt sorry for the bastard. His clothing matched his deteriorating appearance, the suit looking slept-in, hosting more wrinkles than a Beijing street map at the end of tourist season.

Jack turned his attention to Wheeler, who flashed a campaign-quality smile that didn't match up with the thinly veiled hostility in his eyes. Still, the President stood and managed an amiable introduction.

"We are fortunate to have superlative scientific minds hard at work already. DARPA is spearheading the examination and hypothetical applications of our technology windfall." He held out both hands, palms up in greeting. "Many of you know Dr. Kyra Gupta personally if not, undoubtedly, by reputation."

Kyra whispered to the A/V specialist. Flat screens illuminated and the lights dimmed. The man handed Kyra a wireless remote.

This is not her first time in front of a heavy-weight audience, Jack thought. *No wonder she's so relaxed.*

"We've only scratched the surface with regard to our non-terrestrials and their technological capabilities," she began. "Let. Me.

Be. Clear. From the start. We have no knowledge of, nor are we in possession of: spaceships, starships, or an operational Death Star. Nor are we secretly hoarding warp-drives, hyper-drives, or ion drives. There are no lasers, phasers, blasters, or disrupters. We have seen no evidence of working 'transporter systems' or handy-dandy 'wormhole-generators.'"

A slide flashed on the screens, featuring a high-res photo of the Antarctic facility's airlock mechanism—a portal that Leah had opened with the touch of her palm.

"What we have found are clues: exciting, compelling, and mysterious. Our leading theory is that the 'Complex,' as we often refer to it, suffered a malfunction. Whether software, mechanical, or operational error is unknown. We know the interior had once been pressurized. Whether to provide a survivable atmosphere for non-terrestrial hosts, the human subjects, or some other purpose is, again, unknown. Ancient, mummified female remains were discovered near the airlock. Given what we learned from Dr. Leah Andrews's ability to open the airlock with a touch, it's possible that the dead woman opened both the inner and outer airlock doors at the same time. When she died, she was within a meter of the operating panel."

The images on the screen brought Jack straight back to Antarctica. An involuntary shiver coursed down his spine. *What a nightmare. A series of bad dreams, really. And they showed no signs of ending anytime soon.*

"The resulting depressurization, similar to what you might expect if a commercial airliner suffered rapid depressurization, created a shock wave, fracturing the ice and sending an avalanche down the shoulders of the rock formation known as Thor's Hammer. This sheet of ice gathered speed and momentum, shattering into pieces and becoming a full-scale avalanche, entombing the station. Perhaps the non-terrestrial crew 'missed' the fact a human hand with female chemistry would activate the opening mechanism. It's also possible that the mechanism failed by other means."

CIA Director Jorah Frohman, raised his hand, "Does that mean *any* female, not just Dr. Andrews, could have initiated the airlock system?"

Kyra nodded. "Because we salvaged working stasis units, DARPA has tested and proven this theory using our own scientists—starting with me."

"I knew it," Teresa Simpson said with satisfaction.

"What's that, Ms. Simpson?" the President asked.

"Women are destined to rule the universe."

"Well," said Kyra, "we can *infer* that the non-terrestrials *were* humanoid, *possibly* female. The hand pattern, using that term loosely, and shoulder-high position on the access panel hints they were bipedal, with biometrics comparable to that of a human."

Fischer, who hadn't said a word or changed his expression, raised his hand. His voice was raspy and he coughed to clear his throat. "I believe that makes Dr. Andrews...expendable."

Before Jack made a move in Fischer's direction, Teresa Simpson struck like a cobra.

"Oh, now you want to give Leah the old heave-ho? Good luck, Fischer. You do know she has a well-trained, loyal, and lethal security force at her disposal, right? Whereas you're lucky not to be sitting in a federal prison. My advice would be to watch your own back while you're still a free man. Getting rid of her should be the last thing you're worried about. Even if you could. Which you can't."

Fischer nodded. "I'm well aware that Dr. Andrews has an inflexible view regarding my well-being. She made her wishes regarding my future, or lack of, known on more than one occasion. This has nothing to do with Dr. Andrews, personally. It was simply a statement of fact, from a scientific standpoint."

Jack found himself strangely lacking anger at the man. Seeing Fischer in his beat-down state made retaliation, verbal or otherwise, seem pointless.

"Enough," Wheeler said, his voice icy. "The issue of Dr. Andrews has been litigated. At this point, it's best for all parties to move forward."

With impeccable timing, Kyra clicked on the next slide, which featured one of the "pod" units containing a cliff dweller still in stasis.

"Most of the material and mechanisms salvaged from the complex look like the contents of an auto chop shop after a police raid. An understandable result, given the inadequate time spent on site. Contained within it were more than forty such 'stasis units.' Twenty-nine were occupied by 'Ancients,' one having malfunctioned, the Ancient within deceased. To date, the stasis units are the crown jewels of the cache. When discovered, they were still operational—however, within ninety-six hours after breach, they shut down, one by one, in no identifiable order."

Kyra addressed the room at large. "Enough of the whole 'Debbie Downer' thing. We are in possession of technologies that could radically change the fabric of our culture—our very future. The stasis units could provide life-saving, life-extending potential. Colonization of Mars could be within our grasp if we can reverse-engineer this technology. Placing a crew in stasis units prior to launch would allow astronauts to spend months, years, even decades in space, then be awakened upon reaching their destination. The 'Ancients,' as Dr. Andrews dubbed the twenty-eight Native Americans, who spent the better part of eight-hundred years in the units, were effectively shielded from radiation, did not age a day, and suffered no other obvious ill effects from their long isolation."

"Agreed, Dr. Gupta," Admiral Rush said, "That is certainly a treasure beyond our wildest dreams. I have full confidence you will succeed in your charge to 'reverse-engineer' everything in our possession. Now, you lightheartedly mentioned weaponry—my concern, should more of these 'complexes' be discovered. Our number-one national-security concern, far exceeding anything else at this time, is preventing this hyper-technology from falling into foreign hands. I know that DARPA is tasked with using the recovered artifacts to develop a sound search-and-find strategy. What do you have that we can use right now?"

Kyra nodded. "We haven't formulated any scientifically proven methodology concerning finding more complexes. Jack Hobson is working with our team on this critical assignment. While we can theorize on technology-based location solutions, Jack brings a wealth of experience. Not only boots-on-the-ground exploration of Antarctica, but on all seven continents, including some of the most inhospitable environments on earth. Assuming we come up with no viable technological search method, Jack's knowledge and experience may be our best chance of finding another complex."

"Why do you say that?" Wheeler asked.

"Because, Mr. President, we more than seven billion people on this planet. There's hardly any place we haven't already mined, explored, blown up, or torn up, being the less-than-delicate species we are. If there are other complexes, it's likely they've been shielded by advanced technology rendering them invisible. It's our belief, as we have said, that the search should be focused upon Antarctica. However, having been tasked with all possible scenarios—i.e., search every haystack on planet earth—this is what we have."

Jack fought to keep a straight face. He was dying to needle Kyra about schooling Wheeler. He'd have to wait until they were flying back to DARPA. He had a more urgent duty right now: take the heat off Kyra.

Jack cleared his throat and raised a hand. "A thousand years ago, Antarctica was uninhabited and, for all practical purposes, it remains so today. That allowed non-terrestrials free rein, operating within the continent without cultural disruption or contamination beyond what they were already willing to risk. As Dr. Gupta explained, we believe the complex experienced an accident. Otherwise, it would have been discovered long ago by explorers. Thor's Hammer, the rock formation that towered over the site, has been used by pilots as a navigational tool for more than fifty years. It was my accidental fall into a crevasse that brought the existence of the complex to our attention.

"Now, when searching for similar complexes, one signature that we can use is heat. In the case of the Antarctic complex, heat escaping a jammed airlock entry for centuries literally melted a large crevasse, leading directly to the entry. The power system not only did its job for nearly a thousand years, but generated significant heat to melt that amount of ice."

"Dr. Gupta," the President said, "what theories do you have concerning the extraordinary power system that sustained this complex for centuries?"

"We don't have enough data supporting specific theories." Kyra used a remote to advance through a series of slides. She stopped on one of the architectural drawings featuring the complex's exterior. While the station was circular in shape, three pipe-shaped features extended out like a fan from the dome.

"From an initial survey using ground-penetrating radar, the ground team identified three extraordinary culverts. While they might have been tasked to melt ice and pump water for personal or lab use, these culverts exceeded three meters in diameter. The teams used GPR out to a distance of a thousand meters from the complex. The culverts remained contiguous and unending—before the complex was destroyed, that is."

Kyra focused on the Vice Chairman of the Joint Chiefs. "Admiral Rush has a long and distinguished service record commanding both attack and ballistic nuclear submarines. Perhaps he could make an educated deduction."

Admiral Rush didn't miss a beat.

"Electrolytic Oxygen Generators." He shrugged. "These conduits exceed by a huge margin the diameter necessary to supply the complex with pure oxygen, if that was the purpose. Of course, EOG also produces hydrogen. Hydrogen offers an excellent choice for power generation. Extending the culverts well beyond the complex tells me the non-terrestrials funneled a massive volume of water to the complex. Otherwise, the foundation of the complex would be immediately undermined, melting that much ice nearby."

Kyra nodded in agreement. "Our conclusions exactly, Admiral. If the non-terrestrials used known technology, breaking H_2O into its base components of oxygen and hydrogen, they could theoretically have used the hydrogen byproduct of EOG to create power on a massive scale—perhaps enough to run a large city. The water pipes could also have been used to cool a large, traditional-style nuclear reactor. Our teams have not identified mechanisms photographed within the complex that we recognize as traditional nuclear reactors, however."

"Regarding our search for other possible 'complex' sites...." Kyra handed Jack the remote control. "Jack has come up with some unorthodox search methodologies that we estimate offer a Vegas longshot at best."

Jack stood. "The heat signature created by the complex in Antarctica was the result of an accident. It's notable, but not a solid search-and-locate parameter, unless more such accidents occurred. However, we can assume that power generation on a large scale would be common component to all complex sites."

Jack paused. It was dead quiet in the Situation Room. Everyone from the President on down were so focused that even the normal shuffling, side chatter, and coughing had come to a halt.

He continued, knowing he had a captive audience. "Cliff or cave-dwelling cultures are not common, but neither are they rare." Jack clicked through a series of slides. "Examples include these dwellings in Mali, a near duplicate to the dwellings in Mesa Verde." Additional slides flashed on the flat screens. "Cappadocia in central Turkey, Kandovan in Iran, and the Matmata subterranean dwellings in southern Tunisia are other excellent examples. And then there's Guyaju, an ancient cave house located sixty miles from Beijing. Origins unknown. The complex has more than one-hundred and ten stone rooms, the largest cave dwelling ever discovered in China."

Jack paused briefly. "Native Americans lived—in fact, thrived—on the mesas for thousands of years prior to and nearly a thousand years after confining themselves inside the cliffs. Science struggled for years to come up with a logical reason for stuffing yourself into an uncomfortable, dangerous, and illogical cliff-dwelling existence. Can you imagine having to carry water up hundreds of feet from the river, then scaling bare wall in some cases, and then having to do the exact same thing the following day?" Jack grinned. "Well, now we know the why. The question is, did any of these other cultures around the world make a similar sacrifice for the same reason?"

A couple of hands raised as new slides flashed up on the flat screens. For the moment, Jack ignored them. "Perhaps the best example is Cappadocia, Turkey, located near Mount Ararat. Here we have mysterious cliff and cavern dwellings, also quite ancient. As a bonus, they're physically located alongside the biblical references of Noah's Ark.... *But*...I hasten to add, not all cliff dwellings have mysterious beginnings or endings. The Tunisian dwellings, for instance, make perfect sense if you're living in a desert, where hurricane-force sandstorms shred other house-building materials and temperatures commonly run at triple-digit levels. In that context, living underground is a common-sense survival tactic."

"I'd like to add", Kyra said, "that Jack Hobson has climbed on and around Mt. Ararat on three occasions."

Teresa Simpson slapped the conference table, grinning broadly. "Jack! You've been holding back. You found the Ark, and you're keeping it a secret."

Jack played along. "Well, the Catholic Church does have quite a sizable 'keep-quiet' slush-fund." He paused while some at the table scowled and others chuckled. "In all seriousness, though, I saw no Arks and no evidence of a Hyper-Technology Cache on Ararat. There were plenty of ways to get killed, ranging from Kurdish rebels to Kangal dogs the size of small ponies, wild dogs and more—way more."

Wheeler grimaced and crossed his arms. "So, you believe the biblical scripture concerning Noah's Ark could have been an ancient civilization's interpretation of seeing objects they couldn't explain?"

Jack hesitated. "I'm sure we could debate the religious significance and importance of the Ark long into the afternoon. I want to stress that I'm simply tying together facts that match our search parameters. My own personal belief is there's a better chance at finding the Ark than another alien complex buried on Mt. Ararat."

A slide lit the flat screens, featuring an aerial image of Mt. Ararat. "Ten years ago, Jacob Badger, a well-known Ark hunter and pastor of a large ministry located in northern Idaho, said he found a geothermal spring near the summit of Ararat. He reported the pool as measuring some ten meters across where it bubbled up out of the mountain. At some undetermined depth, it appeared the hot spring opened into a vast cavern. Badger and his team of Ark hunters used two-hundred and fifty feet of climbing line, weighted with a rock-filled, nylon bag, in order to measure the depth. According to Badger, at two-hundred feet, the weight hit bottom. He insisted the water was clear enough, even given the depth, for the team to identify a large, 'non-natural' structure. Now, if you're familiar with the physical dimensions of the Ark, the 'find' didn't match the biblical description."

People around the room nodded.

"Badger was pushing sixty-five, but one of the younger guys on the expedition had free-diving experience. Despite Badger's warnings, the kid stripped to his skivvies, ignoring the near-freezing air temperatures and thirty-knot winds on the surface, donned a pair of beat-up plastic swim goggles one of the other climbers used for swimming in hotel pools, tied the climbing line around his waist, took along a knife in case he needed to cut the line, and, *splash*, went into this spring. The water, at near seventy degrees Fahrenheit, felt like jumping into a kettle of coffee compared to standing out in the that icy wind tunnel near the summit of Ararat. He made several attempts to dive, without success. The kid was already sucking air at sixteen-thousand feet altitude; there's hardly enough oxygen to have a conversation, much less hold your breath and kick down without fins.

"After a few attempts, the kid said he needed weight—and suggested the nylon bag filled with stones. They gave it to him, despite the obvious danger. When he submerged this time, he dropped...

well, like a bag of rocks. They'd agreed to a maximum depth of fifty feet for safety. The kid went through fifty feet like greased lightning, and before Badger thought to brake the line, it went slack. The kid had sunk two-hundred feet straight down on one breath of air; nearly impossible for anyone to survive that except world-class free divers. Badger panicked. They hauled on the line, but it got hung up for more than thirty more seconds before they finally managed to reel him to the surface."

Eyebrows arched around the Situation Room. Jack had their full attention now.

"When the kid reached the surface, he yanked off the swim goggles and blood gushed from his eyes. The water pressure at that depth had compressed the swim goggles down on his eye sockets with such force, well...with standard swim goggles, there is no way to equalize pressure like you'd have with a diving mask. Badger tried dragging him out of the water, but the kid pushed away, blinded by the blood flooding his eyes and hysterical. His last words were: 'Pastor Badger! I found it!' Badger and the others tried to force him out of the hot spring, but the kid used the knife he'd carried and slashed Badger across the face, nearly blinding him in one eye. He cut the line above the rock-filled stuff bag, flipped back head-first, and submerged, blood streaming from his crushed eyes." Jack drew in a deep breath. *This part was never easy.* "He never resurfaced."

A collective exhale sounded around the room.

"Badger took this as sign that he had indeed found the remains of the Ark, and the kid's horrible death was Jacob Badger's punishment for seeking out what should have remained concealed: God's direct handiwork on earth. He returned to the States, left his ministry, and has been a hermit ever since."

Wheeler tossed down a pen. "Surely, others have found this spring, investigated further?"

"Search? Yes—for years now. But no one's relocated the spring, which was named 'Jacob's Well' soon after he returned."

"This preacher—he must know how to find it?"

"If he does, he won't tell." Jack shrugged.

Fischer said, "I believe this should be investigated, as soon as possible. While the chances of finding anything related to non-terrestrials seems remote, we cannot leave one stone unturned if there's a hint of evidence that would reveal another complex."

Jack put up his hands. "Well, I'd hardly call this evidence. I was asked to help come up with ideas on how and where we might use the limited data we have to provide search parameters. You can't land a bunch of army rangers in eastern Turkey and start searching Ararat. The Turks aren't ISIS. They've got a formidable military."

Admiral Rush spoke up. "Do we pick this Badger fellow up, hard-court-press him to talk?"

Teresa Simpson made a disgusted sound. "Are you really willing to water-board this old preacher?"

Again, Jack held up his hands. "If I might offer a suggestion here?"

The President nodded.

"Badger and I share common experience. We've both climbed treacherous, high-altitude mountains, and people in our care have died. I've been on Ararat. From a climbing perspective, it presents none of the problems you'd encounter on Everest. In fact, Everest base camp is at a higher elevation than Ararat's summit. If I approach him, on a personal level, perhaps he'd agree to share the location of his spring—as a national-security matter."

Teresa Simpson leaned back in her chair. "Don't you think Badger will put two and two together? Hermit or not, everyone's connected these days. What prevents him from running to the media and selling his story to the highest bidder? 'Jack Hobson, the climber from the mysterious events in Antarctica, is off to find a mysterious hot spring on Mt. Ararat.'"

Jack shrugged. "Aside from my charm and general trustworthiness? Climbers who've survived tough expeditions have a certain bond. Plus, I'll have my armed security along. He'll get the gist of what happens if you leak national secrets."

17

President Wheeler sat on a couch inside the private White House residence. Behind him, through a picture window, the Washington Monument glowed under night lighting. A knock came at the door to the residence. Wheeler opened it and Stanton Fischer stood in the hallway, alongside a secret service escort. Wheeler ushered Fischer into the residence, led him back to the sitting room, and invited him to sit where he liked.

"Stan...we have a problem that needs a solution."

"Would that be Al Paulson?"

Wheeler nodded. "You were in the Situation Room today. He's undermining the authority of the presidency."

"I agree, sir. How can I help?"

"We need a plan to divest my administration of Mr. Paulson."

Fischer blinked. "I don't know if that is possible. We have opposition senators and congressman responsible for the situation we find ourselves in. Any move against Al Paulson would result in an immediate action from them—and others, including the Chairman of the Joint Chiefs, and elements within the military."

"Agreed."

Fischer hesitated, then said, "Either Paulson decides upon his own volition to resign, or, he must be removed in a way that appears we had no hand in it."

Wheeler nodded. "He won't resign voluntarily. No question about that. He's power-mad and he operates well outside rule of law. He's a threat to our country and constitution."

"That leaves only three options," Fischer said. "Accidental death, suicide, or some fatal political action that his allies cannot defend."

"Your critical analysis is astute and on-target, as usual, Stan."

"Do you want me to come up with options, Mr. President?"

Before Wheeler could respond, another knock sounded at the front door. Wheeler answered it, and the same secret service escort waited with another man. Wheeler nodded for the man to enter and closed the door behind. He escorted the man to the sitting room, where he took a seat on the couch opposite Stan Fischer.

"Stan, I'd like you to meet Mr. Krause." Krause nodded but didn't bother to shake Fischer's hand. "Mr. Krause has a remarkable resume."

"Active military?" Fischer asked

"Not for some time," said Krause.

"An interesting name, Mr. Krause. "German ancestry?"

"I wouldn't know." Krause glanced at Wheeler, irritation clearly bordering on anger.

Wheeler intervened. "Let's say that Mr. Krause operates under a number of identities. I think it's better if we stick to business and avoid the personal pleasantries."

"Of course." Fischer shifted uncomfortably on the couch.

"Mr. Krause has unique experience in a variety of black operations. He's also a true patriot and has agreed to provide whatever assistance necessary in returning our government to the proper constitutional balance."

Krause remained stoic and expressionless.

"I've briefed Mr. Krause on everything except the most sensitive elements of the Antarctic operation, so consider him up to speed on our history with Mr. Paulson, including our current predicament and potential solutions."

Finally, Krause spoke up. "You'll find me to be forward, so I apologize in advance. My first question: Why worry about Al Paulson? You've got a war with Russia over what transpired in Antarctica. Rumors are flying about the 'sensitive elements' of that incident, including the discovery of a crashed alien spacecraft. That's currently the best bet in Vegas, but there are others, ranging from a cave full of Nazi gold to a deadly virus discovered under the ice." Krause paused. "Care to enlighten me on which one I should place my bet?"

"I wish I could, Mr. Krause. These are crucial National Security matters."

Krause said, "And Paulson has knowledge of these issues—along with the rest of his entourage. Or so says the news."

"Yes—another reason he's an issue that must be dealt with as soon as possible."

Krause nodded, crossed his arms. "You haven't asked for it, but I'm going to give you my advice—before we get to the point-of-no-return here. Do your job as President: Focus on the Russians and this bizarre blackout situation over the southern end of the globe. Whatever happened in the past, it will be forgotten and forgiven if you get a handle on these challenges and bring them under control."

Fischer raised his hand, as if he were back in high school. "Excuse me, Mr. President. Does Mr. Krause have the details concerning our overriding problem, in New Mexico?"

Krause looked from Wheeler, to Fischer, and then back again. "What problem is that, exactly?"

"Thank you, Stan. I thought I should save that until I had a firm agreement from Mr. Krause to go forward." Wheeler looked Krause directly in the eye. "We do have an agreement?"

"Provided I know all the details that concern this operation, I have agreed." He glanced at Fischer. "However, if your plan is to dribble out the information, then I will disagree to agree."

Wheeler nodded. "Before we can move on to Mr. Paulson, there's something we must have back in our possession—and other, related details."

"Possession and details. Really?" Krause didn't bother to hide his sarcasm. "I'm getting the distinct impression that my initial briefing from you was woefully inadequate."

"Stan, will you please explain to Mr. Krause the details concerning our missing nuclear weapon."

Krause slid forward on the couch. "Nuclear weapon?"

Fischer concisely explained how Al Paulson and his crew were extorting the American people with a nuclear weapon hidden somewhere in the mountains of New Mexico—or so the administration assumed. Fischer didn't mention this was a non-conventional, highly classified Hafnium warhead, or the magnitude of its yield upon detonation.

Krause chuckled when Fischer was done. "You boys really got yourself into a ball of knots, now, didn't you?" He shook his head in disbelief.

Wheeler ignored the slight. "Based upon the information I have provided, what would be your course of action with regard to securing the warhead? We have no choice but to secure it before we can deal with Paulson."

"First," Krause said, "I'd have drones patrolling grids over sections of New Mexico 24/7, just in case you catch unusual activity. Forget looking in the mountains. You said they landed an aircraft. The old pilot who flew the warhead out to its hide, Luke Derringer I think you said the name was, would know the washes that would serve. He'd need cover nearby, and somewhere to stash this warhead."

"We already have drones on that mission, Mr. Krause. So far, nothing has yielded any clues."

"I figured you would and I wouldn't mistake Paulson or his crew for fools, based upon the way they have your king in check right now." Krause paused, appearing to work the problem in his head. "From what Mr. Fischer said, it seems our best source for the location would be this old pilot. If what you say is true, he's the only one who's vulnerable. The location is so remote, it's perfect for a question-and-answer session."

Fischer interrupted. "Mr. Paulson did say they'd moved the warhead into a more secure location—known only to him and Jack Hobson. We can assume that Mr. Kinney is providing security, as his current location is unknown."

"I'll call bullshit on that one," Krause said. "Moving a canister of that size isn't easy. Paulson knows you'd double-cross him in a heartbeat. He wouldn't take a chance you'd spot him with your drones trying to move it."

Wheeler's jaw visibly tightened after Krause mentioned, 'double-cross.'

"Beyond that," Fischer said, "Luke Derringer is protected by Al Paulson. Al Paulson is protected by his congressional cabal, who would move against the Administration at the first sign we were in breach of our agreement. I believe the chances of getting information out of him prior to death from any extended questioning would simply make our problem larger. He'll die, be found, and Paulson will have all the political gravitas to get us pushed out of the White House, while still able to use the nuclear warhead more effectively than ever as a blackmail device."

The president stood. "Okay, you can go, Stan. There're issues I need to speak with Mr. Krause about that don't require your expertise."

Fischer stood and nodded. "Thank you, sir. I will see you in the a.m. for the briefing—however, I want to strongly disagree with this plan, should it involve Mr. Derringer."

Krause gave him a thin smile. "Not to worry, Mr. Fischer. There's no way we'd move on the old pilot, provided what you've told me. We will find another solution." Krause doubled-down on the phony smile. "Nice to meet you. I look forward to working with you on this operation."

Fischer walked to the doorway out of the private residence.

When the door had closed, Wheeler sat back into the couch. "So—reimbursement for an operation of this size and scope?"

"It got a whole lot higher when you mentioned a nuclear weapon. That'll require helicopter support for a team of between five and ten men. Such men do not come cheap, Mr. President. Not only are you buying their expertise, you're buying their silence."

Krause paused for a moment, staring out the window at the Monument.

"Moving Mr. Paulson out of your orbit will be the easy part of this. Getting the information necessary to locate this warhead, and dealing with anyone tasked with sentry duty? That will get—messy." Krause nodded toward the door Fischer had just exited. "He's right. We can't make some blatant move against the pilot. I'd save that for the last option—assuming we had other things fall into place that takes Paulson out of the picture first."

Wheeler nodded. "A situation's developing that may provide me with help on the Paulson problem—or at least keep him occupied for a period of days. However, the warhead, as I've said, remains the number-one deterrent to my goals. Once it's been located and secured, we can move, not only against Paulson, but all of those involved in this nuclear-blackmail coup."

"Then I suggest you make a cup of coffee, Mr. President. Because two things are going to happen: We're going to review this entire operation until I know every detail. And the fee for my services is going up. One more thing. The information regarding the mission in Antarctica, classified beyond Top Secret. Who has had access to this information? I'd like to have Mr. Fischer along with us on the operation. He's your direct point of contact, and of course we want to make sure we're doing this work to your specifications."

Krause turned his attention from the lighted Washington Monument back to Wheeler. "By the way—we don't clean up the mess. We go in fast, do the job, and get out. You'll need another team for mop up."

Wheeler nodded.

Krause gave him curt nod back. "Good. Now, let's get this comprehensive briefing underway."

18

J ack woke from a deep sleep, feeling like he was suffocating inside a mountaineering mummy bag. He reached for the flashlight he always kept next to his side when on a climb. Instead of the flashlight, his hand struck the metallic neck of a table lamp and knocked it to the ground.

It took a moment for Jack to realize he wasn't bivouacked on the shoulder of a mountain, waking from one of those bizarre dreams created by a nauseating blend of stress, oxygen deprivation, and poor nutrition. Instead of a mummy bag, a comforter had tangled itself around his body, and he found himself in the bedroom of a modest log home located on a fifty-acre parcel of federally-owned land in Falls Church, Virginia.

The cozy log house wasn't listed on any Internet booking sites, and even if it were, the listing could hardly do it justice, given all the extras. Resembling a summer camp for adults, the property hosted a total of twenty individual cabins, each situated to provide seclusion from others. They were all connected by a series of dirt roads and deer trails and decorated like the chalets you'd find at an expensive ski resort. While the log exteriors were stained in a single shade of reddish-brown, the interiors featured wood-beamed ceilings, granite kitchens, high-end oak and pine décor, soft leather furniture, landscape paintings, and even antique fly rods. Jack's home had a working wood stove, a rarity in urban environments. Stacked next to the fireplace, a mix of pine and oak firewood cut into ten-inch by two-inch sections, sized perfectly for the stove.

If not for the persistent presence of heavily-armed military police and a fortress-like fence surrounding the camp, Jack might have forgotten he was under constant surveillance, even held prisoner, depending on one's perspective.

The log homes were laid out in a circular pattern around a three-story lodge dubbed 'the clubhouse.' It had an open-air atrium ringed by three massive fireplaces. Built from river rock, the immense chimneys rose three stories to exit the pine ceiling.

A gourmet restaurant occupied one of the clubhouse's ground floor wings. It opened at six a.m. and served the last dinner at ten. Also open from five until midnight was a bar, complete with dance floor and DJ-operated disco. The temporary residents of this secure lodging facility could roll in after a long day, enjoy a cocktail at the bar, watch sports in the lounge, or head over to the game room, which included an impressive collection of old-school pinball machines. Oh, and in case you had to conduct actual government business, the business center offered secure communications and related IT services.

It sounded entertaining, and it might have been under different circumstances. Unfortunately, Jack was the only guest. After his long days at DARPA, he'd make his way over to the excellent gym inside the clubhouse and do a variety of strength training and high-intensity intervals for another hour, then shower, dress, and hit the lounge. There he could order his cocktail of his choice, made to order—no charge. The lounge was hosted by an army veteran/mixologist outfitted in an Armani suit. Staff Sergeant Carlson was as skilled a pro bartender as you'd find in the toniest clubs in Georgetown.

Jack checked his watch. It was past three in the morning, eastern time, and his secure satellite phone was ringing. He'd intended to call Leah earlier, but had gone from resting his eyes one moment to fast-asleep the next.

Jack stared at the blurry LED display. He pushed the phone away until his arm wouldn't extend any farther. He trusted it was fatigue and not early-onset presbyopia. He read a series of numbers: 090-8816, then the prefix 532, followed by another string of digits.

Jack jumped off the bed. 0-9-0 was the satellite country code for Turkey; 8-8-1-6 the Iridium satellite phone system; and 5-3-2 and the following digits were classic Turkish satellite numbers. No question, it was his guide and old friend: Hawar.

And in record time, no less.

He'd just called the warlord earlier that day, using the contact number he'd been given.

Hawar lived in the badlands of eastern Turkey, but as the Kurdish warlord liked to say: *Just because a man grew up without a flush toilet and was schooled in a goat house, do not mistake him for an idiot.*

Hawar was far from that, and he was also equipped with the latest satellite communications gear. The way you contacted Hawar was to send a text to a satellite phone with a contact number. If Hawar's number changed, he sent you an update. He never returned a call or sent a text on the same satellite phone twice. He was after all, an outlaw.

Eastern Turkey, bordered by both Iraq and Iran, was dangerous at the best of times. Without Hawar and his sons, armed to the teeth and offering protection, Jack would have never ventured into the region.

He dialed the number.

"*Elu*," said a hoarse but familiar voice.

"*Demêke tum nebînîwe*," Jack replied in his best Kurdish dialect. It translated as 'Long time, no see.'

"Mr. Jack," Hawar said in near-perfect English. "How are you, my friend?"

Jack answered with another Hawarism. "I'm alive and my family is well, which is more than I can say for many."

"Are you in Turkey?"

"Not yet, but I may have need of your services in the near future."

"This is a very bad time for a holiday in Turkey."

"Yes, I know. This is personal business. I need a guide to the summit of Ararat."

"In the middle of winter? Ararat will still be here this summer, God willing." Hawar paused for a moment, faint static sounds filling the dead air. "You are quite famous, my friend. I was hoping, God willing, that you survived the mysterious events in Antarctica."

"News travels fast." Jack was more than a little surprised that Hawar would know anything about it, given his remote home near the Iranian border.

"Because a man grew up without a flush toilet and was schooled in a goat house, do not mistake him for someone who has no access to CNN."

Jack grinned. "Tell me, do you remember a man named Jacob Badger? The guy who led at least two expeditions searching for the Ark?"

"Of course. He claimed to have located the Ark, and God made him pay a terrible price."

"I don't believe he found the Ark. However, he did locate a hot spring near the summit of Ararat. I'm searching for this location."

"Yes. I know of this spring. It is frozen over most of the time—very hard to locate."

Jack almost fumbled the phone out of his hands. "Can you find it? During the winter?"

"There is no Ark there, my friend."

Jack sucked in a deep breath. "Have you seen the spring?"

"Yes. Yes. Many years ago."

"How large was the opening?"

"Not enough for the great Ark of Noah. Perhaps ten meters. Listen, Mr. Jack: Boiling waters come from the depths of the earth at this location. It's the cauldron of Satan, my friend. God would have nothing to do with this place."

"Do you remember how to find it?"

"In the winter? It's possible. Ararat is my home."

Jack felt a wave of relief. If Jacob Badger could provide a location, along with Hawar's knowledge of Ararat, it was a near certainty he could complete the mission in short order.

"But seriously, Mr. Jack. Risking a climb on Mt. Ararat in winter? Risking the Turkish military and Persian jihadists who would gladly cut off your head for fifty lira.... Why would you do this?"

"I can tell you more when I get to Turkey. If you can guide me and provide protection."

"Your friendship is worth more than any price, Mr. Jack. However, my family thanks you, for your generosity. My sons, they have grown into men since your last trip."

"If they are like their father, they're fierce fighters as well."

"Yes. And you will need such fighters. War rules our region."

"I'll know if I'm headed to Kurdistan within the next forty-eight hours."

"Then I will call you as usual. Say, in twenty-four hours?"

The downside was that it'd be a three a.m. call tomorrow morning. The upside? There was no way Jack would be caught in a meeting and unable to answer his phone.

"That's is perfect," Jack said. "Use the same number."

Hawar cut the connection, and Jack glanced at his watch once more. Past one a.m. in New Mexico. Leah probably wasn't getting much sleep anyway. He hit the speed dial on Leah's satellite phone, and she picked up after only the second ring.

"Jackson! So nice to hear your voice."

"Wow—you sound relaxed. Is everything going well?"

"Fabulous," Leah replied "Our young lady is doing great. No surprises with her, or back at the Settlement. We've got one more day here with Gordon. Not a peep out of him, and K'aalógii is no worse for wear. Hell, I'm tempted to take her into Alamogordo for a Happy Meal and a movie." She switched subjects. "How'd your bigwig meeting with the shit sticks go?"

"If you mean Wheeler and Fischer, surprisingly cordial. Paulson and Teresa both said to say hello."

"Aw. At least someone cares," Leah said. "Hey, my name didn't come up at all, perchance?"

Jack decided bringing up Fischer's comment would send her ballistic, so he dodged. "Nothing that impacts the Settlement. Between the nature of the technology and our military challenges in the Southern Ocean, they don't have much time for the Genesis Settlement.

"This didn't come up at the meeting, but that energy net that's descended over Antarctica appears to be intensifying. We don't know how—we can assume the why—to keep us off the continent. The energy beam emitted by the complex when you touched the entry pad seems to be mimicking a high radiation particle burst, better known as a sunspot. It has infected, for lack of a better term, the atmosphere over Antarctica, making electronic communications of any kind impossible."

"I think I knew that," Leah said. "Do you know," she asked, "how much energy it takes to create inference of that scale and intensity? Immense."

"Teresa Simpson's analogy was sobering. She said, 'If you wanted to Taser a planet, this is exactly how you'd do it.'"

"I never had any illusions we were dealing with cute ETs," Leah said. "I saw how these people were purposely terrified, starved to death, even murdered, kidnapped, and stuffed into alien deep-sleep gadgets. The purpose of a Taser is to disable someone, so you can take them into custody. Sounds like we're being disabled."

"Exactly," he said.

"Again," she said, "I had a pretty good idea of this already. Why is it you're calling, again—unless you JUST had to hear my voice."

Busted.

"Okay," Jack said, unable to hold it back any longer. "I'm just going to spit it out."

"Don't tell me. Gordon ratted us out?"

"No. Nothing like that. One of our key charges at DARPA is leaving no stone unturned in locating other alien complexes."

"Makes sense. No better guy on the planet than Jack Hobson for that job."

"Right," Jack replied, treading lightly. "We have one location that, although evidence-thin, does have potential. Eastern Turkey. On Mt. Ararat."

"That makes sense," Leah said. "You've got the Cappadocia dwellings and a location chock-full of mythology, including the Ark. But you've covered Ararat pretty thoroughly in the past as a guide for Ark-hunters. There's nothing up there—nothing that's easy to locate, anyhow."

He was stunned. Leah had figured out in five seconds what had taken him days of thinking to conclude.

Okay, he thought. *Here it goes.*

"I'm the guy they want to investigate. I've got Hawar available. If this operation launches, I'd do a solo trip to Turkey, hook up with Hawar, check out this hot spring called Jacob's Well, and get the hell out of the country." He waited for the explosion he was sure would come.... Instead—only silence.

After a few seconds, Leah shouted. "Jack! You still there?"

Jack was so stunned; it took a moment to respond. "Honestly, I expected you to have an objection."

"Ha! That'd be slightly hypocritical. Here I am, waiting to get my throat cut, sitting on a human powder keg—and I expect you to hatch an office chair. Fat chance that's gonna happen."

"Seriously?" Now he was bit disappointed. "I could be headed off to my death, and you're just gonna wave a handkerchief as I go?"

"Oh, for God's sake, Climber. Buck-up. You're the best person on the planet to do this. They can't send the military into Turkey without having a two-front war. You'll be in the company of a Kurd warlord who treats you like another son. Unless...."

"Unless what?" He knew there'd be a catch.

"Unless you're taking Paulson along on the climb."

Jack had to chuckle. It wasn't Jack's climbing Leah hated. It was taking rookies like Paulson on eight-thousand-meter peaks, expeditions that entailed a big paycheck and a bigger risk of death.

"Got you there, huh, Jackson? I think this is a goose-chase," Leah said, matter-of-factly. "But, if you find something, at least we have the information. Otherwise we'll be shut out. Plus, I don't want you in Wheeler's crosshairs. Or spending too much time with this Kyra character. Hell, I couldn't have ordered up a better solution—send you out of country."

To Jack's surprise, Leah laughed out loud. Her dilemma with the Ancients must have been stressing her out so much that it made her giddy.

Leah sobered quickly. "Just give me all the details, Jackson. Otherwise I have to sit here and listen to Gordo recite the Periodic Table—again."

Jack sat down on the couch in his log home, feeling strangely energized. The five-hundred-pound gorilla of telling Leah that he might be headed to Turkey had suddenly left his shoulders. He filled her on the details, such as they were, while Leah crunched what he assumed were Corn Nuts in the background, all the while throwing in her two-cents' worth of expert advice. Just like the good old days.

It was a heroin-like high. A monumental, emotional escape, from current events. A Groundhog Day-like déjà vu, back to the early days of their marriage.

Jack could not have been happier at that moment. He knew it wouldn't last, but rediscovering a sensation that he'd thought long gone was pleasurable beyond belief, regardless of the perils of Ararat.

Jack had made another call, earlier in the day. This one to Jacob Badger's home phone in Wallace, Idaho. He'd tasked one of the DARPA staff to find a phone number, if one existed. Less than five minutes later, the staffer came back.

"Got it," he said.

"That fast? Gotta love a billion dollars' worth of high-tech spook gear."

"Didn't need it, sir," said the twenty-something staffer. "I Googled the white pages in Wallace. Came right up."

When Jack called the number, Badger picked right up. Not only that, he also already knew perfectly well who Jack Hobson was. A bit of a surprise, although mountaineering was a small and tight clique. Plus, Jack had become well-known for being involved in the mission to Antarctica.

He leveled with Badger up-front, telling him that he was representing the federal governmental on a mission to Ararat, the existence of which was highly classified and critical to national Security. Any mention of their phone call or subsequent face-to-face meeting must remain secret or, Jack told Badger plainly, the ex-preacher would be detained immediately. For this reason, he needed Badger to make a firm decision over the phone. Either he'd agree to Jack's terms or Jack would terminate the call with no further contact.

To Jack's delight, and relief, Badger had agreed right off the bat. He said he was too curious not to help Jack in any way he could.

Jack signed off, saying he'd be flying by military jet into Wallace, Idaho, as soon as possible the next day.

19

Jack's security escort had him standing on the tarmac at Andrews Air Force base at six a.m. sharp. His pilot, an Air Force captain dressed in a standard commercial airline pilot's uniform, told Jack the weather was expected to moderate, which meant that they were good to go: direct flight from D.C. to Wallace, Idaho.

Jack flew in an unmarked C-21A along with his security team of four. They dressed casually in jeans and T-shirts, their large, down-filled parkas covering an array of weapons and communications gear.

The C-21A was the military's designation for a Learjet 35. This particular aircraft had been tasked for intelligence operations. It was registered by a bogus meat-packing company incorporated in Delaware. Since nearly every grocery chain on the planet dealt with meat providers, it could travel just about anywhere without raising an eyebrow.

Even to Wallace, Idaho.

Upon arrival at the Shoshone County Airport, Jack looked out the window of the C-21. The temperature was a brisk twenty-five degrees, zero breeze. A light snow floated down slowly, almost appearing frozen in place.

Wet, sticky snow. If it got a bit heavier or the wind picked up, they wouldn't be leaving any time soon. Storms and bold pilots were a lethal mix. Jack had learned that lesson several times and survived to tell the tale. He had no interest in testing fate once again.

As the jet taxied, he scanned the margins of the small airfield, looking for Jacob Badger. No sign of him yet, but Jack was hopeful.

It's good to be the boss, he thought, as his security guys scowled while he explained that Badger would be picking him up. His guards would follow along in a standard-issue, government-black, four-wheel drive Suburban that had been dispatched to the small town for their use. In his short time working for the government, Jack had decided that there must be parking lots full of the big vehicles everywhere he traveled. The federal government must have been keeping the GMC Suburban alive, simply through the sheer numbers that they bought each year.

Jack stepped off the plane and headed for the small parking lot alongside the strip. Three of his security team stayed at his side, while the fourth went to secure the Suburban.

Jack spotted Jacob Badger before he caught sight of the man's beat-up Chevy Blazer at the side of the road. Badger looked like any Idaho woodsman, dressed in jeans, a camouflage hunting jacket, high-end but well-worn Sorrel boots, and a black cowboy hat. It had been a few years since he'd seen a photo of the man, and Jack was shocked to find Badger looking so fragile. He appeared a lot older than his actual age.

When Badger reached out and shook Jack's hand, the grip was anything but frail. The thick white scar that cut across his face, from the deceased young man's desperate knife slash, seemed more prominent than he remembered from the photos. Where the knife had cut across his right eye, Badger's brow, lids, and cheek drooped.

The old preacher spoke in a hoarse voice. "You look a little worse for wear than your photos in the news, young Jack." He winked with his good eye. "Still a sight better than I look."

"Locked up in a commercial dryer on spin for a month doesn't even come close to my current lifestyle," Jack said.

Badger chuckled. "I'm guessing brisk Idaho weather isn't much of a burden for a man who's stood on the summit of Mt. Everest countless times."

"The older I get, the less I enjoy cold weather."

"They say it's God's country around here," Badger said without expression. "Are you a Christian, Jack?"

"Hardly. Although, I'm the first to admit, I've spent plenty of time praying on a mountain when things weren't going as planned."

Badger nodded, then gestured at Jack's three-man security detail. "So, what is it? Brass knuckles and batons if I don't talk?"

"I promise not," Jack said, gesturing for the security team to relax. "They're gonna follow us, that's all. Just act like they're not there."

Badger jumped out of the way as the Suburban slid to a stop, sending ice water flying in their direction. "Easy for you to say, Mr. Government Big Shot."

"Right," Jack replied dryly. "Welcome to my world."

Badger led Jack out to the Blazer, opened the dented passenger door, and ushered Jack into the passenger seat. When the old preacher keyed the ignition, the truck's V8 blew a cloud of blue smoke before settling into, more or less, an idle. "You say them boys'll follow us?"

"Trust me on that one," Jack said.

As if tempting fate, Badger stomped on the gas pedal, weaving out of the airport at a speed that had Jack pressing his hands against the dash while searching futilely for a seatbelt.

"Probably been awhile since you rode in an old Blazer held together with baling wire and duct tape?"

"Actually, I had a similar experience not long ago. Off-road, down in New Mexico."

"I've never wrecked yet." Badger's eyes shone. "Not exactly saying you're in God's hands...."

"Close is good enough for me."

"I'm taking you into town. The best buffalo burger you've ever tasted. Those boys wearing them wrap-around sunglasses in the middle of a snowstorm are welcome to come on in, too."

Jack was liking Badger more every minute. The old man was a breath of fresh air compared the bureaucratic dipshits Jack dealt with daily.

"If they have an out-of-the-way table, I'd appreciate it."

Badger just grinned.

20

Badger was right. It was the best buffalo burger he'd ever had. It was also the second time since leaving Antarctica that Jack had felt anything approaching a semblance of normal life. The first had been during his long phone conversation with Leah, after she shooed him off to Ararat.

Badger had selected a booth in a secluded part of the small diner, as requested. Nearby, Jack's security team was also savoring the buffalo burgers, seeming to enjoy the brief escape from oppressive Washington as much as he.

Badger leaned back after finishing the last of the fat-cut, homestyle fries. "You want to tell me how my pilgrimage to Mt. Ararat ties in with the world going to hell in a handbasket?"

"Wish I could," Jack said with sincerity.

"Plenty of stories out there. Care to tell me which ones are false?"

"The hole I've already dug is deep. It's entirely possible I've placed your life in danger just by coming here," Jack said. "I really can't open up as much as I'd like to on anything classified that might or might not have happened in Antarctica."

Badger said, "I doubt very much you're here on a spiritual quest."

"Not much gets past you."

"I've been in the people-game my whole life. If you're gonna build a flock, you have to tie the strings together, way, way ahead of everyone else."

"Okay," Jack sighed, leaning forward. "I *cannot* tell you *exactly* what was found in Antarctica. I *can* say the discovery resulted in the death of more friends and colleagues than I care to think about. I have no doubt the details will be leaked sooner rather than later. For now, it's still highly classified."

"Whatever it is, young Jack, I won't be around to see it. I've got stage-four cancer. Esophageal. My doctor says most likely due to all those church dinners." He grimaced. "When you're the pastor, you're obliged to eat everything. If you don't, it causes all kinds of problems in the congregation. *'Psst! Old lady Willis, her chili was so bad Pastor Badger couldn't eat it. She's goin' to Hell, for sure.'*"

Badger managed a grin. "I suffered the worst heartburn for years. Didn't know I was setting myself up for cancer. I did pray, more than once, that the Almighty would trigger a power outage so I'd have an excuse to leave. But damned if *He* didn't make me suffer through every one of those dinners."

Jack shook his head and held the older man's gaze. "I'm so sorry, Jacob."

Badger dismissed it with a wave of his hand. "So, let's get down to business, young Jack. You want to know how to locate what they like to call Jacob's Well. Why?"

"I can say, honestly, I'm not in search of the Ark."

The wrinkles on Badger's tired face took on the 3D appearance of a raised map. "You know the last time I was there; I was responsible for the death of the nicest young man you'd ever meet. What makes that worse? Every Sunday, while I preached God's love, that young man's mom and daddy and his two sisters sat in the front pew, nodding and smiling like I knew what the hell I was talking about. After a year of that, those reassuring words sounded pretty damned empty. Turned out, maybe my faith wasn't up to the task. I retired. Never went back for Sunday worship after that."

Jack glanced down. "I know exactly how that feels."

"Took years before I forgave God, but I did," Badger continued. "That doesn't mean I don't believe he can be a nasty bastard at times—cause he sure as hell can."

"The articles I read said you found the Ark, and the death of David Samuelson was punishment for hunting and uncovering evidence of God's work on this earth."

Badger nodded. "You know, in a situation like that, you try to make sense of it all. And I believed that, for his family and friends, finding the Ark gave his death some meaning."

The hair stood on Jack's neck. "So, you didn't find the Ark?"

"Nope," Badger said.

Jack's mouth dropped open. Up till now, Badger had seemed as honest a man and preacher he'd ever met. If this were a hoax, he'd just wasted a whole lot of time. He felt the anger bubbling up from deep inside but didn't respond.

"What young David said, with his eyes awash with blood, was—and these are his exact words: 'Pastor Badger—I've found the firmament!'"

Jack was more perplexed than angry. "Sorry. The firmament?"

"From the book of Genesis. 'And God said, "Let there be a firmament in the midst of the waters, and let it divide the waters from the waters." Thus God made the firmament, and divided the waters, which were under the firmament, from the waters that were above the firmament; and it was so. And God called the firmament Heaven.'"

"David thought he'd found Heaven at the bottom of this spring?"

"The ancient Hebrews believed there was a solid 'dome' or 'vault' to heaven."

Jack felt the table sliding away; all sense annoyance evaporated. *Firmament*, he thought. *A solid 'dome' or 'vault.' A near-perfect description of an alien complex.*

"Looks like I struck a chord there, eh?"

"Maybe. I wish I could tell you more. If anyone deserves to know the truth, it's you…. What did you see, if anything, from the surface?"

"There was something down there—I can't say for sure what I saw."

Jack nodded. "Well, any help you provide could save us time. I know it was poor weather and you were never actually sure of the exact location...."

"Yep. That was my story." Badger reached into his shirt pocket, pulled out a folded sheet of yellow-pad paper, and handed it over.

Jack unfolded the sheet. Written in blue ink were GPS coordinates. "You knew how to relocate Jacob's Well all along?"

"I swore the members of my team to silence, but we all knew."

Jack raised his eyebrows. "You lied to keep it secret?"

"Says who?" Badger replied in mock indignation. "I said the weather was awful: true. At the location, it was zero visibility, wind blowing like a hurricane. What I told the press and everyone else who asked was: 'We'd never find it again without guidance from above.'"

Jack snorted at the old man's clever pun, causing his security team to go silent and turn around. "GPS from above, eh? Not divine intervention."

"God works in vague and infuriating ways, young Jack." Badger paused. "One more thing. If you get close, you'll know you're there."

"How's that?"

"Sulfur. It was thick with the stench of sulfur—like Satan himself was hunkered under those waters."

21

Beckam sped over the ice toward the Antonov fuselage, deliberately keeping his speed down, despite his impatience. Damaging the snow machine or flipping and tearing up the empty toboggans was at the bottom of his to-do list. The aluminum toboggans were designed to tow weapons, gear, even injured soldiers, but only for short distances.

The Antarctic sastrugi made for a rough ride, even at slow speeds. Come to think of it, he'd need to line the bottom of the toboggan with padding, both to insulate Danny from the cold and to soften his ride as much as possible.

"Sorry, honey," Beckam said, pushing his way into the cluttered fuselage. "They don't have our reservation for tonight. Looks like we're hitting the road."

"Not a minute too soon, Skipper. Kind of a shame my view will be straight up at the sky."

"You're lucky. It's Antarctica. Not a strip club within ten-thousand kilometers." Beckam started plucking out the soft insulation that lined the old fuselage. "Remind me when we exit this continent-sized freezer, to permanently remove it from any future travel itinerary."

"Roger that," said Frantino quietly.

Beckam slid Frantino out of the fuselage on a ragged section of insulation that would serve as his bed for the foreseeable future.

Almost immediately, Beckam had to stop and catch his breath. Towing the one-hundred and eighty-five-pound SEAL by hand wouldn't have been easy at the best of times. Weakened by the radiation poisoning, the altitude, and the pounding he'd endured during the detonation left him far from full strength.

"How are you holding up?" Beckam asked after taking several deep breaths and readying himself for another pull.

"Ten out of ten, Skipper," Frantino said, a line of perspiration popping out on his forehead.

"Remember...pain is just weakness leaving the body."

"Thanks, Skip," Frantino answered through gritted teeth. "I'll remember than when I enlist in the Marines."

Once Beckam had Frantino next to the aluminum toboggan, he gently slid Danny onto the ice, then began packing the insulation into the sled like an ad-hoc mattress.

"Ready for your ride?"

Frantino nodded.

Beckam pulled him onto the toboggan as gently as he could manage, then piled more insulation around Frantino's sides and over his torso and legs, making him look like a mummy wrapped in an aluminum sarcophagus.

"First-class accommodations, Danny. Way too good for a combat-hardened Frogman."

Frantino didn't respond. Beckam figured the pain from the broken femur had been more than Danny had let on while being hauled to the toboggan.

Driving the Taiga again, he towed Danny in the direction of the Russian gear drop, wincing each time his XO bounced over an imperfection in the ice. Given the distance, time, exposure, and the amalgamation of Frantino's injuries, it seemed unlikely that Danny would survive the trip to Amundsen-Scott. Then again, Beckam couldn't honestly rate his chances of making it all that much higher.

When Beckam reached the Clay twins, they had two Taigas side by side and ready to tow toboggans already loaded with critical gear.

"You boys have been busy. What's on the manifest?"

Lenny unhooked a series of bungee tie-downs on the toboggan behind his snow machine. "We're Gucci, Boss. I dug up ten, twenty-liter cans and Liam's got another ten."

Beckam estimated that the Taigas got around twenty kilometers for each gallon of gas. For three snow machines running together, that meant a range of 650 kilometers. If they dropped one Taiga along the way, the fuel would stretch.

"Find another ten cans of fuel if you can, Len. How much oil did you pack?"

"Shit—oil—never thought about it."

"These things burn a ton of oil—at least a quart every two-hundred kilometers. The Russians will pack cases of it. Grab at least ten quarts. What else you got?"

"I dug out two more pallets and managed to find one of those aluminum bridges you wanted. I got two of those multi-fuel stoves that burn just about anything and at least a hundred Russian MREs."

"IRPs, Lenny. *Individualnovo Ratsiona Pitanee – Povsedyen*, as I recall. Toss one over here." Lenny tossed Beckam a brown cardboard box. Beckam opened the top and confirmed it contained the meal.

Each IRP had a complex mix of foods, and even a small stove for heating and making soups and stews with the ingredients. He studied the Russian stamp on the outside of the pack.

"The good news is they look complete and in good shape," Beckam said. "The bad news is they expired in 2005."

"Anything but Vienna Sausage," Liam said with a shrug.

"You might change your mind when you take a look-see at this stuff" Beckam tossed the IRP back to Lenny. "Remember to take it easy towing the gear. If you try to corner like a Ferrari, you'll flip the rig and break your neck at the same time."

"No worries," said Liam. "We're from Montana. We've been riding snowmobiles since birth. Nothing like running a hundred miles per hour over a frozen lake."

"And sometimes when it wasn't frozen," Lenny said.

The twins laughed and bumped gloved knuckles.

Beckam studied the ice-scape. "The detonation sent substantial energy waves through the ice in all directions. We're bound to run across a thousand variations of frost heaves and crevasses. So, X-Game champions or not, keep your eyes open and take it slow."

22

Senior Lieutenant Grigoriy Ivanovich had been well briefed on his objective: Recon the target and gather intelligence. Engage any Americans only as a last resort. Reconnaissance was the supreme priority on this mission. The first Russian Spetsnaz airborne platoon had parachuted into a 'Myasorubka' fourteen days earlier and been dead within minutes of airdropping the target. More than dead—vaporized.

According to his briefers, the Americans had stumbled across a 'high value target' while trying to steal a junk aircraft off the ice. That's all that was said in the official briefing—beyond the nuclear detonation, that was purposely used to destroy the very 'high value target' they were being send down to recon. You didn't have to work in Star City to know the Americans had stumbled across something of such value, they'd fired the first shots of the next Great War—and used a nuclear weapon to do it. His first thoughts mimicked the rumors of an aircraft of alien origin: the Americans had taken what they could, and then destroyed the rest. If this was truly the case, their mission was essentially meaningless.

Such had been Grigoriy's thoughts during the briefing. The fact that his platoon had now escaped death not once but twice before reaching Antarctica reinforced his already low opinion of humanity in general and a cancer known as the Russian billionaire in particular

The Americans were clearly dead-set against allowing Russia access to Antarctica. It didn't take Grigoriy long to get that message south of the African continent. The Ilyushin 76MD-90A had pulled up to less than a hundred kilometers behind the air-to-air tanker when their airborne gas station had exploded in a fireball.

The Pilot did evasive maneuvers while radioing desperately for any other fuel tanker plane nearby. They hadn't been shot down, and one hour after turning around, they'd reached a back-up tanker with just enough fuel to allow the Ilyushin a second attempt. Once the Ilyushin air-dropped them and all their equipment, it would turn around and need more air-to-air fuel transfer in order to reach the African continent.

Not that he'd been given the choice...but if he had, Grigoriy would have chosen bailing out over Antarctica rather than try and make the return to South Africa. Those chances look infinitely better than the odds of the pilots and crew on the Ilyushin getting home.

When it came to briefings prior to a mission, Grigoriy tended to believe about ten percent of what he was told. Having a pessimistic attitude, especially when it came to Russian intel and motives, had kept him and his men alive on more than one mission.

His platoon had drawn this lethal mission thanks to an assignment in the Ukraine that had gone wrong. Civilians were mowed down during an intense firefight, unfortunately in direct view of news cameras. Following the incident, the entire platoon of highly trained and motivated Spetsnaz commandos had been reassigned to a penal platoon, in which they had now spent fourteen months out of a two-year 'temporary assignment.' The penal platoon had been Stalin's way of dealing with soldiers who didn't follow his orders to the letter. During the Great Patriotic War, penal-platoon inmates had been sent only on the most suicidal of missions.

In true Russian fashion, penal platoons continued after the Great Patriotic War, outliving their creator. It was hazardous duty and to be avoided, yet this was Grigoriy's second time being assigned to a penal platoon.

The first time had been long ago, and it had started simply enough: He'd caught a soldier stealing from the barracks. Instead of confronting him on the spot, he handled his business Spetsnaz-style. He'd alerted several other commandos, all of which earned an instant promotion to sergeant after completion of training.

Grigoriy and his fellow Spetsnaz had crept into the barracks and beaten the thief and his cohorts with locks wrapped in towels until the offender and his bunkmates were unconscious.

Thievery within Spetsnaz was the ultimate expression of treachery and betrayal, and leniency was no way to maintain discipline or set an example within the ranks. Grigoriy's sentence to three months' service in a penal platoon had not been for beating the thief. That was expected and a tradition within the Spetsnaz culture. He'd been punished for beating the thief's bunkmates, who Grigoriy had deemed equally guilty because they hadn't schooled their fellow Spetsnaz properly.

In the ten years since, Grigoriy had risen in the ranks to become one of the most experienced operators within the *Glavnoye razvedyvatel'noye Upravleniye* or GRU, the Main Intelligence Directorate for the Russian military. Grigoriy was fiercely loyal and known for his ability to keep secrets, immune to the kind of drinking and carousing that made Russian soldiers undependable when it came to classified and sensitive information.

Because they could keep their mouths shut, Grigoriy and his men had abundant experience in state-ordered assassinations of foreign nationals and were routinely assigned missions that caused even the most brutal Kremlin bureaucrat to flood a toilet with his breakfast—and last night's dinner.

Only three days prior to this mission, Grigoriy had been ordered to wait on standby while equipping his platoon for an extended, self-sufficient Antarctic airborne deployment. Mission: reconnaissance with a full complement of combat weapons and ammunition to cover practically any eventuality.

Then he had received a mind-blowing briefing about the extraordinary developments on the underside of the globe. Another Spetsnaz platoon had been eliminated upon arrival, along with an unknown number of American SEALs, by detonation of a theoretical nuclear device that left no residual radiation signature.

That caught Grigoriy's attention. It meant that Russia was effectively at war with the United States—not the occasional dustup in some backwater Middle Eastern shithole.

A nuclear war.

Which he and his men would be entering shortly.

Grigoriy had almost convinced himself that they would arrive at the target without being shot down, when the state-of-the-art Ilyushin suddenly lost its lock on both Russian GLONASS and American GPS satellites. The alert came via his headset from the flight crew.

"What was our last known location?" he asked the navigator via the secure comms.

"Two-hundred meters from the Antarctic coast."

"Dead reckoning it is, then. Proceed."

The navigator clicked his response and the big aircraft's engines whined, the Ilyushin tilting perceptibly as it corrected course.

As a backup, the pilots would now be using Inertial Guidance Navigation, a relic of the early rocket age that used analog accelerometers and gyroscopes to maintain a known course. Not a comforting thought....

Three hours later, with no further comment from the flight deck, the platoon received the long-awaited drop alert. In true Spetsnaz style, no one wished his fellows good luck. No one smiled. No one said anything at all.

Remarkably, Grigoriy and his men all hit the ice without injury and quickly assessed the equipment drop, which had also been a success, every pallet touching down without damage. All satellites covering Antarctica, including American GPS and Russian GLONASS, were inoperable, so Grigoriy ordered his second-in-command to do some dead reckoning of his own. The result? The Ilyushin had dropped them more than 150 kilometers east of their intended LZ.

How very Russian. Once again, he'd been screwed by his command, with the satellite-navigation outage running a close second in the race to kill his men. On the positive side, they were in a real shooting war with a formidable enemy. All things considered, it was better than drinking oneself to death in a remote Siberian penal colony.

Reconnaissance was the mission, he reminded himself. Also, one positive note: the enemy would also be technologically deaf-dumb-blind. That lifted Grigoriy's spirits. The loss of navigation and communication systems necessary to operate the American aircraft-carrier battle group did much to level the playing field.

Another ground-leveler? Grigoriy's commandos had been issued the top-secret and still-unproven *Karakatitsa*, or "cuttlefish shells." The shells were a breakthrough in combat garb, using technology discovered while studying the ability of cuttlefish to camouflage themselves. In addition to providing nearly perfect camouflage, the *Karakatitsa* were also impervious to both infrared and thermal targeting. Or so he'd been told. Grigoriy was skeptical on all three claims.

23

Grigoriy applied the brakes and the Taiga 55 slid to a stop. He held a hand up, then closed it into a fist, signaling his men to shut down their snow machines. In the dry, high-altitude atmosphere of Antarctica, the landscape appeared extra sharp, almost painfully clear. Landmarks in the distance seemed eerily close. The clarity made the lazy smoke plumes appear no more than six kilometers ahead, but Grigoriy calculated the distance at closer to fifteen kilometers.

Antarctica, playing tricks on those foolish enough to tread her ice.

He pulled a pair of Swarovski binoculars out of a bag attached to the fuel tank and balanced them on the windscreen of the Taiga in order to steady the image. The series of air-dropped pallets that had supported the now-vaporized Spetsnaz platoon came into crisp focus.

Grigoriy made two immediate observations: his dead-reckoning navigation had been accurate, and someone had blown up the air-dropped supplies. The distance was still too far to get an accurate reading of exactly what had taken place. Either they'd been destroyed by an air strike or spec-ops troops on the ground. Neither circumstance was promising.

Grigoriy spun and addressed a soldier standing next to a Taiga. "Vasily. Analiz."

Vasily Popov opened a gear bag and extracted a Russian-made Soeks Quantum Geiger Counter. He held up the device and swept it in a 360-degree pattern. "All within acceptable levels," he reported.

The commander signaled weapons-ready. He scanned and confirmed: no movement on their flank. They might go the way of the first Spetsnaz platoon if the Americans had dropped fresh commandos into the target zone. Grigoriy started his Taiga, and his men did the same.

Moving cautiously, Grigoriy signaled a stop every kilometer, and they surveyed the drop for movement. Within two kilometers, the view became crisp enough for him to see that the pallets had indeed all been blown up—with the exception of two. Those had been plundered to the point that it was unnecessary for the enemy to waste explosives.

"Americans taking Russian weapons and supplies?"

"Astute observation, Vasily. Why would Americans raid an abandoned Russian air drop?"

"Obviously, not all of them perished in the battle and nuclear detonation. The communications blackout affects them as well as us, so they're stranded."

"I have trained you well, Vasily." Grigoriy raised the binoculars once again. "No movement," he said, wiping at the frozen tears around his eyes.

"What is their mission in such an occurrence?" asked Vasily. "Ambush?"

"Survival," Grigoriy replied. "Anyone approaching the target would have seen smoke from kilometers away. This was not a matter of stealth. They've departed and in chaotic fashion, more concerned with being hunted by the weapons contained in the drop than eliminating any enemy." Grigoriy used the binoculars to examine the burning pallets once again. "They might have left a lethal *podarok*, or perhaps three, for anyone foolish enough to examine the drop up close. We'll approach no closer than one-hundred meters."

Nearing the drop, they ran into Taiga tracks and boot prints leading both toward and away from the drop. That solved the problem of locating the mission target without GPS or GLONASS. They would simply follow the enemy's tracks. Grigoriy crouched and examined boot prints. Spetsnaz soldiers wore a range of winter boots; BKT tactical boots were a preference in Arctic combat. The sole patterns told Grigoriy that the soldiers wore Bannon. A favorite of Navy SEALs.

"*Pachet*," he said. The Russian translation for SEAL.

The entire platoon lifted rifle scopes and scanned the horizon with heightened intensity. After several scans, Grigoriy said, "We recon the perimeter of the drop." He pointed a rifle barrel toward the boot prints. "Either they returned to the site of the battle, or, after loading gear, they left from here, in another direction. If we find outbound tracks, we know how to track them." He turned to Vasily. "Advance to the target. Time for our reconnaissance."

Taiga tracks led Grigoriy and his men directly to the Antonov fuselage. He had been briefed on the Antonov transport that had crashed on takeoff weeks prior to the firefight and disappearance of the Spetnaz platoon, as well as the cascade of events that had ended with him and his men trapped in Antarctica with limited supplies.

The nuclear detonation had blown the fuselage some distance from the original crash location, it appeared. More than likely, they had been using the fuselage as a defensive firing position when the warhead detonated. They had been lucky...if surviving the blast and being trapped in this hell could be called lucky. The Antonov fuselage had been shielded by piles of ice, pushed up into a large mound, when the original ski-way had been plowed. Only that could have saved them from the intense dose of radiation that should have killed them in hours or days this close to ground zero. Clearly, the surviving Americans had occupied the fuselage from the time of the detonation until their departure, which he estimated at having been hours, not days, before.

He turned and found Vasily standing behind him, the same thoughts readable on his face. "How many, Vasily?"

"It appears four, perhaps five survived," Vasily said, pointing out the places in the fuselage where SEALs had bedded down on a variety of cargo blankets and soft insulation. "There are empty plasma bags, used medical. I expect a wide range of injuries from radiation poisoning, impact injuries, perhaps gunshot wounds."

"Radiation level?"

Vasily tapped a mitten on the Geiger counter. "Nominal."

"A clean bomb?"

"A clean bomb with no signature. It's a nuclear blast, but not one we've had any training on."

"The mystery continues," said Grigoriy.

Vasily picked up a gear bag he'd dug out of the wreck. Vienna Sausage cans rattled around inside.

"They ate well," said Grigoriy.

Vasily gave him a wry smile. "Better than Russian infantry anyway."

It was time to move on. Although no American SEALs seemed to be lingering nearby, plenty of danger remained in the surveillance stage of their mission. Grigoriy fully expected to lose lives, perhaps even his own, as they approached what he'd been told was a highly lethal blast zone. Of course, that did not include what he *hadn't* been told.

Grigoriy called out to the rest of the men, "We move on the target. Harness and line on each man. We stop the Taigas a thousand meters from ground zero. On foot at that point."

ᴖᴧᴗᴧᴓ

Grigoriy stood outside the debris field and ice heaves surrounding the crater at what had been ground zero of the mysterious nuclear blast. A debris field of ice and rock rising to a height of thirty-meters or more prevented them from gaining a direct view of the blast crater.

"Find me a safe route to the summit of the debris."

"Da, ser," Vasily responded instantly. He turned to the platoon and issued crisply ordered: *"Skoby. Verevka. Ledorub."*

Crampons. Rope. Ice axe.

Grigoriy nodded his approval. Breaking their necks while climbing the debris was a stupid way to endanger the mission.

The Spetsnaz platoon bustled into action and, within minutes, each soldier wore crampons over boots, had climbing lines attached to harness, and had ice-climbing axes strapped to their wrists.

"Vasily. *Naydite mne marshrut starika!*"

Find me a route that even an old man can climb.

Grigoriy's order solicited good-natured snickers throughout the platoon.

Twenty minutes later, he stood at the top of the crater's debris wall, gaping at the shimmering blue of the blast crater. The surface appeared perfectly smooth. The ice-skating rink in Gorky Park would be proud to contain such perfect ice.

Frozen within the blue crystal were a series of bizarrely shaped, metallic sculptures. Burned and twisted, they stood out from the ice in various shapes and sizes, rising to three or perhaps four meters in height, like a series of blackened and evil apparitions rising from a lake, bedtime stories told to terrorize Russian children from time immemorial. Clearly there had been a large, metallic structure underneath the ice, that despite having been blown with a nuclear warhead, had left these twisted and torn metallic spires. From the size of the blast crater, it was obvious this was a small, single-kiloton detonation. Similar to the Cold War nuclear "suitcase" weapons. Between one and three kilotons, at most.

"*Chto takoye ad?*"

Grigoriy lowered his binoculars. "Those, *tovarisch*, are the remains of what started the next Great Patriotic War."

24

I already talked to Mac," Paulson said over the satellite connection from Washington. "We can get you into Turkey cleaner than the CIA could ever hope."

Jack was sipping a cocktail in the clubhouse lounge, next to the rock fireplace. He'd just tossed two more pieces of wood on the fire, and it was roaring. He said, "Using one of your private charter jets?"

"Yes and no—we rent a jet from a charter that caters to Hollywood studios, transporting actors and film crews around the world. If we can get a bird that has a history of flying film crews into and out of the Middle East, even better."

Jack said, "Given our situation, there's no way I can go through customs—even if you have the NSA or CIA whip up a fake passport. Between facial-recognition software and the bag of cash I need to pay the Kurds, it's not workable."

"We use my air crew to get you in-country, bypassing customs. I'll have the boys in the NSA work up a fake passport you might need while in-country. We'll make you an independent film producer."

"Wait," said Jack. "Bypass customs—how would you manage that?"

"That's normally a trade secret...getting my warbird recovery crews into less-than-friendly countries."

"You mean most of your mechanics, with the exception of Ridley, are former felons and labeled undesirables in every civilized country on the planet."

"You can't even get into Canada with a simple DUI on your record. How am I supposed to conduct business with such unreasonable border-entry rules in place?"

Jack sighed. "How exactly does this work?"

"We fly you into Atatürk Airport. I've got resources in Istanbul. We used to have a good network in Ankara, a lot closer to Ararat, but that's gone cold."

"You mean the Turkish gangster you employed got killed."

"Isn't that what I just said? Anyway, I can get you into Istanbul." Paulson hesitated. "You'll be carrying a large quantity of cash—that's in addition to the cash for your Kurd protection. Hand over the first bundle without comment."

"Got it," Jack said.

"How much will it cost for guidance and protection from your Kurdish warlord?"

"Twenty-five thousand. In euros."

"He won't take dollars?"

Jack repeated, "Euros."

"Guess he hasn't watched euro plummeting against the dollar."

"Maybe he gets a better price buying weapons with euros," Jack said, only half-joking. "Better make it thirty-thousand euros. I can tip Hawar and his sons another five-thousand. Add another ten-thousand for emergency get-me-out-of-trouble money. If Mac's coordinating the air, I need to meet with him and work through all the details. My climbing gear was either vaporized in Antarctica or is at home in Lake Tahoe. I've got a list I can provide. Someone can pick it up for me. I'll need a bogus passport to use in-country, like you said. Two secure satellite phones and three handheld GPS units."

"No problem," Paulson said. "The less Wheeler knows about the details of how I'm getting you past immigration, the better.

There's an excellent chance I can get you into Cappadocia via car. How would you get to Ararat from there?"

I've already arranged for Hawar to pick me up in Cappadocia. East from there, it gets a whole lot more dangerous, so I'm under his protection from Capp to the base of Ararat. Hawar has a family compound near Doğubeyazıt, known to the Kurds as Bazîd. From the compound, it's less than ten kilometers to the base of Ararat. Last time on the mountain, we used horses partway up, then humped gear from there. Ararat, Turkey and Kurdistan are a whole lot less friendly than ten years ago. I don't know his exact plans for getting me up to the Western Plateau. Based on the GPS coordinates, Jacob's Well should be on the eastern flank, near the summit. Likely we'll climb the west flank of the mountain. That route will take us past the Parrott Glacier and on to the Western Plateau."

"Damn—sounds exciting."

"You're welcome to come along."

"I'd have to pass on Ararat, Jack. We spent a lot of time together in tents on Everest. I think you told me just about every way you could get killed in Eastern Turkey, including: torn apart by wild dogs, shot in the back at long range by anyone wanting a few lira and a free lunch, bird flu and bear-sized Kangal shepherd dogs that'd take off your head if you even side-glanced their herd. If you survive all that, there's not even a decent summit to bag at only sixteen-thousand feet."

Jack chuckled. "I knew my big mouth would get me into trouble."

25

Jack didn't wait until noon. His DARPA helicopter transport delivered him to the Camp David helipad precisely at ten a.m. Jack's first impression of the presidential retreat was how much it reminded him of a very comfortable and somewhat modest country estate. Behind the helipad, a first-class skeet range spread out in a fan. He instantly understood how the place would appeal to many presidents, stuck in the White House fishbowl, unable to so much as stretch their legs without incurring a security risk.

A young army captain in his mid-twenties with flight wings pinned on his uniform waited with a golf cart to transport Jack into the camp itself.

The officer saluted; Jack simply nodded and hopped in.

"Where have you got these hooligans locked up?" Jack asked.

"They pretty much have occupied, and held, the Aspen Lodge since they got here."

"Wait. That's the President's house."

"Yes, sir."

"So they dug in—and no amount of force can get them out of the residence?"

"Yes, sir. They have definitely laid down a claim."

"Well, there goes the neighborhood."

The captain returned Jack's smile. "Actually, they're a pretty good crew. Not like a lot of the VIPs we get here, who think we're just a gloried butler service. Their stories are something else, especially after they get a few drinks in 'em. You know, pulling vintage warbirds out of the most inhospitable places on the planet. They can spin quite the yarns."

"They tell you any stories about Antarctica?" Jack asked, eyebrows raised.

The caption's eyes lit. "Yes, sir. How they flew the B-29 off the ice, three engines on fire, after pouring six cases of Russian vodka into the wing tanks to boost the octane of the lousy Russian fuel."

"You actually believe any of those stories?"

"Not one of them, sir." Both the captain and Jack burst out laughing.

"Well—when the truth come out, it will make the stories they're spinning now seem dull in comparison."

The captain nodded and stopped the golf cart in front of the Aspen Lodge. "This is it, sir."

Jack took in the elegant and lovely country home. "I'll probably be an hour, maybe two."

"Anytime, sir. Give us thirty minutes if you can, so the crew can prep the helo."

Jack was escorted up to the front door, and let into the residence. He was met with the smell of fresh coffee and fresh-baked cinnamon buns instead of stale beer and empty tequila bottles. A cackling fire burned in the oversized fireplace that featured a huge rock mantel, complete with the presidential seal, front and center.

Mac Ridley pushed out of a chair, and walked over, taking a pair of reading glasses off his nose. "Jack! Damn, it's good to see a familiar face."

Jack glanced around the Aspen Lodge. "From what Al said, you guys are running wild up here."

"Oh, hell...." Ridley gave him a sly wink. "Where does he come up with those stories?"

Ridley motioned for Jack to sit on one of the couches and picked up an iPad.

"Al says he's got this worked out with you. Getting me into, and out of Istanbul in one piece, side-stepping customs...."

Ridley scrolled through the iPad. "Let's just say smuggling mechanics and craftsman into and out countries is one of our better skillsets. Occasionally, we have to, you know, play fast and loose with the rules." Ridley looked up at Jack. "So, Al says once you're in-country you've got this armed-to-the-teeth warlord who *says* he won't cut your throat after you put a large cash payment into his hands. Where's he supposed to meet you?"

"In Cappadocia. I'll go covert from that point up to Ararat."

"This is about as dumb an idea as I've heard." Ridley shook his head in disgust, or disbelief, then pulled out a satellite phone that matched the one Jack had in his jacket. He put on a pair of reading glasses, trying to focus on the iPad display. Mac fumbled with the phone's keypad until he placed the call. Then he put the phone on 'speaker' and held it between the two of them.

"Mac!" the voice said. "You have my guy there?"

"Right here, Karen. Don't tell me Paulson's sucked you into this nightmare."

"Oh please," said Al Paulson's personal assistant and the single most powerful person at Paulson Global after the billionaire himself. "I could take Wheeler with one hand tied behind my back. That rug-wearing putz wouldn't stand a chance."

Ridley winked at Jack. They both grinned.

"So, what have you cooked up from the rent-an-untraceable-jet department?"

"I immediately thought sexy, fast, and high-maintenance. Code-named Desiree."

Ridley sat back in the couch. "Desiree. That's Paulson's second ex-wife."

"True, but she's smarter than all his other ex-wives combined."

Ridley lifted his eyebrows and nodded in approval. "Good choice. I like it."

Jack shrugged. "So what are we talking about here?"

"The Cessna X—Citation 10. One of the fastest charters available," Karen said over speaker. "This one's logged hours overseas, and with a variety of film crews. Based in southern California. Top speed .965 Mach. So smooth, you can sip champagne out of five-inch pumps in the middle of a thunder-bumper without spilling a drop."

Ridley and Jack had to stifle their laughter.

"Sounds perfect," said Jack.

"I have your swift-princess inbound Westchester County, from Riverside, dead-head, crew only. We'll take possession of the charter, Mac'll get his crew lined up, and you'll be good to go as soon as your heart desires."

26

Marko was ready to snap. The relentless monotony of babysitting Freddy Krueger in the endless cold, eating sawdust-flavored military MREs, and struggling to recharge the battery system operating the PlayStation were mere appetizers in a buffet of discontent.

Jack had included a backup heater that ran on camp-style propane bottles, but it burned gas like a fraternity went through beer kegs during rush. He needed the propane bottles to run the stove, so he used the electric space heaters, and they sucked battery like crazy. It certainly wasn't summer—in fact, it was getting colder. The more he used the heaters, the more time he spent playing videogames, and the faster he depleted the lithium battery pack. Recharging from the mouth of the cavern using the solar panel and wind generator wasn't creating nearly enough electricity to suit him.

His other big issue when Jack had set him up, the toilet situation, was also proving to be an ordeal. He'd set up a latrine deeper into the sandstone cavern, assuming he'd only need it for a few days, not weeks hiding out with the Hafnium bomb. The odor was beginning to make its way back toward the cavern entrance and his happy camp. If he had to spend even another week here, he'd have to move the latrine outdoors, regardless of Jack's insistence that he not leave under any circumstance.

Marko stared at the twelve-foot aluminum sliding ladder they'd used to access the opening of the cavern. In order for him to reach the ground, he needed the ladder. The entrance, at ceiling height above the forest floor, was too far to jump. While he could free-climb the eight or ten feet up to the entrance, it'd be a whole lot easier with the ladder in place. It wouldn't be in sight but for a minute or so. He could drop the ladder and slide down it to the forest floor in a matter of seconds. Then he'd take down the ladder and hide it under pine boughs until he was ready to return to Camp Krueger.

No better time than the present....

Marko walked over to the cavern entrance and peered out. Even though it was late in the afternoon, he still had to squint against the glare. He'd gotten used to the darkness within the cavern.

Turning into a regular vampire, he thought. *Two more hours, gonna be pitch dark out there....*

Marko gave the sky a once-over and decided Jack had been paranoid. The cavern was located within a canyon with substantial tree-cover. The dark of night sealed the deal. He grabbed the ladder from deep inside the cavern and hoisted it, surprised that it felt a whole lot heavier than the last time he'd moved it around.

No surprise. My muscles are already turning into mush in this shithole. Another week and I'll be bedridden if I don't get some fresh air and exercise.

Marko hauled the ladder over to the opening, took one more cursory look, then dropped the bottom of the ladder over the side and allowed it to slide through his hands until it seated on the ground below. He was so stoked about getting a five-minute parole away from Freddy that he nearly forgot to take along the camp shovel and toiletries.

Marko slid straight down the ladder, wasting no time on the rungs. The sound of his boots touching down on a pile of eroded sandstone pebbles, along with the aroma of pine, was exhilarating. Though fresh air flowed in and out of the cavern, there was something about being under the stars that made the outdoors feel like nirvana compared to the stale and dank cavern. For several moments, he was tempted to bolt; use the switchback trails leading up to the canyon rim, then skedaddle to the nearest highway. Flag down any car, truck, or motorcycle—anyone who'd give him a ride out of this nightmare—and disappear.

Jack and Leah would be disappointed. *Actually, Leah doesn't do disappointment*, he thought. *She does revenge.* Leah would kill him and then ransack his wallet for the cost of the bullet.

Marko took care of his personal business while staying on high alert, using the shovel to bury any sign he'd been outside the cavern. He snatched his shovel and toilet gear, then climbed the ladder two rungs at a time, diving back into the cavern and pulling the ladder up and out of sight in under fifteen seconds.

Back inside his lair, Marko did a dance and shouted, "Yeah, baby!" pumping his fists in the air. Then he remembered he'd left the ladder stacked up against the rock the entire time he was outside the cavern, when he should have stashed it out of site in the brush. *Okay, so one minor screw-up....*

Maybe this gig wouldn't be so bad after all. If he could sneak out under cover of darkness, take a leak, stretch, breath in some fresh air, hell, even do five minutes of star-gazing, he'd make it at least another week, maybe two.

27

Leah crossed her arms, trying to conserve body heat, even though she stood near the roaring, communal fire. Leah often spent the evenings listening to the Ancients tell stories, tales that had been passed down for generations. She needed to bring a recording device and capture this living history that was being told by those who'd made that history.

Leah had noticed that, while she stood near the fire, the Ancients did not discuss their current predicament, or what the future might hold. Only when she walked away from the fire, or tucked herself into a sleeping bag, would the Ancients huddle closer and whisper. Although Appanoose was present many nights when he wasn't hosting a sweat lodge or sermonizing at his Basilica, he seemed neither to participate in nor discourage the others' discussions.

Even though it was past midnight, warriors were heating stones in preparing for a sweat-lodge ritual. The lodge, since her return with K'aalógii the day before, had been in constant use. Even more remarkable, Appanoose himself led every ritual. How he did it without collapsing from heat stroke was inexplicable.

"Ant-Arc-Tikke."

His words came back to haunt her frequently. And she still couldn't make any sense of his desire to return to the frozen continent. It made no sense. Why would he want to return to the site of their forced captivity? It went against everything that Leah had learned about the shaman. He was protective to a fault, and he seemed fully aware of where the Ancients had been taken and how they'd been returned back here. Despite Garrett's and her assurances that the alien complex had been destroyed, he still wanted to return to the *Ant-Arc-Tikke*.

Leah glanced up at the sky. The Milky Way cut across the sky in a shimmering belt. She'd never been much of a stargazer. Jack loved to sleep under the stars, and they'd done plenty of huddling together, sleeping under the stars on Jack's various summer camping and fishing trips into the back country. Typically, she'd end up nodding off after a day of brutal backpacking, while Jack continued point out constellations, navigational points of interest, and the occasional satellite streaking across the sky.

Given recent events, she now felt a newfound interest in, respect for, and unease while staring at the night sky. Instead of simple, twinkling pinpoints, Leah imagined an endless number of solar systems orbiting those points of light and hosting an otherworldly intelligence. The stars were no longer a beautiful panorama representing a rich history of harmless human mythology. Now they seemed an endless source of star-predators—mysterious, unstoppable, and lethal.

Not long ago, planet Earth, cradle of all life, protected by a benevolent atmosphere and a magnetic field, with neighbors like Jupiter absorbing most of the killer asteroids that might otherwise have struck home, had seemed impenetrable, invulnerable, infinite.

Lovely Earth. Safe Earth. Orbiting a smallish but stable star, located out in the galactic version of the boondocks—it had nothing to worry about.

No longer.

One of the young fierce femmes approached her and smiled.

Wow, that's a first, Leah thought, both startled and delighted.

Aside from K'aalógii, the Ancients kept their distance. Of course, Leah knew all of them in detail, right down to blood type. The young women who stood beside her had originally been called Number Twelve, having been the Twelfth Ancient examined by Gordo. Numbers were the easiest way to keep track, so each Ancient had been given a standard, hospital-issue plastic medical ID bracelet with a number and a chip that contained all of their medical data.

Leah had tried speaking to each individual in hopes of finding out more about them, including their actual names. Because Navajo was the only language Leah was even close to fluent in, she'd tried communicating in that language. Most of the Ancients were conversant in Navajo and Pueblo, a necessity of having been jammed together in a crowded cliff dwelling for months, perhaps even years.

This particular young lady had sat frozen at first, when Leah first met her. After several attempts to communicate with Twelve, Leah noticed that she'd begun touching her face, her hair, even running her fingers over her teeth, performing what seemed like a self-inventory.

Perfectly normal, she'd thought. She imagined waking from stasis was similar to waking from an extended coma after a bad car accident.

When Twelve finally spoke, it wasn't in Navajo, but Apache. With some tricky translation work, Leah had discovered that her name was Dahteste: Warrior Woman. That small breakthrough felt like eons ago.

Once Leah had learned all of their names, tribal affiliations, and languages, she'd insisted that their true names replace their identification numbers. The sooner Gordo and his minions saw the Ancients as individuals, not lab rats, the sooner they'd be treated like humans. Another memory that felt like years ago, not weeks.

Now Dahteste came closer to Leah than ever before. She hesitated a moment, then reached up and brushed Leah's hair lightly with the back of her hand. "De'nzhone'" she said softly.

'*De'nzhone.*'

For a moment, Leah sat motionless, in shock. Even with her rudimentary knowledge of Apache, Leah understood Dahteste had called her 'beautiful.' The kind word provoked an unexpected rush of emotion.

The shaman abruptly stood from his log throne at the Basilica fire and strode over to the communal fire. He nodded at Leah. "Sa'ah naaghaii bik'eh Hózhó."

Garrett, who'd also been warming himself at the fire, told Leah, "The lodge. He won't let that go"

"Yeah, I got the Hózhó, part," Leah said. Hózhó, in the Navajo language was a single word that described perfection. A spiritual declaration of everything good, versus bad, even evil. A state of living and a state of being: balance, order, beauty, harmony, goodness, and success in every realm. "So, the sweat lodge is his idea of a path to perfection—even beyond purity?"

Appanoose pointed at the lodge again. "Inipi—hózhó."

"Have to give him points for stubbornness," Leah said, feeling a shiver. She also knew the Lakota word for sweat lodge: Inipi. In their language, it also meant 'to live again.'

Clearly, the shaman was dead-set on making her live up to her agreement to enter the sweat lodge—and doing so in front of the entire Settlement. Unprepared to respond in this public forum, Leah wasn't sure how to respond. She was about to tell Garrett to say that they'd would discuss her 'agreement' in the morning, when Dahteste, who had been standing beside her, grasped her wrist with enough strength that she couldn't move her arm in any direction.

She was so shocked and alarmed, she hadn't noticed that K'aalógii had come up to her opposite side and grasped her wrist in the same manner and with similar force. Garrett came closer, suddenly realizing that Leah was struggling to free herself. Before he was able to take a second step, two warriors came up from behind him and restrained him in the same manner.

Appanoose spun on his heels and walked back to the entrance to the sweat lodge. He disappeared inside as Leah and Garrett were walked over and held near the small fire in which the Ancients continued heating stones. K'aalógii and Dahteste released her wrists, and she rubbed them, working the circulation back into her hands. She was thankful they had brought her near the fire.

As best she could, Leah tried asking K'aalógii and Dahteste whether she was being forced into the sweat lodge. Neither replied, although both smiled, K'aalógii with a gleam in her eye, as if she'd just bought the greatest gift in the world for Leah and couldn't wait until it was opened.

Leah stared into the stone-heating fire, absorbing the life-giving warmth while a multiplicity of scenarios played out in her mind's eye. Was this a bluff? The story of the POW being knelt down while a guard fired an unloaded pistol against the prisoner's head, simply for the mental anguish it caused? Would he shove her into the sweat lodge and make Leah beg before allowing her to leave? Yeah, and maybe after some celebratory backslaps with his fellow Ancients, Appanoose would dump a bucket of Gatorade over her head, sit down, and, in perfect English, provide a bullet-point list of beefs and non-negotiable demands.

When Appanoose flipped the door flap up and exited the sweat lodge, Garrett went off. The warriors released him as he repeated the phrase over and over again: "Doo yá'áshǫ́ǫ da." He formed a closed fist and thrust it forward with power, just short of striking the shaman's chest and repeated the phrase, punching out each time he did. It was disrespectful; *No—it was more than that*, Leah thought. *A threat and a promise.*

Doo yá'áshǫ́ǫ da meant intending harm, to do evil, even malevolence. Not in the context of Appanoose doing harm to Leah, but what would happen should harm come to her. Garrett told Appanoose in carefully enunciated language: *If you hurt Leah, you have no idea of the magnitude of the evil shit-storm that will be aimed squarely at your ass.*

The shaman nodded in his sharp, single-nod style, a gesture she'd come to associate with Appanoose being in a relatively agreeable mood.

Garrett said, "He understands and says that no harm will come to the Bóhólníhígíí."

Leah's eyes opened wide. "He called me the boss?"

"Well, he has a few nicknames for you. He uses Nááts'ǫ'oołdísii, when he doesn't think you're listening."

Leah cocked her head. "What does that mean?"

"Dust devil would be the best translation."

"Bastard." Leah shook her head, glancing at Appanoose, who had begun speaking again.

He spoke in clipped Navajo and Lakota. Leah even caught a word or two of Apache. A less-than-subtle reminder that he was in charge.

That's when all hell broke loose. Garrett had first protested in Navajo. Now he shouted a string of good-old fashioned four-letter swear words...in English. At the same time, Dahteste began to gently tug Leah toward the sweat lodge.

"T'ahálo!" Leah said. T'ahálo roughly translated as 'Wait!' in Navajo.

Dahteste and K'aalógii stopped. Leah turned and watched as the warriors restrained Garrett again, seemingly without effort no matter how hard he struggled.

"Garrett! Stop." Something about the way both Dahteste and K'aalógii held her hands, or maybe it was the look in their eyes, had disarmed Leah.

"That bastard. I told him what would happened if he tested me." Normally serene and stoic, Garrett Moon was furious. The veins stuck out on his neck, and his muscles, always toned, bulged as he struggled.

"It's all right. I'll be all right."

Garrett's fury had dissolved. "Leah. Don't," he pleaded.

"It'll be okay," she said. "I believe that." Leah squeezed the hands of her young captors and stepped toward the door flap, where Appanoose already waited, inside.

28

Leah sat cross-legged across from Appanoose, both on the same side of the pyramid-shaped stack of scorching hot rock separating one side of the sweat lodge from the other. Beside her was a large clay pot, filled to the brim with water, containing a clay cup that had sunk to the bottom. She didn't wait for permission but lifted out the cup and dipped it into the pot, filling it with water, then drank deeply. It was blistering hot inside the lodge, but the water was icy cold.

She was just beginning to understand how much work went into one of these rituals. It must have included making sure that a pot contained ice-cold river water inside the superheated lodge.

She dropped the empty cup back into the pot, feeling the ambient heat searing her skin from the outside in. Her eyes watered freely from the lingering smoke. At least the lodge's temperature, while quite hot, wasn't the broiler-set-on-high, skin-burning, scorch she'd experienced the first time she got a look inside.

It didn't take long to figure out what Appanoose did while alone inside the lodge. He handed her a clay cup, now filled to the brim with a steaming brew. All it took was one whiff to suspect what he had concocted. The bitter smell was a reminder

of the one or two times she'd eaten the peyote buttons—a rec-
reational drug she'd given up long ago, largely because it was,
without a doubt, the most god-awful tasting substance she'd ever
had to gag down. Its bitter residue lingered on her tongue for
hours afterward.

She held the cup and said, "Peyōtl."

Peyōtl was the Nahuatl name for peyote, which meant there
was a ninety-percent chance he had no idea what she'd just said.
Still, it was worth a shot.

He simply replied, "Hosh." He lifted an imaginary cup to his
mouth and tipped his head back, the said, "Bitoo."

The translation for Hosh from Navajo to English meant cactus,
which was close enough. There was no doubt from the bitter smell
that he'd steeped a powerful hallucinogen in the water, and she
was expected to drink.

'Bitoo.' *Yeah, right, just drink.* She couldn't help but think of the
grape Flavor-Aid served by Jim Jones in Guyana.

She had two choices now: storm out of the sweat lodge, or drink
the brew and explore whatever 'trip' he had in store for her. Appanoose didn't make any move to prevent her from setting the
cup down and exiting.

Leah drew a deep breath. *Gone this far with these people—
might as well take the plunge.*

She lifted the cup to her lips, held her nose, and gulped. While
it didn't taste like tea served at Her Majesty's annual summer
Queen's Garden Party, it was far from the dreadful flavor of raw
peyote buttons. It tasted bitter, yes, but she also detected sweet
notes, as well as other flavors that she couldn't identify. One thing
was for sure—it was more than simply peyote buttons boiled
down over a fire. Still, she had to assume it included the same
ingredient found in various desert flora that contained psychoac-
tive alkaloids: mescaline.

Leah sipped until the cup was empty and handed it back to Appanoose. For the first time, she saw honest-to-God respect in the
proud man's expression.

The peyote blend might kill me but, damn it, I finally won the bastard over....

Thirty-minutes later, she was back to cursing the shaman under her breath. Leah was experiencing classic side-effects. Nausea and flu-like symptoms, made all the worse by the lodge's heat and the lingering smoke from the outside fire pit. The side-effects lasted one, maybe two hours, as she recalled, but it was pure misery every second it lasted.

Appanoose had been chanting in a low tone the entire time, well aware of what Leah was experiencing. Leah locked him up in a *'This really sucks—thanks so much'* expression, not expecting a reaction.

Wait. Did he just wink? It seemed the cynical of wink you got from a toothless carny when you asked if the spinning whirly-gig ride would make you vomit. Or maybe he hadn't winked at all. The hallucinogen was kicking in....

This isn't your first rodeo. Suck it up, girl. Leah drew in one deep breath after another, resisting the urge to spew in her lap.

Appanoose bowed his head then slowly lifted his hands with palms up and began to chant in a language Leah couldn't translate. It sounded like a combination of Lakota and Apache.

Her knowledge of shamanic rituals told her that the shaman would continue lowering himself deeper into a trance. Leah struggled to do exactly the opposite. She wasn't exactly the designated driver, but if she were going to learn anything, she couldn't allow herself to stare at the river stones, waiting for one to engage her in a lively conversation.

As the shaman's chanting grew louder, she lost peripheral vision first. Once, Jack had gifted her a ride on a High-G aerobatic plane ride. When the pilot pulled the biplane into an impossibly tight turn, she'd felt a similar sensation. Her vision was tunneling, until the image of Appanoose condensed, like coal under a millions of tons of pressure, transforming into a magnificent diamond.

A diamond-like brilliance, at first barely a pinpoint of white light, grew, and soon unfolded, pushing back then overtaking the blackness.

Leah burrowed her fingernails into her thighs, hoping the discomfort might counteract the loss of her wits. As she did so, though, an internal voice encouraged her to unwind, maintain focus on the shaman, ignore the outside world, look inward. Her last physical sensation was not digging her fingernails into her thighs, but digging them into the palms of the shaman, as he held her hands tight and continued to chant.

She hadn't understood a word of the chanting, but now a voice in her head said, "Šóka."

The light grew in brilliance. She wanted nothing more but to shut and shield her mind's eye from the starburst, but she already felt herself tumbling away, dissolving into a million miniature diamonds....

Leah was flying over the mesas and the landscapes with such an intense and vivid awareness that she felt tears streaming down her face and her hair twisting into knots; she smelled the scent of pine and sage brush, and heard a river rushing below her. Suddenly, the water's sounds were replaced by silence. Her speed increased and she raced over the landscape until the mesa tops, the valleys, rivers and canyons, all blurred into a kaleidoscope of color.

29

The landscape was clearly New Mexican, but she knew it was not the modern day. The desert appeared too lush, too green. The mountain peaks were thick with snow and ice, appearing almost glacier-like.

If it were a vision, this trip was beyond her wildest imagination. The suffocating heat and pungent odor of the sweat lodge—gone. Smoke rising in the distance caught Leah's attention. What had appeared, at first, to be miles away, was beneath her. It was a prehistoric village next to a river. The Ancients appeared like a scene out of a painting, representing Indian life as Leah would have expected it to look thousands of years in the past.

A flash of light on the horizon caught her attention. The Ancients on the mesa ran toward the protection of the mesa cliffs amid shouts and warnings.

Oh my God, thought Leah, as the small village was attacked from above. It was something she had imagined and pondered endlessly after rescuing the Ancients from stasis. Now she was witnessing it in real time. A beam of light so bright that Leah had to press her palms into her eyes to stop the pain, that had come out of nowhere. When she pulled her hands away and her vision recovered,

Ancients lay scattered around the village and the base of the mesa.
Had they all been killed?

She screamed in anger, until feeling a light touch on her forearm.
She turned, to find nothing there—still the unseen touch filled her
heart with serenity and calm.

When she looked down at the Ancients once again, they no lon-
ger lay on the ground beneath the mesa cliffs. Instead, they lay en-
cased in the same stasis units she'd found at the Antarctic complex.

The vision dissolved as quickly as it had appeared, and she found
herself looking at a field of brilliant stars, surrounding her, engulf-
ing her, streaming through her—she'd become the center of a cos-
mic snow globe, shaken until not one star remained stationary.

Just as she was beginning to relax and marvel in the indescrib-
able experience of floating within the snow globe, she felt something
like cold liquid metal flowing down her spine and toward her legs.
She was paralyzed, unable to move—and the blackness returned.

Leah was no longer looking at an infinite field of stars. She was
flying again, but over an unfamiliar landscape. This one featured
mountainous terrain. Snaking through the mountains were deep
canyons, in which water flowed and greenery grew thick on the
banks and cliffs. The only terrain that remotely resembled this was
the mountains of the southern island of New Zealand.

Leah felt cold, her exposed skin already porcelain in color from
exposure. Her focus on the cold was drawn away by a sudden inabil-
ity to draw a deep breath. No matter how hard she tried, she couldn't
fill her lungs with enough oxygen necessary to satisfy her body.

A village appeared below, with hundreds of Ancients walking up
and down a mosaic of paths leading from the deep, rich canyons, to
the mountain glacier, where a massive village stood. Wood lodges,
some the size of cathedrals, were anchored into the ice; smoke from
a multitude of chimneys rose above the structures.

It was a city like Leah had never explored, seen, or studied in her
archaeological career.

The people looked familiar, but not their clothing. They wore
what appeared to be an organic weave, like a hemp, but richer.

Leah scanned the horizon and identified at least three more of these cities in the distance. Where was this place? Something only the shaman could answer, she knew. She looked left and right, sweeping the horizon, hoping he might appear, and explain, but she was alone within the vision.

"Where is this?" Leah shouted. "Who are these people?"

She searched in every direction for Appanoose.

She cried out again. "You promised answers!"

One word flooded her mind with such intensity that she saw the letters imprinted on her brain like the afterglow of a lightning strike.

"Yá'ąąsh."

One of the English translations for the single word in Navajo was Heaven. Leah instinctively looked up toward the sky. Not one sun but two shone in the sky. Neither seemed bright as the sun she knew, but together they flooded the sky and the landscape with intense sunlight. She felt a momentary shock, then convulsions wracked her body and the blackness closed in like a cocoon as she struggled to see more.

When her vision returned, she saw ice stretching for as far as she could see, the horizon ending in curved line. Leah immediately looked for the suns. The two suns had been replaced with the single familiar one. The transliterated word that Appanoose had spoken repeated in her head, echoing off her forehead, and then off the back of her skull—never changing.

"Ant-Arc-Tikke...Ant-Arc-Tikke... Ant-Arc-Tikke...Ant-Arc-Tikke."

That's when she realized it. She was now flying over Antarctica. Below lay the complex where the Ancients had been encased in the stasis units, but she saw no wrecked aircraft or the massive crater where the complex had been obliterated. And Thor's Hammer still stood, as it had for millions of years before the Hafnium warhead sheared it from the earth. No avalanche covered the domed facility, and the silver metallic surface reflected the soft Antarctic sunlight in every direction.

She flew on over barren ice, until after what had to be hundreds or thousands of miles passed by in her mind's eyes, another struc-

ture stood. This one featured twin domes—each much larger than the complex she'd discovered—connected to one another by a tube-shaped assembly.

The silver metallic surface of the domes flashed brilliant white, then became transparent. Inside, Leah saw hundreds of the stasis units, each containing a body in deep hibernation.

One line of stasis units stood apart from the rest. They were brightly lit, and their clear, glass-like lids stood open. Even though she didn't count them, she knew there would be exactly twenty-seven units. The same number as the surviving Ancients at the Settlement.

The vision was so peaceful, so serene, Leah intensely regretted removing the Ancients from the complex, and her feelings about the non-terrestrials softened. She understood now: The Ancients had been selected as colonists, tasked with settling new worlds.

It wasn't right, but then again, was this how Earth had been originally populated with humankind? Her thoughts, while at the Settlement, star-gazing and seeing threats coming from the stars now seemed, foolish, immature. How could she have missed the obvious?

She was flooded with a sense of well-being she hadn't experienced since she'd been asked out for the Christmas dance in junior high. It was all fine—no, it was better than fine. Everything was magnificent.

Leah didn't have time to enjoy the sense of well-being. A sense of dread began at her fingertips. As it moved up her arms, so did an intense cold. If that weren't bad enough, suddenly she couldn't breathe. The air, once again, felt too thin; or maybe she was at too high an altitude above the ice.

Leah sucked deeply, working to fill her lungs, but the small amount of oxygen did little to alleviate the growing oxygen debt depriving her brain and organs of vital O_2.

As her sense of dread morphed into terror, she felt, but did not see, an immense buildup of energy flooding both domes. As it did, the ice around the second complex began to fracture. Blocks of ice the size of skyscrapers pushed themselves out of the surface and, *like watermelon seeds squeezed between two fingers, rocketed away from the domes, followed by the intense crack of air parting at supersonic speed, shaking Leah right down to her bones.*

Massive fountains of steam and water exploded from the newly created city-block-sized cavities. Whatever was happening had created so much heat that ice was converting instantly into liquid, then steam.

That wasn't the worst. As the energy within the twin complex intensified, growing in strength and mass, it could clearly not be contained. Leah opened her mouth and screamed at the same time two blinding beams of energy cut holes in the sky, generating enough heat that she felt the skin on her face peeling off in strips.

The blue sky went black; her body convulsed. Leah instinctively knew the energy that cast billions of tons of ice miles in every direction had also stopped her heart.

30

Garrett Moon paced outside the sweat lodge. Leah had been inside for more than four hours, well beyond their agreed time with Appanoose. After being restrained by the Ancient warriors, he been shown a place to sit near the sweat lodge, but not allowed to move for the first two hours. When he finally complained, one of the warriors nodded and allowed him to stand, then walk about, unrestrained.

When the skin flap opened, Appanoose slid his legs out first, then his upper body. He was covered in sweat and his eyes shone with an intensity Garrett hadn't seen before. But it was what lay limp in his arms that caused Garrett to panic.

Appanoose held Leah, her arms and legs dangling and her head lolling back on her shoulders, mouth open and eyes strangely lifeless. The warriors, seeming to have anticipated what would have happened, had brought blankets and spread them next to the fire.

Appanoose looked around, orienting himself to his current surroundings, then laid Leah gently down on the blankets.

Garrett tried to rush over but was instantly restrained. Appanoose laid his cheek next to her mouth. It was obvious that she was no longer breathing. He leaned over, and blew air over her face, gently. On the third breath, Leah arched her back, and drew a deep breath on her own.

The warriors who held Garrett released their iron grip. He pushed them away and ran to her side. Leah's face was white, and her skin cold and clammy. He put his cheek up against her mouth and held his breath, praying that by holding his, he might feel Leah breathe once again.

It took more than fifteen seconds before he felt the lightest of breaths against his cheek. Overcome with relief, he watched K'aalógii and Dahteste bring lit torches and hand them to the warriors, who braced the torches upright with river stones. More wood was added to the fire and the sandy ground near the pit danced with shadows made by the breeze-driven flames.

Appanoose nodded, and Dahteste and K'aalógii knelt beside Leah and began washing her face and hair with water, dribbling some on her lips as they worked.

Garrett told Appanoose he wanted a private audience. Appanoose gave one sharp nod and led Garrett over to the Basilica. Even before the shaman sat across from him, Garrett began speaking his mind in Navajo.

"We trusted you with her life. You've broken your bond with us." He paused. It would have been easy to lose his temper, to shout and make a major scene. It took all of his strength and the training he'd received at the feet of elders on the Navajo reservation to remain calm. He pointed back to where Leah lay unconscious, perhaps dying. "She and she alone saved you from a lifeless death under the ice in Antarctica."

"Nik'ijį' asihígíí éí ayóó'í'óo'ni' bee baa nídidíí'áál," Appanoose replied, inclining his head in Leah's direction.

Garrett hardly expected Appanoose to drop to his knees and give thanks for their rescue, but what he'd said was so unexpected that Garrett didn't know how to respond: *With much affection, she was forgiven for her crimes.*

"Ałk'idą́ą́," Appanoose continued.

She had been forgiven, a long time ago.

The only 'crime' Garrett thought she could have committed, was removing the Ancients from the stasis units.

31

Jack sat at a café, sipping espresso, in the ancient Turkish city of Cappadocia. It'd been nearly twenty-four hours since he'd boarded the Cessna X at Westchester County Airport. The X didn't have the range to fly to Turkey unrefueled, and they'd had to make two stops before landing at Istanbul Atatürk Airport.

His mafia-like entry into Turkey had been smooth as silk. Any question on how terrorists were able to move about the planet without fear of capture were quickly answered by the seamless way a large sum of cash could buy you into and out of just about anywhere.

Before Jack could even exit the aircraft, a blacked-out Mercedes station wagon stopped next to the Citation. A Turk dressed in an army uniform got out of the Mercedes and loaded Jack's duffels into the backseat. The door to the car hadn't even closed before the driver stepped on the gas, headed toward a locked security gate. The driver jumped out of the car, inserted a key into a lock system, and the gate popped open. He swung it wide enough to allow the car to exit, drove through, stopped and locked it again. Without a word he whisked Jack out of the airport, drove for a few minutes, then turned in a parking lot that overlooked the Aegean Sea.

As instructed, Jack handed over the cash to pay for his illegal entry into the country. *Paulson Immigration Services*, as Jack had come to call it, had another car waiting in the same lot. This driver took him straight through to Cappadocia—a distance of nearly 800 kilometers. Needless to say, his ass should have been kicked, but he felt invigorated. The adrenaline buzz of a real adventure never got old.

He'd tried Leah numerous times before leaving, without success. While she'd promised to have the satellite phone handy, he knew she was living on pins and needles after returning to the Settlement and all of its potential for violence waiting, simmering.

For Paulson's benefit, Jack had given a complete briefing on the Ancients and his and Leah's concerns in case something went down while he was in Turkey. Al Paulson hadn't seemed that surprised, or even concerned. He made it obvious that Wheeler was getting more erratic and the Russian/American conflict appeared to be building toward another explosion. The Russians were determined to get troops onto the frozen continent via ship. The Americans equally determined that no Russians ships would draw close enough to the coast that they could offload a division of troops and armor.

As Jack was finishing his second espresso and wishing he could stick around to explore Cappadocia like a proper tourist, a beat-up Toyota truck came to a screeching halt in front of the café.

A young Kurd in his early twenties jumped out, beaming. He wore western style clothing, including worn but clean blue jeans and an Old Navy t-shirt. His hair was shaggy and his beard thin, but when he smiled, his teeth were white and straight.

"Mr. Jack?" He spoke in accented English, his smile growing wider by the second.

"Kajir?" The young boy of twelve or thirteen, who'd helped his father prepare meals on the last Ararat expedition, nearly ten years before, had grown into a man. Jack hardly recognized him. "When did you grow the beard?" he managed.

"It is very good to see you again. My father is very anxious to see you."

A boy of thirteen or fourteen pushed open the creaky passenger door and stood next to his older brother.

"My little brother, Bazi."

"Are we taking this truck to Dogubayazit?"

"Only part way. We must switch trucks before we reach the military checkpoints." He pointed toward the cab. "Mr. Jack."

Jack dropped a wad of currency on the table and stepped to the street, but before Jack could board the small truck, Bazi sped past him and climbed in, claiming the middle seat on the narrow bench. Kajir jammed the Toyota into gear and dropped the worn clutch. The truck lurched forward, gears grinding.

Kajir sped to the corner, spinning the steering wheel to the right. Jack thought for a moment, the Toyota might crash into a produce shop on the opposite side of the street, but the vehicle remained upright and untouched.

Outside Cappadocia, Kajir glanced at his worn Timex Ironman Triathlon watch. "We travel for only three more hours, safely. Then you must ride with the hay."

⊙▿▵▿⊙

Jack dozed as the Toyota weaved through traffic in the style that made driving in the Middle East more dangerous than a Kurdish ambush in the badlands. Finally, the truck slowed, waking Jack. They were rolling into a small village.

"This is where you must switch vehicles, Mr. Jack." Kajir checked the rearview mirror, then slowly navigated the narrow streets, avoiding any unwanted attention.

"Yes!" Kajir pointed into a narrow alleyway. An ancient-looking flatbed truck bearing the familiar Mercedes Benz logo waited, idling. Its bed was stacked high with straw, making it appear top-heavy. Jack hoped it didn't topple before they cleared the narrow streets of the village.

"Mr. Jack," Kajir said. "We load your gear and drive to our village." He pointed toward the large pile of straw. "You must climb underneath. Many Turkish checkpoints on the road. If we are stopped, you must not move or talk."

Jack knew well that corruption and brutality reined at these remote checkpoints. The Turkish military shook down the Kurds at these stops and beatings, sexual assault, even murder were common events. If anything happened at one of the checkpoints, and the Turks found Jack, they wouldn't hesitate to kill him. He'd disappear like so many do in eastern Turkey, just another mystery out in the badlands, never to be solved.

To that end, Jack remembered how he'd told Jacob Badger about dropping a prayer, maybe two on a particularly hazardous climb, or series of events that seemed headed toward lethality.

He decided this situation fit perfect and he said a lengthy prayer under his breath. After a pause, he added that God should give Jacob Badger a break, if it turned out the DECISION was a squeaker, whether to let the old preacher into Heaven, or send him south.

Jacob Badger might have sworn at the Big Man a time—maybe two, but Jack had never met a man whose heart was so much in the right place and who had suffered so, over the death of young David on Ararat.

32

The Turkish soldiers at the roadblock shouted questions at Kajir over the roar of the engine. Kajir answered back in a non-conciliatory tone, sending a tingle down Jack's spine. It felt strangely frustrating to be unable to watch the drama playing out only meters away.

Jack was buried at the bottom of the straw, two duffels tucked in, one on each side. He'd pulled a dirty blanket up over his face, to prevent from smothering and/or having his eyes gouged by the coarse straw. After five hours under the straw, he wasn't sure what was worse: suffocating under the load or the nauseating odor coming from the blankets. The same blankets Bazi said were used for their horses.

More loud voices, and shouting.

If Kajir had given an inch or appeared nervous in any way, the soldiers would have searched the trucks for weapons or contraband. After an exchange of what Jack assumed were a plethora of mutual insults, the truck clunked into gear and lurched through the checkpoint.

Two hours later, Jack had to take a leak and was visualizing a plan to unzip one of the duffels, whilst in prone position, then rifle around the duffel for an empty water bottle, when the truck slowed again.

Not another checkpoint.

Instead of Turkish soldiers shouting and Kajir slamming on the brakes at the last second, the flatbed turned off the paved two-lane highway and trundled down a bumpy dirt road with ruts so deep the truck threatened to tip one side, then the other. The rough ride reminded Jack that he'd better start digging for the water bottle, but thankfully, the truck found smoother footing and after less than a half hour lurched to a stop.

Kurdish voices filled the air from every direction. Hands cleared the straw from the bed of the truck and a voice said, "Come out my friend—it is safe now."

Jack dug himself out from underneath the rough blanket and several feet of tied-down straw. In the soft glow of the lanterns, the people stared at him, eyes bright with curiosity and excitement.

"Mr. Jack!"

Jack recognized the familiar face of Hawar, his guide from ten years ago.

The Kurd had aged considerably. He looked shorter than Jack remembered and his beard, once jet black, was gray and thinning. Hawar wore traditional Kurdish clothing, including baggy pants with cummerbund. Although his body had aged, his eyes remained clear and sharp and his handshake strong. Jack embraced the gray-bearded Kurd, allowing Hawar to kiss him on both cheeks.

"I knew you would someday return, God willing." He grabbed Jack by the hand and led him to the center of the village.

"Your sons have grown into fine young men."

Hawar beamed. "They will climb with us. They have been waiting to climb with Jack Hobson, the famous mountain climber."

Jack told Hawar about being stopped at the checkpoint and the harassment. "What is the situation on Ararat?"

"It is very, very bad, Mr. Jack. Many Kurds have disappeared, many more military have been sent to Kurdistan to search for terrorists and Kurdish rebels. We will be in much danger if confront-ed by Turkish soldiers."

"Let's see if we can avoid that."

"We will climb at night—at least until we reach the glacier," Hawar added. The warlord led Jack into his walled compound, where fresh lamb kebab cooked over an open flame and Jack, thankfully, was able to make the call of nature without a water bottle.

Jack sat outdoors, his parka zipped up, the fire offering wel-come warmth. Coleman lanterns hung on poles around the com-pound provided the light. The food was served while the Kurds chatted and Hawar or one of his sons translated as best they could.

Loud, deep howls sounded outside the compound. Hawar pointed over the wall. "Wild dogs—probing for ways to get at the herds."

"Do you still have those Kangals?" Jack asked.

Hawar nodded.

"Still as big and mean as I remember?"

A ghost of a smile flashed across Hawar's face. "Pray they never see you as a wild dog, Mr. Jack."

33

Beckam swept the endless ice to the right, then to the left. He pulled the binoculars away and wiped at his eyes. It didn't dissipate the fatigue-induced blurring and burning. He was on the bubble for active combat deployment and feeling his age. One thing was true: he no longer had the physical gifts he'd possessed as a twenty-five-year-old, gung-ho SEAL operator.

It was little things that degraded one's combat fitness. In his case: vision. When Beckam got dog tired—not simply physical-workout weary, but combat-mission beat—his first impairment was vision. Only days ago, the Antarctic horizon had been a clear-cut line across the ice. Now, even through binoculars, it looked blurry. The sharp disparities in the horizon now shimmered like diamonds and the lines were anything but clear-cut.

Beckam had restricted their speed to no more than fifteen kilometers per hour. The ice was far from smooth, and he didn't want Danny Frantino bumped around anymore than necessary. Beckam pulled his goggles back into place. "How's your fuel consumption, boys?"

"Good here, Boss," said Liam. "The gauge has hardly moved off full."

"Same here," Lenny added.

They'd raided the Russians for extra fuel before blowing up the balance of the gear with the Russians' own satchel explosives, leaving a string of burning pallets and heavy smoke behind them.

If his estimates were correct, they should cross the South Pole Transverse at 250 kilometers. Then it would be another 250 to Amundsen-Scott.

Beckam had decided to drop one of the Taiga snow machines at 250 klicks, regardless. It would leave them with more fuel in case locating the South Pole turned out to be more elusive than expected. Whether they'd find Amundsen-Scott in one piece, or a smoldering wreck, he couldn't predict.

34

Grigoriy scanned the horizon with the binoculars, holding his breath to keep the image steady. The Taiga tracks told the story well enough. American survivors, also apparently out of contact with their command, had waited long enough and finally decided to find their own way off the ice. There was no confusion regarding which way they had gone. The tracks were fresh and crisp.

Grigoriy had already taken photos and video of ground zero, including detailed video of the fractured and twisted metallic pieces that remained of whatever had been discovered beneath the ice. A thousand meters or more from ground zero, they had also found some assorted, small debris. Grigoriy had ordered his men to pack up to twenty kilos of it for examination in case they made it back to mother Russia.

The American survivors were headed toward the magnetic South Pole.

There's no other reasonable explanation, Grigoriy assured himself.

Without communications and navigation, the Americans' decision made sense.

Grigoriy was sure they planned to bisect the ice highway that connected the American base on the Ross Ice Shelf—McMurdo—with Amundsen-Scott, make a turn south, and follow the highway directly to the South Pole base. During the Antarctic summer months, it was a small city. Finding that mote of civilization would be their chief and perhaps only chance for survival.

Grigoriy had three options: Return to where they had been airdropped and hope that somehow Russian forces located them. Follow the Americans to Amundsen-Scott. Or continue past the ice highway and try to navigate their way to the Vostok Russian Station. Even with GPS navigation, Vostok was more than 1,500 kilometers distant, over barren ice. No possible way to make Vostok. Similarly, the odds of Russian troops arriving at their drop location, loaded with vodka, was laughable. Waiting around was guaranteed death. The best chance at survival appeared to be Amundsen-Scott.

Grigoriy made a silent command decision. Follow the Americans, avoiding contact until they were within a hundred kilometers of the South Pole station. Then, engage before the Americans reached Amundsen-Scott. At most, five Americans had survived, and they'd suffered combat and/or blast-related injuries. Grigoriy, on the other hand, had six Spetsnaz commandos, fresh and combat-ready, with plenty of weaponry for almost any scenario.

Eliminate the Americans, gather additional intelligence, and then occupy Amundsen-Scott. Resupply and hope that GLONASS satellite navigation and communications came back online. It they didn't, then with a large enough resupply he and his men could make for Vostok.

"Your thoughts?" asked Vasily.

Grigoriy smiled. "I was once a student in Moscow. Skating at Gorky Park with a girl I had been smitten with at Winter Festival. The lights, the music, the feel of this girl's hand in mine." Grigory flashed a weary grin. "I think that was the best day of my life."

"What made you think of that?"

"That tranquility of the blue ice filling in ground zero. Such peacefulness after a detonation.... It's...unimaginable." He shrugged and looked at his second-in-command. "I don't know why it reminded me of ice skating at Gorky and the girl. It was such an uncomplicated time. And death?" He shrugged. "Death was only to be found in history books about the Great Patriotic War. We were immortal and invincible."

"Perhaps you will return to Gorky, during Winter Festival, and that same girl, having not aged a day, will see you and come skating into your arms."

Grigoriy nodded but his gaze remained distant. "I think my days at Gorky are behind me. *Your* thoughts?"

"How easily it could have been our platoon instead. Ordered to engage the Americans and secure the target. Vaporized on a mission so secret that our families would never learn the truth."

Grigoriy nodded again. "Our surveillance mission is complete. I've formulated a plan."

"We hunt Americans," Vasily said plainly.

"What makes you think that?"

"We are Spetsnaz—that's what we do."

Grigoriy patted his friend on the shoulder. "Yes, indeed, we are Spetsnaz—but we don't hunt Americans today."

35

Beckam focused the binoculars behind them, scanning in the direction of their tracks for any sign that they had a tail. The sun didn't set during December, the height of the Antarctic summer. While the constant daylight didn't provide any cover, it did protect them from the minus hundred degree Fahrenheit temperatures that would descend down over the ice when the Antarctic winter enveloped the continent. There was no threat of that today, or tomorrow. It was highly unlikely they'd ever see an Antarctic winter, or a summer in Virginia Beach, again.

Even with twenty-four-hour daylight, it wasn't like a clear summer day in Miami Beach.

The temperatures ranged from zero to minus twenty, the sun bright but filtered. A momentary flash glinted suddenly on the horizon.

Reflection off an ice dam—or another set of binoculars?

"Shit," he whispered.

Tactically and strategically, enemy forces, Russian or otherwise, would like nothing more than snatch-and-grab the SEALs, pump them full of drugs, add a variety of physical tortures to extract any intelligence possible about what exactly had been discovered at the alien site. This meant that Beckam had to consider all potential contacts as hostile until they were determined to be non-hostile. Capture was unacceptable, given what they knew.

"Might have company, Frogs," said Beckam.

"Russians collecting rental fees?" Lenny shaded his eyes and scanned the horizon.

"Doubt it's a food truck delivering a hot lunch."

"We sure are popular. Wanted dead or alive by just about everyone with a rifle," Lenny said.

Beckam shook his head, holding back a chuckle. The twins could be less than disciplined at times, but if the clock on his life were about to run out, he could ask for no better crew than Danny, Lenny, and Liam. They'd open the gates of hell on an enemy before taking the express elevator down to be greeted by Satan himself.

36

Grigoriy stood on the seat of the Taiga, using the extra meter to acquire more range out of the Swarovski binoculars. No visible sign of the Americans. The Taiga tracks were still crisp and clean—perhaps too much so.

Grigoriy had ordered his men to slow in order to maintain distance. He could not afford to make contact with the SEAL platoon. They had hundreds of kilometers until they reached Amundsen-Scott. American SEALS, like a Siberian badger, would charge even if cornered. It was pointless to engage them earlier than necessary, unless discovered and risk having to care for wounded and dying so far from their objective.

Given an almost flat ice terrain, and thin, high-altitude and smog-free atmosphere, he could identify objects at approximately fifteen kilometers. Nothing but blowing snow, ice, and then more ice.

Keeping a good tactical distance meant calling a halt every fifteen minutes, scanning the horizon ahead, then continuing at a conservative pace.

He turned to his men. "Keep the 'Karakatitsa' within arm's length. If necessary, I want everyone and everything camouflaged at once."

Grigoriy turned his binoculars to the sky and swept three-hundred and sixty degrees. All clear for many miles. Not one aircraft had overflown them since they'd landed on the ice. He had no reason to think that would change.

Grigoriy thought about his lovely Sasha back in Moscow. *Perhaps the unthinkable had already happened? M.A.D. Mutually assured destruction via intercontinental ballistic weapons on Moscow, Washington, and the balance of all other major cities....* Grigoriy cleared his mind and dropped the binoculars against his chest.

"All clear." With a sweep of his hand, he ordered his reconnaissance platoon to advance.

37

Lenny raised his eyebrows in anticipation. "Ambush?"

Liam studied the terrain. "We won't be much of a surprise out here in the open, Boss."

"Not here," said Beckam. "We need to confiscate a crevasse from Mother Nature." He lifted the binoculars, scanning the bearing toward the magnetic South Pole, their direction of travel. A slight ridge to the left signaled a possible crevasse.

"Liam?"

"That's me."

"See that pressure ridge couple of klicks away?"

"Got it."

I want you to run a straight set of tracks with the Taiga, right toward the pressure ridge. Right up to it. I'm hoping there's a crevasse running parallel to it. If so, we can bridge over it using the aluminum connectors we ripped off from the Russians. I want it to appear we found nothing but a pressure ridge and ran the Taigas right over the top of it. Don't make a bunch of tracks that we have to cover up. If we are being tracked, they'll will think we just kept going...until they're within range and we can identify friend or foe. I'm so irritable, I'm inclined to just open up on them, regardless."

"Yeah, baby." Liam did a little ice dance.

Lenny nodded, his gaze turning deadly. "Challenge SEALs, pay the price."

Beckam added, "Slow learners awarded lead crowns with complimentary 5.56-millimeter thorns."

"Ouch," said Lenny said. "Glad you're on our side, Boss."

"Yeah, well, something about being dropped into a meat grinder and hung out to dry has soured my normally sweet disposition."

***

"We're in business," Beckam said.

Lenny had given a wave and a double thumbs-up signal after checking out the pressure ridge and crevasse.

"Let's get after it, Frogs," Beckam said, simultaneously checking on Frantino, who was lying comfortably inside the toboggan.

Liam climbed aboard the Taiga and waited for Beckam to lead. Once Beckam had pulled forward, Liam realigned his Taiga so his tracks lined up exactly with Beckam's.

Several minutes later, Beckam idled up to within ten meters of Lenny's position at the edge of the crevasse. He shut down the Taiga and walked over to where Lenny stood. The crevasse measured a little less than two meters wide and more than ten meters deep. Even better than Beckam had hoped.

"Watch out, Boss. That first step is a killer," Lenny said.

Beckam nodded. "Excellent choice, Mr. Clay."

"We can use the crevasse to set up an effective ambush, the break in the ice making it natural for trench warfare."

"You won't get that lucky, Len. But you're right. Lethal bad guy set up. I wouldn't want to be on the incoming side. You two unload the aluminum bridging."

Minutes later, a rainbow-shaped aluminum bridge nearly three meters long and a meter and half wide joined the two sides of the crevasse. The Clays secured the bridge with ice screws, courtesy of the Russians.

"Let's get the Taigas across," Beckam said.

Lenny wore a harness and climbing line attached to an ice screw with the line threaded and anchored. Should the Taiga decide to take a dive to the bottom of the crevasse, Lenny and the aluminum bridge would be saved to fight again another day.

Once on the other side, Lenny shielded his eyes, and studied the barren ice leading out toward the Trans-Antarctic-Highway. "How are we going to camo the snow machines? There's no way they won't spot these miles away."

"No need, Len." Beckam pointed in the direction of travel. "You're taking my rig with Danny. We'll load the Taiga and toboggan to the gunwales with fuel, food, and meds. You'll navigate to the Transverse, solo, make a left turn and get Danny to Amundsen-Scott as fast as you can, keeping him comfortable. We're gonna dump the remaining two Taigas in the crevasse. Even with camo, the snow machines would be spotted by a trained eye using binoculars in a hot minute."

Lenny hesitated, and then said, "Boss, I can't do that..."

Beckam held up a hand. "That's an order, Lenny."

Lenny nodded, the look on his face grim. "This operation just keeps getting better. I can't wait to see what's coming next."

Liam grinned. "Tell me about it, bro. I'm the one who has to stay here."

"Yeah. But at least you have a chance to kill some commies."

Beckam said, "If we are being tracked by the Russians, and we do this right, there's a good chance we take out the entire patrol, leaving us with fresh Taigas. If friendlies; we high-five, tell war stories, and ride to Amundsen-Scott like Patton into Messina. If it turns into a cluster, you know where we are. Get Danny medical, then haul ass back with the cavalry, if you find any, and rescue our asses."

Beckam pointed at the aluminum bridge. "You wondered how we were gonna make this work. We unfasten the bridge and force it down into the crevasse, anchor it with some line and screws. *Voilà.* We've got a fighting position."

Liam shouldered his weapon. "That's why you're the boss."

"Inventory the weapons; ours and whatever we poached from the Russian drop. I want to see exactly what kind of toys and ammunition we're bringing to the party."

Beckam worked with Lenny, loading all the fuel, extra food, blankets, and water strapped behind Lenny on the passenger pillion and around Danny in the toboggan. When done, Beckam knelt at the head of the toboggan where Danny lay semi-conscious.

"I'm sending you ahead with Lenny to recon and then take— with extreme violence, if necessary—Amundsen."

Danny Frantino reached a shaky hand out from underneath the blankets. He replied in a weak voice. "You got it, Boss. We'll show those civilians how it's done."

Beckam nodded, his eyes bright, steely. "Make sure Lenny doesn't drink up all the booze. We're showing up right behind you."

"I can't promise we won't be drunk as skunks, draped with adoring and lonely glasses-wearing, uptight, female scientists with a SEAL crush—other than that, you bring it, Boss. We'll be waiting."

Beckam leaned down and kissed Danny Frantino on the forehead, then he stood and said, "Put the spurs to it, Frog."

Lenny gave his brother a bear hug, then Beckam. "Kill everything in front of you, Boss," he said. "Then bring it home."

38

It was dark when Hawar gave the order to move out from the compound. Even at the altitude of five thousand feet, it was ice-cold and windy. Jack wore down-lined climbing pants and a parka, and Hawar had given him traditional clothing to wear over the top of his climbing gear. They would pass villagers on the move to and from Doğubeyazıt.

Having a westerner tagging along would raise questions and be hazardous not just for Jack, but for Hawar and his sons, should someone decided the western infidel would make a profitable target. The idea was to get up and down Ararat quietly. If the Kurds had to pull out automatic weapons and engage in a firefight, likely killing bandits, jihadists, profiteers, or others, it would create more than a few problems.

Hawar and his sons Kajir, Camir, and Bazi led two horses loaded down with food and weapons. From what Jack saw, there was way more, of both, than would be required for this fast turn-around. Hawar must have a weapons and food stash somewhere on the shoulders of Ararat. Hawar's compound was less than eight kilometers from the base of the mountain. It seemed they'd just started when they started climbing up a steep grade, following a series of paths and trails.

There was no moon, but the skies were crystal clear, and the stars—brighter than is ever seen near a city or at lower altitude—provided enough light to navigate the well-worn paths leading up and down the mountain. Jack wondered for just how many thousands of years had this footpath been used by people? Even the stone was worn into steps in places from where feet had been wearing at them since the beginning of civilization.

At just after four in the morning, Hawar told Jack the dawn was nearing and that it was time to stop. Hawar shouted at Kajir, who was walking the lead horse up the steep trail. Kajir acknowledged with a wave, and turned off the trail, cutting across the rock, until he linked up with another trail a hundred meters to the right.

Hawar shouted again, pointing more toward the right. Kajir led the horse up a twisting switchback, while Jack did his best to keep sight of the young Kurd in the darkness.

Suddenly, Kajir and his horse disappeared. Jack stopped, then turned toward Hawar. The Kurd urged him on with a hand wave. The switchback trail disappeared into the mountain, or so Jack thought. The entrance, hidden behind rock shelving was just large enough to swallow the horses. Hawar shouted in Kurd, and Jack immediately stumbled into the rear of the second horse. Kajir had brought the two horses to an abrupt halt.

Hawar pushed past Jack, ducked under the horses and got ahead of Kajir. After a moment, Hawar said two words. Kajir continued with the horses, through two more narrow passages, before the passageway opened into a gaping blackness.

Hawar sparked an ancient gas lantern and a cavern at least thirty meters deep, wide and high, lit up in a soft glow. He motioned Jack over near the entrance, and showed why he had gone ahead of Kajir and the horses. He held a meter and a half-length of line, dyed black, with two steel washers, one on each end. He showed Jack how this attached to matching hooks located about a half a meter off the cavern floor, hidden by a series of well-placed rocks. Anyone entering the cavern, having stumbled across the naturally hidden entrance would have to step over the rock, tripping the line set just where a foot would naturally touch down. Even with a flashlight, the chances of spotting the trip line were near zero. Seated within pockets cut out of the rock walls, hidden behind a pile of stones, were two Chinese anti-personal mines, one on each side of the entrance. If tripped, they would kill everything facing them. Jack nodded, then turned and worked back into the main cavern, watching every step he took.

Protected and out of the howling winds that were driving the wind-chill well below zero, the grotto seemed warm and secure. Several wooden tables lined the walls, along with chairs, blankets, and a plastic tub full of cookware. Stacked along the rock walls, wooden boxes overflowed with weapons and ammunition of nearly every kind, Jack imagined. He'd been right guessing that Hawar was using Jack's climb as a dual purpose expedition.

While Kajir and his brothers tended to the horses, Hawar lit two Whisperlite stoves and hydrated several packages of freeze-dried stew. He spoke in Kurdish to Bazi, who nodded, and ran toward one of the military-green, canvas bags they'd packed onto the horses. He unzipped the bag, laid a blanket down on the rock, and then began pulling one automatic weapon, after another, out of the bag.

"We rest today and wait for darkness, Mr. Jack. Then my sons will lead you up Ararat. Past the Parrott Glacier to the Western Plateau. At the Western Plateau, there is another protected spot you can rest. It is a half-day climb from there to the spring." He put his arm around his youngest son. "Bazi and I will wait here with the horses for your return." He placed a hand to his ear. "Have you heard them? Turkish helicopters, searching below. Does anyone know that you are here, Mr. Jack?"

Jack hesitated. "Is there any other reason they'd be searching the mountain?"

"It could be an exercise." Hawar shook his head. "But I think not."

This can't be a coincidence, Jack thought but didn't say. "The helicopters won't search much above fourteen-thousand feet. Once we reach the Western Plateau, we can climb nonstop. Does Kajir know the way to the spring?"

Hawar nodded. "He has not seen it, but I have told him how to find it."

Jack pulled one of the handheld GPS units out of his parka. "At least the GPS units are working. Hopefully, we won't need them."

"God willing," Hawar said.

Jack woke to the sound of the Whisperlite stoves burning fuel under high pressure. On one stove, Kajir brewed tea, while on the other he was cooking up 'murtuga,' a Kurd breakfast staple of eggs scrambled with butter and flour. Bazi ran over to Jack, dropped on his knees and handed him a steaming cup of traditional Kurd tea brewed with cinnamon and a sizable helping of sugar.

After two sips of the strong tea, Jack felt his energy level rising. He climbed out of the mummy bag and dressed in his climbing gear, sans the traditional Kurd clothing. They were far enough up the mountain it was unlikely they'd run into anyone, especially during the winter, and they'd start the climb under the cover of darkness.

Regardless, both Kajir and Camir were already sporting automatic AK-47s on shoulder straps. They didn't expect to see anyone on the mountain, but open carry of automatic weapons was a deterrent to any unexpected casual or inquisitive conversation. Anyone who saw them coming would quickly disappear. Even after a chance encounter, Jack, Kajir, and Camir would be long gone off the mountain, and Jack headed back toward Cappadocia, before someone could round up a large enough gang necessary to take on the young Kurds armed with automatic weapons.

After Jack dressed, he walked over to the stoves, where he put his hands down near the flame to warm them. Hawar squatted near the stoves, helping Kajir dole out helpings of the egg, flour, and butter combination. "God has given you the gift of a perfect night, Mr. Jack. The weather is clear, the stars bright, and the winds have stopped—for now."

After several hours working up through the rock, still traveling on ancient trails that led toward the Western Plateau, they hit the base of the glacier. Jack dropped his gear to the ice. He said, "Crampons, ice axes and harnesses...from this point on, no one goes anywhere without crampons and an ice axe."

Kajir pointed out the Cehennem Dare glacier.

Jack nodded and gave a low whistle. "You live at the base of one of the most magnificent mountains in the world."

"We are blessed by God, Mr. Jack."

Jack, Kajir, and Camir pushed on through the icy winds, each laden with nearly fifty pounds of gear, not including the AK-47 automatic rifles each of the brothers had slung across his chest.

The icy winter winds and bone-chilling cold was every bit the match for Everest at the worst of times. The fact they were climbing through fourteen-thousand feet, not twenty-five thousand was a life-saver. The air was thick enough to cut with a knife, compared to the eight-thousand meter world-class peaks. Beyond having a whole lot more air to breathe, the extra oxygen molecules in each breath kept a body a whole lot warmer than the thin air at hyper-altitudes.

Kajir stopped and waited for Jack. "The Western Plateau," the young Kurd said, pointing out a false summit, glowing under starlight, several hundred meters in the distance.

Jack nodded, sipping from a water bottle he'd stuffed inside his parka. "How far to camp?"

"Twenty minutes, no more."

"A cavern?"

"Not so much, Mr. Jack."

Jack swore under his breath. He was cold, exhausted, and second-guessing his desire to get out of Washington D.C. Staff Sergeant Carlson mixing endless cocktails while Jack sat in front of the fireplace, in the clubhouse, had never sounded so good as it did right now.

39

Kajir's "not so much" description of the cavern was an understatement. The 'cavern' turned out to be a rock shelf cutting four meters back under the glacier, the ceiling a mere meter in height. Even so, it felt every bit as good as a five-star resort hotel as Jack unslung his backpack and crawled under the overhang, tugging the pack in behind him.

Kajir and Camir followed Jack, chattering in Kurdish and clearly enjoying the climb way more than Jack was. *Youth.* A reminder he might be getting too old for these off-the-cuff, high-altitude trips in the middle of winter.

Jack pulled the GPS from his pocket, slid back out to the entrance to the cavern so he could get satellite signal. The small device did its calculations and gave him a distance to Jacob's Well: slightly less than six kilometers. Jack logged the magnetic bearing in case the GPS satellite dropped off. Back under the overhang, he glanced at his watch. It was still at least three hours until sunrise, and they needed rest.

He told Kajir and Camir to take a load off, they'd rest for six hours. Kajir was delighted. Jack caught something about how, if it were Hawar leading the trip, they'd get an hour of rest and a horse whip across the back of the neck if they failed to move at his command.

"Soup, Mr. Jack?" Kajir scooped air toward his mouth.

"Yes, please."

Camir pulled out the beat up Whisperlite and succeeded in lighting the cantankerous stove. Kajir slid out from underneath the overhang and stuffed a two-quart, dented aluminum pot well above the rim with packed snow and ice. Minutes later, after several more cups of ice went into the pot, all three were sipping reconstituted chicken noodle soup.

"The soup?" Camir asked Jack. "Very good?"

Jack grinned. "Hot soup on the side of a mountain after a brutal day climbing—better than the best restaurant meal in Ankara."

The two young Kurds smiled and again began chatting in Kurdish. Jack was in mountaineering paradise. Stuffed under a rock overhang, the sound of winds howling outside and the Hubble-like view of the sky—the Milky Way so bright and thick it appeared like a solid band bisecting the heavens above. The jet-like sound of a Whisperlite burning gas under high pressure, the warm feel of the steam, and the aroma of the hot soup.

Jack zipped up his parka, pulled a black, wool hat down over his eyes and rested his head on his backpack. He was asleep in less than thirty seconds.

―――

"God has blessed us with another fortunate day, Mr. Jack."

Kajir pulled the Kurdish-style hat down over his forehead, almost to his eyes, keeping as much of the wind out of his face as possible.

Jack had awakened to find the Whisperlite hissing again, and a pot of hot water steaming. Kajir was making tea. He handed a mug to Jack, after adding what looked like a half-cup of sugar to the tea. The winds had moderated, and the sun was already well above the mountain. A near-perfect day. They were high enough up on Ararat that there was no need to continue on in the dark. If all went as planned, they'd be at the location of the hot spring in the afternoon. By the time they got down to the Western Plateau it would be dark again. They'd continue on down in the dark, right back to the cavern where hopefully, Hawar would have hot soup and tea brewing on the stoves when they arrived.

If it went as planned, they'd find Jacob's Well, Jack would rig up his GoPro cameras and two underwater lights on the custom mount made to Jack's specifications. He'd sink a line down into the hot spring and drop the Go-Pros down to around fifty meters, the maximum depth and pressure the camera cases could withstand. He had one Go-Pro set to video straight down, and with the clarity of the water it should easily see to the bottom of the well at seventy meters. The other GoPro would shoot horizontal. That way he'd cover video straight down, and also at a 90-degree angle from the line. The two GoPro's offered redundancy. He's used the GoPro enough to know how easy it was to hit the start button, see a blinking red light, then inadvertently hold the start button again, shutting the camera down. He was determined to shoot a few minutes of GoPro, then get the hell off the mountain. He pulled the GPS out of the jacket; it still held signal.

So far, a near-perfect day indeed.

They resumed their hike fully rested, hydrated, and in good spirits. When the GPS indicated they were within a thousand meters of the coordinates provided by Jacob Badger, he signaled for Kajir and Camir to stop.

"We're close, Jack said.

Kajir looked at the mountain, using his hands to frame the mountain against points on the horizon. He nodded in agreement. "We will go ahead and see if we can locate it."

"Thanks," Jack said. "But don't go swimming until I get there."

Kajir grinned and then took off up the mountain at a jog, with Camir right behind him, both disappearing from sight in a flash.

Youth, once again, bares its ugly head. Jack drew a deep breath, turned, and looked back to the Western Plateau, then turned again to see the East summit and the actual Summit of Mt. Ararat.

No peaks to bag today, he thought wistfully.

Jack got underway again, climbing solo for an hour in Kajir and Camir's crampon tracks. He had just stopped for a breather and to sip a mouthful of water, when the two Kurds appeared upslope, running down toward him, their AK-47s, unslung and in firing position.

What the hell? Jack thought. *This can't be good.*

When the brothers approached within fifty meters Jack saw they were excited and spooked. Eyes opened wide, they swept weapons left and right.

Kajir spoke, while Camir continued scanning the horizon with his rifle barrel. "Mr. Jack. We found the spring!" He bent over and sucked several deep breaths, gassed from the thin air, the excitement, and the sprint down the glacier. Kajir rattled off in Kurdish at Camir, who continuing to sweeping the horizon with his weapon.

"Easy, Kajir, Jack said. "Tell me what you found."

"The spring! We found it. But, Mr. Jack, someone, perhaps soldiers, have been there!"

Jack felt his own head going into swivel mode, looking for signs they were about to be attacked. "How long ago?"

Kajir shook his head. "Very soon ago. There is equipment—you will see...."

<hr />

Jack stared down at Jacob's Well. The three-inch frozen ice cap over the spring had been cut with a task-specific, Husqvarna ice saw. That was a good sign. If the waters had been cold, the ice would be far thicker—perhaps meters thick at this altitude. The Husqvarna lay alongside other gear, scattered haphazardly around the perimeter of the hot spring. A Honeywell Dura winch, normally painted bright yellow, repainted in desert camouflage, had been dragged away from the spring, then disassembled, before being tossed aside.

"Only Israelis have apparatus this...." Kajir struggled for the words in English.

"Brand-new equipment," Jack said.

"Yes!" Kajir said, scanning the horizon.

Jack studied the gear. Whoever had been here had left in a hurry and not bothered to clean up the site—even going as far as dumping the gear into the spring to cover their tracks.

A flash of light emanating from a chunk of cut ice caught his attention. Jack pulled the ice away, exposing a small aluminum cylinder. It was painted white, with the words, DILUENT, circling the cylinder in bold red block letters

Kajir walked over as Jack picked the cylinder off the ice and spun it.

"What is that, Mr. Jack?"

"A cylinder of gas that's used in what's called a Rebreather. A sophisticated type of SCUBA equipment used by Special Operations Commandos—Navy SEALS in particular."

"American commandos searching for the Ark, Mr. Jack?"

Jack shook his head. "No worries there. I know for a fact they weren't searching for the Ark." Jack glanced around the site. "Explore the area. Look for anything that might identify the nationality: uniforms, weapons, writing. Have Camir keep watch for unwanted visitors."

Kajir began digging through the scattered gear while Jack did the same. Pulling up the leftover gear, searching empty gear bags for a uniform, flag, cigarette, lighter—anything that would give them a clue who had already explored the spring.

Jack had rummaged without success when he decided to circle back to the Honeywell. If they'd brought anything up, it would have been near the Honeywell.

Two gear bags had been discarded. The first one was empty; he tossed it aside. The second had something inside—something that had been salvaged from the bottom of Jacob's Well.

The remains of David Samuelson....

40

Leah opened her eyes to a mosaic of light, sounds, and aromas. It took minutes before her vision focused enough that she was able to recognize K'aalógii. Hands gently brushed back Leah's hair as the girl's face stared down at her own.

She opened her mouth to speak, but instead, she was wracked with a cough that felt like she'd hacked up a lobe of her right lung. When the fit subsided and she opened her eyes again, two faces were staring down on her.

"Welcome back to the living," Garrett said, his relief evident in both his voice and countenance. "You were dead when Appanoose carried you out of the lodge."

Leah could barely whisper. "Dead? What are you talking about?"

"When he carried you out of the sweat lodge, you weren't breathing and didn't appear to have a heartbeat. I wanted to do CPR, but the Ancients held me back while Appanoose put you down by the fire and revived you like he'd expected it to happen."

Leah tried to sit up, but her upper body felt like it was weighted down with a hundred pounds of rock. She dropped right back down on the blanket and surveyed her surroundings. She was lying under the mesa overhang, on a bed of pine boughs and blankets, with several more stacked on top of her. She lay between two mounds of hot rocks, the same as those used during for the sweat lodge rituals. Heat radiated off the stones, warming the air around her to create beads of sweat on her forehead.

Sunlight penetrated the overhang, and from the angle of the light, Leah figured it had to be morning. She'd gone into the sweat lodge sometime during the middle of the night, so she'd been unconscious for several hours.

At least.

"How long was I in the sweat lodge?" she croaked.

"I'd say three, maybe four hours," Garrett said. "I tried to intervene several times but they held me back every time."

"You must be exhausted," Leah said. "Staying up all night, wondering if I was going to make it."

"The lodge wasn't last night, Leah. You've been in a coma for more than seventy-two hours."

The shock, and then effort trying to respond to Garrett, triggered another fit of coughing. Suddenly, her mind was flooded with memories of the sweat lodge and what she'd experienced with Appanoose. The shock gave her a burst of strength.

She reached out and grabbed Garrett's forearm. "I saw it all, Garrett. The Ancients, the reason for their capture, the complex, the mountains, two suns in the sky...." Leah drew a deep breath. "Oh my god, Garrett. I saw the end as well...it's all our fault...we've ruined everything."

Before she could continue, Garrett took her hand gently in his. "I know why you saw all those visions. There's no need to panic."

"No need to panic?" This time she managed to keep the coughing down to a few hacks. "You have to believe me when I tell you, Appanoose showed me everything. The Ancients. They weren't part of some random science experiment. They're colonists—destined to settle on another planet. By removing them from stasis, we've set in motion the destruction of Antarctica, maybe even the entire planet. We have to return them to Antarctica. We have to do it now." She had to stop, this coughing fit so intense that she thought she might pass out.

Garrett nodded as she spoke, his only expression a look of quiet concern. "Appanoose showed me why you were unconscious for days—I've been a pain in his ass, to say the least."

"What are you talking about? You're not listening to me!"

"Leah—Appanoose dosed you with a hallucinogen."

Leah dropped her head back onto the blanket. The peyote cock-tail, the heat, the chanting. "It seemed so real," she said, relieved that it might have all been just a drug-induced series of high-definition hallucinations. "That was the doozy of bad trips," she said, managing a faint smile. "Oh, crap. I was supposed to check in with Gordon. He's gonna think I blew him off."

Garrett looked grim. "You can't feel any guilt about that. In fact, I went to grab the satellite phone, to arrange a medical evacuation—checked where we stashed it at the bottom of the green gear bag—and it was gone. So I made for the quad—figured I'd get to somewhere I could make a call, but after about thirty steps I felt cold steel on my neck. When I was able to turn around, I found old 'Noose' standing there, that military blade out, telling me in pretty clear language what would happen to me if I tried leaving the Settlement."

Before Leah had a chance to respond, K'aalógii, who had continued stroking her hair, said, "Díí aláahdi haz'ánii bee baadi-idááł. Da'njahí góne'." She reached into the air with both hands and drew two circles. "Naaki jóhonaa'éí".

This time the young girls' words didn't seem as strange as they once had.

You are the one who will lead us, she had said, *to a place between the Fourth and Sixth... The Fifth Domain.*

"Naaki jóhonaa'éí."

Leah almost could have predicted K'aalógii's next words before she spoke them.

A place that has one plus one suns.

41

The remains of David Samuelson amounted to little more than a mass of twisted climbing line and bones. Jack had a visceral reaction. He backed up, turned around and vomited, tears streamed down his cheeks.

A group of unknown Special Operations soldiers had already obtained and documented the intelligence, then split in a hurry. Wheeler's worst-case scenario—unless it had been Americans.

"Mr. Jack! Mr. Jack!" Kajir sprinted around the perimeter of the spring, something held up in his hand. When he got within ten meters, Jack knew exactly what it was, because he'd gotten cases of them for Marko: MRE. Meals Ready to Eat. American military. The empty wrapper had at one time contained two high-energy bars.

It was all too obvious—and infuriating. Wheeler had sent a Special Operations unit in before Jack arrived, and had already executed a high-altitude dive into the hot spring. Likely one of the divers, freezing his ass off, needed a snack to help ward off hypothermia after exiting the water. It was sloppy, leaving identifying wrappers behind—but, then again, they'd left just about everything else here, except weapons and ammunition.

The fury and anger boiled up. If Jack got back to the states alive, he knew one thing for certain. Wheeler was a dead man.

The bastard set me up, knowing if I took the bait, I'd be out of the country. He was hoping I'd get killed, solving one problem, or making it easier to round up the entire Antarctic crew. Killing two birds with one stone.

This time, Wheeler might just have successful disposed of Jack Hobson, and there wasn't a damn thing Jack could do about it. That might also explain the helicopters searching the shoulders of Ararat. Special Operations were good—but so were the Turks. It's likely, given the messy withdrawal from the well, that the Special Operations team had to blow off the mountain to an extraction in a hurry to avoid capture, or, they had indeed found something extra-terrestrial in nature, and it was imperative they get out alive in order to get the intelligence back to Wheeler.

Jack fumbled inside his pack for the two sat phones. He chose Paulson's phone number, but when he tried to make the connection, nothing. The phone's secure satellite service had been de-activated and he was locked out of the device. He dropped it on the ground and tried the second satellite phone with same result. It wasn't lack of service, which might be explained by the geo-magnetic anomaly reaching into the upper latitudes—the phones were locked down.

Hawar stood at the edge of the cavern, looking down the mountainside without expression. The heavy 'thwack' of military helicopter rotor blades echoed off Ararat from nearly every direction. The horses were safe inside the cavern, but Kajir and Camir and Jack Hobson would be in great danger if they were caught out in the open, returning from the Western Plateau.

Hawar swung an AK over his shoulder and shoved many loaded magazines into a canvas bag. He opened one of the wooden crates and pulled out a rocket-propelled-grenade rifle and five rounds of Iranian high-explosive rounds. That was the maximum load he could carry and maintain any speed while running up the mountain with other weapons and gear. He loaded the rounds into the canvas bag, along with the AK magazines, and slung the RPG gun over his shoulder, using the strap to hold it in place.

He turned to Bazi and said in Kurdish, "I'm going to help Mr. Jack and your brothers. You stay here. You must keep the horses calm. When the helicopters swoop down, it'll spook them." Hawar hesitated and then pointed a finger. "Do not leave the cavern for any reason, Bazi. Do you understand?"

His youngest son, showing no fear, nodded.

***

Jack was kneeling near the remains of David Samuelson, saying a prayer. Kajir and Camir spoke in semi-panicked Kurdish, but Jack paid no attention. He was thinking of the young man's family and how much pain his death must have caused them and Jacob Badger.

"Mr. Jack. We must leave," Kajir said. "We have not heard the helicopters—but that does not mean they will stay low on the mountain."

Jack drew a breath and stood. "These are the remains of a young man about your age. His name was David Samuelson. I want to give him a proper burial."

Kajir stepped back in shock, then nodded his approval.

Jack had seen enough climbers left dead in the mountains, to know that he wasn't allowing that to happen to Samuelson. This young man deserved a proper burial on Ararat. The remains of his body, tangled up in nylon and line, left out on the open was a level of disrespect Jack couldn't stomach.

He chose one of the canvas gear bags to serve as a casket of sorts. He looked around the site and decided upon a small mound on the ice, fifty meters away.

Jack used a folding shovel and chopped away until he had a hole about a half a meter deep. He gently laid the remains into the shallow ice grave and covered it with the cut ice. He dug out pieces of rock near the surface of the ice and began to stack them on top of the ice.

Kajir brought more rock and, within minutes, they had a meter-high rock cairn standing over the burial site.

Jack stood back and said another prayer while Kajir and Camir stood watch, ready to open fire at the slightest movement. Once finished, he returned to the spring and looked down into the waters. He could easily see twenty meters down, but there was nothing, even at that depth, that faintly resembled anything but shaped rock.

Still, even considering the risk, it seemed pointless to have made this entire trip and not shoot the video. Jack retrieved his pack, and dug out climbing line, the aluminum GoPro mount with two camera attachments, and the five pound diving weight that affixed to the bottom of the mount, a guarantee that the camera rig would sink straight down into the spring.

The two GoPro cameras were kept in a padded case. He checked one camera by initializing it. The battery bars registered full and he had a 32G SD card in each camera—enough to video for an hour, or more, at high resolution. The waterproof cases each sported a helmet attachment, and the metallic mount had the corresponding mounts, glued onto two arms. Jack slid each camera into the helmet mounts, making sure each audibly locked in place. He clipped the climbing line onto the aluminum mount, and secured the five-pound lead diving weight with plastic ties.

Jack paused, and took a breath. The next part was critical. If he got this wrong, as simple as it seemed, the entire trip was for nothing. He made sure both cameras were on video record mode, pushed down the button to start the GoPro recording, and double-checked that he saw a constant blinking light on each camera.

He attached two Fenix handheld high intensity underwater dive lights, used by SCUBA divers, to thumb-screw driven friction mounts. One light pointed straight down, one at a ninety-degree angle. Wherever the camera was pointed, the light would illuminate the water around for at least ten meters—thirty plus feet, providing high resolution video, even near the bottom of the spring.

Before he lowered the device into the spring, he checked one last time that each camera featured a blinking red light. With both cameras recording, his rig was ready to go.

Jack allowed the line to slide through his gloves, getting through the thirty meters at a speed of about a meter per five seconds. Jack twisted the line, forcing the mount to do same during the descent. This allowed the Go Pros to video three-hundred and sixty-degrees, capturing every angle down below.

He took his time, despite Kajir's urging that it wasn't safe to remain at the site, even for another minute. Jack nodded, telling the Kurd he'd be done in just a matter of a few minutes. After allowing the line down to a point just short of seventy meters, Jack slowly pulled the cameras up, twisting the line as he did. When the rig reached the surface, he checked that the cameras were still recording, that no water had seeped into the cases. Both were operating perfectly. He detached each camera and placed them back into their padded bag.

He was tempted to just toss the mount and the line into the spring, and be done with it, but his disgust with climbers polluting mountains with garbage of all kinds prevented him from doing that. He coiled the line and stuffed the entire rig back into his pack.

Jack shouldered the pack and told Kajir and Camir, "Time to go."

The expression of relief on their faces told Jack all he needed to know. These seasoned fighters had an instinct for trouble, and they were expecting more than their fair share climbing down the open shoulders of Ararat.

42

Hawar crouched behind a row of boulders, watching the T129 ATAK helicopter gunship working the shoulders of Ararat. He swore under his breath. The helo was a state-of-the-art, lethal, all-weather attack helicopter, a combined effort of Turkish and Italian aerospace companies.

With a crew of two, a 20mm cannon, and a wide variety of rockets and guided missiles in its arsenal, it was a most formidable weapon. Plus, it had the ability to operate up to twenty-thousand feet in altitude. There was nowhere in Turkey that Kurds were safe from the T129.

God-willing, Mr. Jack and his sons had perceived the threat and would stay well-hidden until the helicopter needed to refuel or was called off to work another grid. The Turks only had a handful of the highly advanced attack helicopters, and even fewer deployed. It meant either that the authorities were hunting Mr. Jack or another threat of significance. They would never waste such an important resource pursuing a few Kurdish rebels on Ararat.

When the T129 swung around and suddenly gained altitude, Hawar knew the crew had spotted something.

As the T129 probed the upper reaches of the mountain, Hawar crept out from behind the rocks and started jogging up-mountain, jumping from rock to rock, running around the larger rocks and bounders with the grace only someone born of this land could muster.

⌐◡⌐◡⌐

Jack, Kajir, and Camir moved quickly down the shoulder of Ararat, stumbling and falling on the glacier's ice, using ice-axes to self-ar-rest before getting solid traction with the crampons and running again. They had descended to slightly below the glacier when they heard the first echoes of helicopter blades. Kajir cupped his ears, trying to determine the direction and distance.

Jack scanned the skies around and below them. "Well, I doubt anyone flew up here to give us a courtesy ride off Ararat."

The sudden military activity on the shoulders of Ararat meant either that the special operations team that beat them to Jacob's Well had been made by the Turks or else someone had dropped a dime on Jack and sent the Turks hunting.

"We will be safe once we get to my father and the cavern," Kajir said.

Jack stripped the crampons off and shoved them under rocks. He opened his backpack and pulled all his extra climbing gear, clothing, and food out of the pack to make it lighter. Not only did that make it easier to jog down the mountain, but it also meant that, should he fall, he wouldn't be crushed or battered by the heavy, awkward pack.

The trio had traveled another kilometer or so down the mountainside, when the sound of rotor blades got a whole lot louder. Jack watched as Kajir and Camir simultaneously dived to the ground and slid their thin bodies under rocks that would've hard-ly fit a housecat.

Jack dropped as well, but he had no way to conceal himself. He covered his face even as he realized that his blue climbing parka would be a dead giveaway if the attack helicopter overflew his location.

The T129 opened up with an intense barrage of 20mm cannon fire. The rock around Jack exploded, followed by the sound of the helicopter overflying his position.

Jack checked to make sure he had all his arms and legs and wasn't bleeding out after having been struck by rock shrapnel. He'd gotten lucky. He'd been on the upslope side of a sizable boulder and the helicopter had been firing from downslope. Rock cover wouldn't keep him safe for long, though.

Once the helicopter had passed over, its nose pitched up sharply and the vessel spun 180 degrees to begin another attack run.

This time Jack had no cover between him and the 20mm rounds. He had ten seconds to make a decision: make his body as small as possible or dive *over* the rocks and hope the 20mm shells would either impact the upslope side of the rock or pass over his head.

The choice was really no choice at all, if he wanted to live. He shrugged off the backpack and dived headfirst over the rock, unsure how far he'd have to fall before impacting the rocks downslope of the boulder.

The rounds from the 20mm cannon started blowing rock to pieces even before he hit, nearly three meters below. His bulk thudded into the rock-studded earth and his entire body went numb. He hadn't the strength to rise and dive out of the helicopter's range again. Instead, he lay still, playing dead. A sitting duck.

The pilot pitched up, this time in a leisurely manner, before rotating the helicopter and preparing the final attack run.

A loud *pop* sounded near Jack's position, and a rocket propelled grenade streaked skyward with a whoosh of propellant trailing behind. An instant later, the RPG struck the side of the helicopter's fuselage inches below the main rotor. The explosion separated the rotor from the helicopter, which tumbled in flames toward the steep slope, flinging smoke and aircraft parts in every direction before impacting.

Jack took a moment to perform a quick self-check. It seemed he hadn't broken any bones hurling himself over the boulder. Aside from rock rash and the pain associated with hitting rock and gravel, he was unharmed.

Hawar was working his way up the mountain from less than 200 meters below, a canvas gear bag over one shoulder and the RPG launcher on the other. As he moved toward Jack's position, Jack stood gingerly and retrieved his backpack. He could have simply taken the chips out of the cameras, and left the pack, but after the shoot down, he had a sense he needed all the gear he had—and perhaps more if he were forced to stay out of sight for a period of days, even weeks.

Hawar hugged and kissed his sons, and Jack felt tempted to join the lovefest. Instead, he offered Hawar his sincerest thanks while the boys recounted their climb and discovery in Kurdish.

"The Turks will send aircraft, soldiers, and more helicopters very soon," Hawar said, translating for Jack. "They will hunt for us without stopping because we shot down one of their helicopters."

"I'm truly sorry for all this," Jack said. "I had no intention of putting you in the way of the Turkish military."

"We are all in danger, Mr. Jack." Hawar pointed toward the west—the direction of Istanbul, where Jack was supposed to be picked up by the Cessna X after being smuggled back on to the tarmac at Istanbul airport. "I'm sorry, too, but we cannot take you back, Mr. Jack. Our only choice is to travel east. If you go west, you'll never make it back by yourself. The Turks will set up many roadblocks and it won't take long to find you." Hawar paused long enough for that to sink in. "There is only on way for you to survive, God willing." Hawar pointed toward the east. "The Persian border," he said. "It is still Kurdistan. We have allies there. The Turks won't find us once we cross the border."

Iran.... Jack knew the border was only a few kilometers from Ararat. They could be across in twelve hours or less on foot.

"How long before this area is crawling with Turkish military?"

"Six hours—perhaps less."

"How dangerous is Iran?"

Hawar shrugged. "Normally—I would say not so much, but you are a very valuable and profitable target, my friend. Even Kurds could not turn down so much lira, if offered. The Iranians—they will kill us on sight, should we be caught out in the open." Hawar glanced off to the east. "God will decide, if we are too live—or die." Hawar spun, and begun leading them down to the cavern, where they'd retrieve the horses, and make for the Iranian border.

Jack hesitated for a moment, before falling in behind. He had a chilling sensation, that God had already decided, and Jack was likely to end up like David Samuelson, just another unmarked grave, this one out in the middle of the Iranian badlands

43

Marko studied the forest floor outside the cavern, checking for movement, but also waiting for full-on darkness to settle over the canyon so he could leave for what he'd begun to call his daily 'constitutional.' In common parlance, he had 'to go' and was running out of time if he wanted today's call of nature to take place outside the cavern. The military Meals Ready to Eat were getting to his stomach and his bowels.

Friggin' kill for a veggie burrito.

He winced at the sharp salivary reaction the image provoked. And the consequent urge to go to the bathroom.

A reminder to get the ladder ready to go—every second counted today. Marko shoved the aluminum ladder, positioning it right up to the cavern entrance. He knew he should cool his heels for at least another thirty minutes, make sure it was dark, but that wasn't happening tonight.

Marko slid the ladder over the sandstone, seating the ladder in the same depressions created the first time he decided to do an 'against the rules' walkabout. He grabbed his toilet kit and, instead of dashing to an expedient but environmentally-correct 'spot,' he stretched and looked up at the stars. Without the crushing claustrophobic weight he suffered inside the damp cavern, the need to *immediately* relieve himself dissipated—temporarily, at least.

He spread his arms out wide, opened his mouth, and was tempted to cut loose a monster-sized Tarzan call—New Mexico-style.

Nope...gotta keep it together. So far, he hadn't broken any bones, or been injured since the beginning of this debacle. *No need to provide Leah additional motivation to use my bones as a stress-reliever.*

Marko continued to stretch, drawing in deep breaths as he did. He swung his arms from side to side, then reached down diagonally, brushing the top of his boots with his fingertips—the good ol' high school windmill toe-touch. He hated it then, dressed in gray shorts and the mandatory jock strap. But, damn, it felt good this evening. He continued on for another two minutes, then took care of his immediate business. But instead of dashing for the ladder, he stood away from the wall and studied the sandstone. Not all that safe to climb, but maybe some bouldering, just enough to get the blood moving, and strengthen his body a bit before heading back into the cavern.

I'll be careful. After all, there's no one within fifty miles in any direction.

No one within fifty miles—true. But he hadn't considered three miles, directly overhead.

The General Atomics MQ-9 Reaper drone had been on station for three hours in a standard racetrack pattern at an altitude of fifteen-thousand feet AGL, using classified, infrared surveillance equipment designed to find, differentiate, and target a wide variety of heat-generating targets.

This particular Reaper, along with two more working the eastern side of the Gila National Forest, looked for human heat signatures in five one-hundred-square-mile areas with designations like Anvil, Buckshot, Cobalt, End-run, and Friction.

The Reaper operator had target hits three nights in a row at the same numbers. She rolled video and snapped infrared photos of the target, the video overlaid with the exact Global Positioning coordinates.

After the target disappeared, the operator was ordered to return the drone home to Creech Air Force Base, near Las Vegas, Nevada. The two men standing behind the operator high-fived. They'd identified the target, against long odds. Now, time to go operational.

44

Paulson reduced throttle on the T-38 Talon and began a decent into the abandoned airfield. Everything looked just as he'd last seen it. The two Cessna 172s that sat on the tarmac, sat exactly where they'd been when he'd landed the Gulfstream weeks before. Luke's hot-rodded Cessna, the one Derringer had flown when they'd hidden the Hafnium device, Paulson assumed, was still tucked away in the hanger.

After yesterday's meeting with President Wheeler, he'd requisitioned a T-38 Talon from Andrews and told Teresa Simpson he intended to meet with Gordon, get a first-hand update on the Genesis Settlement. Although he had to refuel at Holloman, he had no intention of sitting through a long-winded briefing with Gordon. He needed a reason to overfly Luke Derringer's airport, and the briefing provided him perfect cover. He didn't want to alarm Teresa, so he'd kept the real reason to himself.

During his meeting with Wheeler, Paulson thought something had changed in the president's attitude. While that should have been a positive step in their working relationship, the man's sudden calm and almost cocky demeanor had set Paulson's internal alarms off.

Something had changed. Something Paulson didn't know about. And that was not good.

There was only one living person who knew enough to throw this whole apple cart under the bus. That was Luke Derringer. The old pilot had refused to leave his remote airfield and, frankly, Paulson figured the stubborn, but frail old man would die long before he gave up Marko's location and their get-out-of-rendition-free card, the Hafnium warhead.

Besides, Wheeler knew well enough that a move against any of the Antarctic team, including Luke Derringer, would 'release the dogs' as Paulson had told Wheeler on numerous occasions. The dogs being the opposition politicians, who would still love to see Wheeler gonzo, despite the negative impact that would have on national security. While not quite an airtight security plan, Paulson allowed Derringer to stay at the airport, instead of sequestering the near centenarian behind military barbwire.

Paulson overflew Luke's airstrip at pattern altitude and on the downwind, checking to make sure some desert dirt-bag hadn't parked a rusted Buick, or anything else for that matter, on the centerline of the runway. The wind direction and approximate speed were exactly what he expected.

Paulson rolled the T-38 gently on to the base leg then final, expecting at any time to see the old man limping out of the FBO, the wooden cane more for appearance than real support.

On short final, Paulson focused on his touchdown point and eased the stick on the T-38 back, walking the rear landing-gear wheels onto the pavement before allowing the nose wheel to settle on the centerline.

Five minutes later, he was parked in front of the FBO. The Talon was decidedly old-school, with much of the navigation done with an iPad strapped to his knee, so the shutdown was fast and easy.

The roar of the T-38 flyby and landing should have brought old Luke Derringer out of the FBO, but no joy. The breeze that helped grease the landing blew dust over the tarmac, magnifying how eerily quiet it was with the jet's turbines spooled down.

Paulson deployed the air stair that allowed him to exit the T-38 without benefit of a standard fighter-jet style boarding ladder. He shielded his eyes from the blowing dust and walked over to the door leading into the FBO. He tried to turn the old brass door handle, but it wouldn't budge. Locked up tight. He pounded on the door.

"Luke! You in there? It's Paulson!"

Nothing but the sound of the wind blowing through wires that secured the radio aerials lining the roof of the FBO. Paulson tried looked through the window on the door. The seventy-year-old glass had the clarity of a vintage coke bottle after years of desert dust polishing.

He pounded on the door again, then hiked around to the back of the building. Luke had converted one of the rear offices into a living space. The door that provided Luke with entry into the living space rear door was unlocked and hanging open. Paulson scanned left and right. He had the impression that someone was watching him from behind. He studied the hangars and abandoned buildings: nothing out of the ordinary.

Paulson focused on the open door, evaluating the chances of getting shot by his own ally. The old pilot was hard of hearing. The likelihood Derringer would shoot first, and ask questions later was a given, if Paulson broke into the building.

Paulson cupped his mouth. Didn't hurt to amplify. "Luke! You in here? It's Al!"

No reply.

Paulson tip-toed in, blocking the door open. In case the old bastard opened up on him, he wanted a quick exit.

"Luke! It's Paulson!"

Paulson turned the corner and peered down the hallway leading to the lounge and the living space. At the end of it, he peeked around the doorway into the living space, ready to bolt should he be met with a barrel.

No Luke Derringer.

Paulson tip-toed toward the lounge and the FBO kitchen.

"Luke!" he shouted.

He peeked around the corner and into the kitchen. What Paulson saw caused him to step back in shock. A man sat strapped in to a wooden office chair. Heavy-duty, black plastic zip ties secured his wrists to the armrests on the chair. His ankles were similarity strapped to the chair legs. The man's chin rested against his chest.

The cause of death was obvious: blunt-force-trauma and blood loss, a lethal side-effect of extended torture. There was a tremendous amount of dried blood coating the body, so confirming the identity took more than a few moments. While the torture scene was horrifying, it was nothing compared to Paulson's astonishment and disbelief when he realized the man wasn't Luke Derringer.

It was Stan Fischer.

Fischer had been dressed in his standard Washington suit, still wearing his jacket. The plastic ties that restrained him to the chair had cut deep into the flesh, a testament to how agonizing the torture had been.

Paulson backed out of the kitchen and checked the hallway both directions, then walked to the counter located inside the lounge. He squatted down and searched around in the storage areas underneath the counter with his hands until he felt the butt of a handgun. He slid it out—one of Luke's Glock 19s—keeping the barrel pointed away from his body. He dropped the clip out and took a look. Full load of fifteen. So Luke hadn't fired the Glock.

Paulson shoved the magazine back into the handgun and checked that the safety was operating properly. If he needed to use the Glock, he didn't want the trigger-safety to hinder him from unleashing fifteen rounds in rapid-fire succession. A simple pull of the trigger disengaged the safety. The Glock was operating perfectly.

He examined the lounge for clues to Fischer's demise. It looked exactly the same as Paulson had seen it less than a month before—other than the horror scene in the kitchen. From the condition of the body, Paulson guessed that Fischer had been tortured and murdered hours prior. Maybe as long as a day before.

Paulson unlocked the front door to the FBO and examined the tarmac. The T-38 was parked exactly where he'd left it, canopy down and locked, no sign the airport was about to be stormed. He went back to the kitchen, standing just outside the doorway, careful to not contaminate the crime scene.

Had Fischer come to take Luke Derringer hostage, work him over for information on how to find the hidden Hafnium weapon? Had Luke turned the tables on him and tortured the younger man to death.

Hardly. It was Luke who had information about the location of the Iso-Hafnium nuclear device. Not Fischer.

Paulson couldn't figure it. In fact, he was still having a hard time believing he'd found one of the President's closest advisors strapped into a chair and tortured to death. Then again, Paulson had said many times that Wheeler had to keep Fischer because he knew where all the skeletons were buried.

True, except for one key point: Fischer had no idea where the Hafnium warhead was hidden.

Paulson walked into the FBO lounge and relocked the door, then wiped his prints off the door handle. When he exited out the rear doorway, he wiped any prints off the door where he'd pushed it open. He proceeded to searched the grounds of the airfield—no sign of Luke Derringer. Either he hadn't been here, or, whoever tortured Fischer had taken him along. Granted, if a smart interrogator wanted to get information out of the old man, torture would be the last way to do it. Perhaps some black-op medical facility would work, where they could use a series of drugs. But normal torture could kill the old man before he had a chance to tell what he knew.

If this was Wheeler's work, then Paulson's intuition that something was off was correct—though Paulson had a hard time imagining what could have happened in the President's world to force this particular outcome.

Paulson stopped. His head spun so he was looking directly at the hanger, where Luke's personal Cessna should still be sitting inside. He jogged over and found the hanger door unlocked. When he pushed it open, Paulson was shocked to find an empty hanger. The Cessna was gone. They only person who'd fly that old bird would be Derringer himself.

It was starting to look like old Luke heard, or smelled a coming attack, and had flown himself out of danger—but to where? Paulson had given him a satellite phone. When he'd explained how to use it, old Luke glazed over. This technology was way too new for Luke Derringer, who didn't know how to use a computer. Even so, if he'd flown to a public airport, he'd have tried to make a phone call. Paulson had stuffed the old man's wallet full of business cards, with direct numbers both for him and for Karen.

It was a mystery, but with a silver lining. It was unlikely they'd gotten a hold of Luke Derringer. That meant the location of the Hafnium warhead should still be secure.

Paulson climbed back into the command seat in the T-38 and spun up the turbines. After dropping and locking the canopy down, he taxied to the end of the runway. Without a word on the radio to announce his intentions to any aircraft in the area, he jammed the throttles forward to take-off power.

There was no feeling in the world like pushing the throttles forward on the super-sonic T-38, but Al Paulson drew no pleasure from the experience today. It was time to dig out his war face.

45

Karen, Al Paulson's Executive Assistant, watched with interest as an overseas phone number lit up the display on her personal mobile phone. She recognized the country code as Turkey's, which meant only one person could be calling: Jack Hobson.

She hit the receive button and put the phone to her ear. Before the caller could speak, she said: "Jack Hobson. Are you in trouble?"

"Karen. I can't tell you how great it is to hear your voice."

Jack sounded hoarse. He always sounded this way after safely delivering Paulson back down to the Base Camp of whatever godawful mountain they happened to be climbing. In addition to the climbing-induced hoarseness, she heard tension in Jack's voice. Something she'd never heard, even on the bad Everest Expeditions. She immediately pulled a yellow pad down, plugged in her headset, and grabbed two pens.

"What's going on?"

"My plan is blown here. We've run into trouble with Turkish Military. There's no way I can get to any major city in western Turkey. In fact, I'm headed toward the Iranian border as we speak, along with my guide and his sons."

Karen's instant response was: "Is Wheeler behind this? I can't believe he'd have the brass to try a stunt like this—he'd have to kill Al to get away with it."

"I'm not a hundred-percent sure. I don't believe in coincidence and I've just run into a few. My government sat phones were mysteriously shut off, and Wheeler clearly sent a team of Special Operators into Turkey on the same mission as mine. American soldiers had already been there, and you can quote this to Al: 'explored it from top to bottom'. They were long gone when I reached the objective. Still, things can happen on a mountain climb, as you know. I'm not sure of anything at this point—except I'm headed for Iran. I'm safe with the Kurds, just over the border—for now. But I need Al to find out what the hell's going on.

"Should I use this number to get back to you?"

"No. The Kurds rotate the satellite phones. I'll call you back in six hours."

46

I t had taken Leah another twenty-four hours before she could walk around the Settlement without sitting down every five minutes to take a breather. She still felt unreasonably hungry and thirsty, which, along with her weakness, meant she probably should have been hospitalized. Given the situation, she settled for river water, beans, and corn.

Over-shadowing everything were K'aalógii's words. That Leah would lead her people "to a place that has one plus one suns." Exactly what she'd seen in her version of the vision quest.

Garrett was nonplussed but tended toward skeptical. He said it could easily be suggestion. Leah gets high as a kite on an unknown hallucinogenic tea. All the while, Appanoose spins this tale, repeating it over and over again, until it's running through her mind like an IMAX movie premiere.

It didn't ring true for Leah. There was so much more. The intense cold, feeling unable to breath, the second Antarctic complex, and all of the penetrating detail. She didn't tell him about the city-block sized blocks of ice, the masses of steam, or the fracturing of the ice for as far as her mind's eye could see. If she had, he might have suggested she not only needed a break from the Settlement, but also a strait-jacket wearing holiday at the Gerald Champion Regional Medical Center in Alamogordo on a '5150' hold.

Leah had come to other private conclusions as well. If Appanoose were human, he differed greatly from the rest of the Ancients. First, he had this overwhelming and uncanny ability to serve as a leader for people from many different tribes. He could talk their talk, serving as the keeper of traditional culture, yet he clearly understood their predicament in the larger world. Having survived his sweat-lodge ritual, Leah now felt strangely certain that the man could transmit, perhaps by touch, information that had been imprinted into his DNA. She held that back from Garrett as well.

Had Appanoose been bio-engineered by the non-terrestrials to do exactly what he did? Keep the traditional culture alive, but prepare the Ancients for their next role as planetary colonists, using a sweat lodge ritual to imprint this information on a need to-know-basis? It dovetailed smoothly with the Ancients' expectations of what a shaman did.

Now that she had most of her strength back, it was time to face off with Appanoose at his Basilica. Her intention: get the satellite phone back and make it clear that if Garrett or she were ever threatened again, the shaman's desire to get back to Antarctica would be 'Put on Ice' forever. He'd never see the outside of a walled compound ever again, much less Antarctica.

And she meant it.

Already after eight in the evening. Leah walked toward the Basilica, where a fire burned bright enough to light up most of the Settlement while Appanoose spoke to a small knot of his followers.

He glanced at her when she got within fifteen meters of the fire. She signaled him with a universally recognizable gesture: hands up in the air with a shrug. 'Let's move this along—you're killing me, here."

47

Appanoose continued his sermon for thirty more minutes after Leah had given him the 'hurry up' signal. With a sharp nod, the Ancients stood, stretched their legs, a couple even smiling and greeting Leah, then patted Garrett on the shoulder, sharing a quiet word with him.

Since her experience with Appanoose in the lodge, both Garret and she had been treated much more like part of the Ancient family, not outsiders. Garrett said the difference in treatment had begun immediately after she exited the sweat lodge. "Aside from the knife point at my neck." Given that this was her first real day of being up and around, the sea-change was still a novel experience.

Appanoose gave one sharp nod; Leah stepped forward as if she'd been urged on with a freshly-charged cattle prod. *Easy, now*, she thought, reminding herself not to instantly respond to his orders. Charlie 'Appanoose' Mason was all his nickname suggested, and more.

Garrett joined her and they sat across from the shaman, precisely where the Ancients' butts had been warming the skins on the logs not two minutes before. She badly wanted to start the conversation, asking questions about the lodge ritual. The longer she'd been awake, the more she felt the experience had been real—not some hypnotic suggestion.

You're doing it again, she warned herself. *Do not knuckle under to the shaman.*

With a snap nod, Appanoose signaled that he was ready to begin. Leah spoke first, using a pretty strong line of semi-fluent Navajo, surprising even herself. "I want the satellite phone back," she said, using English for "satellite phone."

To her shock, Appanoose gave her a single snap nod, then pointed to one of the warriors standing nearby. He spoke curtly to the warrior, who spun and sprinted for the mesa overhang. He returned less than thirty seconds later with the satellite phone in his hand. Appanoose nodded in Leah's direction, and the warrior handed her the phone without a word.

Garrett said, "I wish it had been that easy for me. Guess he didn't want any interference while you were still unconscious."

Leah shrugged. "If he thinks I believe everything I saw, then there'd be no reason for me to use the satellite phone, except to do his bidding."

"He miscalculated there," Garrett said. "That's a first...."

She said, "Maybe," while maintaining her stoic expression.

Appanoose reached out for the satellite phone, and Leah handed it over without comment, already breaking her rule not to jump at his every command.

Although he spoke in Navajo, Leah now understood every word he uttered. One side-effect of her lodge ritual was an unexplainable improvement in her language skills. While she might have to pick words out of a phrase before, the words were now as clear as if they'd been spoken in English.

Appanoose held up the sat phone. "Chidí naat'a'í!"

"Did you hear that, Garrett? He told me to call and get an aircraft."

Instead of expressing shock, Garrett simply and quietly asked Appanoose, matter-of-factly, in Navajo, "Where do you want to go?"

"Shádi'ááhjí Honeezk'azii." Appanoose pointed toward the south and repeated in English. "*Ant-Arc-Tikke.*"

"Chidí naat'a'í?" Leah asked, the frustration evident in her tone.

"Naaki éé'neishoodii bikin," Appanoose replied.

"Oh, shit," she said, shoulders slumping. The shock of his reply had knocked the wind right out of her, emotionally.

"Connected domes.... I guess those could be translated as 'churches,'" Garret said. "Sounds like what you saw during the ritual."

"Right," Leah said without further comment.

"You want to tell me what you really think?" asked Garrett.

"My gut says that Appanoose isn't like the rest of the Ancients. I've even wondered if he's really even human. If he is human, then he's different. Was his DNA altered—beyond what we've already seen? Was he imprinted with information designed to be parceled out to the Ancients, as necessary for survival?"

Seeing Garrett's eyes go flat, she pleaded her case. "It fits the Native American culture. The shaman is the religious leader. He's expected to know everything—even be connected with the supernatural. If the Ancients are colonists, then maybe it's a way to acclimate them to their destiny, provide the skills necessary for survival, without, as Marko says in his Star Trek vernacular: 'ripping the Prime Directive a new asshole.'"

Garrett said, "Perhaps avoiding as much non-terrestrial contamination as possible. The Ancients go to the shaman for guidance, spiritual and otherwise—he has all the answers."

"Exactly," Leah said. "He educates through his sermons at the Basilica or, when he needs more of a supernatural approach, he uses the lodge. I can tell you firsthand, when you've been through that experience, you have no doubt he's a deity."

Garrett sat quiet for a moment. "Well, I suppose that leads to the next question for 'Noose."

"What's that?"

"You said it. Let's ask him if he's human."

She turned toward Appanoose and blurted it straight out in Navajo. "Asdzáníísh bíla'ashdla'ii?" Simply translated: "Are you a human?"

Instead of a reaction, Appanoose simply sat motionless, his stoic expression unchanging while Leah waited on pins and needles for his reply. He turned and looked out toward the forest, then back to Leah and Garrett. He opened his mouth to speak, but instead, suddenly stood. He wasn't the only one who had turned their attention to the east. The entire Settlement had gotten up from the fires and were talking among themselves, walking and pointing toward the east.

Appanoose said, "Chidí naat'a'í. Ahonii'yóí Chidí naat'a'í."

Leah stood; Garrett had done the same. "Aircraft—many aircraft," she translated. "That can only mean on thing. Gordo ratted us out. We've got military helicopters inbound."

48

Grigoriy called the platoon to a halt. He lifted his binoculars while his best sniper Alexi swept the horizon using the scope on his Arctic Warfare Magnum.

"*Ochistit*," Alexi said.

Grigoriy continued scanning without comment. Up until now, the Taiga tracks had continued in a straight line, following the magnetic azimuth toward the magnetic South Pole—the exact compass bearing that intersected the Trans-Antarctic-Highway. But their bearing had changed slightly.

Grigoriy consulted his map. If the Americans wanted to shorten the distance by a few kilometers to Amundsen-Scott, it might explain why they'd suddenly turned a few degrees to the magnetic northwest. Although their shift was slight, it was enough to set off alarms. From what Grigoriy could tell, a pressure ridge of ice cut across the direction they'd chosen, while they easily could have continued straight on the azimuth without such an obstacle.

Suspicious.

"Contact?" Vasily asked, raising another pair of Swarovskis to his face.

"No contact," Grigory responded. "The Americans have altered their heading." He pulled his handheld compass out of his parka. He held it out straight ahead and allowed it to settle until he had an accurate reading. It confirmed his visual observation. The Americans had turned, slightly.

What could explain it? Contact with an aircraft, or a correction to reach coordinates for a rendezvous? Could it simply be poor navigation? A heading change due to sloppiness?

Grigoriy slung the Swarovski binoculars around his neck.

"Vasily. Send one man forward one-thousand meters."

In addition to the SEALs' own MP5s and several hundred rounds of ammunition, the Russians had graciously supplied Beckam with two Kalashnikov AK-12 assault rifles and a KBP A-91 Bullpup assault rifle. Beckam and Liam Clay sorted the weapons and set them up on a line rack they'd built down inside the crevasse. They'd anchored the aluminum bridge pieces' side by side, upside down a meter and half below the edge of the crevasse. Once anchored, the bridge had provided a solid fighting position.

"Feel like you're in France, let's say, 1918?" Beckam asked.

Liam Clay chuckled. "Who said World War I trench warfare ever went out of style? We're snug as a bug in a lethal-ass rug."

Beckam and Liam crouched so that just the white helmets and Beckam's binoculars stood above the crevasse rim. They'd been careful to anchor themselves to the surrounding ice. When the shit hit the fan, Beckam didn't want either one of them tumbling off the bridge and getting wedged in the bottom of the crevasse.

Still on Beckam's wish list were the remote-detonated claymores. Enemy facing anti-personnel mines that shot out thousands of metal shards in a fan shape, killing or injuring everything within the blast fan.

Except they didn't have any....

49

Jack rested a pair of Hawar's worn binoculars against the rock to steady the view and did his best to focus on the airfield. It was located in a relatively barren and desolate section of Iran, about twenty kilometers across the border from Turkey.

Built during the Iran-Iraq War, along with scores more in the desert, it had little of itself remaining, from what Jack saw. A rusted water tower and a twisted clump of steel that might have been the base for a control tower, possibly the target of an Iraq bomber. The fact that there was damage to the control tower was disheartening. It probably meant that the runway had been bombed as well, rendering it unusable—then and today.

Jack lowered the binoculars. "I can't see if the runway's intact. I'll have to sneak over there and check it out. Make sure aircraft can land."

Hawar shook his head, looking like a disapproving school principal after you've been caught shooting spitwads across the room during band practice. "Where did you learn to take such risks? Certainly not from me."

He turned and motioned Kajir over and spoke with him in Kurd, pointing at the airfield, explaining what Jack had said. Kajir responded, then shouldered an AK-47, motioned at Camir, who did the same. Hawar handed them a handheld Garmin GPS unit that featured topography maps, not roads and cities. He switched it on, checked that it had signal, then gave it to Kajir, who stuffed it inside a gear bag he carried with extra AK magazines.

Jack handed the binoculars to Hawar, and the Kurd expertly surveyed the region. He pulled the binoculars down and waved his sons forward with a sweep of his hand. The brothers jogged toward the airfield, weapons over their shoulders, while Hawar minded them with the binoculars.

Hawar's sons would get a GPS waypoint from the center of the runway—critically necessary for navigating into the abandoned airfield.

He glanced at his watch; he was already an hour past the time he told Karen he'd call back, but they couldn't risk more than min-imal communication. He needed to have all the necessary infor-mation before calling her, at least if he had any hope of suggesting a viable way for him to get out of the Middle East—alive.

"If the runway is good," Hawar said, smiling, "God willing, you soon will be on the way home to your wife."

⌧

It had only taken Hawar's sons a matter of minutes to cover the ground between the rock outcropping and the airfield, where they disappeared beyond the wreckage of the control tower.

They'd been gone for more than an hour and Jack was con-cerned. He wanted them to do a thorough check of the runway, but more than sixty minutes seemed excessive. Hawar on the oth-er hand, seemed at ease. He continued scanning the airfield and vicinity. Dust rooster tails plumed in the distance, kicked up by cars and trucks running on a dirt highway perhaps six kilometers away—a constant reminder they were far from out of danger.

"See, Mr. Jack," said Hawar, his voice rich with pride. "They are fine—and they will have your information."

Kajir and Camir sprinted back across the open desert toward the rocks.

"I never doubted for second," Jack said, releasing a long-held inner breath for the boys.

The young men jumped over the rocks and back under the cover of the outcropping. Neither seemed winded by the sprint from the airfield, Jack noted with envy.

They spoke with their father in rapid-fire Kurdish. Hawar nodded then pointed a finger back at the airfield, sweeping from left to right, and asked several more questions. Kajir pointed to the left and answered with a lengthy explanation.

"Kajir says the runway is lengthy. At least three kilometers. The...." Hawar searched for the words, but instead made a horizontal motion with his hand in the meantime. "The black surface of the runway, it is in good condition. However, there are two difficulties." He turned back to Kajir and seemed to be confirming in his own mind what his son had observed before explaining it to Jack.

"The runway has a bomb crater—perhaps one kilometer from the end. Also, an armed vehicle was blown up near the center of the runway. Kajir and Camir, they were able to clear much of the metal—but there are several pieces, including two wheels, they could not move on their own.

"If there were three of us, could we move the wheels and debris?"

Hawar hesitated, then nodded. "Yes, with a strong man like yourself, Mr. Jack, it can be done."

50

After taking off from Luke's airfield, Paulson flew northwest until he was over-flying the city of Grants, New Mexico. He decreased power and altitude, spiraling down to ten-thousand feet. He programmed the auto-pilot to fly the T-38 in a lazy circle following a perimeter around the city, holding at ten-thousand. He dug around in a gear bag and pulled out one of his 'burner' cell phones that he carried for just such an emergency. As he expected, at ten-thousand he had five bars of service on the phone. By circling the city at the same altitude, he'd hold signal with the same towers, preventing the calls from dropping.

He used speed dial, preprogrammed with several numbers, his assistant Karen's being on the top of the list. Once the call connected, he switched to speaker phone and ran the volume to maximum.

"Al Paulson, don't tell me you're in trouble, too."

Paulson's eyes opened wide. "I don't like the sound of 'too'? What the hell's happening?"

"Eight hours ago, I got a call from Jack."

Paulson read her hesitation right away. "That's why I'm calling you on the burner phone. We might *all* have trouble. What's going on with Jack?"

"Where are you calling me from? There's all kinds of background noise?"

"I'm in Grants, New Mexico. Actually flying over the city in a holding pattern, so I have cell service."

"Well," she said, "I've left at least four messages on your satellite phone and tried Mac Ridley as well.

"I've got news," he said. "That's why I'm calling. If Jack's in trouble, I want to hear that first."

"Jack is in trouble. His Ararat adventure has gone sideways. He said to tell you: 'American soldiers had already been there', and quote, 'explored it from top to bottom'. Both of his satellite phones are inoperative. Like his satellite service was intentionally disabled. He's concerned that Wheeler may be involved, as bizarre as that sounds, given everything else on that idiot's plate. Oh—and, the Turkish military got involved. You might know more about that than me. He can't get out of Turkey via Istanbul. He said he was nearly across the border out of Turkey, when I spoke with him."

"What border?"

"With Iran. He said to tell you not to freak out, because he's got the Kurdish warlord guide and his sons for company. He assured me he was safe with the Kurds.

"True enough," Paulson said. "Nobody messes with those Kurdish rebels. Does he have a plan to get out?"

"He's hoping that his suspicions about Wheeler setting him up are paranoia, and you can arrange some kind of military extraction—perhaps near the Iraq border. Otherwise, he says there is an abandoned military airfield about twenty kilometers east of the border. Jack was headed in the direction of that airfield when we spoke." Karen took a breath. "Little reminder here, Al. Whatever disaster Jack is embroiled in—you're the one who convinced him to go. Not to mention, he's risked his life numerous times to save yours.... I'd suggest you find out if Wheeler just signed his own death warrant, because I will personally cut his throat if he's behind this...."

"Although my news is a mystery, it likely concerns Wheeler, so we might all be on the same page." Paulson explained what he'd found at the abandoned airfield.

Karen fell silent for a long moment. "I always told you not to run rough-shod over Wheeler. I told you he had screws loose. But still...it's senseless to torture and kill Stan Fischer."

"You're probably right," Paulson said. "I didn't cut him too much slack—still, I did everything I could to make this work. Didn't matter. Wheeler couldn't process it. His ego couldn't take the slap down. Now, Fischer? He was the consummate boot-licker. I can't see Wheeler ordering someone to torture him and take video just for after dinner entertainment. There's something here that doesn't add up. Big time."

Paulson drew a breath. "First order of business—don't leave the executive suite of Paulson Global for any reason. Call a meeting with security. Tell them you might be getting visitors, although I doubt federal Agents would show up at the door. Have security disable all the elevators leading to the executive floor. Move the staff on down to where they can access working elevators. Make security taste any food they bring in for you first."

"Al!"

"Just kidding.... Here's what I really need, okay?"

He heard her signature notepad paper rustle. "Ready."

"I'm going to give you a list of ranking senators and congressman. You contact them with one simple code word. That word is '*Titanic.*' But...*do not call them* unless you hear from me, or, you don't hear from me. And do not say any more. If you have to do it, they'll understand that Wheeler's gone rogue. That right there is enough to send Wheeler down the river. Is the Citation 10 back in Westchester?"

"Yep. All gassed up, ready for the turn-around to pick up Jack. But there's no way you can go get him in Iran...."

"You said it. I got Jack into this—it's my job to get him out. You said Jack should be calling you soon. I'll need the GPS coordinates for this Iranian airfield. Jack'll have checked out every inch of the field and runway. Make sure you write down every detail he tells you."

"Is that it?"

"When you hear from Jack, call me on the burner. I want to get an update on his personal situation, the exact location of this airport and its runway's status. That's a start."

Paulson clicked the phone off and dropped it back into the gear bag. He grabbed the stick and switched off the autopilot. He banked the T-38 until he'd picked up the heading for Holloman Air Force Base. He had to refuel the T-38 first; then, as they used to say back in his naval-aviator days, he'd 'put the spurs to it.' He might also be on the take-down list, but that didn't matter. He fully intended get Jack out of Iran.

51

Appanoose gathered the Settlement together as the sound of helicopters came closer. He spoke in multiple languages to the Ancients, ordering them to battle. Two of Leah's fierce femmes dashed under the mesa overhang and came out carrying spears and more military knives stolen from perimeter security

Apparently, they took a few more than they owned up to, Leah thought.

The satellite phone that had been returned to her still hung from the lanyard. She flipped the lanyard over her head and tucked the satellite phone inside the flight suit. Garrett stood next to Appanoose, armed with one of the hunting spears.

"Garrett!" she shouted. He trotted over to where she stood. "We can't stay here. They realize that, right? I'm thinking if we can get the Ancients to Silver City, they won't be able to round us up like cattle."

"Not gonna work, Leah." He nodded in the direction of the shaman.

"What?" Leah looked to Appanoose and saw he was leading the Ancients in the direction of the inbound helicopters, not away.

"No! The soldiers inbound will murder everyone in cold blood, if the Ancients resist. You know that. Their only hope's to run toward civilization."

Garrett shook his head. "The shaman made his decision." He drew a breath. "I'm going with them." Garrett pointed out the deer trail leading to the top of the mesa. "Get to the quad and get out of here. Use the satellite phone, call Jack, Al—everyone. Tell them what's happening."

"No! I won't leave them," she said, finding inner strength. "They're depending on me. Their fate's mine as well. I couldn't live with myself, knowing I ran."

She expected Garrett to argue, to try to hammer some sense into her stubborn head. There were good reasons she should save herself—no great reasons, granted—but Garrett simply said, "Breɪv," honoring Leah by using one of the most respected terms in his native language:

Navajo warrior.

52

Much as she'd experienced during the deer hunt, the Ancients disappeared ahead of Garrett and her, ghosting into the darkness without a sound. Garrett ran abreast of Leah, his hand pointing out the direction. They were headed toward the meadow where Appanoose had refused to kill the doe and her bucks. That made sense only if the Ancients were looking for a face-to-face fight, as the clearing was the sole place for miles around that could accommodate more than a couple of helicopters landing at the same time.

She'd told Gordo about the Ancients' exceptional hearing. He had to know they'd hear the helicopters earlier than any human, giving them time to prepare for the incoming troops. Would Gordo have warned the Special Operators? She didn't think so. But even if he had tipped off someone in Washington, they likely would have ignored his advice.

It was a struggle to keep up with Garrett now, the sweat-lodge experience still sapping her endurance. Her legs began to cramp first. Then her lungs began to burn.

I'm exhausted already.

"Go on ahead," she called to Garrett.

No response. Just as Leah opened her mouth to shout once again, a hand covered her lips and nose, then yanked her off the deer trail, dragging her backward for at least ten meters before standing her up again, never freeing her mouth. Leah froze, not sure if they next thing she'd experience would be either a shot to the back of the head or a honed blade slicing through her windpipe and severing her spine.

A second turned her around in place, and suddenly she was looking up at Appanoose. He gave her one nod; she nodded back. He uncovered her mouth and whispered in her ear. A single word: "Shił!"

Leah nodded her understanding. *Stay with him.* She was terrified, but the fact that she could stay by his side gave her the courage she needed to take a deep breath and scan the forest for any sign of the other Ancients or Garrett. She couldn't see more than a handful of meters in any direction, the foliage and cover being so thick. When she turned back to Appanoose, she saw K'aalógii crouching silently next to him. Leah reached out and they clasped hands.

It didn't take long for Leah to figure out the Ancient strategy. They were waiting alongside the main trail leading to the Settlement. It was the most direct route from the meadow where the helicopters would most likely land en masse. Another fatal underestimation of the Ancients and their guerrilla-fighting skills—especially in their own backyard.

Before she could conclude any more, Appanoose was signing in the darkness with his arms and hands, followed by his customary head snap to the Ancients he was signaling. The same ones Leah hadn't seen, though she now realized they stood only meters away.

She hadn't heard anything new, but Appanoose and the Ancients clearly had. She felt rather than heard a slight movement of air as the Ancients sped past her in order to intercept the soldiers on the trail. Moments later, she heard the sound of boots kicking rocks, breaking small branches, even muffled chatter moving toward her from the meadow.

After the lethal silence of the Ancients, these Special Operators sounded like a John Philip Souza brass-band number in a Fourth of July parade.

Which raised another question. *What in the hell had happened to the perimeter security?* It made sense they wouldn't be included on any tactical mission. They didn't have anywhere near the experience of a Special Operations team. Her guess was, someone had told them to stand down, ahead of this mission. That told her that the Special Operations would have whatever leeway necessary to accomplish the mission, without anyone watching over them.

A license to kill, she thought. *James Bond would never agree to such carnage.*

Unfortunately, for the Special Operators, the slaughter they might be expected to implement, wouldn't take place.

There'd be a massacre all right, Leah thought. Only not the one she'd feared. These soldiers had been sent on a suicide mission, and they didn't even know it. How many of them were married, had children at home? What would be their last thoughts as a knife blade slit their throat? Their families—and how they'd never see them again?

Waiting for the ambush felt a thousand times more painful than anticipating Appanoose and his warriors piercing the hearts of the doe and her bucks. She crouched with K'aalógii, unable to cover her ears with her hands as she'd done during the deer hunt because she was holding hands with the young girl. The imminent screaming and death rattles...she'd hear them all in unbearable detail.

Leah heard boots scraping trail, the occasional squeak of the backpacks.

She felt the shaman's hand on her back, gently at first, then not. It pressed her down until she lay flat on the forest floor with K'aalógii still crouching and holding Leah's hand for support. The child didn't seem afraid in the least. A reminder of how horrible her early life had been, living the cliff-dweller's existence.

If Appanoose pressed her down any harder, she feared he might break a rib. It felt like that much pressure.

The approaching soldiers couldn't be more than a few meters down the trail from their position now. She clenched her jaw and waited for the first casualties to be cut down from behind at the end of the column.

Instead, to her shock and amazement, the sound of boots continued down the trail, backpack frames issuing an occasional squeak, even a chuckle or two coming from the commandos, as they compared this forced march in the middle of the night to their workouts during basic training.

She stayed in the pressed-down position for at least another five minutes, even though soldiers were out of human earshot seconds after passing the Ancients. Without warning, Leah was gently lifted to her feet, and released.

Appanoose leaned over and whispered into her ear. "Naabaahii, leɪzi."

Leah nodded as relief swept over her in waves. Appanoose had said, 'Lazy warriors,' his less-than-glowing review of the spec ops unit had shuffled right past the lethal ambush. He could have ordered them killed, the deed done in a matter of seconds, but he had not.

Leah felt a swell of pride and appreciation for the shaman and his noble warriors.

He pointed down the trail toward the meadow and said, "Chidí naat'a'í."

Oh, so he wasn't allowing the soldiers to pass by out of the goodness of his heart; he was two steps ahead. If the Black Hawk crews and security got wind that soldiers had been ambushed, they'd likely take off immediately. Or at the very least, set up a perimeter and shoot at anything and everything coming toward the meadow before flying off at the last second.

Leah estimated it was five or six more kilometers to the meadow. At best they had thirty minutes before the Special Operations team sneaked into the Settlement and figured out it had been deserted.

The Ancients could run that distance in a matter of a few minutes, but not Garrett or her. She'd have to suck it up and run as fast as she could, for as long as she could, hoping to get to the meadow before Appanoose stuck his knife against one of the pilot's throats and told him to fly to Antarctica. The chances the pilot spoke Navajo, Lakota, Apache, or Pueblo were slim to none; so no chance a pilot could convince Appanoose that a Black Hawk couldn't make it anywhere near Antarctica.

No, Leah corrected herself. *Appanoose must already know the helicopters can't take them directly to Antarctica.*

The shaman would also know that the pilots wouldn't speak his languages.

He must have another plan in mind.

Appanoose grabbed her wrists, spun around, and crouched.

Oh, dear. Looks like I'm gonna get the piggy-back ride of my life.

Leah put her arms around his neck, then lifted one leg up at a time into the shaman's grasp. He stood and sprinted down the trail at a speed Leah had only exceeded on the quad. Instinctively, she shut her eyes each time Appanoose jumped over a log or creek or short-cut a switchback to descend straight down the an impossibly steep slope, picking up the path again before Leah dared peek.

When he leapt across a ravine more than ten meters deep, Leah's stomach pushed right up into her throat as they went airborne, then fell almost two stories before he landed on his feet and never missed a step while picking up speed on the upslope.

They'd already gone at least a kilometer before Leah thought about Garrett. Was he getting the same treatment, or being forced to chase after the Ancient's gazelle-like pace, doing the best he could?

It was only after Appanoose stopped and dropped Leah to the forest floor that she found out. One of the warriors came alongside and dropped Garrett's lanky frame right beside her.

Appanoose grabbed Leah's hand and led her through the forest. She knew it was futile, but she tried to make as little noise as possible as she moved with him. When he stopped and crouched, Leah did the same.

K'aalógii came alongside Leah and grasped her hand again.

A crescent moon provided enough light that she could easily make out the helicopters sitting in the meadow. Far from what she'd expected, there was only one Black Hawk in the meadow. But next to it stood a second, much larger helicopter, a Ch-47 Chinook. Probably the same one that the Army had put on TAD at Holloman. It had been used when they transported the Ancients out to the Settlement, and Leah knew they shuttled both civilian and military members of the security perimeter into and out of Holloman, using the over-sized Chinook.

The Chinook was a troop transport that featured a drop-down ramp at the back. It could carry thirty...or was it forty people? There was a complicated equation a pilot had told her, depending upon altitude and fuel, temperatures, and more.

Whatever it was, it could accommodate all the Ancients and a crew with no problem. Strangely, no armed soldiers stood watch over the Chinook. The interior was lit, however. Leah suspected the crew were waiting inside for a radio call.

The Black Hawk was a different story. There were five armed men positioned around the war bird. They appeared to be dressed in civilian-style clothing and none wore a helmet.

These men looked frosty, serious, and prepared to shoot at any sound. Even from a distance, Leah felt a certain vibe coming off this Black Hawk, a night-and-day difference from the Chinook. The Chinook crew probably thought they were on a milk run. The Black Hawk crew was ready to go weapons-free at the sound of a broken twig.

53

Appanoose flashed a series of hand signals. Leah saw right away that the number of signals and the complicated nature of the hand movements after pointing toward the Black Hawk meant that he considered it the more serious threat—and that the take-down would require a complex attack.

Appanoose grasped Leah's hand once again. He made it plain she and K'aalógii were not to move. He dropped her hand and crept toward the edge of the clearing, staying well hidden within the trees.

Leah saw no obvious signal from Appanoose before a small group of warriors and fierce femmes burst from cover and, within seconds, disappeared inside the Chinook through the open rear ramp. The tactic was quick and quiet. No screams, cries, or sounds of any type escaped the Chinook. If the Ancients had killed the crew, they'd done it lightning fast and with lethal silence.

Leah hardly had a chance to draw in a breath before she heard the sound of something knocking on a tree, well out in the forest to the left side of the meadow. It seemed unimaginable the Ancients would make such a bonehead mistake, knowing how many lives were at stake.

The attention of the armed men surrounding the Black Hawk, including the barrels of their assault rifles, spun in the direction of the sound. At that moment, at least ten, perhaps more warriors and fierce femmes came out of the forest and took all five armed guards down in an instant.

Leah saw the muzzle flash of a single weapon shooting from what had to be a sixth man from *inside* the Black Hawk. The shooter got off three rounds before being silenced, but not before a single Ancient, slower than the rest, was caught out in open as he sprinted for the Black Hawk. When the shooter got off the third round, the warrior dropped his arms to his sides and fell into the grass.

With a sick feeling in her gut, Leah knew that it hadn't been an Ancient at all. Garrett Moon, a modern-day Navajo warrior charging the Black Hawk with his brothers and sisters, had been cut down with a single shot.

Leah dropped K'aalógii's hand and sprinted into the meadow, one thing on her mind. Reach Garrett, and hope that he'd just tripped, or heard the shots and dived for the ground, or perhaps been winged in the shoulder.

Appanoose was already kneeling beside Garrett by the time Leah reached him. The shaman was whispering a prayer as Leah dropped to her knees and burst into tears. K'aalógii knelt beside Leah, grasping her hand once again. Leah glanced over and saw tears on her cheeks, but also a hardness in her eyes, the eyes of a child who had witnessed this and much worse, her entire life.

The pain of seeing Garrett Moon lying dead was crushing. The Genesis Settlement had been cursed from the start, and one person deserved the blame for his death, and the death of Juan before him. The blame was on her, and her alone.

Appanoose got up and walked away, allowing Leah time to grieve. Leah stayed by her friend's side until her tears stopped. Finally, she stood, K'aalógii helping her to her feet as she drew several calming breaths. With the last of the tears and a new sense of calm came a repressed fury. If she looked in a mirror, she thought, she'd have seen that same hardness she'd just witnessed in K'aalógii.

With purpose, she walked toward the Black Hawk. Three of the five armed guards lay dead in the meadow, their throats cut before they hit the ground. The sight of three slaughtered men should have horrified her beyond reason. Instead, she simply passed them to where two more men, still alive, lay next to the helicopter, hands pinned down to the middle of their backs by the knee of an Ancient on top of each.

She passed them by as well, stepping to where Appanoose held the Black Hawk flight crew on their knees.

She recognized the crew right off: Captain Hutchinson, Lieutenant Cruz, and Sergeant Bruce. The crew that flew most of the resupplies into and out of the SLZ. The same crew that had flown Jack in only days ago, and Leah and K'aalógii back and forth from the Settlement to Holloman.

To say the expression on Hutchinson's face was one of frozen terror was an understatement. He stammered up at her, "D—Dr. Andrews? Are you going to kill us?"

"That depends."

"On what?" he asked, his eyes wide open and unfocused.

"If you so much as make a sound, or flinch."

Leah spun and stepped to the open door of the Black Hawk. Inside, one man lay on the floor of the helicopter, pinned down by two Ancients in the same way as those lying in the meadow. Beside him lay the assault rifle he'd used to kill Garrett Moon.

The calm and focus that she'd gained after grieving over Garrett's body continued to sooth her. She felt no instant urge to kick this man in the teeth, to bash his skull. The calm was damming back her building rage, a rage that disconnected her from her emotions.

That rage intensified geometrically when she peered into the half-lit interior of the Black Hawk. A bloody body bag rested against the fuselage, while strapped securely to the aluminum bulkhead stood the Hafnium warhead that Marko Kinney had been babysitting.

Leah drew a breath. Then another. The sense of calm detachment cradling her murderous rage prevented her from having the man pinned down and slaughtered on the spot. She boarded the Black Hawk and worked her way back toward the nuclear device and body bag. She knelt and unzipped the bag, revealing stringy blond hair stained crimson.

Marko.

She had to stop for a moment. It was critical that she maintain control. The safety of the Ancients remained her responsibility. The Ancients had to be her overriding focus now.

Once certain she'd regained control, she unzipped the bag the rest of the way, exposing Marko's body. It was the hardest thing she'd ever had to do. Once the zipper reached Marko's boots, she pulled the laces open on one boot and slid a hand down inside a bloody sock. Nothing. Leah calmly turned her attention to the opposite boot, unlacing it, and working her hand down inside the sock.

This time she felt the paper envelope she hoped would still be there. She pulled it out and found it soaked with blood. Leah ripped it open and read the codes that had been sealed into a plastic bag. Jack had been thinking ahead, as usual. Certain that Marko would spill soup or hot cocoa on the list, rendering the access codes for Freddy Kruger unreadable, Jack had sealed them inside a Ziploc sandwich bag before inserting them inside a plain white envelope.

She zipped the codes inside her flight suit, then closed the body bag, wiping her hands on her legs.

"Plasticuffs," she said to the man pinned to the deck. He didn't plead for his life, or moan. He simply nodded toward a gear bag jammed underneath the webbing. Leah slid the bag out, opened it, and dug around inside. It was filled with loaded magazines for the assault rifle, multiple satellite communicators, water, even a couple of energy bars.

There was also a plastic bag filled with plastic handcuffs, a basic staple on any mission in which people would be secured for transport. When Leah had boarded the Chinook on the initial transport to the Settlement, the Ancients had been secured with the same. She'd screamed bloody murder. There was no need to secure their hands, they'd all been heavily sedated. The security personnel had refused to cut off or release the plasticuffs until the Chinook landed and the Ancients removed from the aircraft.

Leah showed Appanoose how to use the plasticuffs on the man pinned down in the helicopter. She told him to secure, the Black Hawk crew: Captain Hutchinson, Lt. Cruz, and Sargent Bruce, also using the plasticuffs. Also the three surviving mystery shooters: the man she'd found pinned down inside the Black Hawk and the two other survivors, with throats still intact, lying face-down in the grass.

Leah glanced at her watch. The Special Operations team would be at the edge of the Settlement by now. The sooner she got off the ground, the safer they'd be.

She took Appanoose aside, and told him to gather Garrett's body off the grass and Marko's body out of the Black Hawk. He gave a sharp single nod and gave directions to the Ancients, who carefully picked Garrett's body up and transported it to the Chinook, returning for Marko just moments later.

When Appanoose stuck his head outside the back of the Chinook, Leah motioned him over once again. She told him to carry the 'ophíye' from the Black Hawk and load it into the Chinook. If he was impressed that she'd actually remembered the Lakota word for 'container,' he didn't give any notice.

He simply gave one sharp head snap, and ran to the Black Hawk, retrieved the Hafnium warhead, and with no more effort than a NFL running back, dodging defenders on a long touchdown run, ran with it toward the back of the Chinook.

She picked up the assault rifle lying on the deck of the Black Hawk and the gear bag filled with the spare magazines.

She considered having Appanoose gather up the other assault rifles lying in the grass but decided against it. The last thing she needed was someone whose idea of an advanced weapon was the steel knives they'd taken off perimeter security getting ahold of an assault rifle and shooting up the helicopter, or anything else, full of holes.

When the Ancients were clear of the Black Hawk, she walked backwards, pointing the barrel of the automatic weapon where she thought the fuel tanks ought to be. Leah held the weapon with both hands, hoping it wasn't set on safety. When she pulled the trigger, she hit the Black Hawk twice, before the barrel jumped into the air. She re-aimed, this time determined to hold down on it, and held the trigger back until the magazine was empty. Although the Black Hawk hadn't caught fire, it was shot full of holes from front to back.

"Fly that," she muttered, before moving to the rear of the Chinook.

54

When Leah walked inside the Chinook, she found the pilots held down by the Ancients, the classic knee in the back, a blade moving around just within peripheral vision as a reminder not to move.

The Black Hawk pilot, Captain Hutchinson and his crew, had been propped against the fuselage of the Chinook, hands plasti-cuffed in their laps. On the opposite side of the fuselage, the three surviving shooters from the Black Hawk were lined up, and cuffed in the same position.

Leah told the Ancients to release the Chinook crew. "I know you—you're out of Holloman, TAD for the Settlement, shuttling security." The crew nodded in unison. "What's your mission?" Leah asked.

"We were told you ordered an evacuation of the Settlement," said the command pilot. That's all the information we were given."

"What happened to perimeter security? They should have been all over this...."

"The civilian contractors were pulled out 48-hours ago. The military inner security was ordered to stand down yesterday..."

"By whom?"

The pilot shrugged. "Sorry, Dr. Andrews. I don't know."

Leah pointed toward the goons. "Who are these guys?"

"We never saw them before the mission briefing yesterday. They launched first. It was only after they gave us a 'go code,' were we to fly to the meadow with the Delta Platoon. The Black Hawk was already at the LZ when we touched down."

"Get the Chinook into the air," Leah said.

The pilot looked confused. He glanced first at his co-pilot, then the loadmaster. "Ah—what about the Delta Platoon, ma'am?"

"They get a special treat—hiking out."

"Destination?" he asked.

"Back to Holloman. Don't rush. I want to enjoy the scenery."

Before the two pilots climbed into the cockpit, Leah had one more piece of advice. "We are flying radio-silent until I say otherwise. I'd expect you to hear from the Delta guys anytime now, wondering what the hell happened to the Ancients. You will not respond."

She looked at the command pilot, then the co-pilot. "The Ancients would like nothing more than to cut your throats with your own knives. That's not going to happen—is it?" The pilots and the loadmaster shook heads with such ferocity, Leah thought their helmets might fly off their heads. "Then I think we're ready to go."

She turned to the loadmaster. "My crew doesn't speak English, but don't make the mistake of thinking they're stupid. Show them how to sit on the webbing. Start with the tall one who looks mean enough to kill and eat a rhino with a butter knife—he'll instruct the others."

The Ancients sat on the webbing, the hardness in their eyes replaced with fear and anxiety as the turbines spun up. Appanoose carried the same stoic expression as always, and he moved up and down the web seats, talking with each, calming them with just a word or two.

He'd make a helluva poker player, Leah thought. *Nothing rattles this guy.*

The pilots raised the ramp, and the Chinook lifted off, dipping the nose to gain speed and altitude. That created renewed panic among the Ancients. Leah and the shaman did what they could to soothe and calm, moving up and down the cabin.

Leah turned her attention to the three black-op goons, yet to be identified. One was heavily bearded, the second clean shaven. They both appeared about the same age. Late 30s-early 40s. The third one was clean shaven and sported a monkey shave haircut as well. He was easily in his mid-50s. Muscular, wrinkled, and wind worn. An old school hard-ass who'd seen it all. He had to be the leader. He was also the one she'd found pinned down inside the Black Hawk. The one who had killed Garrett with that last, three shot burst. Leah stepped over and studied him closer. Then he looked into her eyes, all she saw was contempt.

"You got a name?"

"I've got a few—pick one that works for you."

"How about 'Dead Man Walking'?"

He shrugged. "Good as any."

"I don't believe we've had the pleasure."

No response.

"How did you know how to find Marko and the warhead?"

No response.

"So, it's gonna be like that?"

He glanced up, mocking her. "How about pointing a gun to my head and threatening to blow it off...."

"If I blew your head off, how would I get the information I need?"

He shrugged, then closed his eyes, as if anticipating a restful nap. "It's been a long night. Wake me when we get to Holloman."

"Oh, I doubt you'll make it to Holloman," she said. That got a reaction. His eyes flashed open, but only for a moment.

Leah stood and walked forward to the cockpit. She leaned in and said, "I heard you guys using the radio. I only need one of you to fly the helo, so I guess I just toss a coin...."

Both pilots shouted, 'No!' at the same time. A sharp but brief grin flashed across her face. Jack said he used gallows humor—a psychological tool-of-survival—in situations where people were dying around you.

That one's for you, Climber.

"Lower the ramp," she said. The co-pilot lowered the ramp without comment. She knew it would frighten the Ancients, but she had limited time and had to take the risk. When she turned around, the ramp was already opening, the rush of air and the sound of the turbines and rotors making a deafening roar. The Ancients, for the most part sat frozen in their web seats. Leah nodded at Appanoose.

He was at her side instantly.

She turned toward 'Dead Man Walking.' His expression was pure amusement. He had to shout over the roar. "You plan on tossing me out of the bird if I don't talk?"

"I can see why Fischer hired you for the job," she shouted back. "You think way ahead of the curve."

The other two accomplices also looked amused.

"Let me see if I can't wipe those silly grins off your faces," she shouted over the roar.

Leah leaned against Appanoose and shouted into his ear. One sharp nod told her he understood. He reached over and lifted the bearded thug up but didn't cut his restraints. Appanoose hauled him to the back of the Chinook, spinning him around until his body was prone, lying half in the Chinook, half out on the ramp.

Leah had told Appanoose to take the bearded one and _hold him_ at the open door while she questioned the bald one. Or she thought that's what she said. Over the roar of the wind, the turbines, the rotors, and her deep emotional fatigue, she might not have gotten it exactly right.

She turned and looked at Dead Man Walking. His smirk had grown.

This won't work, she thought. *They know it's a bluff.*

She turned and got Appanoose's attention. She shook her head, a sign she hoped he'd interpret as failure and as an order to pull Beard back aboard the Chinook.

Appanoose gave one sharp nod and, without expression, tossed Beard out the back of the Chinook with no more effort than lobbing a rag doll into the trash.

Leah was so shocked, all she could do was stare out the ramp at the fast-vanishing body as it plummeted to earth.

55

J esus!" said Clean Shave. "What the hell do you want to know?"

"Keep your mouth shut," growled Dead Man Walking.

"You saw Sitting Bull toss Miller out." Clean Shave shook his head. "I'm not going out like that. No way."

To her surprise, Leah felt nothing for the late Miller. Or her other two captives. The memory of Garrett shot dead in front of her eyes, of Marko's broken and bleeding body stuffed in the body bag, had dissolved whatever empathy remained.

"Who's next?" She focused on Clean Shave. "How about you?"

"Just tell me what you want to know," he said, looking more disgusted than fearful.

Leah pointed at the older commando. "What's his name?"

"Krause."

"Shut. Up." Krause struggled futilely to free himself from the restraints.

"Who's running this operation? CIA? NSA? Who ordered this mission? Fischer?"

"We're civilian," Shave said. "All former Special Operators with black-ops experience. We work outside the normal chain of command on classified operations."

"Mercenaries with a leash," Leah said.

Shave shrugged. "Pays better than the service industry."

"Fischer—where is he?"

"He was in charge—right up until—"

"Keep your mouth shut!" Krause was getting so worked up that he sprayed a sheet of spit as he yelled.

"Fischer's dead."

Leah was so stunned, she wondered if she'd heard correctly. "Dead? Why?"

Krause continued to struggle but said nothing.

Shave said, "Fischer had all the intelligence on the operation in Antarctica. That information was worth an incredible amount of money to the Russians." He nodded toward Krause. "He'd already done a job or two for the Russians. The money they offered was off the charts. Krause said Wheeler was already headed for the looney bin. Christ, Wheeler has already told Krause to plan on getting rid of Fischer. Can you imagine?" Shave shook his head in disgust. "Nuts to think he'd get away with that." He glared at Krause. "Oh, and concerning Mr. Fischer, we were supposed to get rid of him—just not quite yet." He shrugged. "We figured once Wheeler was wrapped in a straitjacket, there'd be so much chaos, hell, we'd be long gone to the private island of our choice before anyone asked any questions."

"And Fischer just told you double-crossers everything over a cup of coffee at Starbucks?"

Shave hesitated. "Wasn't quite that easy."

"How did you find out where Marko was hidden? Did you kill Luke Derringer?"

"We never saw him. We heard a Cessna taking off while we were driving toward the airfield in blacked-out 4-wheel drive trucks. If he somehow heard us coming, he had some kind of security—or he was damn lucky and somehow spotted movement in the dark."

"How'd you find Marko?"

"The kid was caught on surveillance by drones working the airspace over New Mexico, using infrared sensors. He never would have been made, except he apparently started wandering around outside his hidey hole at night."

"Marko Kinney was harmless. Why would you kill him?"

Shave nodded toward Krause. "Orders were to eliminate the kid."

"What do you know about the Native Americans?"

"Nothing. That was a Delta Force operation. We were to wait until signaled, then accompany the Chinook to the recovery LZ. From there, we were to take you in the Black Hawk, separately."

"Lemme guess," Leah said. "I was supposed to end up in another body bag." Shave simply looked down. Leah continued, "If Fischer's dead, someone else is in charge. Who?"

Shave hesitated, then nodded at Krause. "He says this came right from the top, the very top—Wheeler."

"What about Al Paulson and Jack Hobson?"

Shave shook his head. "I don't know anything about them."

Krause looked up at Leah, a twisted grin on his face. "Satisfied?"

"Momentarily," she said. Leah motioned toward Appanoose, then pointed two fingers at the goons, then one at the ramp. Appanoose gave one sharp head snap, walked over, grabbed one man with each hand, and dragged them toward the back of the Chinook.

Krause's smug demeanor changed in an instant. Sweat flooded his face and his cheeks puffed as he struggled to breathe. Shave was too stunned to react. Appanoose looked down at the two as they struggled, then up at Leah.

She gave one nod, and the two went out the back of the Chinook without so much as a scream.

Leah didn't have any time to process what she'd just ordered, when there was a sudden commotion on the opposite side of the Chinook. It took only a moment for Leah to jump up and rush over to where K'aalógii was having what appeared to be a grand mal seizure. Appanoose had been even faster than Leah. He turned K'aalógii on her side so she could breathe and placed one hand on her forehead and chanted.

Whatever Appanoose had done, whether it be something to do with his genetic engineering, or just old-school shamanizing, K'aalógii's seizure slowed and then stopped altogether. She appeared to be in a deep sleep, resting comfortably. Several of the fierce femes had also come to K'aalógii's assistance and had her head cradled. They spoke up against her ear in soft tones.

Appanoose looked up and nodded, for once without the arrogant snap she'd almost gotten used too. This nod was gentle, even reassuring that everything would be okay. K'aalógii wasn't in any danger—at least at this moment.

She was relieved that they were headed for Holloman, and would be there in a matter of minutes. Gordon, or his medical team would be standing by, and K'aalógii would be in the best care possible. It had been nearly a week since K'aalógii's testing, there was a good chance that Gordo would have more information about their medical condition, and perhaps, how to treat, even reverse if possible. She pushed her way up to the cockpit with one order: 'Put the spurs to the Chinook.'

56

Paulson had tried a cold shower first. That helped some. Still, he was beat. It was hard to slow down one of the most energetic men on the planet. Billionaire businessmen, who started with nothing didn't get to the top of the pyramid unless they could out-work, out-play, out-socialize, and out-strategize any and all competition.

The shower was connected to his personal office suite, part of a large hangar and building complex at Westchester County Airport that made up his charter and warbird business. After landing the T-38 at Westchester, midnight eastern time, he'd called Ridley at Camp David using a burner phone, bypassing the government-issue satellite phone.

If Jack's sat phones had been disabled intentionally, whoever was behind it had left the Stateside satellite phones working. That made sense if Wheeler was pulling the strings. A good way to eliminate Jack Hobson but not raise hell in Washington.

He'd ordered up a helicopter to fly Ridley from Camp David to Westchester. He told Ridley to have the mechanics still holed up in the Aspen Lodge to maintain a low visibility status—and if they had those shotguns they'd taken off the skeet range, have them handy. His helo order had gone through without a problem. Wheeler seemed to be playing carefully with Paulson.

Paulson had ninety-nine problems, and sleep was pretty much at the bottom of the list, for now. Most pressing: Jack Hobson stuck in western Iran with no way out. Even though he was under the protection of Hawar, news spread fast within tribal communities. The missing Cessna and missing Luke Derringer was also a concern, but given Jack's situation he had to hope that Luke had flown the coop and was holed up out at some log cabin sitting next to a long stretch of hardened desert he'd used as a runway.

It was only a matter of time, perhaps even hours, before it become common knowledge a westerner was hunkered down in Kurdistan. A million dollars in that region bought a lot of weapons and power. It was just a question of time, and nationality, to see who'd drop a dime in order to win the warlord lotto.

His other problem was Wheeler. Had he ordered the murder of Fischer? Why? It made no sense. Leaving a dirty crime scene was sloppy and reckless.

It seemed more logical that someone else was behind this. Perhaps the messy murder scene was planned, a way to be rid of Wheeler in such a way that it created mass confusion and opened the door to a wide range of political and constitutional crises.

Some sort of coup? he asked himself. *Really?*

If this were the case, it had to be military-driven. The Hafnium warhead would have marginal value with the military. These boys had millions of megatons available elsewhere.

Hell, for all Paulson knew, he might be approached to participate in this coup, using his sway over the politicians who opposed Wheeler. In that case, the conspirators would be way too busy to worry about Leah at the Settlement.

The Hafnium warhead only worked as long as everyone agreed to play by the rules. Once Fischer was tortured and murdered—someone had already set off the equivalent of a political nuclear weapon.

Paulson pressed a speed dial number for Teresa Simpson's private cell after glancing at his Breitling. After two in the morning—and the day had yet to get started.

"Hello?" she said sleepily. The burner wouldn't come up with any identification. Only Karen had all his numbers set up in her systems. "Teresa—It's Al."

"Al? Why are you calling me using a phone without a—" She'd figured it out fast. "Look, our situation had gone bad," he said. "I'm going to take a risk, hoping your own phone isn't under surveillance. If so—if can't be helped." Paulson gave Teresa a sanitized version of finding Fischer and a bullet-point list on what he thought could be happening, from Wheeler going over the edge to a coup d'état.

"What do you want me to do?" she asked.

"This is a tough one, T. My advice would be to get out of Washington. Find some cabin out in the backwoods of Maryland and stay out of sight. Kill your phones, stay off the internet—you know the drill."

The phone line went quiet for a moment. Then Teresa responded, "You said Wheeler was acting odd last time you saw him. Out of character. I think the best course of action is for me to sit in on any White House meetings as your deputy tomorrow. As far as I know, you're off to see Gordon for an update, if anyone asks. Nothing can happen to me at the White House, and being there might give me a feel for what's happening. When you get back with Jack, we can team up and figure out how to ride this out—one way or another."

Paulson could not dissuade her from her plan. The former BLM chief was damn near as stubborn as Leah. Finally, he agreed, on the condition that she not return home at night. "Stay over at a friend's house. Make up any excuse, but don't tell anyone where you'll be. Oh, and Teresa?"

"Yeah?"

"You have a handgun at home, by any chance?"

"Sure", she said. "Unregistered. The only way they get that baby is prying it from my cold dead hands."

"Strap it," Paulson said. "But you're African American with a concealed weapon in DC, so don't get pulled over. Christ—I'll never get you out of jail if that happens."

Teresa chuckled. "Truer words...." she said and signed off.

Paulson ordered up another pot of coffee, then studied the aviation charts that he'd laid out on a conference table. The charts covered the Atlantic Ocean, the Med, and most of the Middle East.

Assuming this abandoned airfield in the northwestern corner of Iran was still uninhabited and the runways still solid enough to land and take off, he still faced other challenges. The runway had to be clear of rubble. All it would take to strand them in Iran would be a punctured tire, or, worse, debris in the turbine, creating a multi-million-dollar yard sale when the blades, spinning north of ten-thousand RPMs, exploded into thousands of shards hurling out at super-sonic speeds.

Paulson sighed and rubbed his eyes with both hands.

He had to get into and out of Iran, refuel, and get home.

He needed a plan and he needed it fast....

57

L eah told the pilot to make a standard approach into Holloman. One thing on her side were the orders the Base Commander, Colonel Kelleher, had been given.

There is a classified operation (Top Secret—National Security) near Holloman Air Force Base. Unless notified otherwise, expect to host inbound and outbound air assets attached to this operation. Two interconnected aircraft hangars will be tasked to this operation, indefinitely. The hangars are off-limits to all base personnel. Discussion, theory, supposition, and rumor about this operation is strongly discouraged. Consider information attached to this operation: Sensitive and Compartmentalized.

The two hangars had been codenamed *Dragon One* and *Dragon Two*. Leah had rolled her eyes when she heard the code names. Now, she told the pilot, "Have the Chinook towed into *Dragon Two*," she said. *Dragon One* was where Gordon had set up his small medical city; *Dragon Two* was empty, used mostly for storing supplies and providing classified access and egress.

"Yes, ma'am," the pilot replied, anxiety evident in his voice. No one wanted to be next to earn their wings Leah Andrews-style.

Leah leaned over the pilot. "Has the Delta Platoon checked in?"

"Yes, ma'am. They're pissed off. We haven't returned any of the radio traffic."

"Good job. I don't want to have to drop that ramp again. It gets cold inside with all the heat blown out the back." That's all she had to say, because the pilots looked straight ahead and nodded stiffly in reply.

She'd planned to personally cut Gordon's throat, should she get ahold of him—thinking he'd been the rat who'd sold them out. Thanks to the mercenaries, she'd found out otherwise. With K'aalógii suffering epileptic-like seizures, she needed someone she could trust and count on. Jack was lost in Turkey and her closest Ancient confidant, someone she'd come to lean on heavily, Garrett Moon, was dead.

The approach into Holloman proceeded without a snag, and the Chinook was towed into the hangar. Before she ordered the ramp lowered, Leah picked up the assault rifle belonging to Krause, the same one she'd used to empty a magazine into the Black Hawk, before leaving the meadow. She fished around inside the ammo bag and pulled out a loaded magazine, then walked over to where Hutchinson sat against the fuselage, still wearing his plastic restraints.

"You know what this is?" she asked.

"Yes, ma'am," Hutchinson said. "Heckler and Koch MP5."

"It's empty. How do I reload it?"

Hutchinson glanced over at Cruz, not looking too happy.

"C'mon, Captain. If I wanted you dead, I'd have tossed you out."

Hutchinson said, "Pull back on the charging handle on the front of the weapon. Pull out the empty magazine, push a loaded magazine in, release the charging handle. It's ready to shoot. You might want to push the small lever up, so the weapon is on 'safe' first."

Leah pulled the charging handle back, used her fingers to release the empty magazine, slid a full magazine in and released the charging handle so that it slid forward. "That's it?" she asked.

"The safety is off—push the lever up."

Leah ignored Hutchinson and then leaned into the cockpit. "Lower the ramp." She looked for Appanoose. He sat on the webbing without expression. He simply nodded at Leah but didn't move. *This is your show*, the nod said.

Leah drew a breath, pulled the HK up into firing position, and walked down the ramp. The only person standing inside the hangar was Gordon, who looked the worse for wear.

"Sorry for waking you up, Gordo. As you can guess, our whole Settlement idea has gone to hell in a handbasket. I have the Ancients." She had to stop and force herself from not letting go, crying right on the spot. "Garrett and Marko. Both dead."

For a moment, Gordon did a fish-pulled-up-from-depth imitation. His eyes looked like they were bulging, and his mouth opened and closed. He paled visibility.

"Look Gordo. We have plenty of time to sit down and bawl our eyes out over a bottle of Jimmy Beam. Right now, we've got to focus."

All Gordon could manage was, "You have the Ancients? Are they safe?"

Leah nodded. "I don't know for how long. We're pretty much trapped here at Holloman."

He shook his head, still partially dazed. "I always wondered, if we were visited by extraterrestrials, what the outcome would be. As it turns out, we're the real monsters."

"Don't cut them too much slack, Gordo. Remember why we're in this situation." She pointed the assault rifle toward the Chinook. "Although K'aalógii is resting comfortably, she needs medical attention. She suffered some kind of seizure on the Chinook on our approach to Holloman. Appanoose was able to soothe her and she's sleeping now. I know the helicopter ride, and everything that has gone down tonight has been stressful, but I'm pretty sure this has more to do with the physiological changes. Sorry I've been out of touch," Leah added. "My past few days have been—out of the ordinary is all I can say right now."

"Take me to her," Gordon said.

Leah led Gordon up the Chinook ramp. K'aalógii lay on the aluminum floor, covered with blankets. He leaned down and examined her for a minute.

"Her heart rate is accelerated. Appears she's running a fever, but hard to know exactly what her normal temp should be."

"Could it be stress?" Leah asked.

"Stress could make her metabolic anomalies symptomatic," Gordon said. "You asked me what we discovered while having Ms. K'aalógii as our very helpful guest. Their metabolic deviations are accelerating. Almost as if they are being re-engineered to thrive in a different biosphere."

Leah thought back to the vision quest—and what she'd experienced. "Would this biosphere include a thin atmosphere, cold temperatures, and steep, mountainous terrain?"

Gordon stopped the examination. "Exactly. A substantial increase in red blood cell counts, increasing lung capacity, larger, more powerful heart, presenting with elevated rate, hyper-metabolism, body temperature intensification, skin thickening, accumulative muscle mass. How did you know?"

Not the best time to recount about my lodge 'trip.'

Instead, she asked, "Could our atmosphere become toxic to someone undergoing these—modifications?"

"Impossible to say. We are in uncharted waters, medically."

"Can you slow this down?"

"Unknown," Gordo said. "However, if stress triggered the symptoms, a strong sedative may reverse them, temporarily."

Appanoose walked over to Gordon, looking him up and down, and not in a manner that put the doctor at ease. The shaman made it obvious he remembered Gordon from their removal from stasis—and the awkward, initial medical testing that had taken place soon thereafter.

After making Gordon suitably uncomfortable, Appanoose turned toward Leah. He crouched and lightly touched K'aalógii on the forehead.

He said one word: "Ashch'ąh."

"What did he say?" Gordon asked.

"A state of sleep from which one may not wake up. A more modern translation would be: coma."

"Miss K'aalógii is not in a coma," Gordon said.

Leah turned to Appanoose. "Ałhosh' as'ahgóó?"

He offered a single head shake.

"I asked him if she needed a long sleep. You saw his reaction. A definite no."

"What's the difference?" Gordon asked.

"C'mon Gordo. You know better than anyone, the difference between a long sleep and a coma. You don't wake from a coma."

Appanoose spoke again, this time with more urgency. He raised both hands toward the top of the Chinook fuselage and looked up as he spoke.

"Sǫ' shik'éí "Ashch'ąh."

"Oh my god," Leah said. "I get it. He's saying she needs the long sleep from which you don't wake. The sleep provided by the 'Star People'."

"The stasis units," Gordon said. "By disconnecting them from the stasis units, perhaps we inadvertently initiated a biological time bomb." His eyes opened wide, as if he'd just had an epiphany. "What if the Ancients were never supposed to awaken on Earth? What if they were adapted to live on some other world, with an eco-system conducive to these metabolic and physiological modifications?"

Leah nodded. The good doctor had put his finger on it precisely—and without needing to hear about her visions of the same. She felt fatigue pulling her toward the deck of the Chinook. She sucked in a breath, steadied herself. "Good thinking, Gordo. Now tell me something I don't know."

58

W hat's the status of the stasis units?" Leah asked.
Gordon shook his head. "Non-functional, I'm afraid.
One by one, they all shut down, the last one seven
days after the Ancients were extracted. We only have one of the
units here; the rest were shipped out to Dr. Gupta at DARPA. Apparently, they were able to do some research prior to the final
unit shutting down. But even if we could insert Ms. K'aalógii
into a functioning stasis unit, I think it's simplistic and unreal-
istic to think it would arrest her new physiological processes.
For all we know, the units were tailored specifically to each Ancient."

Leah whispered to Appanoose. He gave one sharp head nod in
the affirmative. Then she knelt and stroked K'aalógii's hair.

"I'll be the first to admit it's a long shot, Gordo. But I know
where we'll find more stasis units—*operating* stasis units."

"Jack found another complex?"

"Not as far as I know. The ones I'm talking about are in Antarctica. Somewhere near the South Pole. They're contained within
two inter-connected complexes large enough to make the one we
found look like a dinghy next to a supertanker."

Gordo's mouth hung open. "Wait. How do you know about this other complex?"

Leah stood and replied matter-of-factly, "In a sweat-lodge vision-quest, high as a kite on the shaman's personal stash of peyote."

Gordon looked even more shocked, but Leah didn't pause. "We're taking a long trip, Gordo. I need you to source enough flight suits and cold weather gear to outfit all the Ancients. Can you sedate K'aalógii?"

Gordon nodded. "I'll arrange to have her put under with Propofol. We can check and see if that alleviates the symptoms and maintains her vitals in a safe range."

Leah held up a hand. "Isn't that the stuff that killed Michael Jackson?"

"It is...but I guarantee we only administer the thriller dose, not the killer." Gordo shrugged and offered his best semblance of a grin.

"You're learning from Jack I see."

"What's that?"

"Gallows humor, Gordo. It's what's gonna get us through this."

She whispered to Appanoose, who gave a single nod.

"Appanoose will help you get the Ancients off the Chinook," she told Gordon. "They'll need to use the bathrooms. Show him where; he'll instruct the others."

"Ah...what about the ladies?"

"You've got women working in there, Gordo. Get a couple of them and figure it out." Leah wasn't finished. "These people eat nonstop. Probably starving by now. Get your dining facility cooking up corn and beans, and more of that chicken noodle soup. No jalapeno. And no Hostess Cupcakes—got that?"

Gordon nodded.

A wave of emotion flooded through Leah. She had to pause, and wipe tears off her cheek. "One other thing. Can you get a couple of your people to escort Marko and Garrett to your...morgue?"

Gordon paused, closed his eyes for a moment, his shoulders

drooped. He regained his composure, and nodded, pulling strength from Leah herself, it appeared.

"Dr. Andrews?"

Leah spun around. The Black Hawk crew still sat against the bulkhead, restrained with plasticuffs. The Chinook pilots sat in the cockpit. All eyes were on her.

Hutchinson said, "What happens with us?"

"I haven't decided yet," she responded, honestly.

She signaled to Appanoose and whispered to him in Navajo. He replied with one sharp head nod. Then he went forward to the cockpit and pulled the command pilot out of the Chinook cockpit, sat him down next to the Black Hawk pilots.

Leah fished around for more plastic restraints. She nodded again to Appanoose. He yanked the co-pilot out of the cockpit and Leah repeated the plasticuff procedure with both men and the loadmaster as well.

Once done, she said, "You sit tight—and make no trouble for me. Got it?" The helicopter crews nodded in unison. "Wait," she said. She told Appanoose to cut Hutchinson free. "You're coming with me."

59

Leah escorted Hutchinson to a small side door near the corner of the hangar that led out to the tarmac. Before opening it, she said, "I want you to look out there and tell me if there's an airplane that can fly to Antarctica. I don't want to shoot you in the back, so keep it friendly and don't try to set the base record in the hundred-meter dash."

"No, ma'am. Wouldn't even think of it." Hutchinson hesitated, even after Leah had pulled open the door. "I'm really sorry about Mr. Moon, ma'am. We all thought he was really cool—and he was a pilot, too."

"Captain, you have no idea the shitstorm we've had to survive for what seems like forever. If I seem...harsh, you'll have to forgive me."

"Yes, ma'am. Those of us assigned to the Settlement, we all really believed in what you were doing. We're not like those guys we had onboard the bird."

"I hope that's true. It seems we're surrounded by people who want us dead, and for no good reason.... Now take a look and tell me what we've got."

Leah kept a hand on the back of Captain Hutchinson's flight suit while they stepped outside the hangar. A line of F-22 Raptor fighters and two C-130 Hercules sat on the apron, also two C-17 Globemaster transports.

"What've we got, Captain?"

"The F-22s are no good, unless you're flying them yourself."

"Nope," Leah said. "My flying skills are limited to backseat driving in a Cessna 172. I also need room for all the Ancients, a medical team and gear."

"The two C-130s would work. Are you planning to land on ice?"

"Yes on the landing, nope on the C-130. I flew back from Antarctica on a C-130. Slow as molasses and had to be refueled like a dozen times, or so it seemed. I need something that doesn't have to be refueled, is fast, comfortable, and can handle all my gear."

She pointed toward the C-17 Globemaster: a massive four-engine jet transport that looked as if you could load half a city block, cars and all, in the cargo hold. "What about those big boys?"

"It won't make Antarctica, ma'am. It has a range of around seven-thousand miles. Gotta be eight-thousand, maybe nine-thousand, just to reach the continent from here." He shook his head. "It's heavy, like five-hundred thousand pounds loaded. Maybe three-hundred thousand with fuel. It would crash land on a non-prepared runway."

"Any runways that might support that monster in Antarctica?"

"McMurdo. Amundsen-Scott won't work for the C-17. The only place you can land the C-17 is on the Ross Ice Shelf at McMurdo. It's too heavy to land on the snow runway at the South Pole."

"Damn." *Roadblocks at every turn.*

"The C-17 could make it with one inflight refueling though,"

"Something that big can be refueled inflight?"

"Yes, ma'am. United States Air Force. Global. Airborne. Range," Hutchinson said, proudly.

"How much is Holloman worth, Captain? With all the aircraft and facilities?" *She could use the Hafnium warhead one more time if she had to.*

"Billions. There's a couple billion in jets, sitting right in front of us with the F-22s and the C-17s. The Globemasters are two-hundred and fifty million dollars—each. That's just a fraction of what's here." Hutchinson studied the tarmac and their surroundings. "Ah, Dr. Andrews. Probably not a good idea to stand out here, exposed like this. The Delta Platoon will be headed back and I suspect their mission will simply be re-tasked to take the two hangars. A Delta sniper could get you from a thousand meters, easy, standing out in the open."

"I appreciate the heads-up, and I know how those guys operate. But they'll be trying to figure out what happened to their helo for another two hours."

"Were you in the military? You seem to know a lot about military logistics—or lack of."

"Far from it. Let's just say I've had a career's worth of military BS in the last few weeks."

"We're you able to engage with the SEAL platoon the RUMINT said was dropped in to take you off the ice?"

"Rumint?"

"Oh, sorry. That's military for a mix of rumor and intel."

"Heroes in every sense of the word, Captain. The only military I've run into worth a damn.... Present company excluded."

Once back inside the hangar, Leah said. "You hungry, Captain?"

"Yes, ma'am. The last time we ate was last night."

"I need you for another fifteen minutes, then I'm going to cut you and rest of the helicopter crews loose."

Hutch eased visibly, grinning.

"That happy to be freed, Captain?"

"No, ma'am. I've got to take a leak so bad my back teeth are floating. I think I can hold it for fifteen more minutes."

"Oh, for Christ's sake. Go to the hanger restroom and meet me back at the rear of the Chinook." She raised her eyebrows, but not the barrel of the HK. "Remember. I still have your crew tied up. Don't make me shoot each one between the eyes because you disappeared."

She barely heard the 'Yes, ma'am," as he sprinted toward the hangar restrooms.

60

L ess than eight hours after his brief conversation with Teresa Simpson, Paulson sat in the command seat of the Cessna Citation X. He was in the process of setting up the computerized navigation systems that would fly the aircraft first to Lisbon, Portugal, for fuel, then on to Istanbul, Turkey, to refuel again, then out over the waters of the Black Sea. He'd tried to avoid Istanbul but given the Citation X's range of 3,700 miles, it couldn't be helped.

If all went as planned, Paulson would inform Air Traffic Control he was descending down to five-hundred feet AGL so his 'onboard photographers' could shoot video of the Black Sea for an up-coming documentary. From there, he'd put the spurs to it, go feet-dry on the Turkish border and fly the five-hundred or so miles at sand level, cross the Iranian border, land at the airfield, pick Hobson up, exit the same way, and roll into Athens, Greece, on fumes.

The most important piece of information had come less than three hours ago. Jack had called Karen back and given her a run-down on the airfield. A single runway, about eight-thousand feet long, with a bomb crater rendering some two-thousand feet on the north end unusable. That left six-thousand feet for the Citation. For landing, that was no problem. The jet required less than four-thousand feet of runway. For take-off, it was a whole lot dicier. They'd be fine, assuming Jack's measurements were correct and the runway was solid for six-thousand. The X needed five-thousand plus for takeoff. It'd be running light, which would help; a breeze down the center line would be nice as well.

Which reminded him of something he'd forgotten. Paulson wanted to make sure they had a wind reference. If the airfield was missing a windsock, he'd need another way to determine wind direction and wind speed.

Although not a pilot, Jack Hobson was a seasoned airman. He was experienced at guiding aircraft into and out of tight places. Many of them not even airports—just a long stretch of grass, gravel, lake, river, you name it. Paulson had to count on the fact that Jack would know they'd need a reference for landing—and make that happen. The most important item he had: GPS coordinates for the center of the runway: *39.631803, 44.600669.*

Paulson pushed the reading glasses up on his forehead and leaned back onto the command pilot seat, talking to himself.

"This isn't going to work. This is about a dumb-ass plan as I've ever attempted."

Paulson had sent Ridley on a visual inspection of the aircraft's exterior, looking for signs of hydraulic leaks, loose fittings, anything that could jeopardize the flight.

"Bird looks good, Al." Ridley said, poking his head into the small cockpit. "I can guarantee it will get you into Iran—from there it's up to you to keep us from augering-in on some Persian mountaintop."

Paulson glanced up, the reading glasses now back down on his nose.

"Christ," Ridley growled. "If you can't set up the aircraft without those soda-bottle reading glasses, how the hell are you gonna fly this thing, in the dark, low on the deck?"

"I won't need these glasses for flying the mountains." Paulson reached down into his bag and pulled out another pair, with lenses equally thick. "These are ones I need to see distance."

"Jesus, Mary, and Joseph," Ridley said. "You honestly think this is a workable plan, Al?"

Paulson pushed the glasses back up on his head, his expression grim. "We've done a lot of flying and lying together, Mac. Truthfully, this is a cluster. If we don't get shot down after crossing the border into eastern Turkey, or shot down over northern Iran, or auger-in at any of the above, we'll probably run out of gas before reaching the first safe refuel location in Athens. And even that's dodgy close."

61

After his visit to the hangar bathroom, Captain Hutchinson stood at the rear of the Chinook. Leah had already told the balance of the helo crews they'd be freed in a matter of minutes. The amount of squirming indicated they had to 'go' as well.

"Captain, come on up here."

The Chinook was empty with the exception of the restrained helo crews and the Hafnium warhead. Leah pointed to the warhead sitting in the cradle.

"You know what that is, Captain?"

"No, ma'am. Custom beer keg?"

"Good one. I'll introduce you to my husband if we live through this. You two will get along just fine." She took four steps to reach the warhead and knelt next to it.

"Come on over—get a closer look."

Hutchinson walked over and knelt beside Leah.

"This is a classified, top secret nuclear warhead."

Hutch stood and stumbled back two steps.

"It's called an Iso-Hafnium warhead, and the monster explosion that took place in Antarctica? That was just one of these bad boys…. The only reason I'm alive, talking to you now—is that we had this one hidden near the Gila National Forest. How we obtained the warhead is a long story, and should we survive, my husband Jack will tell it to you for hours on end."

Leah stood. "President Wheeler and his flunky named Stan Fischer tried to kill us on multiple occasions. While it might sound crazy, we used this warhead as blackmail to keep ourselves alive." She shrugged. "And it did, in fact, do that job."

Hutchinson nodded, his face grim. "Yes, ma'am. Guessing the KIA—Marko, I think you said his name was—was part of your crew."

Leah nodded. "Marko Kinney was about your age. We don't know what happened to Luke Derringer, a pilot who lived at a nearby airfield." She paused, then glanced up at Hutchinson. "You did overhear the conversation I had with the goons…."

"Yes, ma'am. Couldn't help but listen in on that Gucci-level spook intelligence."

"I'm going to need you up to speed here in a moment. Anything you overheard bother you, Captain?"

Hutchinson opened his eyes wide, and for the first since she'd been working with the Army pilot, he looking genuinely pissed off. "Yes, ma'am. Sounds like our president has gone off his rocker, hiring some ex-black ops thugs to clean up his mess." Hutchinson was just getting warmed up. "Turns out the lead dog, Krause, is a slimy double-agent. He knocks off some Wheeler advisor, killing two birds with one stone."

"Fischer. Stan Fischer, Captain."

Hutchinson nodded. "Right. Fischer. So, Krause kills Fischer to get rid of one of Mr. Wheeler's liabilities, but before he does that, Krause water-boards Fischer with a knife blade, until he is satisfied he knows every detail about the Antarctica operation. He might have sold that 'secret squirrel' to the Russians for a stack of 'cheddar' that reaches right into the stratosphere." Hutchinson shrugged. "President Wheeler should have known. You live with pigs, you're gonna get dirty. Krause then murdered two of your crew in cold blood and won the big prize: flying lessons, out the back of the Hook." Hutchinson grinned wicked. "Play stupid games, win stupid prizes."

"Secret squirrel?" Leah asked, unable to prevent herself from shaking her head in disbelief. "Cheddar, Captain?"

"Ah, yes, ma'am. Secret squirrel. That's helicopter pilot talk for ultra-top secret. You won't hear it around here much...it's more of an Afghanistan thing. Cheddar—big wad of cash."

"Excellent," Leah said. "I'll remember not to recite my ATM pin in you're ever in line behind me." Leah picked up Krause's bag and fished around for the satellite phone that had been tucked in under the HK magazines and energy bars. "I cannot talk to this asshole without going ballistic. I'm trying to be a little more...user-friendly—with people that is.... Therefore, to avoid going off the rails, and embarrassing myself, probably even saying stuff that would be better off held close to my vest, you'll have the pleasure."

"This asshole?"

"President Wheeler," Leah said, powering up the satellite communicator, hoping that the number she needed would be keyed into the phone on speed-dial or re-dial, and easily identifiable. Sure enough, the only number listed was labeled POTUS.

Hutchinson's eyes opened wide. "You want me to talk to the president of the United States?"

"He won't be for long, if that makes it any easier."

Hutchinson stood at attention. "I'm good, ma'am—just a little shocked."

"Get used to it, Captain. The shocks come at such a rate, pretty soon you'll go numb."

Leah dialed Krause's sat phone and the president answered almost immediately. "Hello? Hello? Hello?" in rapid succession. The man sounded on the edge. She handed the phone to Captain Hutchinson.

"The President is on the phone. Introduce yourself, Captain. Tell him whose 'wonderful' company you're in—where you're at, and why." She whispered, "Leave Krause out for the moment. We'll get to that."

Hutchinson did as he was instructed. He had to stop numerous times while Wheeler interrupted. Leah heard Wheeler's voice an octave higher than normal, his breathing ragged.

"If he hasn't yet had a stroke, Captain, I'd like you to tell him what happened to Mr. Fischer—not that we know, exactly."

"Dr. Andrews said to tell you that Mr. Fischer is dead. Killed by Mr. Krause."

High-pitched screaming dominated the other end of the line for a few moments.

Hutchinson looked over at Leah as he spoke to the President. "Ah...no, sir. Mr. Krause is not here. He went off the ramp of the Hook—I mean the Chinook, sir."

Hutchinson nodded while decoding the screaming. "No, sir. He didn't walk off. He was thrown off. Guesstimate, three-thousand AGL...and at cruise speed. Sir." The line was dead silent. Then came measured, controlled questioning.

Hutchinson nodded once again. "Ah, no, sir. I'm not at liberty to discuss who exactly threw Mr. Krause out the back of the Hook." He nodded again. "Three of his men were killed when Dr. Leah's Ancients cut their throats, capturing my Black Hawk. Two others accepted the Red Bull Challenge as well, sir. That's right. Off the ramp—approximately the same altitude."

"Captain, before he has a stroke, kindly relate our conversation with Krause and company. Hit the highlights, as we discussed."

After Hutchinson ran down everything that had happened overnight, there was a longer pause on Wheeler's end of the connection. Leah wondered if the president had disconnected the call. Wheeler came back and Leah heard the president ask who, including Dr. Andrews, had overheard the conversations with Krause and his crew.

"There are multiple witnesses, Mr. President. Including military personnel unattached to the operation." Hutchinson looked over at Leah and winked. "No sir, I'm not at liberty to disclose those identities—for good reason, as I'm sure you'd agree."

The kid's getting into the groove. Leah was thankful to have another ally. There was only one more item that she needed to have confirmed by an independent source.

"Time for the bombshell," she whispered to Hutchinson. She nodded in the direction of the Hafnium bomb. "Tell him it's Groundhog Day all over again, Captain. I have the Hafnium warhead in my possession."

Hutchinson relayed the information, as told.

Leah pulled a zipper on her flight suit, and pulled out the plastic bag, covered in Marko's blood, opened it and pulled out the typed sheets with both the code to the weapon, and the lengthy, and complicated initializing and de-initializing instructions. Leah was anticipating Wheeler's next question.

"Yes, sir. She's holding what appear to be codes of some kind. Little hard to see, sir, the plastic bag is covered Mr. Kinney's blood. Sir."

Leah indicated it was time to hand over the phone. Hutchinson handed it over and stepped away. "I'm really all out of threats, Wheeler. No matter how many times you get hit over the head with a bat, you return to the same self-destructive behavior. Believe it or not, I'm doing you a favor. I'm leaving the country for an active war zone...."

She paused a moment while he raged, waiting for him to fall silent.

"You can calculate the odds of me getting off the ice in Antarctica alive as slim—perhaps none. Why I'm heading to Antarctica is on a need-to-know basis—and you have no need to know. The Ancients are with me, along with Dr. Gordon and a select medical team." She paused to draw a deep breath and refocus. Wheeler hadn't even bothered to respond, so she took a two more breaths. "I honestly have no idea if Jack and Al, are alive. I've tried both of them on satellite phones. No success."

"They are alive, as far as I know," Wheeler said, breathless and wheezing. The stress of poor decision-making was having a lethal effect on his health. She could hear it in every labored breath. It was pointless to further humiliate or threaten a man who was soon to be dead. She needed him to do two more things.

"There are two C-17s here at Holloman. I need one to fly me down to McMurdo. My pilots tell me that it has a range of 7,000 miles, so we'll need at least one inflight refueling."

"Might not be possible," Wheeler, said over the satellite phone, his wheezing getting worse. "The energy beam—triggered when you accessed the complex—has created a communication black-out over the Antarctic. Not just communications, all navigational tools necessary for aircraft navigation. We've already lost several aircraft under Visual Flight Rules and suffered ten fatalities when a transport went into the sea after losing contact on final approach with the Bush."

"Then you better have a few good pilots here at Holloman, be-cause I'm going even if we have to navigate with divining rods. Grant my wishes and you're rid of me—once and for all."

62

Leah stood at the mirror in the bathroom, distantly regarding the stranger staring back. The creases in her cheeks and lines of fatigue around her eyes told a tale that she didn't care to hear again. Leah leaned heavily on the sink; she didn't have the strength to stand any longer. Not only was she bone-tired, she also faced an impossible road ahead.

Even if she got the Ancients to Antarctica, she lacked the skills to search for the second complex. The Ancients, on the other hand, had been bio-engineered to withstand cold temperatures and high altitudes. With Appanoose leading them, perhaps they'd find what he seemed so sure, was there.

Leah was almost to the point that she didn't care anymore. Even if it was a certainty the Ancients would die on Antarctica, at least they'd be free and making those final decisions themselves—for themselves. She closed her eyes for a moment. Only the sound of the door to the bathroom opening prevented her from dropping into REM sleep still leaning against the sink.

"Dr. Andrews?" A soft female voice spoke.

Leah turned around. One of Gordon's laboratory technicians stood at the door. She held several freshly laundered towels, a fresh flight suit, and toiletries. "We know you must be exhausted. I put together some things for you.... I can take you to our personal shower trailer if you'd like to freshen up?"

Leah struggled to ignore the cramping quad muscles in the front of her legs. A sure sign she was dehydrated, in addition to the crushing fatigue.

"That'd be nice," she said, following the lab tech out of the bathroom and into the adjoining hangar.

⌐⊻⌐⊻⌐

The twenty-minute hot shower, shampoo, soap, and skin cream supplied by the lab tech did wonders both for her state of mind and her body. Once she'd dressed in a fresh flight suit, with her hair pulled back into a single ponytail, her next thoughts were food.

Leah asked where she could get something to eat, and one of the medical personal pointed out a large trailer located in the center of the hangar. Leah walked over toward the trailer, still trying to free her muscles from the cramping. When she opened the door and stepped into the mess-hall-in-a-trailer, she was shocked to see the crew from both the Black Hawk and the Chinook sitting together at one table, drinking coffee and talking non-stop, hands flying as they no doubt described the flight from the meadow back to Holloman and everything that had gone down during said flight.

"What the hell are you boys doing here? I was pretty sure when I cut off the restraints, I said you were free to go. Why aren't you being debriefed by the Base Commander?"

Captain Hutchinson looked at his fellow pilots and crew. They all nodded in agreement. It appeared he'd been tasked with whatever they wanted to say.

"Spit it out, Captain. You of all people know that I don't have all day."

"Yes, ma'am. Well, uh...we'd like to go with you—to Antarctica."

"Yeah. Right. Look—you guys aren't in any trouble. You were my hostages. Remember?"

"Yes, ma'am. It's just—well, we're talking about history here. I mean, history that will stand right up with Moses on the Mount."

She looked from Hutchinson to the other officers. "What the hell are you talking about?"

"We were all onboard the Hook during the call with the President. We know that you're headed to Antarctica to return the Ancients to an extra-terrestrial base—if it's really there. I mean, if that's not the bomb of all bombs to tell your grandchildren, I don't know what is."

Leah crossed her arms. She had to admire the chutzpah, even it reminded her a bit too much of Jack when he went over the top on some adventure. "If I said yes, you'd be classified AWOL and domestic terrorists. Your military careers would be over. If you survived, and the chances of that are near zero, you'd spend the rest of your life in Leavenworth. There won't be any grandchildren, Captain."

Before Hutchinson could continue, his co-pilot Lieutenant Cruz spoke up. "And we're helicopter pilots, ma'am. You might need helicopter pilots, you know, to find this place, ferry the Ancients...."

Strange, it almost sounded as if he were pleading.

"I guess you guys didn't hear a word I said... I'll have to refuse your generous offer..."

All six of the crew hung their heads in a physical display of infinite disappointment. It wasn't a stretch to remember how badly she'd wanted to go to Antarctica—how stubborn Jack could be when he had a goal in mind, no matter that it would kill him and whoever else he took along.

Six young, strong, well-educated men with piloting skills and combat experience, who say, 'How high?' every time I tell them to jump...?

"Okay. If you guys are trying to win the beat-dog Academy Award, you've done it."

They looked up, fresh hope in their eyes.

"This is how it goes down. You are still my hostages. That won't keep you from getting killed on the ice, but maybe keep you out of prison, on the slim chance you survive and make it home." She pointed at Hutchinson. "I have a job for your crew. Get on the phone with the Base Commander. Do you know him?"

"Yes, ma'am."

"Your job is to gather as much cold weather gear as you can. I told Dr. Gordon to do this, but he's got plenty on his plate already. Those one-piece winter suits the aircraft handlers and mechanic use would be a good start. Parkas, hats, mittens, not gloves. Trust me when I say your hands will freeze in gloves, even during the summer. Kelleher will have already been told by President Wheeler to provide whatever we need. He may ask questions. Remember: You are my hostages. You know nothing." Leah hesitated. "We're headed into a war zone. Gather automatic weapons and plenty of ammo and magazines. No bazookas, though—got it?"

Hutchinson nodded.

"That was a test, Captain. You CANNOT gather automatic weapons! You're a hostage. Don't forget it."

The look of horror on Hutchinson's face would have Leah busting a gut in the old days. Instead, she simply continued, "Make up a list, tell Kelleher what 'I' want, then have him deliver it to Gordon."

Leah addressed the Chinook crew. "The Ancients have metabolisms working way, way faster than ours. They eat—a lot. I need you to have the mess hall cook up, and package up as much corn and beans as possible. Also, get several cases of the MREs and a hundred gallons of water."

The crews sat there, frozen in place. Leah clapped her hands. "That's it, boys. Get to it!"

They stood as one.

"Wait" Leah shouted. They all froze. "Hutchinson. You stay for a second."

The other five bolted.

"Yes, ma'am?"

"The warhead is still in the rear inside the Chinook."

"Do you want us to load it into the Globemaster?"

"Negative, Captain." Leah reached into her flight suit and brought out the two sheets of paper with the codes to the Hafnium warhead. "I think Freddy Kruger's done his job. Do you have a lighter, Captain?"

"No ma'am. I don't smoke."

"Excellent, Captain. That was a test. If you smoked, I'd have to leave you behind. Second-hand smoke is a killer."

Hutchinson stood frozen for a second, not grasping her sense of humor. Then he grinned. "No ma'am. Never touch those things."

"Go over to the grill. See if they have wooden matches, or a lighter of some kind."

Hutchinson was back in a moment with a standard barbeque-style grill lighter. He handed over to Leah. She lit the two sheets at the bottom with the lighter, allowing them to burn up until she had to drop them on an empty plate on the table. In seconds, all that remained was a pile of smoking ash.

"Tell Dr. Gordon the warhead is disarmed and now his responsibility. He'll be thrilled."

"Yes, ma'am. Anything else?"

"I have a whole list for you. Get to it."

Hutchinson disappeared without another word. Leah sat for a moment, catching her breath. Then she stood and pushed away from the table. The mess-hall aroma was better than any Michelin-rated restaurant's, and suddenly she was starving.

63

"D r. Andrews."

A hand was on her shoulder, gently waking her. Leah looked up. She was still in the mess hall. After eating the bacon, eggs, and a mound of hash browns, she'd fallen asleep right at the table, her head down on her folded arms.

Gordon stood over her.

"We're ready to go."

"We are?" Leah glanced down at her watch. Had she really slept at the table for nearly three hours?

"We decided not to wake you—you're exhausted. The C-17's fueled, the crew is aboard, the young helicopter pilots have been a godsend. They gathered enough cold weather gear to outfit an entire brigade, the same for hot food in heated containers, plus water. They've all had medical training, which allowed me to leave my personnel here—most have families."

"What about K'aalógii?"

"She's under with Propofol. Doing fine. All her vital signs have fallen into a range I'm comfortable with—I did take a liberty with the Ancients, however."

"Yeah?"

"I gave all of them, with the exception of Appanoose, a sedative. We want to avoid the stress of the flight bringing on symptomatic disorders, if it can be avoided."

"Good, thinking, Gordo. What's left to do?"

"Get you on board the aircraft—you're the last one on the manifest still in the hangar."

Leah stood and stretched. The cramps were gone and the food, along with the deep sleep, made her felt as if she might pull this off.

"Let's do it, Gordo. We're burning daylight."

Gordon nodded, but before he could open the door leading out of the mess hall, Leah said. "Coffee. I gotta have coffee."

In moments, the mess chef handed her a steaming cup, and a large thermos to go with it. "Thanks," she told him. "You might have just saved Dr. Gordon's life."

The C-17 Globemaster looked large when parked down the tarmac. Now that it was backed up to *Dragon Two*, it wasn't simply large, it was massive. Leah stopped for a second and stared at the behemoth. *This'll be like landing a 747 on a frozen lake. What could possibly go wrong?*

Like the Chinook, it featured a cargo-loading ramp large enough to load battle tanks. The interior of the aircraft could have doubled for an airport terminal; it was that enormous. The forward part of the aircraft had been fitted with temporary airline style seating. The Ancients, sporting flight suits, slumped back in the seats, asleep. The exception: Appanoose. He stood with his arms crossed, studying the fuselage.

When he saw Leah, he ran toward the loading ramp, the excited expression on the normally stoic shaman's face a shocking change from the norm. He hovered over her like a mother hen as she worked through the fuselage, grabbing her arm twice when she tripped on the equipment tie-downs. Leah whispered to him in Navajo. One head snap said he understood. She'd told him she'd be speaking with the crew, without using that exact terminology. That he should sit, that everything was yisdá. Translation: The Ancients were in a safe place.

On the way to the cockpit, she motioned to Captain Hutchinson. He jumped up and walked alongside. "You're with me, Captain. I need to chat with the pilot of this rig."

Leah squeezed into the cockpit shocked to see the gray-haired Base Commander in the command pilot seat. "Colonel, Kelleher. You really didn't need to join us for what might be a one-way trip...."

Kelleher replied with a mix of arrogance and irritation. "This is an expensive and critical piece of military hardware—and the pilots are not expendable. I've got almost fifteen-hundred hours in the Globemaster, and there's no way I'm letting this aircraft depart without taking personal responsibility for both."

Leah noted that, in addition to a co-pilot, three additional pilots were crammed into the cockpit. One man and two women. "Colonel, looks like you invited the entire pilot staff at Holloman. Why?"

"This is a long and dangerous flight," he snapped. "I'm not current on air-to-air refueling, so Major Jane West and her crew will handle the refueling. The two other pilots are the primary crew on the second Globemaster. I want to have plenty of relief backing us up in case this gets hairy."

Major West, sitting in the co-pilot seat, smiled, and Leah nodded in return. "I don't know exactly what President Wheeler told you regarding my status and our mission. Care to give me a quick briefing?"

Kelleher softened a bit. "He said the aircraft was at your disposal, not to ask any questions, and do exactly as Dr. Andrews asked." He turned around in the command seat. "We have set up navigation to take us direct to McMurdo. Is there a secondary?"

"McMurdo, unless you hear from me otherwise." She glanced at the pilots. "I know about the geo-magnetic disturbance that is blacking out Antarctica. I told Wheeler I was going to Murdo with divining rods if necessary. I'm not particularly interested in killing everyone onboard, but I am going to Antarctica. What are the chances we can land on the Ross Ice Shelf without crashing?"

Kelleher nodded in the direction of the pilot sitting in the co-pilot seat. "Major West flew into McMurdo not long ago, part of the big airlift operation to evacuate McMurdo personnel after the detonation in Antarctica. She knows more about the approach than I do."

Major Jane West held up a chart that featured the Antarctic continent. A number of concentric circles had been printed over the chart. "The geo-magnetic disturbance gets stronger the closer you get to the original ground zero coordinates. If you said you were flying to Amundsen-Scott in a bird with skis, like a C-130 for instance, I would have taken my wings off and tossed them on the Colonel's desk. There's no way I'm flying that route. There have been a number of aircraft who have tried to penetrate deep into Antarctica, that have simply disappeared for unknown reasons. One theory is this disturbance is disrupting the computer-controlled flight control systems, beyond just the loss of GPS signals needed for navigation, causing them to crash."

West pointed to the Ross Ice Shelf on the chart. "You can see that we are on the outer circle here. We won't have GPS or any satellite communications the last two-hundred nautical. That means we're flying VFR, Visual Flight Rules, into the ice runway at Murdo." She shook her head. "If the weather goes bad, we can't do it, without killing everyone onboard and losing the aircraft."

Leah nodded. "Thank you, Major. We'll worry about that problem when we cross it." She thought about her prepared speech. It didn't seem necessary, given how much pressure Wheeler had put on Kelleher to 'get her to Antarctica,' but how often had she been lied to and double-crossed?

"I want to issue a warning to you, Colonel, and to your crew."

Kelleher couldn't help himself and rolled his eyes.

Arrogant bastard, about to get a schooling.

"Captain Hutchinson. Do you consider me a person that you should test on any level?"

"No, ma'am," Hutchinson said crisply.

"What happened to the last guy who messed with me?"

"Ah—you had the big fella toss him out the back of the Hook."

"Was the Chinook on the ground, Captain?"

"No, ma'am—at least three-thousand AGL."

The change was instantaneous. Kelleher went from arrogant bird-colonel to white-faced and sweating.

Leah continue to press. "Captain Hutchinson. Do you have any doubt, if Colonel Kelleher or his crew were to cross me, I would hesitate to drop the ramp and throw the Colonel out?"

"None whatsoever, ma'am."

"What advice would you have for anyone on this flight who decided they wanted to test me?"

The young captain hesitated, then said, "Ah—don't fly any higher than you're willing to fall?"

She patted him on the shoulder. "Excellent. I couldn't have selected a better hostage."

As Leah was climbing back out of the cockpit, she heard Kelleher ask Hutchinson if she had really ordered a person tossed out of the Chinook. His response, totally uncoached, was precious. "Three traitors went off the ramp. Sir."

Leah continued into the cargo bay without comment.

64

The Citation X flew over the Black Sea at an altitude of ten-thousand feet. Paulson informed the ATC, as planned, that he carried photographers and would be descending to five-hundred feet and flying visual flight rules for an undermined period of time.

Once cleared, Paulson dropped the nose of the X and descended to an altitude of five-hundred and fifty feet over the surface of the Black Sea, flying the heading he'd charted to take them over the coast of Turkey and into Iran just after nightfall.

At fifty miles out, Paulson shut off the navigation lights and pressed forward on the yoke, dropping the Citation to within two hundred feet of the water's surface while pushing the throttles until the jet was speeding at more than four-hundred knots.

"This is it, Mac. Any last words?"

"Yeah. Don't hit the ground—or anything else for that matter."

"I have the coast in sight," Paulson said, minutes later.

He glanced at Ridley, who was holding on for dear life. The nose of the X pitched up and then down as Paulson flew it down as low as fifty feet, leapfrogging obstacles at nearly five-hundred knots of indicated airspeed.

"Like riding a bike," Paulson said as beads of sweat ran down Ridley's face. "Once a fighter pilot, always a fighter pilot."

"Remember, Al. I'm the one who had to fix up those jets every time you busted something—which was often."

"Iranian airspace in eight minutes," Paulson called out." I sure hope Jack got the runway clear of debris and hung up a windsock; otherwise we're going to make a hell of a fireball."

Jack Hobson was hidden between the buildings of the rundown Iranian airfield. He should have been looking to the northwest, the direction Paulson would be coming in at low altitude, if he hadn't already been killed in a crash. Instead, Jack was using a pair of binoculars to study the traffic on the dirt highway that crossed south of the airfield by a matter of a few kilometers. The traffic was about half civilian and half military this close to the border. So far, no one had turned north toward the airfield, but that would change the instant a jet came screaming overhead.

He swung binoculars over to where the ragged windsock still flew over the airport. The wind was blowing out of the north. That meant Paulson would have to overfly the airport, make a one-hundred-and-eighty degree turn, land, avoid the bomb crater, turn around, get Jack aboard, taxi to the end of the runway, and takeoff.

From touchdown, Jack estimated it would take five minutes to slow the jet, turn it around, pick him up, high-speed taxi, turn around again, and pour the coal to it.

Hawar and his sons Kajir and Camir also hid behind the buildings, with weapons ready. Bazi held the horses at the nearby rock-outcropping they'd hidden within, waiting for Paulson's approach.

Jack had tried to convince the Kurds to leave. Even if he got off safe, they'd still be stuck on the ground. If Iranian solders showed up, they'd have to fight their way out. Hawar said he did not fear

Iranian soldiers, only the wrath of God for leaving Jack at the airfield solo after guaranteeing his protection. *That*, he said, was something to fear.

"Who could argue with that?" Jack had said, thankful for the armed company.

He was swinging the binoculars back toward the road once again, when he heard the turbine whine of a medium-sized jet approaching from the north, already within a half mile of the runway. Either Al had guessed the wind direction or seen the windsock in the pre-dawn light. He was setting up for a right-hand pattern. He'd fly past the runway, make a descending turn to base, then final, and set the jet down on the numbers. Without blowing the tires—Jack hoped.

He swung the binoculars back toward the highway—nothing turning toward the runway at high speed. All that praying he'd been doing might have paid off—he'd have to tell Badger...if he made it out alive. The old preacher would be thrilled.

The jet had made the turn and was on short final. Jack wasn't sure if Paulson was going to make the runway, he was down so low over the sand on a flat final approach, nose high, rolling in more throttle, not pulling the throttles back to idle, as Jack expected.

The rear gear touched down no more than five feet from the end of the tarmac, the nose gear swiftly followed, and dust flew when both brakes and reverses were applied. Jack didn't see a whole lot of dust. He turned to hug Hawar, Kajir, and Camir, saying his goodbyes before sprinting for the slowing aircraft.

The jet's hatch dropped down even before the jet had stopped and Mac Ridley's creased smile was the first thing that popped out of the open door. Jack ran to catch up, reached up, and Ridley reached out, grabbing Jack by the wrist and pulling him up as Jack touched maybe one of the stairs before throwing himself inside the Citation.

Ridley operated the door closing mechanism and Paulson swung the aircraft around so fast it pinned Jack against the fuselage. Paulson taxied down the three-thousand feet he'd used on landing in less than a minute, jammed on the brakes, swung the jet one-hundred and eighty degrees once again, and firewalled the throttles, causing both Ridley and Jack to tumble back toward the rear of the aircraft.

Once they were airborne, Ridley climbed up and plopped himself into the co-pilot's while Jack worked his head and shoulders into the cockpit. He got a side glance at Paulson and was shocked to see how worn he looked. This was a man who normally needed two hours a sleep at night and happily worked the other twenty-two. Even on Everest, he'd never seen Paulson looking this beat.

Paulson spun around for a moment and grinned. "You look like hell, Jack. When was the last time you slept?"

"I was going to say the same," Jack said. "Does that mean my suspicions were right? Wheeler's gone nuts and all hell is breaking loose?"

Paulson kept his eyes on the terrain as the X rolled over the four-hundred knot mark, and he held the altitude at less than two-hundred feet AGL, just about to cross the Turkish border, headed for the Black Sea again.

"Mac. Fill Jack in. If I so much as sneeze, we're going to make a large pile of scrap aluminum."

Ridley turned, grabbed a thermos of coffee and a bag of sweet rolls. "Yeah—what we have here is a class-a-number-one cluster-funk."

"Leah," Jack said. "Where's Leah?"

"She's still at the Settlement," Ridley said. "Last time we checked, the trouble-maker hadn't cut her throat."

"Mac!" Paulson said.

Ridley shrugged and grinned. "C'mon, Al. Just keeping it real." Then he added, "Don't worry about Leah. From what Al thinks, this might some kind of governmental coup—Leah's the least of their problems. Plus, she's surrounded by the Indians. Al says they turned out to be a lot less like nervous squirrels and more like pissed off wolverines. I'd bet she's sitting by the fire, listening to them tell stories, and having a hot cup of—well whatever those people drink. No worries."

Jack suddenly dug into his filthy backpack, and pulled out the two GoPro cameras. He removed them from the protective water and shock proof clear cases, and pulled the SD cards out of both. While the newer GoPro cameras had a playback feature, it was so small, it was hard to make out detail, especially in a low-light environment.

"Anyone got a laptop?" Jack asked.

Ridley pointed to a bag stuffed underneath a seat. Inside was a MacBook. Jack opened it—after he'd gotten the password from Ridley. It was one he wouldn't want to have to repeat in mixed company.

Jack pushed the disk into the slot and waited. When it opened on the home screen, he clicked on it and found several files. The first three had been testing the GoPro. The only thing on those files would be Jack's own mug, while he examined the camera, making sure it was operating. The fourth file was the one that had the goods: any video taken down inside the hot spring. He pulled it up, and was immediately thrilled to find a clear, well-lit underwater image.

He clicked on the file, and the camera, this one facing vertically down, began sinking, jerky at times, down into Jacob's Well. He only had to view the video for a minute to determine that what David Samuelson had seen was neither the filament, nor another alien complex. It was simply, a dome-shaped rock, polished smooth over time, perhaps by a glacier that had once slid over the top of it.

"Well?" Ridley was looking back at Jack. Paulson had no idea what he had been doing, he was still focused on getting them out to sea while avoiding both the ground, and anything resembling an air-to-air missile.

Jack shook his head. "Nothing worth risking our lives over."

Ridley simply flashed him a told-you-so look. "I think it's time we started looking out for ourselves. Each and every damn time we've stuck our neck out, we've been burned."

Jack nodded on agreement. "What's your plan, Mac?"

Ridley pointed a finger. "I tell you what my damn plan is—if they're trying to kill me, I'll give them a shot at it, while I'm coming at them with a Desert Eagle aimed right between their eyes."

Jack grinned. "Now that's a plan I can get behind."

65

A lexi had the sniper scope up to his eye before Grigoriy could pull his Swarovski glasses from the gear bag. "Contact?"

Grigoriy seated the Swarovskis against his face. "Negative," he answered.

The sudden change of direction was wrong, Grigoriy thought. *Unnecessary.* SEALS didn't make arbitrary changes in direction unless something else was in play. "Distance to the pressure ridge?" he asked.

"Estimating three-thousand," Alexi responded without hesitation.

Grigoriy spun, focusing the binocs on their flank. Clear. He then scanned three-hundred and sixty degrees, his combat-honed alarm system still activated. "Forward 300 meters. Keep the Taigas in single file."

***

"Contact," Beckam said.

"Hell, yeah," Liam breathed, his eye pinned to his scope.

It was too far out to make out any details other than several points on the horizon that were non-natural, having just appeared minutes ago.

"I'm not making out any movement," Beckam said.

"Same here, Boss."

"Probably saw the change in direction on the Taigas."

"Maybe they're spooked. Probably tucking tail right around and head for Vladivostok."

Beckam chuckled. "Or it's SEALS, following Russian Taiga tracks, thinking those sneaky bastards are setting up an ambush."

"Too slow for SEALs," Liam said.

Beckam nodded. "Elements of the Spetsnaz. Reconnaissance, probably. They don't want to make contact."

"Bitches already made their first mistake," Liam said.

<hr/>

Grigoriy studied the pressure ridge from two-thousand meters out. He pulled the glasses away from his face and said in Russian: *"Truten."*

Vasily dug into a gear bag and lifted out a metallic case about the size of a carry-on piece of travel luggage. He opened the case: inside was a device resembling a high-tech version of a radio-control toy. It was made of aluminum and featured four propellers run by electric motors. Mounted on the bottom of the aluminum frame was a high-resolution camera on a pivot system that allowed the operator to move the camera nearly three-hundred and sixty degrees.

Alexi handed Grigoriy a pair of virtual-reality goggles and a twin toggle controller with a wide variety of switches and buttons aligned around the aluminum-encased remote. The last item he pulled out was a lithium battery the size of a brick. He was confident the drone also would work to a range of two kilometers. They'd tested handheld radios to that distance, without apparent negative effect by the atmospheric disturbance. The radio control drone could operate well beyond two kilometers, out of sight even, and on its own, with a highly sophisticated onboard computer system. He didn't intent to test it past two kilometers.

"Transmitter is on," Grigoriy said after flipping a switch. A red light lit on the transmitter panel. Vasily waited until the blinking red light on the transmitter had gone solid, then slid the battery into a compartment on the drone.

He made sure the electrical contacts were connected, then shut and locked the battery door. He switched the drone on, and a series of lights blinked to life. Three beeps later, the computer brain in the drone had initialized, and the light on transmitter had turned from solid red to green. The *Truten* was prepped and ready to fly.

Vasily held the drone over his head, and Grigoriy pushed the right lever up a notch. All four props spun up, and the drone took off, rising vertically to fifteen meters above the ice. Grigoriy hit a switch that placed the drone in an autopilot hover, then fitted the VR glasses over his eyes. He felt the switch that initiated the camera link and within a second, the panorama of Antarctica spread out before him. He tested the controls, overriding the hover autopilot. He'd hand fly the drone, but if he ever took his hands away from the controls it would spontaneously begin a hover and stay there until instructed otherwise or until the battery ran out of power. When operated in conjunction with GLONASS, he could send the drone out and it would automatically return when instructed and land, no additional control necessary. With both GLONASS and GPS systems offline, Grigoriy would be hand-flying the miniature craft.

He pushed the left stick forward and the drone accelerated away from the platoon in a flash. Grigoriy increased power and the drone gained altitude. He brought it up to 100 meters above ground level, the HD camera giving him a magnificent view of the pressure ridge and the horizon ahead. It had an effective range of between two and five kilometers but needed a line-of-sight connection between the drone and the transmitter for Grigoriy to maintain control. If the drone lost contact, it would simply go into a standard hover.

No matter, he thought. In a matter of seconds, *we'll see exactly what lies beyond that pressure ridge.*

66

Beckam was holding down on the drone with his MP5 as it flew up the center of the crevasse toward their position. The drone pilot had dropped altitude and speed as he homed in on the crevasse.

Beckam sighted on the drone through his scope; an easy shot flying straight at them at less than a fifty-meter altitude. When it got within sixty meters of their position and on line to overfly them, he opened-up with a short burst. The drone exploded into a shower of plastic and aluminum.

"Nice shot, Boss!" said Liam.

"If they had the camera pod aimed forward," Beckam said, "they already *made* us and our strength. From the angle of the camera, it appeared to be scanning the crevasse straight down. For all they know, we've got an entire company of SEALs lined up in here, ready to charge out like the light brigade."

"How long will that slow them down?"

"Wouldn't slow me at all if we had our guys and our weapons. I'd just set up a couple of light mortars, standoff half a mile away and lay down a line of fire on the crevasse."

Before Liam replied, the whistle of an incoming Russian mortar round signaled the Russian's thinking was close to his own. The first round went fifty meters long and a hundred meters to the left of their position.

Beckam was right. He'd shot down the drone before the Russians were able to make their position, strength, and capability. That bought them a couple of minutes before the commander got a bead on the crevasse and then walked those mortars laterally in both directions, killing them before they had a chance to return fire.

"Get me the extra coils of line."

Liam grabbed two coils of line hooked up on the wall of the crevasse.

"Clip onto the line through a pulley and drop the line down to the bottom of the crevasse. We're going to rappel down as far as we can go." Beckam unwound the line. "The chance of hitting us with the mortars are zero. We'll see how long it takes for the Russians to get curious and take a peek into the crevasse."

"Love it, Boss. What did Schwarzenegger say in the Predator movie? 'Dug in like an Alabama tick'?"

"Jesse Ventura, but the analogy is dead-on. We're gonna make ourselves a real pain in the ass to dig out."

67

Grigoriy crouched behind the snow machine, the Swarovskis pressed against his eye sockets, watching the mortars detonate as the team worked the range until they were hitting the crevasse. He watched two rounds in a row drop inside. "Progulki vlevo i vpravo."

The mortar team did as they were instructed, walking rounds left and then right, hoping to kill everything pinned down inside the crevasse.

Grigoriy didn't leave the cover provided by the snow machine but lifted up a bit in order to get a scan of the target zone. A thousand meters might seem safe, but an expert sniper could blow his head off even at that range.

Even with the mortars, he'd be lucky to eliminate the SEALs. They'd need a direct hit on their position, and even then, a smart commander would have his platoon spread out, working the natural terrain features inside the crevasse, providing cover from the mortar shrapnel. There'd been no return fire from the American position. Aside from one or perhaps two snipers with rifles and spotters looking over the lip of the crevasse, the commander had the balance of his guys dug in, saving ammunition, waiting for

Grigoriy to tire of the mortars and move up to take on the soldiers directly.

If only we had a 'crocodile,' he thought. *Five minutes with that and we'd flush them all out.*

Crocodile was a term Russian soldiers used for a lethal ground-attack helicopter: The M-24. The heavily armed gunship would make fast work of anyone, crevasse, or not, with a combination of machine guns and rockets.

If this were the deserts of Syria, Grigoriy could leisurely continue mortaring, while sipping hot coffee and munching sugar cookies. Down at the bottom of the world, they carried a total of thirty mortar rounds. The temperature hovered around minus twenty Celsius, at last check. And they only had food for another five days, ten if they went on half rations.

When he really thought about it, having no attack helicopters was likely the least of their problems.

68

Beckam and Clay had wedged themselves more than ten meters down in the crevasse, backs pressed against one wall, boots braced against the opposite side. The six mortar shells so far had bracketed them on the left, right, front and rear. Wedged this far down in the crevasse, it would have to be a perfect shot to kill them.

"They can't keep this up long, Boss. I think we got 'em right where we want them."

Beckam grunted. "Either they think we're dead or wounded."

"What's their best play, Boss?"

"They've got to keep moving. Getting side-tracked by us, running through their supplies and ammo in sub-zero temperatures.... If roles were reversed, I'd first try and eliminate or injure them, then cripple their ability to travel—wave bye-bye on my way to Amundsen-Scott. But we have no transportation. Pointless to waste ammo when the Antarctic will do the job for them."

Beckam heard the snow machines cranking up before moving off, quickly picking up speed and giving the crevasse a wide berth.

It wouldn't take long for the Russians to pick up Lenny and Danny's tracks. Hopefully pinning the Russians down for six hours had given the boys a solid head start for Amundsen. That wouldn't solve their problems, unless air support miraculously appeared or American troops had already made their way to Amundsen and set up a forward command post.

He'd have to leave it up to Lenny to come up with inventive ways to defend Amundsen if the civilians had not been evacuated.

"Oh, hell yeah, Skipper!" Liam was celebrating. "We kicked their ass! They're tucking tails and running."

Beckam grinned. "Yeah, we really kicked their ass, Frog. One problem."

"What's that?"

"We dumped the Taigas into the crevasse. No way we can winch snow machines up after wedging them in the ice, thirty meters down."

Liam was so stoked; he couldn't be deterred. "Couple of meat-eaters like ourselves—we'll walk to Amundsen Scott. We don't need no stinking snow machines."

Beckam nodded. 'I'm climbing up, take a look see."

When he got to the edge of the crevasse and was able to look out on the horizon, the Spetsnaz were already moving out of sight. Probably picked up Lenny's trail already.

"Okay, Frog. Have it your way. Let's walk it."

"Shit, yeah!" hollered Liam from down blow.

"Once you get up here, pull up one of those toboggans. We take all the gear we can on the sled, fix up a couple of harnesses, and get to it."

One hour later, with a light breeze blowing, and the remaining gear and ammo salvaged out of the crevasse, Beckam was ready to go. He'd used climbing line to configure a waist harness system that allowed the two SEALs to pull the sled.

Beckam glanced over at Liam, who was fitting an MP5 over his harness.

"I'm all set, Boss."

Beckam nodded. He paused for a second, still wondering how the boys ahead were doing. He hoped the crevasse stand-off showed the Spetsnaz that SEALs had teeth and would bite, regardless of the situation. A bit of caution on the Russians' part might be the small advantage Lenny and Danny needed to get to Amundsen. Once there, though, a whole new set of problems would arise.

One problem at a time, Beckam reminded himself.

"Any parting words, boss?"

Beckam grinned. "Embrace the suck, Frog."

Liam nodded, pulled a balaclava up over his nose, and took off at such a fast pace, Beckam had to jog to keep up.

Three or four hundred kilometers to Amundsen-Scott.

We're SEALs—piece of cake.

69

L eah woke to a light shake on the shoulder. Captain Hutchinson knelt next to her. "We're ready to refuel, Dr. Andrews. I thought you'd want to watch this from the cockpit. It's an amazing sight."

Leah nodded, then stretched and glanced at her watch. They'd already been in the air eight hours. She stood and twisted around, taking in a view of the Ancients. Most of them still slept. Appanoose, who remained wide awake and standing, had been silent so far.

She was shocked to find Colonel Kelleher hard asleep in the seat next to her. Then she remembered that Jane West had been tapped to command the refueling maneuver. Leah worked her hands along the seat tops, making her way toward the cockpit. The sun was about to set to the west, the last rays reflecting off the waves of the endless Atlantic Ocean below.

Major West was in the command pilot seat. Leah looked forward, expecting to find a refueling jet ahead, but the horizon was clear. The two jump seats at the rear of the cockpit were empty, so Leah slid into one of them.

"Hutchinson said you were refueling," Leah said. "I don't see a flying gas can."

West turned. "We're still thirty minutes north of the tanker. The weather is clear, light to zero turbulence—should be a piece of cake."

"Trust me when I say, I'm bad luck," Leah said wearily. "If anything can go wrong, it will."

"As pilots, we pretty much live with Murphy day and night. It's never the first thing that goes wrong that will kill you—it's when Murph decides he'll throw a few at you, all at once. We call that the Cascade to Hell."

"In my case, he threw me in an elevator and cut the cables. Cascaded my ass into a free-falling elevator."

Major West smiled, and Leah couldn't help but laugh.

"Can I ask you a question, Dr. Andrews?"

Leah expected the pilot wanted more detail about the operation in Antarctica—past and present. That was fine. Leah had already decided that everyone aboard deserved to know the whole truth.

"Sure—and just call me Leah."

When West turned, she flashed a sly smile, not exactly what Leah had been expecting. "So—your hostage—Captain Hutchinson. Is he single? Not for me, of course—but Captain Ross.... Char's just a wee bit smitten."

Charlotte nodded. "I'd like to have him as my hostage—for a month in Tahiti."

The pilots burst out laughing. Leah felt the galaxy-wide divide between her reality, an endlessly looping horror movie, and the 'normal' life these young military women were still enjoying.

"On a serious note," Major West said, apparently noting that Dr. Leah Andrews hadn't laughed, "we're coming up on this refueling and both Char and I will be super busy. But, we'd love to have you sit up front, and after the refueling, tell us *everything*. Colonel Kelleher said something about 'compartmentalized intelligence' and national security, then clammed up."

As it turned out, Leah slept through the entire refueling. When she woke, the tanker was a series of blinking lights in the distance. Captain Hutchinson was sitting in the starboard jump seat, headset on, regaling Captain Charlotte Ross with tales of flying for the Genesis Settlement.

Leah found herself grinning, despite the situation. The grin evaporated when she thought how much Jack would have loved to jump into this conversation.

Major Jane West said, "Leah—we've got time. Anything you'd like to share on the Genesis Settlement and the discovery in Antarctica—that would be awesome."

"Okay," Leah said. She glanced over at Hutchinson. "This will take a while. How about if you gather coffee and food for me and the ladies. Check on Kelleher—wake him if he's still sleeping."

"Belay that order, Captain," West said. "Leave sleeping dogs lie."

"Isn't Kelleher flying the approach into Antarctica?" Leah asked.

"Oh, hell no," West said with conviction. "First off, he's not our boss. We just happened to be flying through Holloman. Second, all he's flown outside of a desk for the last however-many years is a T-38 around the pattern, a few hours per month to stay current. Third, *I'm* responsible for this aircraft, not Colonel Kelleher. This plane's signed out to me; I fly it nearly every day. No one takes this bird onto the ice but Char and me."

West and Ross high-fived, as if they'd planned it. Then West said, "I let Kelleher fly the first leg, as a courtesy. You know, allow the Base Commander a chance to blow off some testosterone. After two hours, he was already nodding off." She turned in her seat, dead serious. "I hope you read me on this, Leah."

"Got it, and I got your back. Besides, I've already landed on the ice with guys flying the plane. I can tell you first-hand—total nightmare."

The pilots laughed and high-fived again, and even Hutchinson had his hand in on this one.

"I'm on the food," Hutchinson said. "Should I have Gordo knock out the Colonel with a Sleeping Beauty?"

Leah chuckled at his use of 'Gordo' instead of Dr. Gordon. If she didn't know better, she'd swear that Marko Kinney had been reincarnated into Hutchinson—with a few...well, more than a few... upgrades. Something about that filled her, at least momentarily, with a sense of well-being. "Sure. Tell Gordo to go short on the sedative, though."

Hutchinson was gone in a flash.

"Oh. Yeah," Charlotte said. "He's a keeper. Didn't even try to 'mansplain' why we shouldn't drink coffee while flying the airplane."

Leah couldn't hold back a momentary grin. "You ladies mind if I ask you a question?"

"Shoot," said West. "We're an open book."

Leah said, "I've pretty much hijacked this aircraft, forcing you to fly on what we all agree is a hazardous mission. Not to mention, we're right on the cusp of the greatest crisis for mankind, with unimaginable cultural, hyper-technology, and power shifting consequences, even a war with Russia, and yet, you two seem pretty calm and cool."

Charlotte looked at Jane West, and then nodded, like she should answer.

West said, "Remember we've been at war, mentally, since our first day at the Academy. We've never known peace time, as military officers. Char and I have been flying into and out of combat zones our entire careers. We've had to run ass-over-teakettle for the bird, when an Afghan farmer, oh, I mean 'Taliban Fighter' sets up a mortar in order to take a pot shot at a big juicy Globemaster, maybe ten minutes after unloading a hundred-thousand-pounds of One-Five-Five artillery destined to pound Taliban targets out at Camp Wilderness." West hesitated. "We've medevaced wounded to Ramstein, who are then rushed to Landstuhl Medical Center, more times than I'd care to count. That goes double for the KIA we've flown back into Dover."

West glanced over at Charlotte Ross. "Honestly, Leah, our biggest worry is what happens when we punch out of our flying jobs and have to return to civilian life. Neither one of us can wait at a green light for more than three seconds before screaming a string of four-letter greetings to the Prius that takes ten seconds to move its ass."

When West turned to look at Leah, the stress was written across her face. "We've gotten so numb—we'd just go on like it's another day at the office. We had a few, well more than a few shots one night, and Char and I decided, regardless if the world is going to hell in a handbasket, that wouldn't keep us from enjoying every day we're alive and in one-piece."

Hutchinson was back minutes later, loaded with coffee, sandwiches made by the mess hall, plus cookies and waters. When everyone had something to eat, Leah told them the whole story, starting at the beginning....

<hr />

An hour later, Leah had finished, and the facial expressions on Major West and Captain Ross had dramatically changed. Gone were the easygoing pilots who'd seen it all and were sure they'd faced worse in Iraq and Afghanistan. Their expressions had turned sober and serious. Even Hutchinson had fallen quiet.

Major West broke the silence. "Your husband's missing somewhere in Turkey—all your friends: KIA. Our government: taking a cue from North Korea on how to get rid of adversaries. I'd say it sucks, except that doesn't even come close. It makes the whole, alien part of the story seem meaningless—and that should be impossible to do.... So, what's your plan—once we land at Murdo?"

"Yeah...still working on that part," Leah said.

"And everything is based upon these visions you had while going all Timothy-Leary in the sweat lodge?"

Leah slumped back into the seat. Suddenly she felt like an idiot.

Had manipulation by the shaman, her fatigue, and the devastating deaths of Garrett and Marko damaged her psyche enough that she'd led herself down a delusional path? Was Wheeler right? Was she certifiably crazy?

Before she could respond, Major West said, "We are processing a situation way beyond our ability to understand. The technology is thousands, perhaps millions of years ahead of our own. It seems totally reasonable, to me, that this shaman was subject to 'special programming,' especially if he's supposed to lead them somewhere else. This visions in the sweat lodge—it was completely different than anything you've experienced, even using peyote buttons?"

Devastated by the thought that she was leading these amazing young officers on a lethal fool's errand, Leah could only manage a nod.

"Okay then," West said. "Char, get a chart—no, better yet, get a good-sized map of Antarctica out of the flight case." She turned to Leah. "Take the map back to your shaman buddy. Show it to him. Make him point out where this alien complex sits. If he 'transferred' this information to you, maybe it's like an old-fashioned fax. The original always has the sharpest information."

70

President William Wheeler fell back into the couch in the private residence. At first, he'd thought he could still beat them. But, hour by hour, the reality had sunk in.

There was no one he could blame except himself. Beaten...no, destroyed by a group of homegrown terrorists, led by a corporate raider who, in normal circumstances, would be licking the bottoms of his shoes. No, not even the most powerful political fireman could douse this roaring inferno and save his administration.

Wheeler pushed himself off the couch and steadied himself against the dizziness. Gravity was pulling his pants toward the carpet, his belt no longer able to prevent their fall.

He unfastened the belt, intending to tightened it an additional notch. When he looked down, he saw the belt was already on the last notch. To tighten the belt any more, he'd have to cut another hole in it.

Wheeler counted back four notches, to where the belt had a well-worn crease, from back when he'd thought he looked great in the mirror, even if he needed to lose five or ten pounds.

Back in the heady, early days of his administration, winning the election, putting into action his vision for the country and the world—that seemed a lifetime away. As his realm began to collapse, like a bubble, shrinking in size, he'd had to pull the belt tighter as well. It was ironic that most people would dream about the problem of having their belt grow too long. For Wheeler, though, it signaled defeat. Each notch one step closer to the end.

Wheeler carefully refastened the belt and pulled his pants up to the point he thought they'd stay in place, at least for a few minutes. That's all that would be required. He shuffled toward a chair, where his suit jacket had been folded and laid across the back. He put the jacket on, making sure to button it.

He walked into his bedroom, then into the closet. At the bottom of a box full of old magazines, where he'd been featured as an up and coming public servant, Wheeler pulled out an ancient handgun. Given to him by his father, it was a Remington 1911, handed down to his father by his grandfather and used during World War II during the invasion of Italy. It hadn't been fired for decades but was loaded with a full magazine, exactly as it had been when his father handed it over to him some twenty years prior.

Wheeler felt the cold steel, and it reminded him of home, growing up in Michigan. Summers on the lakes, winters building endless snowmen, and riding his wooden toboggan down the small hill behind his house.

He drew a deep breath, then walked to a dining table, where he sat and placed the 1911 on the surface. He pushed the handgun back for a moment, having second thoughts. Was this to be his legacy? Or was there still a ray of hope, a path back to his true destiny as the most successful and loved president of the United States since John F. Kennedy?

Teresa Simpson was in West Wing of the White House, waiting anxiously for the daily security briefing with the President, when all hell broke loose. Secret Service came running from every direction, several wielding fully automatic weapons.

"What is going on?" she shouted to one of agents running past.

"Shelter in place, ma'am. For your own protection."

"Why?"

"The President has been shot in the private residence."

Teresa shut the door to her office, heart racing. Shelter-in-place, the president shot? That meant there was an active shooter in the White House. She wondered if she should barricade the door shut. This was a scenario that she'd trained for on several occasions, but to think it might be happening for real was almost paralyzing. Had Paulson's guess about a coup correct? Brazenly taking place right inside the White House?'

Her terror ramped up a whole lot higher when the brass handle knob turned and the door was shoved open. To her immense relief, it was Kerrie Handleson, one of the executive assistants. Tears were running down her cheek and she seemed on the edge of breaking down.

"No," she moaned to Teresa. "No. No. No."

"What's happening?" Teresa said, holding Kerrie's shoulders and looking her in the eye.

"President Wheeler shot himself."

71

Leah sat in the port jump seat, her emotions a complicated mix of excitement and dread. She was excited one moment, that the Ancients were back on track, returning to their genuine purpose—not the flawed Settlement. The next moment she felt only fear, dread, and darkness.

Leah had gotten a huge boost when she'd flattened the plastic continental map of Antarctica on the floor of the C-17's fuselage and told the shaman, "Ha'át'éegi."

Without hesitation, Appanoose slammed his forefinger down on the map. The good news was that he apparently knew, without doubt, where to find this twin-domed complex.

The bad news was that Appanoose's spot was a thousand kilometers from McMurdo. Leah had no idea how they'd travel that distance on open ice. Jane told her that McMurdo had specially designed trucks, snow cats, and fuel. Thousands of gallons of fuel were necessary to run the convoys between Murdo and Amundsen-Scott. With some skills at hotwiring, she'd have plenty of transportation at her beck and call. Given that they were headed off on the Transverse, a prepared ice highway, they might want to stick with the snow cats, except that they burned a whole lot more fuel. She'd have to make that call when she got there.

Leah looked out the windscreen and down on the ice below. Barren for as far as the eye could see. She had flashbacks of making a similar flight in the Caribou, her biggest concern then had been having to use some makeshift toilet.

Colonel Kelleher sat in the other jump seat. Upon waking, he'd immediately demanded control of the aircraft, challenging Jane West and insisting she turn the Globemaster over to him.

As Leah promised, she'd backed up Major West, but Kelleher had continued to argue.

Finally, Leah held up a hand. "Colonel." She placed her forefinger and thumb less than an inch apart. "I'm this close to ordering the crew to lower the ramp and having your ass tossed off the aircraft."

That had shut him up.

Major West had told Leah about the McMurdo evacuation, immediately after the event in Antarctica. They managed to evacuate all nine-hundred, or so residents off before the geo-magnetic net had fully engulfed the continent. This meant that they'd be landing at a ghost town.

"There!"

Leah looked out the windscreen. Captain Ross was pointing out the right side of the aircraft. In the distance, Leah could make out the buildings and structures that made up the McMurdo complex. Unlike GPS navigation, which brought aircraft in on an exact route, flying by dead-reckoning and inertial guidance was more like hand-grenade combat. Close was good enough.

"Great job, Char," said West, as she banked the Globemaster, now flying at twelve-thousand feet over the Ross Ice Shelf in clear conditions. When the Globemaster overflew the ski-way at three-thousand AGL, even Leah could see it was in perfect condition.

"Maybe your luck is changing." West told her. Charlotte Ross and Jane West got busy configuring the Globemaster for landing. Colonel Kelleher continued to backseat-fly, but the women ignored him.

"How long till we touchdown?" Leah asked.

"Fifteen minutes," Charlotte replied. "Make sure everyone is buckled up in back—and ready for a ski-way landing. The tires make a helluva roar on the ice, and the reversers will kick up ice onto the fuselage."

Leah got up from the jump seat and worked her way into the cargo hold. Gordon had dosed the Ancients an hour ago with another shot of sedative in preparation for landing. He looked up, and gave her a rare thumbs-up. Adventure was growing on Gordon, it seemed.

Appanoose stood near the aircraft bulkhead. Leah pointed toward one of the empty seats. He gave one nod, then sat in the nearest empty seat. He pulled up on the seat belt, looked at it only for a moment, then snapped it together with some guidance from Leah.

She walked to the back of the seats and found Captain Hutchinson and the two helo crews sitting on the fuselage, a box full of cartridges and a stack of magazines beside them. Hutchinson said, "I thought we better get some magazines loaded—never know what we'll run into out there."

"Good thinking."

"How far, ma'am?" asked Lieutenant Cruz.

"How far to where, lieutenant?"

"To where we're headed?"

"A long way. Is this your first time in Antarctica?"

"Yes, ma'am. Looks pretty exciting from what we saw out the windscreen."

"Don't let that fool you—this place is a stone-cold killer."

Leah felt the landing gear coming down, heard the sound the air buffeting the gear and tires. They were on final approach into the ski-way.

She thought about working her way back to the cockpit but decided against it. Instead, she plopped down next to the shaman, who had his eyes closed and was chanting in Lakota.

Even alien-juiced Ancients didn't like to fly, she thought, a wry grin edging up the corners of her lips.

One hour later, Leah stood on the ice, bundled up but still freezing. A breeze was blowing from the west, cutting through the layers. The Ancients stood next to her, in a group, also bundled but apparently unaffected by the cold, chattering away in a multitude of native languages, pointing out the structures and the landscape.

Hutchinson and the helicopter pilots were rushing around, unloading snow machines off the Globemaster ramp, hooking up the toboggans, and loading medical gear and food and water. Gordo had been right. The young men were a godsend.

Gordon said he'd take K'aalógii off the Propofol once they'd reached altitude in the Globemaster, and the plane was pressured to eight-thousand feet. With the increase in altitude, he was confident that her symptoms could be managed. Leah hoped Gordon was right. Everything was simply an educated guess, concerning the changes on physiology.

Major Jane West walked down the ramp, and then ran over to Leah, wrapping her arms around her and hugged. "We're so worried for you," she said. "Are you sure you want to do this? We can load everyone back up and get you and the Ancients out of here."

"Honestly, Jane. I'd love to do that."

She nodded eagerly. "We can have everyone back aboard and be gone in twenty minutes."

Before Leah responded, Kelleher was shouting out the rear of the ramp.

"Major West. Let's go! If the weather degrades we could be stuck here for months! Come on! Now!"

Jane rolled her eyes. "Hate to say it, but he's right. We're flying Visual Flight Rules until we get back into the Southern Ocean. What do you think?"

Leah smiled but shook her head. "These people have a destiny. An amazing, wonderful, fabulous destiny—and I'm responsible for destroying that. I have to get them back to a place where they have another chance."

Jane took a deep breath, then leaned over and hugged Leah so tight it squeezed half the wind out of her.

"You have a satellite phone?"

Leah nodded. "Not that it'll do any good."

Jane tucked a piece of paper with a number and email address. "When you're ready to get the hell out of here—you call, text, email, whatever. Got it? I fuel the bird and we're coming back for you."

Leah hugged Jane back before the pilot turned around and sprinted for the ramp, where Kelleher was still signaling for her get aboard.

"Captain Hutchinson!" Leah shouted.

"Yes, ma'am!"

"Let's get everyone inside Murdo and crank some heat. What's on my Christmas list, Captain?"

"Ah—long-range snowcats and lots of gas."

"Exactly." She nodded toward the structures. "Start moving the Ancients away from the Globemaster. Kelleher's got an itchy take-off finger, and we don't wanna be in his way."

Hutchinson signaled to the other pilots and they started leading everyone toward the buildings in the distance. Two of the pilots operated the snow machines with K'aalógii and the medical gear onboard and Gordon riding on the back. Murdo had a full hospital, which he would make full use of, as needed.

At the front of the procession, Appanoose led the Ancients. She'd gotten them this far. It was up to Appanoose to get them the rest of the way to the connected dome complex—if it existed.

What a switch from the old days, working as an archaeologist, worried sick every second of every day when Jack was off on some world-class summit climb. She had to trust that, true to form, Jack was tough as they come and a survivor, along with Al Paulson and Teresa Simpson.

Captain Hutchinson ran up to her as the Globemaster was spooling up the number one engine. "I know there's this weird interference, but we stole several satellite phones from Holloman."

Leah nodded. "Long shot, Captain. I have one, too."

"We can always hope the interference dissipates. Call in a C-130. Get us out of here?"

"Don't you remember what you were taught in high school?"

"Ah—well, I didn't pay too much attention in high school, so probably not."

"Hope is not a method...."

Hutchinson looked at her with a blank expression, then burst out laughing.

"Good one, doc. I'll have to spread that one around."

Leah waved him off, then studied the horizon ahead. Hope might not be a method, but that's all she had right now...and it was in critically low supply.

What was it Commander Beckam said?

Embrace the suck. Get comfortable with the uncomfortable....

Well, there was plenty of suck, and she had a feeling it was gonna get a whole lot worse. Searching for a needle in a haystack in the most inhospitable place on the planet.... That was bad enough. Then there was the part of her vision that she hadn't mentioned to anyone: the two massive bursts of energy, ice blocks the size of skyscrapers. If one part of her vision were true, wouldn't that mean all of it had to be true?

"Jack Hobson," she said out loud. "If you're out there, get your ass down here and save me!"

"Did you say something, Dr. Andrews?" Hutchinson asked.

"Nothing you have to be worried about, Captain. Let's get to work."

Hutchinson gave her a salute, then ran ahead to help lead the Ancients toward McMurdo—and their destiny.

EPILOGUE

I *was born at night, but not last night.* **That's what Luke** Derringer had said for more years than he could remember any time some shifty actor tried to pull a fast one over on him.

The boys who were sneaking up on the airfield, off-road, in the middle of night had another thing coming if they thought Luke Derringer was gonna be caught with his pants down, waiting for his head to be blown off.

Sound carried over the desert. Hell, he hadn't even been outside when he sensed something was off. For someone in his 90s, Luke had pretty good hearing, but you didn't live in the desert your whole life without picking up some instincts along the way.

He picked up a set of binoculars that sat on the counter of the FBO lounge, then walked out back toward the World War II-era hangar than had originally been constructed out of tin, then patched up with aluminum over the years. He'd learned decades ago that he could hear aircraft inbound from the south much, much earlier if he happened to be working on something behind the hangar.

Countless winter storms had battered the south side of the hangar over the years, slowly bending the tin and aluminum siding into a slight concave shape. If he stood in the right spot, the magnified the sound of inbound aircraft, gave him an extra minute or two to brew up fresh hot coffee, maybe even open a box of donuts if he had any in the kitchen, before an aircraft landed.

Tonight, as he stood on the 'spot' behind the hangar, he heard trucks working their way across the washes, the crunch of their tires running through gravel.

He walked around the hangar, braced an arm on the wall, and lifted the heavy binoculars to his eyes. It was moonless, still, and the stars shone bright, their light reflecting dimly off the sand and rock. The low growl of the engines and sound of the tires across open desert intensified as the two trucks rolled over the top of a small hill; then the noise faded as they dipped down into a wash.

The next time the convoy reached the top of a hill, Luke made out two trucks. The lead vehicle was clearly struggling to get through the loose sand and soil. It stopped, backed down the hill, out of Luke's sight, then tried another path up the rise that featured more solid ground.

Bet that's making 'em madder than a wet hen, he thought. *Wasting time. They should have scouted it out by foot first.*

They would've been a whole lot smarter to come by plane, Luke thought. *Hell, I would've welcomed 'em with open arms and hot coffee.*

Luke carried one of his two Glock handguns at all times. Trouble rarely visited his remote airstrip, but that didn't mean he was unprepared for it.

Luke estimated they were still at least a mile, perhaps a mile and a half out. He hobbled around to the front doors of the hangar, spun the combination on the padlock and removed the chain that secured the two doors closed. He slid one door open, then went to the other door and rolled it as far as it would go.

Luke walked into the hangar, picked up a flashlight he kept on a table near the entrance, and checked out the Cessna 172 parked in the middle of the building. He disconnected a battery trickle charger, pulling it well out of the way, and removed the wheel chocks. He opened the left door on the Cessna and worked his way into the pilot's seat. The keys were in the ignition, right where he always left them. He thought for a moment maybe he ought to leave a note for Paulson, but then whoever was sneaking up on him would find it first.

Plus, he didn't want to take a chance his trick knee might fail him as he tried to hobble back to the Cessna. He'd be as helpless as a capsized turtle on a hot summer road.

Instead, Luke put his feet on the rudder pedals, engaging the brakes, and turned the key, certain the Cessna would fire before the prop had rotated twice. Sure enough, the engine roared to life immediately. He pushed the throttle forward enough to move the Cessna out of the hangar and onto the tarmac.

That done, he climbed gingerly out of the Cessna, limped back to the hangar, and pulled the doors shut again. There was something inside him that wouldn't let him leave a hangar door open.

Hell, in days it'd be filled with sand and the next poor slob who ran the airport would have a helluva time getting it cleaned up.

That done, he pulled himself back into the idling Cessna. He didn't need to glance at the gas gauge to know he only had a few gallons in the wing tanks. The last time he'd flown the Cessna was when he'd been looking for a hiding place for the nuke. Leaving an airplane stored with less than a full tank of fuel would get you a long winded tongue-lashing from old Luke. It allowed water to build up in the tanks, a stone-cold killer if that water caused corrosion or worked its way into the engine.

It was sloppy and stupid but somehow, amid the excitement of finding the hiding spot, and then arguing with Al Paulson about Luke's desire to stay at the airfield, he'd forget to top off the fuel... even though he'd remembered to hook up the trickle charger.

Damn fool.

There was a reason he hadn't passed a flight physical in years and had no business flying as pilot-in-command.

He taxied out to the runway, skipping the run-up.

If you're gonna make flyin' mistakes, might as well go whole-hog.

He pushed the throttle into the firewall, and the Cessna leaped forward. With no passengers and no gas, the plane was running mighty light. He pulled back on the yoke and had it off the ground in less than two-hundred feet. He flew straight out from the runway before banking, making a heading toward the southeast. He estimated he had about thirty minutes of fuel, give or take.

Luke leveled the aircraft at two-thousand feet above ground level, running the motor as lean as he could. He needed to conserve what little fuel remained.

He'd have to fly restricted airspace over the northern corner of White Sands, due to his bingo fuel situation.

One more error, old man…. Let's see how long you can keep it up.

He was flying for the Sierra Blanca mountain range, near Ruidoso. He'd always considered it one of the most beautiful regions of New Mexico. Once you got into the Sierra Blanca, the land looked a whole more like the Rocky Mountains than New Mexico. Miles and miles of green forest.

Luke had to climb some as he reached the foothills of the range, and that little bit of climbing did it. The engine gave its first cough, then coughed a couple more times, caught again, and then stopped for good.

Luke had enjoyed an amazing life. He had no complaints, nothing left undone. He felt at peace. This part of his life had been on his mind for some time now. Somehow, the idea that someone would find him lying in bed, half mummified, having died there alone, never had seemed…dignified. He'd never been the kind of man to leave a mess for others.

Luke listened to the sound of the wind whistling through the wing supports and the prop, said a prayer, checked once again that the forest below was uninhabited, then reached down to the trim wheel, dialing in plenty of down trim. The nose of the Cessna immediately dropped. He leaned back and folded his arms against his chest, a smile on his face.

Damn right…this is the way you go out.

Luke started humming a song from his youth. "In the Mood."

At Las Alamos, during the Manhattan Project, Saturday night at the dorms was something to see. The 'punch' made out of ethyl alcohol liberated from laboratory stock would magically appear and Glenn Miller's music soon followed. They worked like dogs on the 'Gadget,' but don't let it ever be said they didn't have some fun, too.

A smile crossed the old man's face as the Cessna picked up speed and disappeared into the tall pine and fir forest of the Sierra Blanca.

Afterword

Thank you for reading *ICE GENESIS*. Writing, editing, and producing a professional quality INDIE novel is an incredibly challenging and expensive undertaking. We try and give you, the reader, an amazing experience, at just a fraction of the price of legacy publishers. Sometimes, we make mistakes. If you find any mistakes in *ICE GENESIS*, send me a note at kevin@writingthrillers.com. We can fix those mistakes in a heartbeat! I'm always thrilled to get feedback on the ICE series. Please stop by my website www.writingthrillers.com and send me an email or drop in at Kevin Tinto on Facebook. If you enjoyed *ICE* and *ICE GENESIS*, please tell a friend or two. And please help out by rating *ICE* and *ICE GENESIS* by writing a short review at Amazon. REVIEWS ARE EVERYTHING!

Cliff Hangers?

ICE GENESIS is book two in a three book series. We work hard not to leave readers on the edge of a cliff hanger. But with any story that is simply too rich to tell in one novel, we have to end *ICE* and *ICE GENESIS* somewhere!

The last volume in the Leah and Jack Trilogy is *ICE REVELATION*. That is well underway at the date of IG publication (March, 26th, 2018). *ICE REVELATION:* Fall, 2018.

Acknowledgments

Producing a (readable) novel without a professional editor is like trying to make an Olympic team without a coach. Ed Stackler is the best. There are plenty of editors who can correct messy English. Ed took ownership of my characters and plot lines, and guided me along throughout the twists and turns of *ICE*, many times, over a period of nearly TEN years. Without Ed's guidance and professional help, *ICE* wouldn't exist.

For *ICE GENESIS*, Ed had to dig even deeper. Without his invaluable coaching and assistance, it is safe to say that *ICE GENESIS* would be just another mediocre novel, lost in a sea of others. Not everyone will love *ICE GENESIS*. But, for those of you who do—thank Ed Stackler. Oh...better not leave out MY MOM, who waded through endless line-edits, through countless drafts—some good, some bad. She is blisteringly fast—a critical skill when the author is on a deadline.

Dedication

This book is dedicated to you, dear reader. Thank you for taking the journey with Leah and Jackson, and their crew. I sincerely hope *ICE GENESIS* gave you the thrill ride that I intended. I would also like to thank the following individuals for guiding me along the way: Mic Grandfield for his eagle eye and knowledge of all things mechanical and Susan Grandfield-Engenluyff and Bob Engenluyff for line edits and coaching. Most important, my wife Laurie for the support, and taking care of everything while I was working seven-days-a-week on *GENESIS*. Could not do this without her.

Also Maggee and Willie. There's only one eye between two dogs, but that never slows them down. Goldens Rule. And BIG JACK, too.

Kevin Tinto

is a full-time writer based in Tiburon, California. *ICE* was his first book, and has sold more than 300,000 copies. The ICE Trilogy will be complete with *ICE REVELATION*, due fall 2018. He is also writing *VORTEX*, a stand-alone thriller, due 2019. Check his website at: http://www.writingthrillers.com for the latest information and updates!

Made in the USA
Middletown, DE
13 January 2019